CITY OF STRANGERS

CITY OF STRANGERS

A JACK LIFFEY MYSTERY

John Shannon

An Otto Penzler Book

CARROLL & GRAF PUBLISHERS

New York

For Patrick Millikin

CITY OF STRANGERS

An Otto Penzler Book
Carroll & Graf Publishers
An Imprint of Avalon Publishing Group Inc.
161 William Street, 16th Floor
New York, NY 10038

First Carroll & Graf edition 2003

Library of Congress Cataloging-in-Publication Data is available.

ISBN: 0-7867-1163-9

Printed in the United States of America

Distributed by Publishers Group West

AUTHOR'S NOTE

This novel was written before the terrible events of September 11, 2001, and it deals with many parallel themes, with terrorists and Islamic fury toward the West. I think it is even more important today for all of us to avoid the easy demonization of "evil." We need to do our best to understand the resentments that have been left behind by a century of anti-colonial struggle, which are far more social and political than religious. Let me be clear: I believe in the secular values of the West, I reject terrorism utterly. But the anger of many poor and politicized Moslems deserves its hearing.

"If you crammed a ship full of human bodies till it burst, the loneliness inside it would be so great that they would turn to ice."

—Brecht

One

Purity of Heart

"This will make a bloody great noise."

Pejman had been educated for a few years in London, and he always wanted you to hear it in his diction. His delicate fingers screwed down the thumb nut on the last wire of the complex pipe bomb, as the other three boys began to backpedal up the dry yellow hillside.

"That's the point," Fariborz insisted. "We're not out to damage anything." At least that was the agreement, though he watched Iman closely for his reaction at moments like this. Iman was the most implacable of them, and Fariborz wouldn't put it past the heavyset boy to go over the top into real violence sooner or later.

"The point, my brother of the rigid scruples, is in fact testing the igniter," Pejman said as he hurried to catch up, and they all scrambled up the slope away from the device. Pejman was the most technologically inclined. He explained he was using a cheap microchip to count off a five-minute delay before sending a spark from a charged capacitor into a tiny flake of permanganate imbedded among ordinary match heads. The match heads were themselves nesting in crude black powder packed into an iron pipe. Eventually, if all went as intended, devices just like it would erupt in a gallon

1

can of paint and send bright color splashing across their target buildings, houses of pornography, of corruption, of social shame.

Pejman had shown them how to grind charcoal briquettes to carbon powder, then sulfur and the potassium nitrate that was still sold in some drugstores to prevent randy German shepherds from getting their bright red erections. He told them that at Kilmeston School in England, the story had gone around for generations that the cooking staff folded potassium nitrate—saltpeter—into the mashed potatoes every Friday dinner.

They lay themselves flat just on the crest of the hill, and Pejman checked his Rolex. "Three minutes." He fussed with the buttons on his watch so it would count down the time for them.

There was a strange clarity in the air that frightened Fariborz, as if everything was too schematic all of a sudden. Every object seemed to have a hard edge, a border that pushed away everything else, and the ordinary world was a million miles away from him. He felt like an impostor, and he wanted to be back in his parents' house.

How do I know this is the right thing? he asked himself.

"In the name of God, the Merciful, the Compassionate," Iman began to chant in his guttural baritone, and they all followed along. It was in a heavily Persian-accented Arabic. None of them spoke Arabic well, but they knew these phrases, the most repeated *surah* in all Islam.

"Praise belongs to God, the Lord of all Being," they took up, "the All-merciful, the All-compassionate, the Master of the Day of Doom. . . ."

A helicopter was circling far above the Santa Clarita Hills where they lay, and then Fariborz noticed it seemed to be descending toward them. His skin crawled. Had someone betrayed them? "Pej!"

They all craned their necks upward.

"Dogturd!" Pejman snapped. It was the nearest thing to a curse he allowed himself. None of them swore, or sinned, to the best of their ability. This deeply felt project of acquiring *safa*—purity of heart—was an uphill struggle when everything around you was so exhaustively compromised by the values and practices of the West. "Maybe it's nothing."

"Let's run," Fariborz said. "We'll hear it if it works."

The helicopter continued to descend, swelling like a nightmare.

Iman looked from helicopter to pipe bomb to helicopter. "Time?"

"One minute-fifty."

"We can't risk it. I declare a delay." He sprinted back down the slope. He had always been the most decisive of them, even rash. Iman had been the one who first suggested, a year earlier, that they form the group, then he had argued for the gradual strategic withdrawal from their schoolmates.

"Iman, no!"

Pejman put a restraining hand on Fariborz's shoulder. "He'll be all right. All he has to do is yank the igniter out."

The helicopter swung in a wide circle as Iman giant-stepped down the weedy hillside toward the bomb. Fariborz held his breath and he felt the strange sense of distance coming over him again. Everything receded like some trick of perspective. Voices came to him through cotton wool, muffled. He could barely move a finger. Some inner voice told him this was not the path of *safa*.

"Let it be okay," Yahya whimpered. He was a tiny quiet frightened boy and almost never spoke.

"Don't sweat it."

Iman reached the pipe bomb and squatted.

"He's got over a minute," Pejman said calmly.

And at that instant the world changed. They saw Iman leap into the air. A moment later, the blast was like the flat of a giant hand slapping their faces.

"God is great," Pejman intoned.

"Oh, shit!" Fariborz said. And all of a sudden forming their own Ansar-e Hizbollah in Los Angeles did not seem such a wonderful idea after all.

San Vicente ran at an angle to the city grid, a shortcut for some drivers, an irritation for others. Traffic on the broad diagonal ran in intermittent spurts, out of sync with the lights on the grid. Jack Liffey loitered a half block away, early for his appointment, and his eye caught on a leather-skinned old man at the crosswalk. The man took two steps forward into the street, said something aloud, then retreated two steps and spoke again. There were no cars to chase him back. He continued this little dance for a while, and a woman lugging shopping bags gave him a wide berth, pretending not to see him.

Forward, forward—assertion—back, back—declaration. The man wore serge trousers, a white shirt with bloused sleeves, and a scarf around his neck that looked Middle Eastern.

Two teenage boys came along and flanked the old man, mimicking his actions once to mock him, and then laughed easily and moved on.

When Jack Liffey came forward, he could pick out the old man's words. "Mother, may I?" he said at the curb, and then at the farther end of his short orbit, "Oh, better wait." The words never varied, nor did the actions, by so much as an inch. It was like a learned rite of prayer—forward, forward, *Mary and Joseph*, back, back, *Mother of God*.

Jack Liffey stopped next to the man and took his arm. "Can I help you across, sir?"

There was a tiny twitch of the man's head, and then a warm smile. "Thank you so much."

There were no cars close and they made it across easily before disengaging. The man had seemed spry enough.

"Are you okay?"

"I'll be all right for a while." The man smoothed his thick graying hair back from his forehead to show a small scar. "I was one of the last experimental subjects to be given a prefrontal lobotomy. Lobo means wolf. Things are manageable mostly. Malleable. Mandible. Margarine. Once in a while the machinery in my head sticks in a groove, and I have to wait for a Good Samaritan. Bless you kindly."

"You're very welcome." The man walked away normally, gave a little Charlie Chaplin heel-click and kept on going.

Jack Liffey thought of all the monstrous things that had been done to people in the name of normalizing their psyches: generations of leeches, candling, whippings, electroshocks, carving apart lobes of the brain. It didn't help his sour feelings about psychiatry that he was heading for a psychologist's office just then, even if it wasn't for treatment. He winced and massaged his chest, reacting to a curious palpitation he'd been feeling recently.

The place was a little blue house on the edge of West Hollywood that had been converted into an office for two psychotherapists and a masseur. He went up the steps into a waiting room where a young woman sat glaring fiercely at the floor. There was a little box screwed to the wall with three pushbuttons, three lights, and three names. He pressed Aaron Auslander, MFCC, PhD, and watched the appropriate red bulb light up, then sat and picked up a magazine called *Self*. That seemed pretty appropriate. He didn't really like the idea of sitting there looking like a patient, but money was money, and Auslander had called with a job.

The door opened a foot, and a cheerful woman's head came through the gap, saw the glowering young woman and beamed. "Marilyn, come in."

Marilyn jumped to her feet with such energy that it took her a few inches up off the floor. "I'm coming *now!*" she snapped. And then they were both gone.

He had gone to college with Aaron Auslander, roomed with him and two others for a semester in the basement of an old building in downtown Long Beach. Aaron had had the reputation of being a whiz, but it turned out that what he basically had was a photographic memory which he had used to avoid any real work. He had come from a very rich family, with almost as much family trouble as money—a cold dad who was psychologically absent and a mom who had to be carted off one day screaming for love. Jack Liffey wondered if you ever really got over something like that. He hadn't seen Aaron for thirty years, though they still had friends in common, and he always found it mildly interesting to observe how people changed over long stretches of time—or didn't.

"Hey there, long time."

He'd been caught looking the other way, something he hated. "Hello, Aaron. It sure is."

"I don't use 'Aaron' much anymore." Jack Liffey had forgotten how tall the man was, probably six-four, handsome, tidy and capable-looking in his khakis and blue button-down shirt.

"What do you use? Herr Doktor?"

He smiled. "Dicky."

"Really?"

"It's a long story, and not very instructive. Come in."

Jack Liffey followed him through a couple of turns of hallway, past a door where somebody seemed to be yelling in outrage, into a pleasant interview room with two white couches angled into one corner and the big authority chair facing them. He considered grabbing the authority chair himself but decided against it. On the near sofa, he had to inch himself away from a potted palm that teased his head with its fronds. "That thing's dangerous," he complained.

"I've been meaning to move it."

Auslander subsided into the big chair and they listened to a fan hum for a moment. It was a tiny space heater. The room was chilly, but the heater didn't seem to be taking the edge off it. "How have you been doing, Jacko?"

Jack Liffey remembered that—his old classmate's penchant for making up off-center nicknames that nobody else used. He'd never liked to discourage it because it seemed to represent the only spark of creativity the man possessed, but the nickname made his teeth hurt. "I don't use 'Jacko' much. 'Jack' is pretty hard to beat."

"Sure. Sorry." He seemed subdued. "Okay, let's set it out on the table. My daughter's a runaway. No, that's an assumption. She's just gone."

"I'm sorry . . . Dicky. How old is she?"

"Seventeen. It wasn't anger at Helen and me, really it wasn't. We were close. Close enough so she told us she'd been having intimate relations with her boyfriend."

Intimate relations, Jack Liffey mused. He wondered if she had used those very words. It reminded him of a reporter for *Stars and Stripes* he'd met in a bar overseas, complaining idly about euphemism: "We couldn't use the word 'rape' then. Imagine, a woman runs out of a house screaming, "Help, help, I've been criminally assaulted!"

"She also told us she had broken off with him." He let out a big sigh. "Did you hear about the group of boys who disappeared from Kennedy School?"

"The Iranians? Who hasn't?" It had been on the news for weeks, four Iranian boys disappearing all at once, but the story had finally died down when nobody could find a trace of them. They'd all been seniors at Kennedy-Westridge Academy, a fancy prep school in the Valley, and all, by repute, had recently fallen into the earnest practice of Islam. Reading between the lines in some of the stories, you could discern that the rich Anglo twerps at the school had probably hazed the Iranian boys to a fine pitch.

A bloodcurdling screech penetrated the wall from a nearby room, and they both made a point of not commenting on it. It suggested bamboo slivers going under fingernails. The space heater cycled down, having decided the room was warm enough.

"Becky's boyfriend Fariborz was one of the Kennedy Persians. They disappeared just about when she did. I can't really believe it was a coincidence, but it was Fariborz's sudden seriousness about religion that got her to break it off with him. I don't think she would have gone away with them—she's too headstrong. But it scares me, Jack. Religion always does—cults. Adolescents have such a need to commit to something big and meaningful and shocking. I know because I became a Maoist right at the height of things, just about when you got drafted."

"I was a bit of a radical after I got back from 'Nam, too. Briefly. I got over it."

"I've seen that kind of belief, adopted out of teen rebellion, get its claws in deep into some kids. It has something to do with having to construct a new father and a new sense of who you are."

And sometimes they probably just believe it all, Jack Liffey thought. "You're not saying she adopted Islam and fled to Iran so she could spend the rest of her life wearing a big bedspread?"

"I don't know what I'm saying, and I don't think being supercilious is going to help much."

"Sorry."

"I've learned to be respectful of Islam, up to a point. Anyway, I've talked to the boy's father and to people at Kennedy, and they'll all be happy to speak to you. You're the one who's supposed to be expert at finding kids."

The heater cycled on again. There was no discernible change in the temperature of the air, but it did start toasting his left ankle.

"What do you know about the father?"

"He's secular, a very successful businessman in Beverly Hills. His wife is an Iranian Jew. Almost half the Iranians in L.A. are Jewish, though nobody else in L.A. seems to realize it. His family left well before the Ayatollah, so they've been here a long time and you don't have to worry if they were Shah's henchmen, if, in fact, you worry about things like that. Talk to him. Talk to the wife. It may be a lead to Becky."

Jack Liffey noticed that the man was familiar enough with the Iranian community to say simply *shah,* the way they did, instead of *the* shah, the way the rest of the country did. "How long has she been gone?"

The tall man thought about it for a while. "The delay may seem terrible, but we've taken other steps in the meantime. Two months now. We've pretty much exhausted trying to find Rebecca directly, which is why I'm asking you to try looking for the boys, too."

"I'm the last resort. I'm used to that."

"And it's not just for that—picking you as last resort, I mean. Your name came up when I saw Lon and Virginia the other night."

There was some other agenda percolating here, and Jack Liffey couldn't quite see it.

"There's a condition to the job."

"There always is," Jack Liffey said. "Whose toes are too delicate to step on?"

"You have an impatient streak, don't you? To my way of thinking, a detective would be better off sitting back and letting things happen at their own pace. After all, impatience is a kind of insecurity."

This know-it-all confidence could be pretty maddening, Jack Liffey thought, particularly in a therapist, but then he had a hunch

Dicky Auslander was no great shakes at the job. So far his idea of psychology sounded more like a tape of an old *Reader's Digest* article.

"Must be because I never got to fuck my mother and kill my father," Jack Liffey said.

The tall man nodded slowly. "Virginia said you're having a bad time."

That stopped Jack Liffey in his tracks.

"After Marlena left you," Dicky added.

"Mind your own business."

"I'll pay your normal detective rate, but one condition of this job is reporting in to me a couple times a week and using any extra time to talk to me about yourself."

"That's just completely out of the question, Dicky."

"We used to be friends. Are you afraid of it?"

Jack Liffey stared back hard. The heater cycled on, then off right away. That was the way gratification tended to work, too, he thought idly, but he had no intention of talking that over with a therapist, or anything else. The stare went on quite a while, before Aaron Auslander cracked and had to speak. As Jack Liffey guessed, he could mad-dog the man at will. That helped restore some of the balance.

"What is it about therapy that frightens you? Revealing yourself?"

"Remember that personality test we had to take at State? 'Are you *still* afraid of doorknobs?' There's no way you can answer that. Just agreeing to talk about your psyche means you're crazy as a loon."

"Doorknobs scare me to death," Aaron Auslander said evenly.

Jack Liffey laughed. It was almost the first human thing the man had said to him. "I can carry my own water, thank you."

Auslander gave a little shrug with open palms. "So, just come in and report and *chat* with me twice a week. Is it so terrible? I promise we'll talk in a way that will please you. Starting Wednesday at ten."

"The only way this would please me is if you came down from the rafters on a string and quacked like Groucho Marx's duck."

* * *

From the brow of the hill, the faraway high-rises of the West Side poked up through a brown haze like the last signs of Atlantis sinking into a muddy sea. For years, Jack Liffey used to walk Loco up here near the retired nuns' home in the Baldwin Hills, and together he and Loco had discovered the square of lawn at the very lip of the hill where you could look across the intervening plain of habitation to the Santa Monica Mountains. On a clear day, your view stretched all the way from the blue Pacific at Santa Monica on the far west to the tiny urban island of downtown L.A. Loco had liked it here, too, sniffing up a storm at whatever wild scent trails crossed the lawn. Jack Liffey wasn't sure why he'd eventually got out of the habit of coming here.

He looked down into the top of a pine tree where a red-tailed hawk had once nested. Each spring it had raised one or two nestlings, and he had watched it circle away, eye him warily, then bring back food or nest materials. He'd never seen the mate. Then one year it had just stopped coming. Died, presumably. Where did dead birds go? You almost never saw them on the ground. He realized he'd been thinking a lot recently about mortality.

Auslander had been right enough, in his crude way. The fact that Marlena had left him for a religious nut had knocked him right out of his orbit, and he wasn't sure what the crisis was all about anymore. A real inconsolable fondness for Marlena? Yet another midlife crisis? Could loss actually leave you damaged? He'd already had one genuine soul crisis some years back, when his marriage to Kathy, Maeve's mom, and his comfy aerospace job had both gone south at about the same time. Back then he had dipped badly into drugs and drink, and he had cranked himself back out of the hole notch-by-notch only as an act of pure will. He'd made himself over into a drug-free, alcohol-free child-finding detective. Maybe his willpower was starting to wear thin. He'd thought he was okay for quite some time, but this new loss had blindsided him.

He sat down on the grass and clutched his knees, looking through the haze at street after street of houses. It reminded him of a train trip to New York that he had taken as a child with his parents. He'd had a sleeper, and after lights-out, he had lain there, curtain tucked around his neck, forehead to the chilled glass, peering out into the vastness. The rolling motion of the train, the velvety dark, and here and there a little pocket of fuzzy light drifting past in the distance. He could still taste the wonder he had felt then. Every smudge of light was a town that he would never know, every bright pinprick a home. Thousands upon thousands of lives went on outside his ken. Why had he felt so vividly that those lives out there were real and his was only made up?

After a few minutes on the grass, with Loco nuzzling his leg and him scratching the dog's ears, Jack Liffey realized he was crying a little.

Two

Disenchantment Will Never Prevail

Farshad Bayat's shop was called LA ROX, and because it was all in capitals, Jack Liffey couldn't work out whether it was meant to be La Rox or L.A. Rox. All in all, he wasn't very fond of cute ad-spellings, departures like *Sell-a-bration* and *Rite-weigh,* because they just seemed to crank up the level of anxiety, a world that didn't believe in its own rules. Extra anxiety he could do without.

The northern reaches of Robertson Boulevard here, spreading up the flank of Beverly Hills, were all interior designers and antiques and retro shops where they sold Roy Rogers bedspreads and Buck Rogers aluminum furniture at wildly inflated prices. Stripped pine tables out of Iowa farmhouses cost more here than fine hardwood furniture from France—at least, for as long as the music executives coveted that particular look.

The front window of Bayat's was surrounded by smooth river-bottom stone, and so was everything inside. A showroom showed off rocky stub walls and rock chimneys, stone fences, kitchens done up like caves. He wasn't quite sure where the subliminal signals came from, but something told him the rocks were fake. A bored, chunky Middle Eastern woman dismissed him with disdain when he said he wasn't buying and had him wait in a fancy anteroom.

There was a wonderful big stone fireplace, and through an open door, he could see a whole crew of Latinos out back unloading cartons from a truck. A skinny foreman in a red vest and one of the Latino workers were holding up butane lighters against each other and flicking them for some reason, as if seeing whose flame was taller. Then the foreman started yelling at the worker, noticed the door was open, and kicked it shut.

Jack Liffey tried not to doze off in the armchair. He'd had a bad night, waking in sweat in some unsettled state between dread and rage, unable to get back to sleep. He was sure the proximate cause was a blind date last weekend that a friend had set up for him, a real knockout of a redhead who had seemed okay until she started proselytizing him with a goofy therapeutic test that involved holding tiny bags of foodstuffs against his cheek and yanking on his arm like a slot machine, looking for the food that would make his arm muscles weaker. Subclinical allergies, she had explained, or energy misorbits, as if he were a proton missing one of its electrons.

He had put up with it for a while and then he'd got a bit wiseass as she yanked his arm once again, something about his eyes spinning around like a slot machine to show three turnips, and she'd got mad and kicked him out of her apartment overlooking the marina. He didn't really want to be like that, but sometimes he couldn't help it. He wondered if he ought to start drinking again, just a nip or two to help him be a little more sociable to the next gorgeous fruitcake who came along and wanted him to do away with his extra vein poisons by barking like a dog or something.

All in all, he knew he was not really going to revert to the demon rum. It had cost him his first marriage, and he'd been sober ever since. He'd stayed off drugs, too; part of a pact he had made with his ego to prove his strength of character. But for all the propitiating fires he'd lit to these particular abstemious gods, nothing much seemed to be working out for him except an extra helping of anxiety and this new little flutter in his chest.

His second big relationship, with Marlena, had crashed and burned, and now he'd missed several child-support payments so he couldn't even see his daughter. The detective business wasn't really paying off—another bad choice—and his miserable condo was still worth less than he'd paid for it. At a certain point in life, you had to find a way to face the discovery that you weren't a charmed soul after all, and things might just not work out for the best for you.

It was no wonder his friends like Lon and Virginia were ratting him out to the psychiatric community. If only he could get over the bad nights, the sweats and sleepless stretches, he was sure he could take care of the rest by himself.

The bored dark woman came back and beckoned. Following her out the door, he couldn't help hearing the faint *scritch-scritch* in the quiet office as her nylons rubbed together at the thigh. He felt a chill, like hearing a fingernail on a blackboard. She pointed to a door down a hallway and left him to his own devices. Reception-ists never liked him much, but he was inured to that. The Timex and the cheap shoes always gave him away as a low roller.

Farshad Bayat rose from a desk with a welcoming smile. He was handsome, fortyish and had a receding hairline. They're Aryans, same stock as Europeans, he remembered reading somewhere, and sure enough, from the planes of his face, this man could have been a German count or a French university professor. Jack Liffey wanted to like him, for no discernible reason.

"Mr. Liffey. Mr. Dicky Auslander called me about you."

Jack Liffey smiled involuntarily. "I can't get over 'Dicky.' I knew him in college as 'Aaron.' "

They shook hands. "Some men attract nicknames naturally," Bayat said, "as if they were born with an extra helping of charisma. My roommate at UCLA was called Zorro. He was considered a swordsman—as you might guess." His voice had only a hint of an accent, a kind of extra precision in the consonants.

Jack Liffey was happy the man could joke about something like womanizing. It suggested the interview wouldn't have to be con-ducted in the gloom of intense cultural sensitivity, tiptoeing across the eggshells of contrary beliefs.

Bayat gestured and they both sat. The desk was unusual, a thick rosewood slab laid on a base made of the same stones as everything else around, including one wall of the office.

"I guess you deal in rocks," Jack Liffey observed.

He smiled. "I guess I do." The man picked up a stone with two hands and tossed it across the office. Jack Liffey prepared himself for a heavy catch but it was as light as balsa. As he'd guessed, LA ROX were in fact fake. He turned the thing over in his hands, about the shape of a flattened squash, with a hollow back.

"There are other manufactured rocks, of course, but they tend to be very heavy or to look and feel like plastic. I invented a process for cross-linking polymers with a small amount of ground stone. The only thing I can't manage is the cool feel of stone. There just isn't enough substance to act as a heat sink." The man seemed to be worried about something, then his smile reappeared, like cloud shadows scudding away to expose a sunny plain.

Jack Liffey looked at the surface of the stone and it looked grainy, just like granite. "Looks pretty good."

"The wall in front of the store looked fake, though, didn't it?" Bayat asked.

"A bit."

The man wasn't offended. "It took me a long time to work it out. In the first generation, there were only twenty distinct shapes. I finally decided that our subconscious minds are sensitive to that. We must have a very sophisticated facility for pattern recognition. When I increased the number of molds to thirty-six, it seemed to work much better, but science never stands still. What do you think of this?"

He tossed another half-stone across the room; this one was heavier and seemed to slosh in Jack Liffey's hands. The flat back was sealed over.

"It's filled with water, plus a little air space so it won't explode if it freezes. You put that on an exterior wall facing the sun and you've got a passive solar house, storing heat during the day and releasing it at night. These are very popular in Arizona and Colorado."

Jack Liffey leaned forward to deposit the stone on a corner of the big desk. "I didn't really come here to talk about your rocks."

The man's smile stayed, but the warmth drained out of it. "No, of course. You want to talk about Fariborz."

"And Becky."

At her name, he seemed to grow more thoughtful. But at that moment the woman opened the door and looked in. "Mr. Bayat, the factory called." Then she talked for a while in what must have been Farsi, and the man's face went even murkier.

"According to NAFTA regulations, that should not be a problem. I'll call them back."

She ducked out, and the man studied his desktop for a moment. Jack Liffey had the distinct impression something was not right here.

"I will do everything I can to help you," he said at last, so earnestly that he seemed to have just discovered some deep need to convince Jack Liffey of his desire to help. "Fariborz was living away from home, at Kennedy School, when he disappeared with the other three." His face registered distaste. "The news called them the Kennedy Four, like some sixties gang of radicals."

"Were you here in the sixties?"

"No, I came in the late seventies for graduate school, not long before the Ayatollah's triumph. My wife is Jewish so we had little desire to go back. The Revolutionary Guard weren't very benevolent to Jews—though it's a shame; Islam has a long tradition of tolerance. Of course, the fanatics were far worse to the Baha'is. Jews and Christians are what's called People of the Book, and they predated Islam after all. But Baha'i is only one hundred and fifty years old, and the militants don't recognize any religion founded after Mohammed's time. Most of the Baha'is who escaped live in Santa Monica and West L.A. now." He smiled lightly. "You tell me a Persian's religion, and I'll tell you where he lives in Southern California. The ethnic Armenians, all Christians, went to Glendale. The Jews to Beverly Hills and Westwood. Moslems are in the South Bay and scattered around, though a lot of the Moslems here are basically secular. I don't think the militants in Iran were entirely aware of what they were doing, but in retrospect you can see that one consequence of the Iranian revolution was purging the country of its secular middle class."

"Do you consider yourself a Moslem?"

"I'm not very religious, but in some ways—" he shrugged—"the values and the culture run very deep. There's a strong sense of family and proper behavior and respect. I drink alcohol only very rarely. This made it harder to argue with my son when he started to become a fanatic."

"How do you mean?"

"I had no trouble seeing quite clearly what bothered Fariborz about the West. Not just halter tops in the supermarket and sex on TV and drunkenness and cruelty to women. There's a kind of separation of every individual from every other individual. You and I, Mr. Liffey, if we went to Iran now, I am sure we would both dislike a lot of things we would see; but there are other things I think we would both admire. I've been back. There is a deep concern for right behavior and politeness, for being a good host and a good neighbor. It takes a fairly sophisticated worldview to value other things highly enough to put up with the terrible loneliness and apartness in the West. I feel the loss every day, as an exile, but also as an individual. I'm no longer rooted in any place, the way I once was. No one here is rooted."

Jack Liffey was tempted to share something of his own sense of loss and isolation, but he had to stay alert to other things. The man's face kept saying something other than his words. Something was going on under the surface here and it was off-center, like a bent axle, joggling a cart and continually thrusting a kind of disquiet up into the ordinary.

"The fierceness of teenagers leaves no room for gray areas," Bayat added. "Everything has to be perfect right this minute, or it must be obliterated. Fariborz smashed his electric guitar against a tree and burned all his fiction, mostly mystery novels."

Jack Liffey had read a little about the Kennedy Four that morning in back numbers of the *Times* at the library. They had supposedly turned themselves into purist religious zealots, then stayed away from classes, then left school altogether. But the news articles had tapered off about three weeks after the boys disappeared. There hadn't been a word on them in a month. "Do you have any guesses where they are?"

He shook his head slowly. "I hired a detective after they'd been gone a week, but he got nowhere. They might even be in Iran by now, or in some Pakistani *madrasa* up along the Afghani border, or some Hezbollah camp, or just holed up in Mexico reciting the Koran to each other. I hope very much for the latter."

"Why do you say Mexico?"

"Fariborz knows it well and speaks Spanish. I've owned a small *maquiladora* in Tijuana for many years. Where these are made." He indicated the rocks.

"Is there any way Becky's disappearance could be linked to theirs?"

His expression darkened again. He shook his head slightly, but it wasn't really a denial, just a gesture of helplessness. "It's a preposterous coincidence if it isn't connected, don't you agree? But she was not a Moslem and not a zealot in any sense, Mr. Liffey. In fact, she'd been growing apart from Fariborz because of his growing religious fervor. She came to me to complain about it."

"What did she say?"

"Just asked if I could talk to him. He wouldn't see her any longer without a chaperone present. He insisted she wear long sleeves and dresses that went to the ground. She said she loved him very much. She seemed a fine girl, though I hardly know her. I hope very much that you find her."

"So does her father."

"Is he paying you well enough for you to be thorough?"

Jack Liffey wondered if the man was aware of the insult in his words, but he decided not to rise to it. Perhaps he only meant paying well enough to cover expenses. "I wouldn't have taken the job otherwise."

Farshad Bayat leaned forward a little, and a tension came over him. It was so hard to read signals across cultures. "I will pay you a large reward if you find her."

"That isn't necessary." Though not unwelcome, he thought. Some agenda was whirring away beneath the surface.

"I will pay you even more than Mr. Auslander has promised you, but you must do one thing for me. Report to me first, then tell her father. That's all I ask."

This was getting odder and odder. "Why do you want that?"

The man shrugged. "Finding Becky may be the key to finding Fariborz and his friends. No matter how long I've lived in this country, I never quite understand how Americans' minds work. Mr. Auslander has promised to let me know the minute she's found, but he may sequester the girl, or choose to keep silent for his own reasons, or he may just forget me. If she is connected to Fariborz, I have a feeling I will need to move quickly to trace from her to him. That's all I ask. Let me know if you find her and let me talk to her right away. I will make it worth your while."

"I'll consider it."

"Would a retainer solidify your consideration?"

"Let's leave it there. I have a client already."

The man leaned back in his chair, as if deciding not to push any harder. "You're welcome to come to my home and talk to his mother and see my son's possessions, if you think it will help."

They talked some more, but Jack Liffey didn't learn much more useful information about the boy. Fariborz Bayat had been very mannerly from an early age, studious, kind to the old and infirm. He had been interested in literature and poetry, and then music, hanging out with a mixed bag of boys in junior high, Anglos, American Jews, a Palestinian Arab. But once at Kennedy, he had been thrown together with other Persians. The father, too, suspected that the other boys at the elite school had been cool to the Persians. None of the families of the other three missing boys lived in Beverly Hills. They were from Torrance, Sherman Oaks in the Valley, and Santa Monica.

Jack Liffey couldn't work out quite what was so unnerving about Farshad Bayat. His reasons for wanting to have the first words with the missing girl didn't ring true, but there was something else as well, a tremor of mental activity that overtook the man a little too often, as if he was tuned to some distant signal Jack Liffey couldn't hear. And the girl's name had something to do with the signal. Becky Auslander was the ghost at this feast, all right, but he had no idea what feast it was.

He left out the back, through the loading dock, just to get a different perspective on the place. Giant numbered wooden bins of the various species of ROX lined a long concrete warehouse, and a crew of Latinos pushed rolling containers along the bins, counting out a number of ROX from each bin according to the paperwork they carried.

Two young Latinos squatted out in the alley on a smoke break. Only peasant farmers could squat comfortably on their heels like that.

"*Buenas días,*" Jack Liffey said.

"*Buenas.*"

The second man just watched him suspiciously.

"Is Mr. Bayat a good boss?"

He knew they weren't likely to say much, but he might be able to read something in their manner.

"*Es Señor Bayat un buen jefe?*" he repeated.

They did their best to pretend they didn't understand him, but he figured it was a straightforward enough sentence, even in his execrable Spanish, much of which had been learned from Auto Club tour guides, discussions with waiters in Ensenada and Chico Cervantes mystery novels.

The workers were practiced at shrugging. All that he learned was that they were Mexican-born, probably illegals.

"Have a good day," he said, and sauntered on down the alley. The stake truck being off-loaded had *Baja California del Norte* plates, with the *frontera* inscription that basically meant T.J. Another unsurprising fact to store away.

A newspaper rack caught his eye with a giant headline before he reached his car. L.A. wasn't a street-edition town, a headline that big really had to mean something.

Teen Kills 8 at Playschool

The editors managed to work in a little information above the fold, a berserk sixteen-year-old, distraught about breaking up with an older girlfriend who worked at Wonder Playland, had run a bulldozer back and forth through the preschool in Brentwood. Jack Liffey stopped reading. Life was random enough, he thought, and he felt dismal enough already. He didn't need any more insight just then on the sorrowful burdens of the human condition. And, like most crazed tragedies, there was nothing really to be learned from it.

Returning south, he noticed a huge concrete faux Gothic church that he'd seen a hundred times without it ever registering. He parked on the side street and stared up at the flying buttresses. He wondered if the concrete detailing up high was decaying in the rain and smog. The owners who now lived in Frank Lloyd Wright's experimental L.A. homes had learned to their chagrin just how vulnerable poured concrete was, with the maverick architect who had inspired *The Fountainhead* insisting on intricate cast-concrete Mayan designs that eroded to mush in a few decades. Jack Liffey felt his hands tremble a little.

He got out and craned his neck up at the flat gray surface that showed the marks of the wooden forms where it had been poured, unlike the limestone fabric of a European cathedral. Still, the building was impressive. He pushed in at a heavy carved wood door, past a rack of pamphlets about ministering to darker-skinned peoples overseas, past a little font where a brown woman in a shawl was dipping her hand in holy water, and then on into the dim nave. The stained-glass windows were dazzling, a lot of blues and reds that really vibrated in the sunlight.

He slipped into a pew in the cool echoey dimness. There was a kneeling rail in front of him that his long-long-ago childhood Protestant church had never had. And Marlena's Bible-thumping, tongue-talking, millennarian church probably wouldn't have had, either. Marlena. *Give me that full gospel,* he thought. Don't give me any of that 90 percent gospel, no, sir. Actually the only part of the gospel they seemed interested in was Revelations, all those Mediterranean fever-dreams about pale horsemen and approaching hellfire.

He settled back and listened to a kind of beating of the air in the vast space. No, it seemed a real sound, small, far-off and agonized, behind a door or a wall. Something in pain. He smelled floor polish and burning wax. An apse near him was blocked off by a rack of flickering candles in red glass. All these sensations seemed to burn his nerves, as if his axons were overcharged. He could even feel his own pulse beating against the inside of this skin. Just hold still for a minute, hold still, he thought.

Jack Liffey wondered what in hell he was doing there. There was an inkling that maybe he was reaching out to hit the pause button on his life for a few moments. Nothing really religious. Just a whim to commune in some way with that ancient craving to do one's best in the world or be part of something bigger and grander.

Then he heard the odd sound again and noticed a number of small people making their way on their knees around the outside aisles, moving from numbered station to station. His spine prickled as if he had blundered in by accident on something extremely private. An old man crabbed sideways on his knees and stopped directly between Jack Liffey and icon No. 9 on the wall. The little man bowed his head and started to weep quietly, his shoulders shuddering. Jack Liffey had an overpowering urge to hug him, comfort him, tell him it would be all right.

Instead he thought about Marlena. He had let her go without a big scene, graciously, blessing her new union with the big Bible-thumper. But why not? What good would anything else have done? Making a scene wouldn't have kept her.

He tried to stand up to go back outside and return to the world but he couldn't. He kept trying ineffectually. It was like a car with a dying battery, grinding and grinding, getting weaker in that futile way that would leave him stranded, far from home.

Hey, anyone there? he called in his head. *I really think I'm doing my best here.* But, of course, there was no answer.

Something landed on the back of his bare forearm, and he wondered if the church had flies. He looked down and saw a drop of water. A second teardrop hit and he thought, Shit, not again! He knelt to see what kneeling on that hard bar was like, rested his arms on the pew ahead, and then he wept uncontrollably over the back of the pew for a while. A part of him watched, fascinated, and decided he'd never quite done anything like this before. His previous crises had run to alcoholic blur, but otherwise had been pretty much under his conscious control.

Jack Liffey had seen it before, parked along this stretch of Fairfax on his way home. It appeared to be some mid-70s boat-sized GM product, Buick or Oldsmobile, but you couldn't tell because it was completely covered with a blanket of tiny brown teddy bears glued to every surface. There was only an oval left to see out the windshield, and he wondered if that was enough to make it legal. And what would a sudden rainstorm do to it, a billion soggy little bears?

It had been hard enough to tear himself away from the church, and now this. A sign on the roof of the car said, *Disenchantment will never prevail.*

A deferred message from above, he supposed, since he'd been offered no revelation in the church.

Maeve looked up from *Wuthering Heights* to see her mother hovering tentatively in the doorway of her bedroom. Tentative wasn't her mother's style, so she knew something was up. "Did I forget to do something?"

"No, no. I was just wondering if you'd seen your father recently."

Maeve wriggled, set a fancy leather bookmark between pages, adjusted the footrest of the old recliner—generally did all she could to stall. "I'm not sure how you want me to answer. I know he's missed two support payments." That was the deal. No child support, no visits—though Maeve was almost sixteen years old now.

Her mom grimaced and waggled a hand, erasing that idea right out of the air. "I'm not on the warpath. I saw Alice at the market, and she said she and Warren ran into Jack somewhere and he looked like he was in pretty bad shape. He took losing Marlena hard, didn't he?"

Maeve felt a chill on her spine. The deal was, adults were supposed to take care of themselves, quite privately, so you could have your *own* growing-up crises and they could attend to *you*, but it never seemed to work out that way. Her mom had a running problem, too, with her new husband, Bradley, who labored under what Maeve had come to see as a small-man complex, which meant you could never cross him directly, but had to work around him in some way that his tiny brain would not notice. As far as she was concerned, Brad could shrivel up and die any day he liked, but Maeve loved her real father to distraction, unreservedly, with an ache that went all the way through her.

"He and Mar got along pretty well, but they didn't have very much in common," Maeve said. "She was going to one of those churches where they think Jesus already has his landing gear down. I think when she left him, it just brought out a lot of his other stuff."

Maeve could see her mother decide consciously to leave the snotty comment about Jesus alone. "Do you think he's drinking?"

It was drink, long ago, and the disorder that went with it, that had ended up sending Maeve to Two-family City. "No, he's pretty firm on that now."

"Alice said she'd never seen anyone so downcast and unsteady. Would you like to go see him?"

Maeve felt herself light up. "Really?"

"You're on school break. Why don't you go cheer him up."

Maeve was up out of the chair in an instant, hugging her mother. "Oh, thank you, Mom."

"I care for Jack, too."

Jack Liffey adjusted the hard chair to face the wall of his apartment. He took off his wristwatch and set it in front of him. He rested his palms flat on his knees, closed his eyes, and started to inhale deeply the way a meditation-besotted blind date had insisted on showing him, sucking air into every nook and cranny of his lungs that he could visualize. Then he exhaled until his belly tucked in under his ribs and his throat creaked a little. He carried on this way while repeating in his head one of the mantras she had suggested: *I'm strong today, I'm forgiving.* Whatever.

After about fifteen minutes, he'd end up good and buzzed for a while. You could call it meditation if you wanted, but he figured what he was really doing was altering his blood chemistry, hyper-ventilating. It was probably the way mystics and sufis and dervishes had always cranked themselves up to the point where they heard their gods talking to them. He knew it knocked his blood pressure back and left him woozy, so it was as good a substitute as he knew for a stiff shot of single-malt scotch.

About two-thirds of the way through his allotted time, Loco stirred and started to pace restlessly, with an odd little purring. It disturbed his concentration. He thought he'd preempted this by giving the dog its obligatory five minutes of affection. Loco was half coyote and did not usually make much in the way of demands on the human world.

The purr became a mewl. Something was up and then the rasp-angry doorbell sounded. *Damn*, he thought. *Meditatus interruptus.* Still, he was already getting a bit lightheaded. Loco was leaping at the knob as if trying to work out its mechanics.

And there was Maeve, grinning, carrying her little suitcase, and she launched herself into his arms just as the dog launched itself at her. "I missed you, Daddy."

"Oh, me, too, sweet stuff."

She bent down to hug Loco, which gave Jack Liffey a chance to rub his eyes surreptitiously. So much sudden love going around was more than he could handle.

Three

Liffey & Liffey Investigations

"Pretty gutless, Dad."

With Maeve's extra weight onboard, the old VW labored down to third gear, about 48 mph, heading over the Sepulveda Pass toward the Valley. It was lugging so badly now he had to drop to second. He'd had the car for almost a year now and he still wasn't really used to it. The horrible engine noise of the air-cooled beast unnerved him on long trips, like a Greyhound bus running up his tail.

"The price was right," he yelled over the engine.

Chris Johnson had virtually given it to him—$500, he'd said, whenever he could afford it—after his trusty old AMC Concord had given its life, in effect, to save him from a couple of thugs. The VW hadn't proved its loyalty like that yet.

"Can we go to the electronics store first?" she pleaded.

He was combining her errand to buy some gizmo with his own trip to Kennedy School to start looking into the missing kids. He had always had this primitive spirit of economy that gave him a deep satisfaction in dual-purpose chores, like someone who'd gone through the Depression and hoarded coupons. His father had seemed to spend half his life catching him coming out of rooms and telling him to turn out the lights.

"And then I drop you at the North Hollywood Library for a few hours."

"We'll see," she said. He could sense another agenda turning over deep in her psyche.

"How is it you're on vacation in October, hon?"

She grimaced. "I've explained that already, Dad. I'm on C-track. It's not like when you were a kid anymore. We've got year-round school. It's more efficient, and the kids don't have to help bring in the summer crops anymore."

"Really?" He stayed deadpan. "Who *does* bring in the crops?"

"Illegals, of course."

He glanced at her and she nodded quickly. "Okay, okay, *undocumented* workers. I didn't mean anything."

"I know some of those expressions are a bit absurd," he conceded. "*Differently abled*—as if a bunch of folks just decided one day they'd prefer riding around in wheelchairs. But it never hurts to call people what they'd like to be called. It's just politeness. If redneck assholes want to be known as the cranially challenged, that's fine with me."

She smiled. "We had a big discussion of *Huck Finn* in Mrs. Beecher's class before we started reading it. You can bet what it was about."

"The N-word. It gives me the willies, too. I know it really pays off in the book when Huck finally connects with Jim, but I still can't say it."

"When we read some out loud in class, we read it as *Negro*. Negro Jim. It was a weird compromise. Do you think it would have been better to say the bad word?"

"You know, punkin, I think for some questions there just isn't a right answer. I love Twain, but that word carries freight now that you simply can't ignore. Someday you can read Brecht's *Caucasian Chalk Circle* and we can talk about it. He set up a really intractable dispute, between two pig-headed groups, and he thought he'd worked out an answer, but I think it's the most dangerous possible answer." It was wonderful to have a daughter you could actually talk to, he thought.

That perked her up. "*Caucasian Chalk Circle*. I'm there, dude."
She studied him for a moment as he drove. "You know I've started
dating."

His heart fell through to the soles of his feet and then bounced,
but it didn't make it all the way back up. He tried not to let the
trepidation show. "Would I like him?"

"You'd adore him. He's into computers and teaching himself
Greek. He's smarter than me."

"Not a chance."

"Anyway, we're just good friends."

He figured that meant she wasn't sleeping with him yet, but he
decided it was best not to edge into that area *at all*. In any case, she
was spinning her life off into that zone where he would sooner or
later have to trust her.

"When you're ready, I'll be happy to meet him. I won't bite. But
if he's never heard of Brecht, I'll be merciless."

"You? You're a pussycat." She hugged his arm and after enjoying
it for a moment, he wriggled free enough to slam the shift back up
into third and see if the poor old 1200-cc engine could hold it up
the slope.

Fariborz folded his hands and stared at the ketchup bottle on the
Formica table in front of him as if it were his lost childhood.
America was the only country he had ever known, born and raised
here, and the bottle pretty much symbolized it for him, but he felt
utterly outside it all now. The folk-rock music and the comfortable
home and driving his dad's Land Rover Discovery and simply going
into a 7-Eleven for a Coke and feeling like he had a right to be
there. He knew he had done it to himself, but that didn't make it
any easier. Pejman had lived in London for a few years, which gave
him some perspective so he may not have felt quite as lost now, but
Fariborz felt as if he had cast himself into coldest outer space.

He had ratcheted up his bravado day by day, watching himself
do it, feeling his resolve hardening and growing more adamant, letting it build and mutually reinforce with a small circle of like-
minded friends until they forced one another to take themselves at

their word. Suddenly they had to act out their challenges, and—
wham!—he found himself on the far side of a hole torn in his
reality, stuck fast in a completely different place. And then, by
default somehow, they all found themselves closeted with a truly
fanatical cabal of grown men from a desert culture that meant
nothing at all to them. He ached physically, in a place right under
his stomach, ached to be home. But there was no going back; he
could see that.

"Almost midday. Almost time to pray," Pejman said, checking
his watch.

"We should wait for the sheik."

Sheik Arad was the leader of the religious compound in Mar
Vista, which was not far from the sparkling new mosque in Culver
City that the Saudis had built for L.A.'s Moslems, but the sheik
wouldn't go near it because he was from Sudan and he hated the
Saudi regime with a deadly ferocity. The boys hadn't wanted to
come to the sheik—his intensity had terrified them—but they
couldn't think of anybody else who would be able, discreetly, to get
Iman the medical treatment for his mangled hand.

"Pej, I insist we're still just going to attack symbols of impurity."
In fact, he was pretty sure Sheik Arad had other ideas altogether.
"We can stink-bomb cinemas where they show pornographic
movies, and paint-bomb the headquarters of *Hustler* magazine and
the shops where they put scandalous lingerie in their windows. And
we have to do this when the buildings are unoccupied. Maybe it
will awaken the sleepy conscience of many Christians, too."

He had said this many times before, in one form or another, but
he felt his stilted diction shifting weirdly. It was almost as if he were
being taken over by a djinn who had to translate everything from
medieval Arabic. He had sensed it first at the beginning of their
Retreat, trying to think of it as an attempt to purify his speech and
become more precise and careful, but now he felt estranged even
from the part of his brain that generated language.

"All these scandalous things interfere with our own freedom of
religion," Pejman agreed. "There is no way to worship in purity
when you're forced to wade through filth every day."

They were like two boys whistling past a cemetery. They guessed neither of them had the strength of character to hold out against the ferocity of the Sudani band—not face-to-face—and if they weren't on the alert they'd find themselves so beholden that they'd end up reluctantly but inevitably sitting in a big truck heading toward some federal building. Or they would be packed off, will-less, to a desert training camp in Libya or even Pakistan.

"Man, I want a Big Mac," Pejman said. "With fries." He seemed to work out his distress by thinking about food, while Fariborz tended to fret and repeat himself. Yahya just lay on the sofa across the room, whimpering.

"He may not be back in time. Let's pray now."

They took up their little prayer rugs, bought from Ikea, and carried them into the living room. The house had not been built conveniently on a *quibla* axis, so none of its walls truly faced Mecca, but the sheikh had set up a portable *mihrab* niche on the east wall, canted a little to indicate true east. In an uncharacteristic moment of levity months earlier, in a similar apartment room on their retreat, Pejman had spoken of praying to Palm Springs, which was pretty much due east of L.A.

They stirred Yahya and took turns in the bathroom tub washing their faces, hands and feet. Then they unrolled their prayer rugs and prostrated themselves, touching their foreheads down.

"In the name of Allah, the compassionate, the merciful. . . ."

"Two points," she suggested. Maeve and her father played a running game of finding oddities around town and keeping score. To date the highest was four points, awarded for the giant acupuncture needles that she had found stuck into the earth around L.A. by art students, ostensibly to prevent earthquakes. The average point-award was only two, for oddities like the absurdly undersized horse under John Wayne on the statue at Wilshire and La Cienega.

This ought to be equal to the horse: a giant flying saucer was permanently crashed into the entrance of the electronics store.

Customers had to enter under the saucer and past a jeep that had been death-rayed in half. Dummies of 1950s soldiers were firing old M-ls at Martians who were firing ray guns back at them.

"It's all a little too self-consciously cute," Jack Liffey demurred. "Corporate eccentricity makes for a different fish entirely."

"I know what you mean, but it still hits the spirit of oddity."

"I'll be a good sport. Two points. What are you buying?"

"I used up Mom's blank card-stock making business cards. They have this really cool paper that's preprinted with color designs, and you can run it through your computer to put your name on it, and then snap off expensive-looking business cards."

"Supplies are over there." Halfway there, he noticed that the computer monitors and printers were arrayed on a long counter that was held up by the arm of a giant squid that had ripped up through the flooring. Now he didn't feel quite so bad about awarding those points. To enhance the shock, they had even reproduced a fainting victim in the aisle with paramedics clustered around her, her blouse ripped open and her skin gone ashen. The store decor was so bizarre that it took him several seconds to notice that the paramedics were moving. One of them slapped cardio paddles on the woman's chest, and yelled "Clear!"

He got between the scene and Maeve and herded her toward the tall shelves of computer paper. It was a natural reaction, this urge to shield Maeve from harsh reality, but he realized it was a bit patronizing for a fifteen-year-old. "Do I get to take a point back if I tell you there was a genuine fainting victim on the floor beside the giant squid?"

"Huh?" She turned back immediately. He waited while she rubbernecked with a group of others in a little semicircle and after a while she came sheepishly back to where he was toying with a little laptop. He wished he could afford it, but he hadn't had a computer to call his own since aerospace, and that had been before Bill Gates—ancient history.

"It's not fainting." Maeve looked a little green. "The woman is dead."

"I'm sorry I said anything." He put his arm around her shoulder, wanting to feel her substance, suddenly struck by the fragility of the world.

"That's the first dead person I've ever seen," she said. "It's funny. Something's really gone when you're dead. She looked like a dummy of a real person."

He'd seen a small portion of death in Vietnam and a few times since, but he let it go. There didn't seem anything really to say. Dead was dead, and if you thought about it too much, you'd start getting a whiff of your own mortality and then the bad sweats would kick in. "How'd you use up your mom's card stock?" he asked idly.

"I made some business cards for me. See how neat?"

She handed him a card.

"Whoa!" He came to a dead stop. "Whoa, whoa, whoa."

Liffey & Liffey Investigations
Runaway and missing children found

She had listed her own cell-phone number. It was more dignified and better looking than his own business card that Marlena had made up for him two years earlier at her Mailboxes 'R' Us shop, with his name in some weird cowboy script and a big eyeball on it. But this idea was not even negotiable.

"Hon, we can't have this. No, no, no."

"It's just a kind of joke."

"How come I don't believe you? Remember all the trouble you got in last year?" Trying to help him out, she'd gotten in well over her head with a gang of bikers.

"I saved your life, didn't I?"

"Thank you very much, but I don't want you trying it again."

"Dad, think of all the things I could find out from young people that you never could."

"It's very touching that you want to help me, hon, but I fell into this job myself only when I was desperate. It's not a career path for a bright young woman. It's just not."

"I could just ask questions for you."

"Maeve, no. Have I ever denied you anything before?"

"A Porsche. A strapless evening gown. A thong bikini."

"But seriously, *no*. If nothing else, your mom would roast both of us very slowly over an open fire." He had an inspiration. "The first thing she would do is cut off our visits for good until your eighteenth birthday—you know that."

That seemed to strike a chord with her and her face clouded over. "Awww. We don't have to tell her."

"How long before she catches on when you come home in your new shoulder holster and fedora?"

"Dad!"

"We can't lie to your mom, hon, and anyway I don't want you trailing around after me, playing detective. It might be dangerous for me, you know? How about I promise to keep you up-to-date on everything I'm doing, if you'll promise to butt out?" He'd already told her about the Kennedy Four and the missing girl.

She pouted.

"Deal?"

She swallowed some words that might have been an assent, but he knew he'd better not let it rest there.

"Are we agreed?" he insisted. "I need an unmistakable affirmative here, Maeve Mary. No crossed fingers behind your back."

She nodded and showed both hands. "Okay."

And he believed her because she'd never lied to him about anything important before.

A weird electronic chime sounded in the school hallway, nothing like the raucous bell of his own high-school days. That was fine with him, because he knew just how visceral his reaction would be to that school-bell sound, and he did not want to be carried back to all the social dread and sexual confusion and all that unhappiness.

Suddenly every classroom door swung open and boys in blue blazers burst out like thoroughbreds clearing the gates. The sound level rose instantly as they hurried every which way.

"Thank you, Captain Obvious!" one voice wailed.

"Well, bust a can of whoop-ass."

"So then Mary is all, 'Duh,' and I'm like, 'Come *on!*' "

Jack Liffey was having a displaced moment. He was sure it was all English, but it wasn't coming into focus.

He stopped the nearest boy, who had a weird haircut, short on top and long at the fringes. "Can you tell me where the office is?"

"No time to flirt, man. That way." The boy waved a hand dismissively and hurried on.

As Jack Liffey passed among the tidy students, generally ignored, he realized suddenly that they were all white. One tall boy far down the hall might have been a light-skinned African-American, but he was too far away to tell for sure. And there were no girls. He was surprised because he'd read that Kennedy, the ritziest boys' school in Southern California had merged with Westridge, one of the ritziest girls' schools, but there was no evidence of it.

Eventually he reached an office. A printed metal label in a Plexiglas holder beside the door said:

Mr. Christopher Hogle, B.A., M.A.
Dean of Community Affairs
Basketball Coach
Gymnastics

There was also a cutout photograph of a basketball taped haphazardly to the door, with the words in felt pen: *Hogle Rips and Rules.*

The door was open, so he rapped as he went in. A woman at the front looked up, but behind her an extremely tall man beckoned and Jack Liffey went right past her, through a swing gate into the office proper. That pleased him no end because he didn't get on with receptionists. He hated coming on strong with people so far down the food chain, particularly as they were generally just doing their job keeping out riffraff like him. The problem was that gatekeepers rubbed a raw nerve in him.

"Mr. Liffey, I presume?"

"Mr. Hogle. Now I understand the basketball on the door."

Hogle had to be seven feet tall, and thin as a stringbean. He reached far down to shake hands. Jack Liffey wouldn't have referred to his height, but the jokey familiarity of the man's "I presume" invited it.

"I was once third-string center under Kareem Abdul-Jabbar. He was Lew Alcindor then, at UCLA. A pro team in Europe wanted to give me a tryout, but I knew better. Just because you're tall. . . ." He shrugged.

"Fair enough."

"Have a seat. 'Kareem' means 'generous' in both Arabic and Farsi, and he was, if he let you get close to him. I'm just happy to have touched the hem." There was a stiff chair by the desk, the kind of thing bureaucrats used the world over to keep a petitioner uncomfortable. There was no choice so he sat.

"The hem of celebrity?"

"Let's say expertise. You want to talk about the missing young men, don't you?"

An out-of-whack sprinkler on the lawn outside slapped the window glass hard with spray. He was surprised a place so mon-eyed allowed that much disorder.

"And about the girl, too. By the way, what's Community Affairs?"

He shrugged. "Public relations. Making sure the neighbors aren't offended. Talking to private detectives." An edge had entered his voice.

"I just find missing kids."

"The girl wasn't a student here. Her dad switched her to Taunton over the hill when we started merging the boys and girls."

"Her Iranian boyfriend was here."

"And you're going to ask me about the rumors about the hazing of minorities."

So that's what the edge was about, Jack Liffey thought. He let it sit, so the man's own nerves would do the hard work.

"Every student in Kennedy-Westridge is mandated to take a ten-week cultural-sensitivity course. In my experience, we're far better than your average L.A. high school, with its warring cliques and race rumbles."

"How many blacks and Latinos do you have?"

He glared. "Some. We give scholarships."

"Look, I don't care if you kick over Jewish headstones at night, I really don't, and I figure your gracious kids probably don't do things like that, either. I just want to talk to any of them who knew Fariborz Bayat. I could find them indirectly—it wouldn't be that hard—or I can do it through you."

The tall man thought about it for a moment. "You can do it through Mr. Toussaint. He was their counselor, and he's right down the hall. I'm sorry if I seem overly sensitive on this issue. We've taken a pasting on this, and it's really not a bad place." He explained what great, sensitive kids they had, offering anecdotes approaching the some-of-my-best-friends-are-colored variety. Jack Liffey just let him run down on his own.

"After all, the rich are pretty much like you and me," he concluded.

"Except they have a lot more money," Jack Liffey said. Who was he paraphrasing? He remembered: Hemingway, allegedly responding to Scott Fitzgerald, though Fitzgerald had been maintaining that the rich were *different* from you and me.

"I'm surprised that I didn't see any girls out there," Jack Liffey said. He seemed to have been dismissed so he stood up.

"We're merging grade by grade. You'll see them in the early grades."

"Doesn't it narrow the gene pool a lot, putting all the ruling class into the same school?" Jack Liffey said at the door.

The man didn't appear to like the expression "ruling class" very much, but he was Community Relations and wouldn't let himself be baited.

"We try to encourage suitable mates," he said drily.

Four

How We Meet Loss

This office also had a metal nameplate by the door:

Mr. Broyard Toussaint, M.A. D.Ed.
Dean of Bilingual Students
French
Spanish
Biology

But this time there was no receptionist. A man opened at his knock and peered out quizzically. What the sign didn't say was that Broyard Toussaint was black, or—as they said in Louisiana—*hi-yella,* which meant he had Anglo features and was nearly light enough to pass.

"Hello?"

"Hello, did Mr. Hogle call you about me?"

"He did that very thing, about fifteen seconds ago, if you're Jack Liffey. Come in. Excuse the clutter. I wear a lot of hats at Kennedy, and I seem to need a lot of space to park them all."

The room was full of piles of books and manila folders, all with limp white bookmarks sticking out of them. The man shifted a pile of books off the only free chair, and Jack Liffey sat.

"Kennedy has a lot of odd euphemisms," Jack Liffey said. "Does 'Dean of Bilingual Students' mean that you counsel the non-Anglos?"

He smiled. "It does indeed. The term sucks, as the kids say, but there's a logic to it. Those outside the dominant culture tend to share common problems, no matter where they come from."

"Especially at a place like Kennedy, where 'dominant' really means something."

Toussaint's smile tightened. "That has been said, but I assure you we're not one of those vicious Eastern boarding schools, not at all. There's a little cultural hazing, but more often a sensitive young man from another culture will just read the signals wrong, and think he's being dissed, as the boys say, when it's nothing of the sort. Add that to all the usual adolescent struggles with identity. . . . One likes to think one can empathize with that."

"Louisiana?" Jack Liffey suggested.

"My folks moved to Chicago when I was fifteen, but I'm from Cajun country, near Lafayette. Where the white Cajuns still swear there is no such thing as a black Cajun."

"And you're living proof."

Toussaint smiled disarmingly and waved at a poster of an old black man, bellowing over an accordion. "And a lot of other people like me, whole schools of music, styles of cooking. I always found that kind of tetchiness in rural white culture supremely silly— almost entertaining, in fact—but some of my friends tended to go the other way entirely and get a little pissed off."

"I can understand that. So how's the back of the bus at Kennedy?"

"Apropos of the Iranian boys?" Toussaint asked.

"Yes."

"They met each other here in the dorm and became close friends. It doesn't necessarily mean they were driven together by prejudice. Or strictly racist prejudice. School cliques form along a lot more lines than one remembers from our day—goths, football jocks, techies, stoners—it's endless."

"So the four Iranian boys just happened to get together because they were the only Edith Wharton fans at Kennedy?"

The man went quiet for a moment, then gave a small shrug. "Listen, for a while now, all things Middle Eastern have remained pretty unpopular in this country. And it's not getting any better. There was some hazing, one admits. They were called 'ragheads' and 'camel jockeys,' as if Iranians were Arabs. But the lads only magnified their isolation when they became flamboyantly Moslem. Which was their right, of course, of course," he added quickly.

"They weren't from religious families, were they?"

"No. But . . ." He shrugged. "The boys definitely found their way to Islam, whatever their parents felt. Adolescence is a time of heartfelt and consuming belief, as one probably only remembers dimly, and Islam provides the opportunity for that in spades."

" 'Dimly' is right. My adolescence was a bad dream I try to forget."

"For most of us. I think I know why adolescence was so utterly horrible for all of us, *and* why, at the very same time, it's possible to look back on it as if it weren't."

"Meaning?"

"When one looks back now, we recognize that all those terrible things that we dreaded every day *didn't* happen. When we say we want to live it over again, we'd do it only if we could hang onto the knowledge that we didn't actually slip and fall at the senior prom."

Toussaint was beginning to sound like Dicky Auslander.

"Well, I don't envy that time at all, only the stamina I had. I could run a mile in 5:50."

The man seemed to refocus all at once. "One is interested in Fariborz Bayat, true?"

"True."

"Bayat was the smartest of the boys, but I don't believe he was the ringleader—that's a terrible word to use. I apologize. The boy who gravitated to Islam first and needed it the most was probably Iman Behrooz. He's from a broken home, and he really resented his father's leaving the family. Behrooz developed a very stiff and unforgiving moralism out of that betrayal, and the other boys picked some of it up from him. They started reading the Koran together and whatever else they could find to reconnect themselves with Persian culture. They refused to wear the school tie any longer—I believe in Iran neckties have come to represent Western decadence. As proof of how tolerant one tries to be at Kennedy-Westridge, the administration gave them permission to doff the tie as long as they buttoned their shirts up to the neck. We also helped them set up a do-it-yourself class in classical Arabic."

"Did they have an Islamic mentor? Here or outside school?"

The man thought about it for a moment.

"Yes. As Persians, one would have expected them to find a Shia mentor, but the man they found wasn't. The Shias are the division of the faith that relies heavily on clergy—imams and ayatollahs."

"Refresh my memory on Islam." He knew roughly, but he was interested in what the received wisdom had been at the school.

"I'm not a scholar of Islam, but as their advisor one had to bone up a little. Most of the Moslem world is Sunni, something like eight-five percent. The Shiites split off to follow a caliph named Ali soon after Mohammed died, and they're mostly in Iran and Southern Iraq today. They erected their form of Islam on top of an old Persian belief in the divine right of kings so the Shias tended to grant their leaders papal infallibility. Anyway, Southern California is a little short of Persian ayatollahs, but the lads did locate a Sunni sheik who was fierce enough for Iman Behrooz."

He shrugged apologetically. "One finds that many Christian sects also have their militia leaders and fanatics."

"Let's hold the editorials. Does he have a name?"

"Sheik Arad. I have no idea what his title means, but he's got a little group around him. The boys didn't stay with him long."

"Do you know why not?"

"One gathers from Fariborz Bayat that Sheik Arad was a pretty hair-raising character. Bayat was fairly open with me, at least at first. The sheik's like some ancient prophet. One either drops everything to follow him out into the desert, or else one can go to hell."

The peculiar electronic tone now sounded again out in the hall, and even at one remove from the clanging bell that he remembered, the summons gave him a chill. Broyard Toussaint perked up. "I'm going to have to go. I'm invigilating a biology exam."

"*Invigilating?*"

He smiled. "Fancy old prep-school word for proctoring." He gathered up a handful of papers.

"Quickly, then, do you think the boys might have followed this sheik out into the desert?"

"Mar Vista, actually. His school. It was the first place the police checked, as one might guess, plus the second and third. It appears not."

Jack Liffey followed Toussaint out of his office, just as a flood of students washed past. There were a few girls, after all, wearing beige skirts and navy blazers. "Do you have a guess?"

"Hold up, friendasaurus!" a boy bellowed about an inch from Jack Liffey's ear.

"That's cold, dude!"

"I'd suggest you talk to Billy de Villiers. He was Fariborz Bayat's good friend. Call me right after school and I'll arrange it. I wish you good luck on finding the boys. One liked Bayat quite a lot."

"Well, *laissez les bons temps rouler!*"

Toussaint smiled tartly. "One's accent sucks, my friend."

"Sit." The tall, thin Arab named Hassan indicated a spot on the floor with the flat of his hand, as if pointing with a single finger would be rude. A dull red patterned carpet, about three feet by six, had been laid over the beige wall-to-wall of the tract house. Nearby, the sheik sat cross-legged in front of several plates of food on another small carpet, boiled lamb and pots of stewed vegetables that he was plucking out with a piece of limp flatbread and stuffing into his mouth.

"Thanks, sure." Fariborz was fighting a tendency to talk to them in a kind of stilted baby-talk, trying to make sure these strange men understood him. What he was also trying to do was keep some contact with the commonplace amidst so much that was unfamiliar, even alarming. Two men in turbans who looked like identical twin wrestlers waited behind the sheik with their arms crossed. They looked different from the others, less bronzed, with longer faces, and the boys had learned they were Afghanis, rumored to be former Taliban.

He and Pejman sat uncomfortably, crossing their legs. Yahya was still cowering in the room that they'd been assigned and would not come out with them.

Sheik Arad chewed with his mouth open, smacking and snicking. He made some wordlike noise, perhaps acknowledging them, but they could not make it out. The religious leader was not at all what Fariborz had expected, but they had seen him several times now and they had grown less disturbed by his peculiarities. One eye had a cataract, giving him a permanent wild squint, and his legs were withered—at least what little Fariborz had ever seen of them peeking from under his robe. The boys themselves had given up eating meat sometime back, manufacturing a kind of ascetic Islam for themselves, so they had all been put off by the sheik's carnivorous diet and his table manners. Letting meat juices run out of one's mouth did not fit their idea of a holy man's eating habits, but they had only Hollywood films and their own conjectures to match against this reality. And Arad was definitely real.

"You want eat?" the sheik said. This time they could just make out the words in his guttural croak. The good eye came up to pierce their souls while the other one seemed to be contemplating infinity.

"A little, thank you."

"Give them eat." He waved a hand flamboyantly, his robe flapping like a bird's limp wing. Hassan brought the boys plates. Actually, they wanted to ask him if they could leave Iman to recover at this small Mar Vista religious center while they went back to their own place, a furnished apartment rented under a false name in Burbank. Unfortunately, Fariborz was having trouble working up his courage to ask *anything*.

The sheik said something else that failed to compute. Pejman reached out for a piece of the flatbread.

"Other hand!" the sheik roared. "What wrong with you? Don' your mothers teach you *nothing* here? That is the hand you use to clean up your ass!"

Pejman snatched back his left hand, seeming suddenly to shrink into himself.

Our mothers teach us to *wash* our hands, Fariborz thought—but it was not something he was going to say aloud.

"This country is a despair. I lack the strength to confront it every time." Then the sheik seemed to come to some more clement decision in himself. "I conclude you will become good students soon enough. As good as born Arabs."

Fariborz said nothing. Better than born Arabs, he thought. They knew that Persia had a rich civilization that went back thousands of years before Islam and had been the wellspring of a great deal of Islamic scholarship and culture for much of the last thousand. Islamic mysticism and Sufism had developed there, astronomy, Ibn Sina, the prince of physicians, and generations of great poets like Omar Khayyam and the greatest of all, Rumi. The men in the sheik's entourage by and large represented the outposts and backwaters of Islam. But he tried not to hold it against them. He reminded himself that a fool could come from a big city, and a saint might be born in a village.

As if reading their thoughts, the sheik used the flat of his hand, palm up, to indicate his guards. "They are from Afghanistan, the home of Tamerlane." He poked the same hand at himself. "I am from Sudan, birthplace of the Mahdi." Then he indicated Hassan. "He is from Morocco, the great west of Islam. Yet we are all one. The Umma reveals that the group bond does not depend upon blood, but upon faith in Him."

"May the blessing and peace of God be upon Him," the boys said in unison.

Fariborz tried the overcooked and smoky food, but did not like it very much. A voice kept speaking inside him. Time to reconsider, it said. But reconsider what? At every stage they had been driven by logic and devotion. They were young and inexperienced, dropped from somewhere far above into company they could not quite assimilate, and could not seem to assimilate them. He had been living with this heightened disquiet for quite some time now.

For years Fariborz had felt out of place and alone. He was an impostor, constantly having to adjust his disguise amongst Americans so he wouldn't be found out. But his disguise would no longer work here. He had built himself up as a devout Moslem among Christians and Jews, as a Persian among Americans, and these ploys had served as a cloak of protection for very personal fears he sensed within himself. But here they were all Moslems, and he no longer had a cloak against the deeper loneliness.

The sheik chewed noisily, then extracted a chunk of gristle from his mouth and set it on a nearby plate. Fariborz took a deep breath. "We seek permission, sir, to leave our wounded friend with you and return to our own base."

He could feel the tension in Pejman. Sheik Arad brought his good eye around to them. The room was tense with command and submission to command.

"No propositions," the sheik asserted. "There will be no designs outside the grand design. You learners will go to our southern *madrasa* with Hassan."

"But, sir—"

His good eye slitted and became even fiercer, and the Afghani bodyguards seemed to lean closer. "I don't never take no refusals."

This time the woman who sat in Auslander's waiting room appeared more or less normal. She was thin and pretty and blond, with her eyes buried in a magazine called *Beginnings*. She didn't even look up as he crossed the room to press Auslander's button. Almost immediately, the man's head appeared and nodded him in.

"I wasn't sure you'd come."

"I wasn't sure, either. I've been to the boys' school but there's not much to report yet."

"I didn't expect much yet."

Jack Liffey sat exactly where he had sat before and stared at the seascape print, obviously meant to be soothing. Fierce surf pounded down on some jagged rocks. Maybe it would actually be soothing once the sea's rasp had smoothed the earth down to a billiard ball, he thought.

"Would you like some coffee?"

"No."

They were both silent for a while.

"So, losing Marlena surprised you with its power. It knocked you for a loop."

Jack Liffey said nothing.

"That's what I hear, anyway. I imagine it shook up your sense of yourself and your own strengths. It made it hard to get out of bed in the morning. Made you rethink a lot of your life and wonder where you're heading."

Jack Liffey wondered if the door across the office led to the outside world. The window shade was pretty bright, and his sense of the geography of the complicated hallway suggested he was probably at the rear, with the backyard just beyond. He could just walk out.

"Sooner or later that happens to all of us, if we suffer enough of a loss, or a truly unexpected loss. The emotional power of it isn't really a mystery, or it shouldn't be. Loss is more or less the primal experience. The first separation from the mother, the first realization that we're not the center of the universe, the best friend–playmate who moves away. A large enough loss delivers us straight back to childhood. I mean, emotionally."

Jack Liffey wondered if Dicky Auslander, in his years of dispensing facile advice to desperate people, had ever had one of them come across the room and punch him out. He figured it might even be good for the man, might improve his sense of perspective.

"A place of consolation is gone with the loss, and you're helpless about it. But as an adult, you no longer have the defenses of childhood, so it's really worse. You can't invent some kind of magic meaning for your loss. You know better now. Loss is just loss."

He noticed that Auslander had buttoned his open-necked shirt wrong, an extra buttonhole flying high under his chin. He thought about striding across the office, pushing him down in the chair, and then wrenching the shirt open to rebutton it for him. It would be very satisfying.

"The anguish of loss is like being trapped in a moment of time that can never change, never get better," Auslander pontificated.

"Like right now. If we go on glaring at each other for fifty-five minutes, it's going to get pretty boring."

"I thought there was a rule in psychology that the party in question has to ask for help to do any good."

"It's not hard and fast. There's such a thing as *intervention* when things get bad. As Lon and Virginia tried to do for you, by talking to me. It's a sign they care for you."

Once more there was a faint but terrible shriek from one of the other rooms. It was weak, yet quite distinct. And as it came again, over and over like a ritual of pain giving, then tailed off, they both looked at the wall as if they could see through it to that horrible distress. It reminded him that there were other, haunted, worlds all around, overlapping his, and many were much worse. "Count your blessings," Auslander suggested.

"I thought you said something about a way to make this entertaining."

Auslander readjusted his lanky body and grimaced. "Are you comfortable?"

"Yes, Aaron."

"Let's try this. You're a detective, right? The single most popular genre of popular fiction—I think I'm right in this—is detective novels, broadly construed to include what they call police procedurals and crime novels and similar things. Let's agree to look at your life as if it's fiction. I'll interrogate you on why you feel a need to go around detecting things, and just so it's fair, you can pretend I'm the author of your life. I'm the big, bad guy who's devising your adventures and leaving you so forlorn, taking away Marlena, et cetera, et cetera. You can interrogate me on why I should want to write about a detective in the first place, let alone punish him so much."

"*Aaron—*"

"Come on, Jack. Give us a break. What are you so afraid of?"

"I'm not really a detective, Dicky." Somehow, using the nickname gave him enough of an edge to keep from losing his cool. "I was a tech writer in aerospace before the whole industry eighty-sixed in Southern California and promoted me to a small part of the peace dividend. I was at a loss and I fell into this job. It's a long story, but eight or nine years ago—maybe more—a guy from South Africa contacted me. I'd known him years and years ago, and his teenage daughter was hitching around the U.S. and she had stopped writing all of a sudden, her last letter home postmarked Hollywood. He sent me her photo and, as a courtesy, I made a bunch of copies and posted it around and asked some questions up on the Strip. Sure enough, I found out she'd been sucked into this cult up in Canyon Country—you know, that goofy minister who lured all the lost kids up to his sweatshop and put them to work making multicolored leather jackets.

"He had a business sense I guess, if you count a knack for enslaving lost kids a business sense, but otherwise he was a complete paranoid loon. He did everything but wear a tinfoil hat to keep the beams from space from controlling him, and he had guys with guns posted all around his leather-jacket ranch up in Acton. I hired an ex-cop to go up there with me and get the girl out, but the cop turned out to be such a rum-dum, I had to do most of the snatch myself. Which I did pretty damn well, if I do say so myself, and I got her home, and when the aerospace job vanished, it occurred to me that locating missing kids was something I could do."

"It's more than that," Auslander suggested after a few pregnant moments. "That first time may have been an accident for you, but then you kept on doing it."

Jack Liffey shrugged. "Finding lost kids isn't such a bad calling, all in all. I can't stand the thought of a child being abused—I never could."

There was a crash next door and then a tense silence. It only interrupted them for a few moments.

"Do some role playing, Jack," Auslander insisted. "Think of me as your author and complain about your lot. What are you afraid of?"

He wondered if he was ever going to be able to get out of there without obliging this loon.

"Not a fucking chance."

Auslander smiled and rocked a little in his big executive chair. "I think I write about you because I need a hero, somebody brave and tireless and honest who can go out and turn up rocks and see what's underneath. And, of course, take all the punishment that entails."

If only this guy really were in charge, Jack Liffey thought. If only he could walk over there and give Auslander a big punch in the face for all his troubles.

"If you feel compelled to be a mystery writer, Dicky, write about somebody else. Leave me alone."

"Do you really think you've turned children's lives around?"

It sounded like a sincere question, and it gave him pause. Jack Liffey thought back over the last few years. Not counting the runaways that he'd found within a few days, hanging out at the Golden Cup on Hollywood Boulevard and nursing their sexual ambivalence, or the lost kids where he'd done no more than post a few notices and call in the cops, there had been five memorable cases that he could recall.

"Okay, Dicky. Here's the ones I remember."

The first had involved a young Chicano who had lost his mother and was now in Hermosillo, Mexico with his grandmother, a schoolteacher, and probably a lot better off than hanging out with his tagger crew in East L.A. The second, he'd tracked down a precocious and rather insufferable teenage girl who had fancied herself a filmmaker and now wrote him regularly to keep him up-to-date on her progress toward an anthropology degree at Columbia. Lately she had begun writing about the hollowness and cultural imperialism of anthropology, and had begun talking of going into the Peace Corps. After that, he'd located a boy who had been pretty far gone down the road to seeing himself as a religious savior and he'd brought him back to his parents. That boy, too, still wrote Jack Liffey from time to time, and after a year of community college, he'd ended up running a conservation camp, what the State had once called a reform school, far out in the Owens Valley on the eastern flank of the Sierras. The semiholy road.

A young Vietnamese student he'd been hired to find turned out to have been dead before he even took the case, so there wasn't much he could have done for her, but an older Vietnamese woman he'd met in that case had gone on to marry a conservative state senator from Orange County and got him to cosponsor a number of gay-rights bills that no other Republican would touch. That had to be a plus of some kind. And just a year earlier, he'd linked up with a little African-American girl who had remained friends with his own daughter, and was assiduously banging out folktales about magic on a secondhand computer he'd bought her with some of the reward money from her grandparents.

Of course, these lives might have worked out okay without him—it was the kind of thing you would never know—but he liked thinking he might have given each of them a nudge in the right direction.

"Jeez, Jack, I'm glad I created you. You might have saved more kids than me." He wasn't sure irony wasn't leaking in now. "You're my existential hero, and for hundreds and hundreds of readers."

"*Hundreds?* I want an author with a bigger publisher."

Five

The Angry Finger of Islam

"Over to you. Give me eighteen," Maeve exulted.

It was a real fatherly dilemma he faced, having seen the word the instant she had played B-L-O-W across on his C-R-U-M-B down on the Scrabble board. He had another B, and he had a J and an O, too, and there were three empty spaces after blow that would put him right onto the triple word at the edge and give him—let's see—sixty-three points with the triple word. Too bad there was no blow*jeb*. He had an E, and he'd go for that. Even Loco would have approved of that, and he was pretty protective.

The dog lay across Maeve's feet, as if afraid Maeve would go away again if he didn't stay in affectionate contact. Maeve had won the feral beast's heart with gobs of love, as opposed to the carefully metered affection Jack Liffey himself had offered, on his theory of consistency: You offered today only what you were willing to offer every day. There was still a coyote wanderlust that flattened out Loco's yellow canine eyes from time to time, leaving them depthless and a bit panicky. But, for some reason, the dog hadn't put up much of a fuss at giving up the big yard at Marlena's to retrench to Jack Liffey's enclosed condo and patio, at least as long as Maeve appeared from time to time.

"Would you accept 'btfsplk'?" he said. "It's Urdu for the little dark cloud that hangs over your head to make you gloomy."

"That's not Urdu," she said scornfully. "It's Dogpatch."

"You *do* know more than Dickens and the Brontës."

"I bet you've never heard of Puff Daddy," she challenged.

"That some kind of snake? I think Bugs Bunny is the high-water mark of American popular culture, and I can skip everything that came after. Bugs minds his own business in that fine cocky Brooklyn way, gnawing on his carrot, but if you cross him he'll get back to you, first with wit and then with a terrible vengeance."

"Yes, Dad, I've heard of Bugs Bunny."

He laid down two tiles. "I'll have to settle for Jot. Ten points."

She rotated the board gingerly on the dining table. "What's your next move going to be in the Becky case?"

Case, he thought. "The standard move, from page 209 of *Detecting for Dummies.*"

"*Dad.* You promised. I lay off if you keep me informed."

"A promise is a promise." Between their next few moves, he told her what he had learned that day about the boy. His next step, he thought, would be to get his friend Art Castro to find out what he could about Sheik Arad—Castro was a real detective in a big agency downtown with decades of files and lots of contacts and resources, even little microphones in martini olives—and Art owed him a favor.

Later that evening, he planned to go talk to Billy de Villiers, Fariborz's friend from school, he told her. He wasn't a boarder like the others, and it was just a jaunt over to Venice to his home.

"Looks like you got it covered."

"You can read or watch your favorite TV show while I go talk to Billy."

"My favorite show was on last night—*Bowling for Blowjobs.*"

His back stiffened. Kathy had warned him that Maeve was getting mouthy. "Maeve Mary!"

She smirked. "I could tell the letters you had. Right onto a triple word and a million points, but Victorian prudery held you back."

"It's not something a man discusses with his fifteen-year-old daughter."

"Almost sixteen."

"Almost counts only in horseshoes."

"What's horseshoes?"

"Doesn't anybody play it anymore?" he asked. "I'm sure I've seen the metal posts in the park."

"Oh, *that* thing. How does 'almost' count?"

"A ringer counts three points—that's when the horseshoe clangs onto the post and stays on. I think 'almost' means it's lying less than one horseshoe-width from the post. That's one point."

"If somebody puts it on the Internet, it'll be big."

His old CD player came to an end and started to recycle some Chicago blues, J. B. Hutto and Junior Wells. More old-guy stuff to her, he figured, but she ought to pick up a bit of it. The kids who knew only the current popular culture were going to end up terribly deprived, all that in-your-face testosterone, no shadings of emotion.

"I'd hate to see a simple old American game turned into some digital racket with machine guns and splattered goop. Simplicity is its beauty."

"You're still changing the subject, Dad. I know what a blowjob is. Remember when I walked in on you and Mar in the bathroom?"

"I'd rather not talk about Marlena, either." He was still changing the subject, of course, but he really *didn't* want to talk about Marlena.

She stared hard at him, with real tenderness. "Have you been sad about Mar, Dad?"

He wondered if everyone had joined the Let's-Help-Jack Club. "Sure, some. I guess it was the shock. It was like a horse kicked me, actually."

"You know, you two were *super* different."

"I know that, hon, but she had a really big heart, and that meant a lot to me." He felt himself choking up a little, and he stepped hard on it.

Maeve hurriedly came around the table and sat on his lap to hug him. "So do you, Dad. You've got a heart the size of a Cadillac."

He held himself rigid to keep from giving in to the emotion, but he felt his eyes start to burn. This was getting altogether too frequent and too exasperating, he thought.

"A VW-size heart is good enough for me," he said, as evenly as he could.

The de Villiers house was the tiniest of bungalows on a little walking path called Florita Court, face-to-face with a half dozen other bungalows separated by handkerchief-sized lawns and tiny plots of geraniums and pansies that were all fading now into eerie evening shadow. He wondered how somebody living here could afford Kennedy-Westridge.

The peephole darkened up. "Mr. Liffey?" It was a mellow voice through the door, with a strange accent, like British run through a sieve. He had called ahead and heard the same accent.

"Jack Liffey. Mrs. Aneliese de Villiers?"

He heard a chain come away and then several bolts, like a New York door. He was actually a little stunned when he saw her, a lot of flyaway blond hair and a face that could launch quite a few ships, though maybe not a thousand. Probably late forties, but looking less.

"Please come in."

She backed away. Or the rest of her backed away, but her breasts pretty much stayed right there, making the cottage seem even smaller than it was.

"Thanks. Is Billy available?"

"He's closeted in the bedroom, working on his computer. You have no idea how precious privacy can be in a house this small." She pronounced it *PRIV*-a-cee.

"I can try hard."

She smiled and lit him up like a searchlight. Her eyes were the deepest blue, the blue of the sky high up in the mountains above the dustiest layers of the atmosphere. "Please sit down for a few moments. Our agreement is he finishes his algebra before TV or any other interruptions."

"Bless you," he said. "And all who sail with you. I don't know many mothers who could enforce that these days." He sat on a threadbare sofa of some dark indeterminate pattern.

"Could I get you something to drink?"

"Water would be fine."

"I have some tolerable cabernet, and various types of mixed drinks."

"No, thanks." As she left to fetch him the water from a tiny side kitchen, he looked over the room. Pattern on pattern, wallpaper and rug and curtain, plus a print of a shaggy Highland bull. The room looked prewar British, or what he would have guessed was prewar British, mostly from watching PBS. "Where are you from?" he called.

"Zambia, though it was called Northern Rhodesia when we left. It was long ago, when we were trying to hold on to it. Anyone who could count knew it was time to go. And I didn't like the ugly way the whites talked about the blacks. My husband and I took what was called the 'chicken run,' and never looked back. We lost a small business in Lusaka in the process, like a lot of white refugees."

"Is Billy Zambian?"

"Oh, no. He was born here."

"And his father?"

There was a tiny hard glitter in her eyes. "I no longer need to punish myself over him, or deceive or compromise myself. I'm quite fortunate."

"Whoa, I detect anger."

"Quite a lot of rage, actually. The less said . . . Do you have children, Mr. Liffey?"

"Jack, please. A wonderful daughter who knows more about Victorian literature than I do, about Billy's age. Her mother and I are divorced as well."

Aneliese de Villiers sat down in an overstuffed chair and smoothed her cotton skirt over her knees; but when she was through smoothing, even more knee seemed to show. They were nice knees. "It's been quite a transformation from our youth, hasn't it?" she suggested. "I didn't know a single child in my school whose parents were divorced."

He thought for a moment. "I knew one in my neighborhood, but just one. It seemed like an immense tragedy for the poor boy, hush-hush, not to be talked about. I think we both grew up in a strange postwar moment in history that will never be repeated. Our fathers came through the Depression and then the big war, desperate to make everything as stable and peaceful and respectable as possible. They pretty much did, but then our generation blew it." He thought of Marlena again and decided to change the subject. "Do you miss Africa?"

"It gets into your blood. But I've made a life here."

He was about to ask about her life here when the inner door opened and a handsome boy with short hair came through.

"Come in and sit with us, Billy. This is Mr. Liffey, the man who wants to ask you about Fariborz."

The boy came across and offered a polite friendly hand. Nothing surly or distant at all, and Jack Liffey wondered if he'd somehow woken in a parallel world that was populated with tidy, obedient, attentive children. The boy sat gently on the edge of the sofa. He was wearing a T-shirt with a big photo of Jim Morrison.

"Pleased to meet you, sir. Fari was my best friend until all that Persian Mafia stuff. Or whatever you want to call it."

Jack Liffey half-wished the mother would leave, to let the boy talk more freely, but the other half found the woman so agreeable to look at that he was glad she was staying. And where was there to go in that tiny cottage, anyway? "How long had you known . . . you called him 'Fari'?"

"Uh-huh. Sometimes he was Frankie, too, until he got hyper-Persian. We met the first week we were at K-W three years ago—we were put in the same rush group when we were freshmen. We both loved old rock from the sixties, like Hendrix and The Doors, and we wrote poetry together. Song lyrics, really. He set them to music with his guitar. A few months ago, he smashed the guitar and burned his copies of the songs. It was Iman's doing. That little Hitler thought he was some kind of ayatollah, purifying his circle."

"Do you have any idea where they went?"

"No."

"Would you tell me if you did?"

"I wouldn't protect those creeps for all the tea in China."

"Billy." His mother leaned forward. Apparently, negativity was frowned upon in this household.

"They *are* creeps, Mom. I'm sorry, but they are. They made Fari drop me so he couldn't even speak to me anymore. I could see it hurting him, but he went and did it. He was my only real friend there. The rest of them don't like poor kids very much."

There was something hysterical welling up inside the boy, some emotion that he had long suppressed leaking upward, seeping into his speech patterns and visibly thickening his features. Jack Liffey could see the pain in the mother's face.

"It's not the *money,* they say." Sarcasm dripped from his voice. "No, not at *all*—it's just that you don't share our *experiences.* You're not part of our *world.* You wouldn't *understand* so many things that are *important* to us."

His mother covered her eyes, and Jack Liffey tried to change the subject. "What about Becky Auslander? Did she have the same experience you did with the Persians?"

"Becky," the boy repeated, and there was an even harder note in his voice. "The one good thing about this whole Persian Mafia was breaking up Fariborz's relationship with that little bitch."

Aneliese de Villiers gasped a little, then covered her mouth to prevent more.

"She was a money-grubber. Fari was one of the richest boys in the school, and that's all Becky was after, believe me."

Jack Liffey secretly savored this criticism of Auslander's daughter. "So why did she disappear at the same time the Persian boys did? Do you have any idea?"

He shrugged elaborately. "Maybe her Gucci watch stopped and she committed suicide."

"*Billy!* Whatever you think of the young woman, you mustn't joke about suicide."

"I'm sorry." But he wasn't. "Fari never saw her for what she was. *Never.* You know, she never split a tab, not once, even for Cokes. It was Iman who made Fari give her up, but for the wrong reasons. Probably because she was an infidel or some such word. I don't know why I'm so mad at *her.* She was a climber, but it's those *jerks* who snubbed me. Now I don't have any friends at all at Kennedy! Not one!"

There was a choked sob. Jack Liffey had had his eye on the mother's pain at that instant so he missed the heave as the boy jumped to his feet. He bolted out the front door, leaving it open.

"Billy!" She stood up, but her own emotion ran down before she got far. She stood forlornly on the tiny porch for a moment and then came back inside and closed the door softly. "I'm sorry, Mr. Liffey."

"*Jack*. Mr. Liffey was my dad."

"He's not usually like this *at all*. I've been thinking for some time that I should pull him out of Kennedy. It seemed like such an opportunity for him when it came up, but I always had mixed feelings."

"Is his father paying?" He wondered if that was an impertinence, but she didn't seem to mind.

"It's a scholarship I heard about at work, but the kids there are so snobbish. I think he's been trying to please me by staying. He's a very giving boy. I wish he'd learn to please himself more."

"It looks like he's starting to learn," he offered.

She nodded. "Or cracking under the strain. Are you sure I can't get you something, Jack?"

"I'm sure, but have something yourself."

"I believe I will." He helped her open a bottle of Chilean cabernet in the cramped kitchen, and she told him that she drove her son over the hill to the school every morning before going on to work as a secretary in the fund-raising department of the Braille Institute near L.A. City College. He sniffed the wine on the air as she held a big goblet and he was sorely tempted. The wine wasn't the only temptation going, of course. She touched his arm briefly as they went back to the living room and his skin burned where her fingers had been.

"When Billy calms down, I'd like to talk to him again. Do you think that would be all right?"

"I'd like that," she said. And it seemed more of a response to what he'd really been asking.

* * *

Hassan drove the beat-up old panel truck like a rodeo cowboy on a bull. Away from Sheik Arad, he wore a permanent grin, as if a bawdy joke had just occurred to him. But Fariborz did not think the tall, thin man had ever heard a bawdy joke, or would know what to do with one. Fariborz had to cling to the door handle and a big strap bolted to the floor where a passenger seat had once been. The only seat was the driver's seat.

"Western-inspired socialism has failed," the man called over the roar of the old engine. "Nationalism has failed. Islam has shown that it is the only force in the world that can fill the great vacuum. Praise Allah."

"Praise Allah. How did you end up in America?" Fariborz asked.

"Had to get out. I was just starting at Hassan the First University in Settat. My namesake. That's near Casablanca. We formed an Islamic association the first month." He grinned. "Some of us issued a declaration for an end to kings and other backwardness. And we declared for *shari'a* law and an Islamic republic. They shut the whole university down the next day."

"I thought Morocco was an Islamic country."

"Of course. This is a Christian country. What would happen if somebody declared mandatory poverty and turning the other cheek, eh?"

He *did* seem to have a sense of humor. "I see what you mean. But why come to America?"

"My father was a poor artisan. He hammered brass in a shop in the souk in Marrakech and sold it to tourists. Tray tables and other junk. He saved his money for years to make a better life for me. He saw it all going up in smoke, and he was furious at me. I had a cousin in Detroit, so I was sent to stay with him and study at a community college for a while. Detroit is the Arab capital of America. That's were I met the sheik. He saved me from a life of drifting along with the secular tides."

Hassan sat back in the torn and patched bucket seat and clung to the wheel with both hands. The rest of the truck was a litter of oily tools and cable. For the first time, Fariborz noticed that Hassan wore a Captain Midnight decoder ring on his little finger, the kind of thing you got in a plastic bubble in a gum machine. On the dash there was an utterly anomalous bumper sticker that said: *If we're not supposed to eat animals, how come they're made out of meat?* He wondered if it was left over from a previous owner.

"He is quite an inspiration if you give him a chance."

A backhanded compliment, Fariborz thought. At least the man acknowledged that there were things about the sheik that could seem disconcerting. Fariborz readjusted himself where he squatted, trying not to jounce too much as the stiff suspension hammered over the freeway joints. The stump of Iman's wrist was wrapped tight and he was knocked out on painkillers, his condition stabilized by a sympathetic doctor Sheik Arad had brought in. They were headed now to some redoubt the sheik maintained near the Mexican border. He called it a *madrasa*—a religious school—but Fariborz guessed the location had been chosen more for quick getaways.

"Islam alone can inspire the young and give them a positive vision, a sense of allegiance. We are the forward finger of Islam pressed on the raw nerve of decadence."

The finger is a long, long way from home, Fariborz thought, with or without a decoder ring. "How did the sheik end up in America? Sudan is really an Islamic country."

The driver was silent a moment. "It was the will of Allah."

"Of course. But Allah usually works through human motivations," Fariborz said. "There must be a reason."

"Do you mean reason as objective, or reason as cause, or reason as logic, or reason as justification?"

This Moroccan's a lot smarter than he seems, Fariborz thought. "I mean, did he have some purpose coming to America?"

"Can you see into the mind of God?"

"Sheik Arad is not God."

"He is favored of God. I myself have watched him look into a man's heart and pluck out his secrets. I have seen him predict the winds. At night he sits on his carpet and soars out the window high over the city and observes everything that happens."

"You're not serious?"

Hassan bellowed a laugh, but it was hard to tell what it meant.

"Don't mistake yourself. Sheik Arad can do many damn strange things."

People were never simple, Fariborz thought. You just convinced yourself that someone like Hassan was shrewd and intelligent, and then he rubbed this eccentric Aladdin's lamp hidden away in his mind and out flew djinns and magic carpets that made you wonder.

"Beware how you judge, Fariborz, lad. Sheik Arad is not a sophisticated man, it is true, but he knows what is right and wrong and how to make things right. All the meanings will be revealed to you in time."

Fariborz subsided. His anxiety had only increased with the talk of the sheik, and the enigma of Hassan's character. He rolled onto his left side so he could speak quietly to Pejman, in the back with Yahya. Pejman looked tense and lost and forsaken, though Fariborz might have been projecting his own feelings a bit. He didn't much mind being the angry finger of Islam, if it pointed out evil and corruption in a forceful way, but he didn't want to hurt anyone in the process, and he was worried that the sheik's circle did not share those sentiments at all. He was pretty sure that none of his friends would go along with real violence, except maybe Iman. But Iman probably hadn't thought about much but pain and the loss of his hand for several days now.

"Pejman, you remember that night of the suitcase? . . . " Of course he knew his friend did, they all did—it was the moment when everything had started to go wrong, when they had hurried back to their apartment in confusion—but talking about it had been taboo for weeks now.

"Shoot, Fari, how could I forget?" That night Pejman had gone on to declare, almost sacrilegiously, that the event taking place was *their* flight from Mecca. He meant that that night marked a point in their own lives that would remain as much a milestone to them as Mohammed's night flight to Yathrib to escape his murderers, the night when Allah intervened to save the Prophet's life, the date that now marks year zero of the Islamic calendar.

"I know."

"Do not despair, Allah is with us," Pejman said, echoing what the Prophet had said the night of the flight to Yathrib, but there was no confidence in his own voice. To save Mohammed, God had placed a spiderweb across the cave mouth to divert the murderers, but Fariborz could find no parallel assistance in their own affairs, none at all.

He had to ask it for the hundredth time, because he had been in another room when it all went down. "Are you *sure* it was Becky?"

Pejman's eyes firmed up with hostility, but he didn't reply.

"What do you think has become of her?"

"She was *your* girlfriend, Fari. You never let yourself see what she was. We could have done so much with that money."

In his heart of hearts, Fariborz was not so sure he wanted a suitcase full of hundred-dollar bills. The world was simpler and purer this way, even though it seemed to be turning out a lot more dangerous.

Six

The Smell of Rotting Meat

"Alina, this is Maeve. Can I talk to Eremy?"

"Sho 'nuff," Alina drawled.

Eremy's family came from what Alina was now calling the "Deep South" of Armenia—Iran, in fact—and for some reason, probably reading *Gone with the Wind* last year, Eremy's older sister had got it into her head to play at being "Southern." There had been a large Armenian community in Iran since the eighteenth century, but as far as Maeve knew there had never been a single one of them named Scarlett.

"I'll get her for y'all."

Maeve waited out on the tiny patio of her dad's condo with her cell phone tucked secretly against her ear in case her dad came back suddenly. He didn't know yet that her mom had given her the cell phone, and she didn't want to flaunt it when he could barely afford an old sit-on-the-table black model with no modern features at all. Eremy was speed-dial 3, her third-best friend.

"Maeve!"

"Femme 2 of the Fabulous Femmes."

"It's great to hear from you at last. We've been missing out on days and days of sun. When are you going to come back to beachland?"

"Not right away. I'm staying with my dad up in Culver City." She looked around over the patio wall, nobody in earshot, and changed to a conspiratorial tone. "But we could get together for some detective work."

"That's cold!"

"My dad is looking for some runaway Iranian boys, and they have something to do with a guy called Sheik Arad."

Maeve heard a groan. "You *do* know we're Christians, Maevie, don't you? My family doesn't have much truck with Moslems," Eremy complained. "My big brother calls them 'sand niggers.' "

"That's not very nice. I just need to try to find out where this sheik hangs out."

There was a long silence. A group of very young black kids sauntered past the patio, talking breathlessly about a girl who had apparently been flashing her breasts at the condo pool. Maeve instinctively tuned into their excitement and almost missed Eremy's reply.

"You know, if he calls himself a sheik, he isn't any kind of Iranian guy at all. He's some sort of Ay-rab."

"You always said you wanted to get in on being a detective. I didn't say it would fall in our lap. And you've got a car."

"Okay, okay. I can try my uncle Armen. He's got a Middle Eastern grocery in Venice. They get Lebanese and Syrians and Pakis and all kinds. I'll bet he knows something about this sheik."

"Don't call my cell. I'll call you."

"Great, solid. Let's do this."

He took Fairfax up to the 10, and instead of the usual orange-seller beside the on-ramp, there was an old man in the tattered coat of a marching band with a lot of braid. He had a forlorn-looking monkey on a chain and held out a hand-lettered cardboard sign at the passing cars: *Please Help. Flatulent Monkey. Need $$ for Vet.*

Jack Liffey laughed out loud. He was feeling pretty good for some reason, and he thought of tossing the inventive organ-grinder some change, but the traffic flow was too fast and carried him up and onto the Santa Monica going east. He found his head a bit buzzy. He wasn't sleeping well, but once he came fully awake that morning he found his weeks-long gloom was on the wane, and he wondered if it was something as simple as meeting Aneliese that had done it to him. It sure seemed to have improved his general disposition. Something had, anyway. He was still too many years past fifty, Marlena was still gone, and his life still seemed stalled out near zero; but inexplicably, he felt a lot better about things for the moment.

Downtown, he pulled into the *L.A. Times* parking structure on Spring, picked the name of a city-desk reporter at random, and told the guard he was having lunch with him. Then he exited out the side of the place and walked the opposite way over to the Bradbury Building. Inside the Bradbury, the ornate grillwork and terra-cotta tiles never failed to delight him, like dropping through a thin crust of L.A. reality into turn-of-the-century New Orleans. The central light-well also had open-cage elevators that clattered upward in a leisurely way. Rosewood Agency was up on the sixth floor, behind pebbled glass doors set into dark wood.

He usually had trouble with the receptionist, so he tried to blow past her. "Art Castro is expecting me. I know where his office is."

"Uh, sir." She stood up with a look of panic, a weird tall haircut swaying a bit with its own momentum. "I don't think you do."

Down the hall, he noticed that the door to Art's big corner office didn't have a name on it anymore. Jack Liffey wondered how you could do much better than the view that room had afforded Castro out over the city, two big windows pointing north and east. From way up here, even the area called the Nickel didn't look so bad, though up close it was wall-to-wall homeless.

"He's in 401A," she said. "Down two floors."

"Rosewood's expanding."

"Kind of," she said dubiously.

He went back out and found a marble stairwell that took him down to four. The door marked 401A had a smaller version of the Rosewood logo, the famous never-squinting eye that Pinkerton created. There did not appear to be a 401B. He rapped once and went in, startling Art up out of his newspaper. The room could probably have held enough brooms and mops to tidy up a floor of the building, but not much more. Where a window should have been, there was a big sheet-metal air-conditioning duct that split in two and headed left and right. The desk and a filing cabinet took up most of the rest of the space.

"Uh-oh," Jack Liffey said right away.

"You said it."

"I'd say it looks like Art Castro screwed the pooch."

His friend made a face. "Art Castro failed to exercise due diligence at a critical juncture in an investigation." He stood and shook hands and gestured Jack Liffey into a stiff wood chair with an embroidered pillow on it. He moved the chair a bit and then found he had to move it right back in order to shut the door in the cramped space.

"What does *that* mean?" He and Art went way back as friends, to the tail end of the antiwar movement, when they'd stood side by side to toss their medals back at the Federal Building on Wilshire, though Art had had some real medals, including a Bronze Star, and in his case the medals didn't get past the Vietnam theater ribbon and a good conduct.

"I was toking a bit and nodded off in Wilmington just as some bad-doers pilfered one of those forty-foot shipping containers full of Teva sandals. Did you know the drivers they get to haul those shipping containers from the docks to the rail yard up in East L.A. aren't even union? Those cheap bastards in the Harbor Department have been resisting the union for years. Anyway, serves them right. A couple illegals with fake names drove the sandals straight into Mexico, where they vanished into a million bodegas, and I got demoted from associate to employee. Kind of like being busted down to PFC. And my old lady sort of threw me out, too, having been jawing at me overtime for months about the evils of weed. I think she'll let me back after a bit. What I shoulda done, I shoulda ingested a little crank to stay up on top, but I like the mellow way too much. All around, it hasn't been a tip-top month. I just don't feel the deal, at all, Jack."

"I'm really sorry, man. Anything else? Boils? Gambling losses?"

"Don't even start about my prostate." The phone rang and he glared at it, then picked it up. "Castro."

He nodded for a while, but there was an edge to it. "The will is legit. Nobody could find another one, no matter what she says. Let her litigate, if she feels that way. She oughta be the one in trouble, you know, she hopped him up with so much Viagra they needed a chain saw to cut it down at the morgue. She fucked him to death. She admitted to me she didn't really mean to overdo the blue pills, she just got tired of waiting for wood on the old guy."

He hung up and glared again. "I didn't work on stuff like that before the Fall, I tell you that for free. What do you need from me, Jack?"

"I don't know if you're in a position to do this, but I might actually be able to feed you something back that would put you in good stead. Maybe that would help you with the people in charge here. Sheik Arad. Heard of him?"

He frowned. "You know, when I was in high school, *sheeks* were rubbers and we pronounced it that way. When did this 'shake' stuff start?"

"I think it always was. We just didn't know any better. Maybe we say 'Trojans' wrong, too."

Art Castro put his big brogues up on the desk. "So?"

"Anything you can find out about him and his circle."

"What's your stake in this?"

"It's complicated."

"It always is, *hermano.*"

Jack Liffey told him about the Auslander girl and the Kennedy Four who had gone missing at the same time, and the fact that someone had tied the boys vaguely to the sheik. "I think he's Sudanese, like about half the mad bombers in the known world, the guys who hit those embassies in Africa, a couple of the 9-11s, I think. That's about all I know."

"I'll try our database and I'll try a friend upstairs who's into the spook stuff, but don't count on a lot. When your stock goes down, it's hard to trade up." He offered a sudden feral grin. "Then again, the rules no longer apply."

"Your stock will always be A-plus with me, Art."

He eyed Jack Liffey for a moment, as if wondering about his

sincerity, but decided it was okay and acknowledged it with a nod. "We're still getting away with it, *carnal*. All lapses are temporary."

"It hurts!" Iman complained.

Fariborz was trying to feed him soup that Hassan had warmed up before he left, but he seemed too distracted by the pain in his hand.

"You can take another Darvocet, but you've only got three left."

"I need it now. Man, I need it."

They were in the back room of a two-room cottage, and Yahya was peering out the small window into the blanched expanse that Fariborz had already checked out. "Where are we?"

"We went south, then east," Fariborz said. It was rolling desert land a lot like the arid hills he knew just east of Tecate, which was probably just across the border from them. They were on the edge of a scabby little habitation, not even a town, and at the nearest shack a half mile away a fat, dark woman had been pounding on a bunch of rugs on the clothesline for a long time. None of them knew whether they were prisoners or accomplices, though they'd been left completely unattended when Hassan drove off. "We're someplace where it wouldn't be hard to find gila monsters and scorpions."

"Don't leave me, man," Iman begged.

"I'm not planning to. Don't worry."

"What's that woman doing?" Yahya asked in an aggrieved tone.

"You mean with the rugs? She's beating them."

"What's that?"

"Haven't you ever heard of that? It's how people used to clean the dust out of them."

"My dad spreads them out on the driveway and scrubs them down with soapy water and a pushbroom." He considered that thought for a moment. "I want to go home."

"Not just now, Yahya."

Pejman came in from the bathroom, drying off his hair. "Somebody else. You're up. At least there's hot water."

"Dibs," Yahya said. He grabbed up the big plastic bag that was his suitcase and lugged it into the bathroom.

"Fari," Iman started plaintively.

"Uh-huh."

"We can't go home now. We've gotta go along with these guys, even if they are Arabs."

"I guess so, but we've got to find out what they want from us. I'm not going to hurt anybody. It's against Islam."

"I'm *already* hurt." He lifted the mangled hand and Fariborz could see it was starting to seep again through the bandages.

Fariborz took the hand and set it gently on a towel in his lap, grimaced and slowly began to unwind the bandages. "Everything went bad really fast. But that's no excuse to do more wrong. I think what we've got to do is do something good to make up for the harm that happened to you." He was just thinking out loud. "It may not get us back in balance, but it seems like all we can do."

"Like what?"

"I don't know."

"Don't go dreamy and sissy, Fari."

"*Allugatu l'arabiyattu salah,*" Pejman read haltingly from a worn old mimeographed book.

"Oh, no it's *not*," Fariborz insisted.

"What was that?" Iman asked. He had never learned much Arabic.

Pejman looked up from the old book he had picked up. " 'Arabic is an easy language,' " he translated.

"Arabic is hard," Fariborz insisted with his new ruminative air. "Life is hard. Duty is hard. Belief is hard. If there's something easy, you guys tell me what it is."

Riding down the rickety cage elevator, it suddenly occurred to Jack Liffey that it was still the girl he was really after, and he'd been altogether too willing to take Auslander's word for the fact that his earlier detectives had exhausted all the possibilities for finding her directly. Taunton was her school, not far west of downtown, in the heart of old-money Hancock Park. He'd been out there before on another job, so he figured he might have a leg up.

The school had been built up around an old Tudor-style mansion at the corner that still served as the entrance, the front steps guarded by drowsy concrete lions. He parked right behind a lime green Facel Vega and nodded to the lions going in, but they didn't seem to remember him. He pushed his way in the heavy doors to a place with a lot more ambiance than Kennedy-Westridge. There were worn hexagonal terra-cotta tiles like the refectory of a monastery, and a chair rail down the wall made of shiny mahogany.

He asked for the headmistress by name—Mrs. Plumkill—and told the girl at the desk that the woman knew him. The headmistress must have recognized his name because she came straight out. She wore round wire-rims and looked as thin and severe as ever, as if she really belonged in a porn film wearing a black leather SS coat and nothing else.

"Mr. Liffey, please come in."

Her office had a lot of dark paneling and an overworked baroque desk.

"Do you remember me from three years ago? I was looking for Lee Borowsky. Actually, I found her."

The woman nodded. "And in so doing you caused Taunton's good name not a whit of embarrassment whatsoever. I thank you."

"If I had, I guess I'd've been frog-marched out of here by two big guys with tattoos about now."

She laughed, and he remembered that about her. A ready laugh that belied the severe look. "Something like that. You never come to see us in the good times, Jack. You just come by when there's trouble. Only one of our girls has gone missing recently, so I assume that's the occasion for this visit."

"Becky Auslander. I'm afraid so."

"We had police at the time, two jurisdictions. We had FBI, and we had a big detective agency from downtown."

Rosewood, Jack Liffey thought. Maybe Art Castro was completely out of the loop now. "Now what you get is me," he said. "Life is a steady decline of expectations."

She laughed again. "I don't see it that way. The FBI man couldn't have said something witty to save his life."

"They breed them like that on a farm down in Alabama. It's the way Hoover liked them. When he wasn't wearing black bras. And it's why they didn't figure out 9-11. I'm working for the girl's father, if you want to call him."

"I think I can trust you. I'll do more than I did for the others. I'll summon her best friend and let you talk to her in my office. Is that to your liking?"

"It's to my utter delight."

She smiled as she walked past him, resting her hand for a moment on his shoulder. "It's *Miss* Plumkill, by the way, Mr. Liffey. Not Mrs."

He sat stunned. She had actually flirted with him. An image of Aneliese de Villiers flashed past in his mind. Was there something about finding yourself attracted anew to a woman and perking up about it that suddenly made you emit a haze of pheromones to attract other women? He didn't quite think Miss Plumkill was his type, but the hand on his shoulder unsettled all his preconceptions and pushed things around, like thick ice breaking up under great pressure on an arctic sea.

Miss Plumkill came back in, another light touch on his shoulder, inflaming the spot that was already asimmer. "The girl's name is Tiffany Caution. I know it sounds like the heroine of one of those sixties spy movies, but her father is very big in building tract housing. You've heard of Caution Contractors?"

It was the biggest developer in the city, with a finger in every major scandal—the collapse of the Red Line tunnel, the overpriced high school built over a toxic dump. "I sure have, but I never knew it was a proper noun."

"Be careful of her. I'll be in the next room."

"Uh-oh."

"She's a man-eater. I predict she won't last out her senior year if she finds any rich prospects that are edible."

"Thanks for the warning, but I'm poor as a churchmouse." He might have added that she could probably do pretty well in the man-eating department herself.

"I think Tiffany would chew on just about any man to stay in practice." While they waited, she asked him about the earlier job, Lee Borowsky, who had never made it back to Taunton, and he gave her a potted summary of the case, minus the torrid affair he had had with her mother, a faded movie star. That part had left him shaken for a long time, ruminating over the power of celebrity to alter your perceptions and corrupt your purposes. For the first time, he realized that his relationship with the wonderfully ordinary Marlena Cruz might have been something of a rebound from all that.

The door opened, and a young woman came in. She had the Taunton woolly gray pleated skirt and a blue blazer over a white blouse. The plain-looking girl had long blond hair and fierce direct eyes, and somehow he sensed a lot of pent-up sorrows, rages, and despairs. "Mr. Jack Liffey, this is Rebecca's friend, Tiffany Caution." The girl gave him a limp hand that caressed his palm lightly in secret. "I'll leave you two to talk."

The headmistress closed the door softly, and her shadow soon disappeared from the frosted glass. "I'm working for Becky's father," he said. "I seem to be just about his last chance to find Rebecca."

He sat in the desk chair but rolled it away from the over-ornate desk, into the open to make himself less imposing, and gestured for the girl to sit in the other chair. She made sure a lot of thigh showed as she sat, and then spread her knees, daring him to look up her skirt. He could go several ways with this, he thought. This girl was real trouble.

"Could you tell me about Becky?"

"Beck has really big tits, genuine honkers."

"That'll be a help." And instantly regretted showing any response at all. "Did she have any hobbies?" He regretted his follow-up question, too.

"You mean, like making *quilts?* Mostly she liked buying lingerie, putting on makeup, and fucking boys. On the whole, fucking was probably top on the charts."

The girl had slipped into the past tense, but it might not have meant anything. Her expression was still deadpan, daring him to rise to the sexual bait. "Miss Caution, I've never forced a young woman to return to her parents if she didn't want to go home. You don't have to protect her from a deprogrammer here, if she's off doing something she believes in, or even if she's just living with some guy she fell in love with. I'll leave her alone. But the world can still be tough on a young woman, no matter how invulnerable she thinks she is, and I need to find out for her father if she's okay."

"Did ol' Plumkisser come on to you just now? I'll bet she did, didn't she? You got a nice bulge there, and she needs it bad." She tugged her skirt up even more. "Wouldn't you rather know what a tight young pussy is like?"

The air conditioner came on with a whine, and a puff of air out of the overhead vent stirred papers on the desk. It was like an evil spirit passing through the room.

"What sports did Rebecca like?" he tried doggedly, mostly to buy time. He hadn't worked out how to deal with this girl. Growing up in the 1950s, he'd never heard a girl talk remotely like this, but more recently he'd heard plenty of gutter mouth from girls while hunting runaways. In his experience, those who had grown up privileged were often the worst.

His persistence now seemed to catch her attention at last. "We used to go surfing and in-line skating over in Venice, until Beck realized you only meet dodos that way. They may look good in tight shorts, but they'll end up driving a truck or working for some-body else. Guys with money don't hang out at the beach. Poor Fari didn't know what hit him when she zeroed her sights. She showed him a few tricks until she had him whimpering for more."

"Until he got religion."

"Stupid camel jockeys. He gave up really good head for a lot of moonwash and banging his forehead on a carpet. Beck was just get-ting to think she had a meal ticket. Was she mad when he turned oh-so pure on her—really furious. She even went to his crib and talked to his dad, played sweet sixteen, but no luck."

Jack Liffey couldn't quite put his finger on her attitude. He was trying hard to keep his eyes on her face.

"I think it was the first time Beck had ever been rejected, and she was really zoned about it."

With her eyes firmly on him, the girl undid a button of her blouse, then slid her hand slowly inside and started apparently massaging one of her nipples. It aroused and enraged him at the same time. He didn't believe in physical punishment, but this one needed a spanking.

"Do you know what rotting meat smells like?" he asked, out of the blue.

Her hand withdrew and her eyes wrinkled up a little.

"That sweet horrible smell that makes everyone want to throw up. Like decay and garbage and fermenting old fruit in the gutter, with maggots crawling over it." He let the anger show in his voice. "That's what happens to you inside when you start disrespecting yourself. Your flesh starts to turn rancid. Your bones go soft and won't hold up your weight. Your muscles lose their force. It all starts to smell like rot, and nobody with any integrity, nobody with a good nose, wants to be anywhere near you." He went on like that for a while, just a big stick to knock her off balance, until she tried to interrupt with some smart comment.

"Just sit still!" he snapped. "Your act would make any decent human being sick to his stomach, the way you punish yourself in public, but I know better than that. I know it's only a snivel. There's a scared little girl in there trying to shock the world because she thinks nobody likes her. Her parents don't give a damn, they're busy with their own life, and no boy has ever wanted her for anything but sex. They take her out to get into her pants on the first date, and then they walk away and brag behind her back about what a lay she was and never call her again, and even the girls won't have anything to do with her anymore; they turn up their nose or ignore her."

At first she'd gone stony-faced and tried to brazen it out. It took a while, but he saw self-pity creeping over her as she listened and his rap started to frighten her. It was just a cold reading, a fortune-teller's trick, but it was amazing how you could take control of someone else's self-image and shift it bodily, just by suggesting forcefully enough a new way of looking at themselves. And since everything was pretty much true of everybody, all you really needed to make it all work was your own strength of character.

In another minute or two, she was sobbing uncontrollably. It had been touch and go, of course. She might have cried rape on him or clung to her pain, or run out of the room, but it had been worth a try. Jack Liffey didn't like to give up on anybody that young.

"Tiffany, can you tell me *anything* about Becky you didn't tell the police?"

She nodded, just faintly. "I'm sorry I was so awful, Mr. Liffey." She tugged the skirt back down and sat primly. She was having a hard time talking, but finally got herself partway back. "I really don't want to be like that. What can I do? Beck was my only friend. I'm such a mess."

"Why don't you begin by talking to Miss Plumkill. Start simple, then work up to what's really bothering you. She has a heart and a great sense of humor. You'd like her if you gave her a chance." He was not about to volunteer his own services as camp counselor. She was just too volatile, and too willing to run up the sexual pirate flag.

"Really?"

"I'll tell her you want to make a fresh start. You'll be a lot happier, I promise."

"Thanks, Mr. Liffey. I'll give it a try."

He had no idea whether this was just an act, a whim that would burn off with the moment. "About Becky . . ."

"Uh-huh. I do know something I never told. Beck told me that she had some way to get even with the Iranian boys. This was right about when they all disappeared. I didn't want any part of it, so she didn't tell me what it was, but she looked like the cat that ate the canary or whatever."

"Leave aside the boys for the moment. Was Becky the sort of girl to run away from home?"

"Oh, sure. She hated her parents. She said her dad drove her crazy constantly trying to explain her own head to her. Just imagine how awful that is. You can't even squeak without being analyzed to death. I think she ran away a lot of times."

They talked some more in relative calm, but the troubled Tiffany didn't know anything more about Rebecca Auslander that helped him much. Then he went out and spoke to the headmistress, who was stunned when he told her Tiffany Caution seemed to want to come around and reenter the human race.

"I should hire you on a consulting basis for our problem girls."

"No, thanks. It's far too terrifying."

The headmistress insisted on getting his phone number, anyway. She electrified the space around them with her eyes, but there was already far too much erotic catnip on the air.

He fled the school.

Seven

Money Eats the Soul

In the *Times* that morning, sandwiched between the relentless department-store ads of women with come-hither eyes showing off push-up bras, there was a small report on page 17 about a truck bound from Mexico to L.A. that had been hijacked and driven out into rural Riverside County, somewhere near Lake Elsinore, where it had been looted of its contents. A Mexican national driving the truck had been killed execution-style. The truck and trailer had then been shot up with automatic weapons and torched. The Riverside sheriff's department suggested that it was an unusually brutal attack for a hijacking and looked more like something the Arellanos or one of the other Baja drug cartels would offer as an object lesson.

What had caught his eye was the fact that the truck was owned by a Los Angeles manufacturer of decorative stone surfacing called LA ROX. Jack Liffey telephoned, but a chastened-sounding Farshad Bayat wouldn't talk about the hijacking on the phone. He agreed to meet him at home late in the afternoon.

A half hour later, Jack Liffey was only a few blocks from his condo, idling at a light, when he noticed two grizzled old men in antiquated military uniforms with tin hats and puttees leading a string of mules up Jefferson, like sourdoughs planning to dig for gold in the Ross-Dress-for-Less parking lot. The old men looked pretty happy about things, and waved now and then at the traffic. One of them carried a bugle which he brought to his lips now and then and blatted.

Each mule wore a blue saddle blanket fringed with gold, and the last two carried big professionally printed signs on their backs that waggled hypnotically with the stolid mule shamble. The first said, *Bring Back Muleskinners*. And the second said, *The U.S. Army Has Never Lost a War in Which Mules Were Used*.

Jack Liffey mused for a moment about the claim, something he had never really considered, of course. It occurred to him that the United States had never really won a war in which jets were used, either. Depending on how you scored Korea. Iraq wasn't a war, it was a cruel turkey shoot against a hopeless underequipped army. One of the mules dumped on the sidewalk just as the light changed and the mule behind it sidestepped the pile with great delicacy.

He drove on, giving the procession a little wave. Things had been grainy and unpleasant for a long time, the boundaries blurring wherever he looked—but now he saw that it was all distinct; it was all simple; it was all funny. He was headed up to West Hollywood to talk to Dicky Auslander, MFCC, PhD, and that was the funniest part of all.

"Come on in, Jack."

"Sure, Dicky. *Dicky* . . . I'm getting to like the name."

Jack Liffey wasn't sure but he thought Auslander frowned a little at that, walking ahead of him. He followed him into the interview room and sat on the sofa as Auslander scribbled something on a yellow pad. The man had finally moved the plant a foot from the sofa, leaving the patient more headroom. Through the wall there was an irregular dull bapping sound, like a fist into a catcher's mitt, over and over. "What's going on?"

"My partner does marriage counseling, and sometimes he encourages them to use pugil sticks."

"Those big rubber Q-tips that people hit each other with?"

"That's the thing."

"Seems pretty childish for old married couples."

"We're all pretty childish, given a sufficiently charitable perspective, Jack. Wouldn't you like a few minutes go at your ex? Some people can burrow down into it, get out their hostilities and use the anger to help them do some of the growing up they never managed."

"If that's the game, I'll just go back to making model airplanes."

"Would you really?" Auslander asked as he sat.

"No, Dicky, I really wouldn't. I liked the smell of the glue, though." Never give a psychologist an inch, even in jest, he thought. "What would you say if I reported that some people describe your daughter as a ruthless social climber?"

That stopped the man for a moment, and the bapping next door seemed to redouble as somebody cried out angrily in pain. Auslander pursed his lips and seemed to try to blow through his mouth while the lips were closed. "I thought I suggested you start by looking for the Iranian boys."

"You shrink the heads, I find the kids. I won't tell you what's childish behavior, and you don't tell me how to do my job."

He nodded glumly.

"I'll find your daughter, Dicky, if you really want her found. It's what I do."

"Why wouldn't I?"

"I don't know. Nobody seems to have liked her very much, and some say she didn't like you very much."

He sighed and real pain flitted across his features. "Her younger sister is the sweetest girl you can imagine. Sometimes they just turn out a certain way and there's nothing you did, and not a damn thing you can do to change it. Rebecca is a handful, but she's still my daughter and I love her. Just the way you love Maeve."

Maybe not *just*, Jack Liffey demurred in his head. "When she was young, did you go on family vacations?"

"Some."

"Where?"

Auslander seemed to think it over, like a burglar holding back his

alibi. "The Russian River when she was very young, before it
became a hundred percent gay. Then Roatan in Honduras—that's a
fancy resort island off the east coast. Ensenada a couple of times
when she was a teen. She seemed to like Ensenada—I think because
she met a boy at the University of Baja there. I sent a guy to look
for her down there, but he got nowhere."

"Does she speak Spanish?"

"She took it in school. Probably not very well." He looked a bit
sheepish. "There's a reason I wasn't very serious about looking in
Mexico, Jack. Rebecca has a nasty racist streak. I don't know
where it came from. Neither my wife nor I ever disparaged minorities in front of her. I suppose it's classism as much as racism. She
seems to scorn any group that has a high percentage of poor
people—blacks, Central Americans, Mexicans. You only had to see
the disdain on her face when she looked at somebody a bit ragged.
And she kept using words like 'beaner' and 'greaseball.' Since it was
mostly the well-off who'd fled Iran, she didn't mind them so much
as a minority."

"And they're Aryans who seem to own a lot of Rolexes."

"There's that."

Bap-bap-*whap*. There was a sudden explosion of cursing behind
the wall, and Jack Liffey smiled to himself. Nothing like growing
up fast.

"Have you found out anything?"

"Just things to think about. There's no point in me getting your
hopes up."

"How about your own life? You look a little less tense than the
last time I saw you."

That was disconcerting. If somebody like Dicky Auslander could
read him that easily, he really *did* need help. And there had been
nothing more than a vague expression of interest from a woman—
two women—to brighten up his horizon. "I guess it's just getting
my teeth into a job. It always perks me up."

"Not a new woman?"

"Nope."

"Let's return to our little metaphor of life, all right?"

"You know what I'd like *not* to do, Dicky? I'd like *not* to do that again."

"Come on, indulge my metaphor. I'm the author of the detective story of your life. And you've got this burning sensation in your soul, something that you've just got to complain about."

"If you want to be accurate, that detective-story thing isn't a metaphor, Dicky. It's a paradigm."

"You're the one who took English lit. Are you still pissed off at me for writing a story that leaves you so unhappy? I mean, because I took away so many things that you thought you could rely on?"

Jack Liffey glared a moment and then decided the only way out of this nightmare was to humor the man. "I wouldn't be opposed to having all the normal stuff in life fall *into* my lap instead of *out* of it, yeah, sure. Home, wife, job, money. And I don't like feeling I'm stuck outside the amusement park without a ticket, looking in over the hedge while everybody else is having fun on the Matterhorn ride. But I reckon that's just the human condition."

"Not necessarily. I think you have a tendency to romanticize being an outsider."

It was lucky there was nothing within reach to throw, Jack Liffey thought. It was no wonder this guy's daughter's soul had gotten all twisted up.

"It's an ordinary human tendency to romanticize what we seem to be stuck with, even the bad stuff, so we can value it and live with it. Let's put it in terms you can buy into. Dostoyevsky romanticized his pain. Twain romanticized his cynicism. Hemingway romanticized his penis. Romanticizing only gets in the way if you need to be really grounded in reality."

"I guess I missed that lit class that covered Hemingway's penis."

"You know there's still a lot of gender socialization that goes on. It might stem from something vaguely like Jung's collective unconscious. Maybe some deep survivals of what we had to learn to reproduce the species. Whatever. You can think of it as sex-linked hormones working their magic on the chemical processes in the brain. But girls and boys really do develop in different ways."

"No shit. Let me write that down."

"*Something* impels girls to be nurturers. They practice it all the time by engaging with their dolls, with their pets, with one another—overengaging, really. You can see them cooing and petting all the time. If that practice never matures, if it freezes at some immature level, it leads to a kind of gross sentimentality. They grow up clinging to things furiously. They gasp and weep at news of far-away car wrecks that hurt people they never knew. They become immobilized by emotion. They can't make transitions. The trait is frozen way beyond a useful sympathy, it becomes a *need.*"

Dicky Auslander uncrossed his legs and recrossed them the opposite way. His hands fiddled with a pen in a way that suggested he had once been a heavy smoker. Jack Liffey figured he was thinking out loud, just working out some article he was working on for *Psychology for Idiots.*

"On the other side, boys are the guardians of the tribe, the warriors. Why? I don't know. We're thousands of years past the need for all that, but it's still there. So instead of engaging, boys stand off a ways, on guard. They develop a critical distance. I'll bet you used to sit in the front row of the science-fiction movie, making fun of all the bad science and implausibility. The wiseguy is a kind of practice for being a warrior. Look at the African-American boys practicing their dozens game on their street corners, developing their social confidence. And if most of us boys think we've got to learn to be warriors for the race, you've got it even worse, Mr. Detective. You're the guy I send out there in the hard rain to find those in trouble—even my own daughter."

"You're getting your 'yous' mixed up there. You're either God or you're Dicky with the missing daughter." But you couldn't divert the man once he got up a head of steam.

"And I just might be sending you out ill-equipped on your mission. A boy's critical distance can fail to mature, too, leaving you stuck in this outsider persona. You end up thinking you're Camus or somebody. You feel you can never really belong anywhere. You've got your nose pushed right up against a big, cold window that's going to shut you out forever. Other people go inside and let their hair down and laugh in the dance hall. Not you."

"You go to a lot of dance halls?"

"Unfortunately, the only trustworthy knowledge of the world comes from direct contact. So the more you're stuck with this picture of yourself as a romantic outsider, the more you're doomed to work on secondhand information, to be untouchable, insulated from real life."

"I'll point that out the next time somebody takes a shot at me." He'd been shot twice on his last big job, saved from death only by brute good luck. One bullet had left him with two cracked ribs, and another had accomplished what the ER people called a through-and-through at the left shoulder that had left him with an arm he couldn't lift above the horizontal. He also had a metal plate in his head from another job. All in all, he didn't feel very untouchable.

"This isn't literal. It's about your psyche and what goes on inside there."

"Fine, Dicky. But you know the profound truth I've noticed about men and women? I've noticed women absolutely never rob liquor stores. I think they're probably just more evolved than we are."

There was one hard *bap-bap-bap* next door, and then a terrible shriek and a dying moan.

"Fifty-five minutes must be up," Jack Liffey said.

Auslander looked a little concerned at the sound of the last blow. "Think it over. Maybe we can go back together and rewrite a chapter or two of your career—you've got a few years left. Maybe we can write a happy ending—get you feeling like you belong here with the rest of us. Most of the things in life don't really torment us per se, Jack—it's just the way we end up thinking about them that torments us."

"Wait'll you get yourself a messy divorce or two, Dicky. I find you can really look hard at the way you *think* about something like that and, what the hell, there's a reality in there that actually hurts."

"Same time, three days."

"You doing sex with Trev?"

Eremy had to shout over the noisy Triumph TR3 engine. Sixteen and a half, and she had her license, plus access to a really righteous car. Maeve was envious.

"Good grief, no!" Maeve called back.

"You haven't touched his penis yet?"

"No. We just kiss, and a little tongue. A couple times I let him touch my breast, but only over the bra."

Eremy grinned and shifted down, roaring, then stopped for the red light. Her brother Petros had taught her how to drive the restored sports car, double-clutching and matching revs by rolling her foot from brake to gas, and she loved it all, though it was really still his car. "I let Jarrod do it on my stomach. Not inside. It wasn't much fun, but then he did me with his finger. Haven't you let anybody do that?"

"Is it great?"

"Oh, wow. Like, the earth *moves,* Maevie. I get shooting stars right now thinking about it." One of her hands went toward her blouse and Maeve could see her nipple had hardened up against the thin blouse.

"You mean like Maria, the Rabbit?" *For Whom the Bell Tolls* had been the last-but-one book in their reading club.

"Yeah. Just like that. Wouldn't our parents drop a load if they knew!"

"I have a feeling that happens every generation. You know, *everybody* ends up doing all these things eventually."

"Yeah, but it's worse when your folks come from some old country where women have to pretend they're a kind of inferior species. Like, they could try to arrange a marriage to some old geezer I don't even know, with warts all over his face, and then I'd shoot myself."

"Would they ever do that?"

"I don't think so, but they sent Petros home to Armenia this summer."

"No wonder you've got his car. He's not over there looking for a wife?"

"I bet that's what they had in mind. You know, Mom and Dad've never even been in Armenia, not the real thing. It was still

Soviet Armenia when they left for Iran and they couldn't visit." She
made a big helpless gesture with one arm. "But you'd *think* we
were still living there. All they ever talk about is the Armenian
genocide, the *horrible terrible* Armenian genocide. Man, like
nobody else ever died."

"What's that?"

She slammed the brakes hard for a light, and Maeve had to brace
herself against the dash. "I forget nobody else knows about it. I
think it was in World War I and the Turks were ruling most of
Armenia and they were Moslems. The Turks decided to wipe out
the Armenians who were Christians. They killed a million people or
something like that and drove the rest of them out into the desert
and took their property. I suppose it really was a pretty big deal,
but I'm tired of hearing about it, you know? Mostly my folks get
worked up because Turkey still denies that it ever happened. It's
weird you can kill a whole country and say it didn't happen."

"It's worse than weird," Maeve said.

"Here's the street."

They turned off Lincoln onto a tiny lane called Leeward, heading
for the building Eremy's uncle Armen had told her about. Apparently Sheik Arad was fairly well known in the Venice area. The man
had gathered a circle of followers around him and bought an ordinary ranch house that he turned into a compound that functioned
as a mosque and school and social center for those who scorned the
big official Saudi-financed mosque not far away.

"Anyway, that explains why there's no love lost between Armenians and Moslems."

"There's a lot of different Moslems." Maeve tried to be broad-
minded. "I imagine people in Malaya are pretty different from
people ten thousand miles away in Turkey."

"Not if you ask my dad. He thinks they're all bloodthirsty
Christian-killers." She laughed. "Even Moslem babies, they're born
with little-bitty scimitars in their hands. Whoa!" She slowed way
down, the engine popping and crackling.

A head-high stucco wall completely surrounded the house, right
at the sidewalk. There was a solid wood door in the wall, and a

speaker contraption to talk to the occupants, plus a mail slot. The only other visible feature, at the corner, was a small sign, blue on white, that was in Arabic characters except for the street address.

"That's it," Eremy said as the old car sputtered past.

They went around the block and drifted past again, without seeing anything more. The fence was so tall, they couldn't see the house. "I don't know how we're going to find out what's inside," Maeve said.

"I do. Did you see that carport?"

"Huh-uh."

Eremy drove halfway around the block and parked. An unfenced frame house directly behind the sheik's compound had a big flat-roofed carport off the side, a few feet taller than the compound's wall. The house looked dark and abandoned in the middle of the day. Maeve smiled to herself. She finally had a sleuthing partner even bolder than herself. The last time she'd gone off detecting, she'd had to supply all the grit herself.

"Look at this." Eremy reached under the seat and handed Maeve a strange-looking pair of binoculars. She pressed a button and Maeve almost dropped them when they started to vibrate softly in her hand. "They're image-stabilized. Weird, isn't it."

Maeve tried to move the binoculars and felt them resist the movement, as if they were held in place by invisible rubber bands.

"That's really cool."

"We can see right into enemy territory from the business-class seats up on the roof."

"No, no, no, it was doubles, double four. I get to jump sixteen points."

"You can't take them separately."

Hassan and Pejman were playing backgammon on a card table, but they disagreed mightily about the rules. Iman had doped himself into a comatose sleep with the last Darvocet, Yahya was reading *Teach Yourself Arabic,* taking notes on the margins of an old Mickey Spillane paperback, and Fariborz sat by himself in a resin bucket chair across the small room, feeling very apart, watching them all draw away from him palpably on some wave of quantum physics that he did not understand.

None of them were actually moving, he was well aware of that, but they seemed to be receding, diminishing, growing more unap-proachable, and their voices were muffling into a kind of cottony stupor.

"You can't stop on the same point *I'm* on!"

Fariborz wondered if this would go on until he shrank to a point at the geographic center of the room and then, with a little pop, went out of existence altogether. It was impossible to locate himself in his own body. Nothing he did seemed right any longer. It was all just putting one foot in front of the other.

They argued loudly, and he thought, "It's only gestures. There's no way to redeem this." His own motives had come to seem like comforting lies, or vanities. He had just gone on an inner search for ways to make himself feel righteous. But he couldn't find his way through the thicket of motives to the righteousness itself. What was left was emptiness and inertia.

"You must be Mr. Liffey." She had gorgeous long hair, shiny black, falling in waves over the shoulders of a gold cashmere sweater. "I'm Ruth Bayat. Come in, please. Farshad is in his Persian room." She didn't offer a hand; there was still that much Iran in her, and there was an edge of some sort to the words "Persian room."

The house was tidy and very white, and what furniture he saw was pretty ornate, with a lot of gold leaf. She brought him to a side door that looked as if it should lead to the garage, but, instead, he went through into another world.

"Wow!" It had once been a garage all right, but now it was a grotto, the walls crafted of what was probably the same substance as LA ROX, but all in one irregular surface. A waterfall dripped and trickled diagonally along one wall, descending from pool to pool, and the red-tiled floor was dotted with big patterned cush-ions. There were several leafy potted hibiscus, and he had no idea how they kept them alive inside the windowless cavern.

Farshad Bayat and another man sat on cushions wearing

comfortable-looking sweats. They were not far from a raised platform on the side that looked as if it was for musicians. There
were none there at the moment, only a portable stereo on the
edge of the platform that offered a soft plucked music with
female vocals. He remembered that Lawrence Durrell described
Egyptian music as sounding like a sinus being ground to powder,
probably because it wasn't the eight-tone harmonics of the West.
This was sweet and clean, lilting, though something about it was
clearly Middle Eastern.

"Mr. Liffey." Both men stood, and he shook hands with Bayat
and then the second man, who had a face made of the same rock as
the walls. Nothing stirred in his expression.

"Mahmoud Khalili. My factory manager and expediter."

"I'll leave you gentlemen in the Persia of man's dreams," Mrs.
Bayat said, with the same edge.

Bayat smiled. "My wife thinks this room is a ridiculous indul-
gence. We have poetry nights in here, we've had the great poet
Ahmed Shaloo standing right there, we've had famous Persian
singers like Mohammed Reza Shajarian." He pointed to a skinny
stringed instrument on a stand. "That's a Persian *tar*. The guitar
was named for it, but it's really more like a lute. I love this place,
it's my sanctum. Please sit."

At the back of the platform he noticed an old color-organ from
the '50s—one of those strange contraptions that flashed colored
lights through a grille depending on the pitch of the music. It was
turned on and offering mostly yellow and green with the pulse of
the Persian singing.

They settled on pillows and Bayat offered a big plate of food off
a dwarf's table, the soft flatbread called lavash, sliced cucumber,
tomato, onion, feta cheese, and leaves that smelled like mint. He
declined, but Bayat wouldn't accept his refusal to a glass of tea
from a pot that rested on a little samovar, and the second man held
out for him a glass mug of sugar cubes.

"Thanks."

Jack Liffey didn't drink tea much, but he put in a sugar cube and
nursed it. Rather than talking right away about the hijacking, Bayat

talked about Iranian music and poetry and how important they were to the culture, and he asked after Jack Liffey's family and his health, and Jack Liffey did his best to reciprocate the elaborate courtesy. He noticed now that there were an incongruous treadmill and a stair stepper in the far corner of the cave, probably survivals of the room's previous life as a gym or junk room. The second man didn't talk at all, but watched with a predator's eye.

"You're very gracious, you Persians," Jack Liffey said after they had been talking long-winded pleasantries several minutes longer than anyone with even the vaguest goal in life could have borne. He hoped it might break the stranglehold of the man's civility.

Bayat nodded and smiled. "It drives many Americans crazy, I know. Even Iranians who have lived here for a while. It's called *taarof*. How would you translate that?" he asked the other man.

Mahmoud shrugged, without softening his expression in the least. "Sweet talk, perhaps."

Bayat laughed softly. "You know, Mr. Liffey, after so many years here, I think in English and talk on the telephone in English, and I do a lot of business in English; but I still make judgments about people in Farsi, deep in my head. Some things are like that."

"I don't speak Spanish well," the second man said, the first information he had volunteered. "Even living there half the time."

"May I ask about the hijacking now?" Jack Liffey requested.

Bayat sobered with a small nod. "You mean, could it have anything to do with my son's disappearance? I don't see how. Whatever my son has become, he and his friends are not running around California with Uzis, hijacking trucks."

"Do you have any idea at all why someone would go after one of your deliveries, and hit it so viciously?"

Bayat shook his head. Jack Liffey asked them as many questions as he could come up with about the hijacking, but still they professed to know nothing whatever about the crime.

"Do you suppose someone across the border could have hidden drugs in your truck?"

Bayat considered the idea in silence for a moment. He seemed to approach a watershed, then step across it on purpose. "All right,

Mr. Liffey, that's why Mahmoud is up here. He will be looking into that very suspicion at both ends. If there was somebody putting contraband on the trucks at *that* end, they had to be tied to someone here to off-load."

"What is an expediter?" Jack Liffey asked.

"Some of it you don't want to know," Bayat said, and he seemed to cheer up again. Mahmoud grunted and walked bandy-legged across the grotto to the treadmill. He flicked it on with a whirr and started to walk vigorously. He didn't seem in any rush to get down to his smuggling investigation.

"Doing business in Mexico still involves a variety of unofficial costs," Bayat went on. "There are many people in politics and various ministries and elsewhere who have to be satisfied. It gets even more complicated as the PRI weakens and Mexico becomes a true multiparty country. There are that many more interests to consider."

"There's no bribery north of the border?"

"I'm sure there is. But it's more subtle, and it's not a good idea to count on it for easing your path. Mahmoud and I met in the garment business downtown, when I was briefly trying my hand at what's known as the rag trade. There were a lot of . . . secondary costs involved in getting shipments through customs, getting them into stores, and Mahmoud taught me about them. It was a very cut-throat business. Have you seen the garment district in L.A. recently, Mr. Liffey?"

"A bit."

"Fifteen years ago it was just old tenements, used as small factories, a few hundred of them, with a handful of sewing machines working away in each one. The streets were dead outside, full of litter. Now the whole district is a bazaar, with storefronts and shops everywhere. There're flags and bright colors and crowds. We did that. Persians are a bazaar people. We transformed L.A.'s garment district into the biggest and brightest clothing bazaar in the entire world. With a little help from some Israelis and Koreans, of course, and all those Mexican women who are hard at work at the machines. But mostly it was Iranian capital and Iranian energy. On the way, a little money changed hands in unusual ways."

The song came to an end, then another started up with more of a wailing trill, the woman's voice continually changing key and swelling up out of itself. It echoed a bit and reinforced the foreignness that pervaded the grotto. Mahmoud Kahlili was breathing heavily now as the expensive treadmill started tilting itself uphill.

"Bribery isn't really my concern," Jack Liffey said. "I'm curious about Mexico, though. You suggested once that your son might have gone there." He decided not to mention that he'd had a second hint about Mexico, because it involved the girl who had interested Bayat so much last time, and he didn't quite trust the man. For all the man's courtesy and charm and sweet talk—whatever that Farsi word was—Jack Liffey still had an overactive instinct that told him something was wrong deep in the bowels of LA ROX. "Can you tell me if Fariborz spent much time there?"

"The family did. For a while, we had Sea-Doos and we went to San Felipe quite a lot to run them around in the Gulf of California, but we all got tired of it. They just make a lot of noise. Last summer, he said he wanted to earn some money and I arranged for him to work in the plant for a couple of months, adding up the accounts, things like that. Mahmoud let him stay in a hospitality apartment we keep in the fancy zone of T.J. up near the country club. He's not there now; it's been checked."

"I'm sure."

"You have no word on the girl?" It was his first direct query about the search, and it was curious that it wasn't about his own son.

Jack Liffey shook his head. "Nor the boys. I'm just getting started. Did you ever meet her?"

"Only that once. She came to try to get me to intervene—she was that upset over Fariborz' religious mania." He shrugged. "What could I do? Other than that, Fariborz came home from school most weekends, but he never brought girls to meet us. He used to be a normal boy, off with his friends, playing his guitar. I don't mean he wasn't polite with his family, but he was very private and he had already pulled himself back a little from us as most adolescents do."

A small buzzer went off across the room and the treadmill

slowed to a stop as it sank to horizontal. Mahmoud got down and toweled off.

"We will keep you informed, Mr. Liffey, if there are any developments in regard to the hijacking."

The stiff business diction seemed to be a dismissal. "Thanks." Jack Liffey levered up off the uncomfortable pillow and tugged his trousers straight. "Do you ever think of going home?"

"I don't know if Iran is my home any longer. There's a lot in the country I miss, and I'm not really at home here either, but Islamic law is not my cup of tea. My wife certainly would never go back. She is Jewish, and whatever they claim about toleration, no Jew will ever trust that regime. The revolution had to come, though, you know."

"What do you mean?"

"The old regime was corrupt to the root. I don't just mean Shah's people took money. I mean the way things were run, every business, every ministry, it all bred that way of thinking: Money was all, money was god. Eventually that kind of thinking makes smart money scared. They say over the last two years of Shah, a billion dollars a month left the country. You can't let money surround you as if it were the air you breathe. You can't let it have that much importance in your world. It eats the soul."

"Then my soul's in a pretty safe place," Jack Liffey said.

Eight

Boysmeat

"These are super-duper." They lay side by side on their stomachs, passing the lightly vibrating binoculars back and forth. The instrument seemed to have a mind of its own and resisted being passed, as if it longed to stay with the previous user.

"Way cool."

Maeve wished they had brought up a blanket or some kind of padding. The roof of the carport was made of angular pebbles over tar. Some of the pebbles were bigger than others, and sharp edges poked uncomfortably through her light cotton blouse and her cut-off jeans at several points.

"Seen anybody yet?"

"Nope." They could see over the compound wall straight into the rear of the ranch house that was almost all uncurtained glass. Inside, a slab floor was covered by dozens of reddish carpets. The only furniture was a folding card table pushed up against the wall, and there was a tall stack of identical cardboard cartons like the ones you'd see in a stereo store for the latest boom box. She could read the word "Sonovox" on each one. At the far right they could see the corner of a deep-blue tiled counter, upon which a box of Famous Amos chocolate-chip cookies rested, taunting them. Cookies that reminded them they hadn't eaten any lunch.

"I'm drooling," Eremy said.

"For sure, Miss E."

"Let's break in and grab them."

"No," Maeve objected. "I'm not committing a felony for a Famous Amos."

Maeve now took her turn at the binoculars and eventually scanned to a stack of papers on the edge of the card table. The papers were fanned out a bit so she could tell they were all photocopies of the same thing, which looked like a hand-drawn map. An annoying reflection on the window blocked a clear view, but the 20-power binoculars brought the map near enough to make out a lot. There was a heavy black line, probably a main road, and a grid of smaller lines with a mix of Arabic and English for legends and labels. The most prominent word looked like *Potrero*. On one of the roads at the edge, someone had drawn a cartoon rendering of a house, like a kindergarten doodle with steep eaves and a centered door. A big arrow pointed to the house from an inscription in Arabic.

She rested her elbows firmly on the roof and tried to make a tripod by stiffening her neck to firm up the image completely. The road by the house read something like Chuckawalla, and the only crossroad looked like Hope Street. She handed the binoculars back to Eremy and sketched what she could of the map on the back of one of her Liffey & Liffey business cards.

"Maybe we best try again later, when somebody's home," Eremy suggested.

But just as Maeve tucked the card into her shirt pocket, there was a rumble, both noise and a vibration in the carport roof. A big lowered 1950s car gunned up the drive and came to a stop in the carport. It revved its engine once with that rough-sounding *blat-blat-pop* of a hot rod and then shut off. This was not going to be Grandmother home from bingo, Maeve thought.

Car doors opened and slammed, and then there was an ominous silence.

"Waaal, Cletis, was you seein' what ah thunk ah saw?"

"Sho' did, Bubba. Coupla young dollies, hunkered down like possums on the roof. Most excellent."

Eremy and Maeve made frightened faces at one another. The accents didn't sound real, as if the young men were just larding on the hillbilly for fun.

Two black T-shirts came into view, both saying *To Hell and Back*. But it was the hair that Maeve noticed first. Both young men—maybe eighteen or twenty—were shaven bald, except for a line of tall hair-spikes that were dyed, respectively, green and purple, Mohawked down the middle of their heads from front to back. Maeve had seen hairdos like that in movies but almost never in person. One of them had zigzags and barbed-wire tattoos all the way up and down his arms. These guys really and truly wanted to be called freaks.

"Didn't the ol' man say we get to do jes' what we want with any strays that wander into the yard?"

"Uh-huh. Just *whatever.*"

Eremy sat up and dangled her bare legs brazenly. "Southern cracker boys," she observed with disdain. "The lowest form of animate life except for pond algae."

"*Eremy,*" Maeve tried to hush her.

"Don' you go messin' with us, girlie. You want to come down with us and rip it up some? Got us some beer and Mary-J." He waggled a very long tongue obscenely up at them. It was a real shock. Outside of that guy in the band KISS, Maeve had never seen a tongue stick out so far.

"Ugh."

"We certainly don't."

The boys seemed to notice the binoculars. "Look there, Bubba. They got them a set of bye-noculars. Musta been spying on the camel jockeys over there doin' they thing. This one looks like an Ayrab her-ownself."

"I am not," Eremy insisted. "I'm Armenian and one hundred percent Christian."

"You got you an awful lot of one hundred percent leg, Armenia girl. Looks like it go all the way up."

Eremy teased them by dangling her legs even farther, hiking her shirt to show some midriff. But Maeve grabbed her shoulder and tugged her back up roughly. Eremy seemed to be determined to get them into trouble.

"What do we do with these cuties, Cletis?" Cletis, if it was his name, was the one with the green hair.

"Let's start by givin' them a eyeful of real men workin' they bodies, see some real washboard abs to get they little pussies aw' wet." He stripped off his T-shirt, and Maeve had to admit to herself his upper body was pretty buff. "Bet you ain't seen nothing like this."

Maeve noticed that down in the overgrown grass there were a lot of weights and a couple of workout benches. The purple-spiked one yanked a barbell out of the weeds and started doing speed presses, the big iron weights clanging at the top and bottom of each repetition. His companion now stripped off his shirt, too, and began curling a heavier-looking set of blue weights, up to his chest and back. His arm muscles looked huge, bulging tremendously as they stretched his barbed-wire tattoos.

"What are we going to do?" Maeve whispered.

"We just watch them be morons. This is fun."

"It *is* not. We've got to get out of here."

"They aren't gonna hurt us. Don't be a wussie."

Between sets, the boys struck stylized muscleman poses for the girls, fists front and back, arms and legs crooked at angles. Purple-spikes could grunt and tense himself up all at once in a peculiar way that brought up the definition of every one of his upper body muscles. In that instant he seemed to morph into the carapace of a huge insect. Maeve wondered why anyone thought looking like that was attractive. But finally, tired of showing off, they positioned themselves directly under the roof, their hard-eyed faces craning upward.

"Come on down now. Come to Papa."

"Party down now."

"Huh-uh," Maeve said. "I don't think so."

Then Green-spikes got the idea to spray them down with a hose. He hooked up a brass nozzle. First a fine spray bloomed overhead, sprinkling down on them and driving them to the trellis where they'd climbed up, and then Eremy squealed as a hard gush hit her straight on as she was climbing down. Maeve hoped the binoculars she was carrying were waterproof, and then she was gasping herself as cold water smashed into her. She heard Eremy coughing, and cleared the water out of her eyes to see Purple-spikes holding Eremy tight and kissing her. Maeve was mortified to see that both of their cotton shirts were soaked through and nearly transparent. Eremy wore a blue bra.

"I'll scream rape if you touch me," Maeve threatened.

"Act cool, girlie. We just got to punish you for being bad, trespass and all, then you can run home to Mama."

Eremy ripped herself away from the boy grabbing her. "Do what to punish us?"

"Come on, have we raped you?" Purple-spikes complained.

He pointed at a Ping-Pong table next to the house. "You bend over and take a swat, that's it. That's pretty lenientatious I'd say, for trespassers."

"Promise only one?"

"Scout's honor." Maeve noticed that the boy's accent had completely disappeared. She didn't think they were hillbillies at all, and she doubted they were named Cletis and Bubba, either.

Eremy made a disgusted noise, but she gave an elaborate shrug and bent forward over the edge of the table. "Get it over with, dorko."

"Bare bottom. It's gotta be, tweak."

Eremy snorted again, but quickly tugged the back of her jeans down several inches. Blue panties clung to the denim and bared her buttocks. Purple-spikes hauled back with a Ping-Pong paddle and took a wide swipe at her, but stopped a few inches short. "Just a warm-up. Nice little butt buds there, girlie. Gets the ol' juices flowing."

"Get it over with or forget it."

This time he swiped around with a full swing and let the paddle hit. There was a resounding slap, and Eremy flinched but refused to cry out. She tugged her jeans back up and pulled away from the table, with a flush spreading across her face.

All eyes went to Maeve. "No way, just no *way* at all."

"You gotta, girl. It's the deal. Then you're out of here. Else we turn you over to the Ay-rabs."

That was an alternative she hadn't thought of. The sheik would probably tell her dad, and he'd go through the roof and send her home. She glared for a moment, wondering how she'd gotten into this predicament in the first place. After all, she told herself, it would only be a single sharp pain, and then it would be over. She'd been paddled once in a hazing ritual for a school club and it hadn't been that bad. Maeve took two steps and flung her chest down on the Ping-Pong table. *"Primitives."*

"Pants."

"You can do it right through the cloth."

"Huh-uh. This is the real deal here, girl, bare cheeks."

Maeve gritted her teeth and felt the breeze as she tugged her jeans down, just past the curve of her buttocks. There were so many emotions roaring through her that she felt like fainting. There was fear and shame and, to her horror, even a little of what seemed like sexual excitement.

"Panties, too."

She hoped they were clean. She worked the elastic down just below her bottom and waited. Maeve closed her eyes tight, hearing the footsteps of one of the boys slide toward her on the concrete patio. There was the testing swish of the paddle in the air, and a crow nearby added its derisive caw. Thanks, crow, she thought, and then she yelped as a hand jammed down hard between her shoulder blades to hold her down on the table and the other hand snaked up between her thighs and fondled her, a single insistent finger trying hard to poke inside.

"Stop it! *Stop!*"

"You just a bitty wet, ain't it so?" The accent was back.

She wriggled away and wrenched her panties up. Maeve could

feel her vision narrow to a small cone and go bright red. "You bastard, you liar!"

Green-spikes, the one covered with tattoos, stood there grinning at her, his eyebrows raised, and then he brought his finger up ostentatiously and licked it. She tried to slap him but he caught the blow, and then she ran toward the Triumph, tears streaming down her face. Eremy was ahead of her, and the car coughed to life. Her face burned. All she could feel was humiliation and hatred. If she'd had a weapon, she would have killed both boys, she knew it.

"Don't you *dare* tell Trevor, or anyone," Maeve said between gasps and coughs.

"Let's go take a bath for about a week."

Hassan had shown them what do with the boom box, repeatedly and annoyingly, as if they were utter dummies. The brand name on the black plastic was Sonovox, basically a no-name cheapo. The top of the case had been neatly removed and the works of the radio, only a small circuit card, had been moved to the side, behind one of the stereo speakers. The CD and tape sections had been gutted to leave the whole center of the unit empty. Then a rectangular packet about the size and shape of a pound of butter went into the bottom, a little wired spindle was inserted gently through the waxed paper into the pliable substance in the package, and then a five-pound bag of Globe flour went on top before the case was sealed up again.

They knelt out on the scrubby desert, far out some unknown two-track road, and Pejman took his turn and went through the steps while Fariborz observed, and they made doubly sure it was done the way they'd been told. Hassan waited at the crest of a hillock fifty yards away. Fariborz felt a chill. The whole scene was far too much like the afternoon they had left their pipe bomb in the Santa Clarita hills, the second of those fateful moments that, taken together, had changed their lives forever.

"Praise belongs to God."

"The lord of all being, the all-merciful."

They surveyed the work and then sealed the top of the plastic case with superglue as they'd been shown. Their eyes met for a moment. The only reason Fariborz wasn't more worried was because the device was so small. This couldn't have been meant to do much damage, though he had no idea what the bag of flour was for. Maybe a stand-in for paint, like their own paint bombs.

"You take off and I'll hit the switch," Fariborz said.

"No, you."

Fariborz gave him a push and the smaller boy started to run back toward the hill. When he was safely away, Fariborz reached out gingerly and flicked up the ON switch. The radio started to play some top-forty number, a guitar, drum and horn, yet another derivative eight-bar blues-based wail. Some lyric about regret and spurned love. He longed to do it better, put a little backbeat into it, words with more edge. He could almost feel the strings bowing tight against the frets under the fingers of his right hand. He was left-handed, and he had taught himself to play the guitar upside down, just like Hendrix, following Jimi's invented fingerings that he watched over and over on video. Then he felt the regret washing over him again: that music was his distant past.

They had been told the radio would play for exactly five minutes, wired to a timer, and then blow. Or until somebody hit the OFF switch. But it wouldn't switch off. If he were to switch off, it would blow instantly. That thought gave him another chill. Something about the accessibility of that tiny chrome switch; the force it contained seemed to dare his hand to reach over and flick it down. It was like standing at the edge of a precipice—that terrible vacuum that tugged you toward the edge.

The teen lament wailed on. Fariborz wondered if Allah could really be leading him down this profoundly distressing course. A month or so back things had seemed so much clearer, his decisions God-directed, each step leading forward and upward to soothe some wounded place in him. There had been a real satisfaction in the tight group of them buckling down to studies and serious reading, Arabic and the Koran and their own Persian history. He'd had a sense of his murky and unhappy life clarifying before his eyes, of newfound purpose and deep satisfying moral activity. The four

of them had come together as a cell, led more or less by him and
Iman together, brain and brawn, as Pejman had joked, but that was
not the real distinction between them.

"We have to get past our softness," Iman had insisted. "That's
the West in us. It's sentimentality. If you're always afraid of
breaking eggs, you can't ever cook."

But that's stupid—you can always cook *without* eggs if you
want, Fariborz had thought. There was always another way to do
something. Still, at the time, he had talked himself into the neces-
sity of hardening themselves for action. They were the forerun-
ners and had to get people's attention by making a little noise,
risking a little material destruction. Not hurt people, though.
They were all firm on that. That was wrong, definitely against
Islam, and it would be counterproductive, too. It would make
everyone hate them.

All they had to do was find some conspicuous and newsworthy
ways to thumb their noses at pornography, prostitution, usury, and
hate-mongering. Stink bombs. Paint bombs. Clever posters. It
would win people over to see what they were doing. People would
watch the six-o'clock news and secretly delight as the new moral
Batman swooped down unexpectedly, once again discomfiting the
foul and sinful.

In the best of all possible worlds, they might even get national
publicity and begin to wake the moral conscience of the West.
And even if their tactics turned out to be a bit too strong, or
poorly chosen, or ineffective, they knew they were ultimately in
the right. They were on the positive side of History, moving things
toward the good. That was what he and Iman had felt at the time,
with great certainty, and only now did Fariborz fear that some
of that certainty had been manufactured within himself, pumped
up out of loyalty to Iman, or maybe responding to something
else within himself, something he dared not even think too
closely about.

Suddenly Fariborz noticed that Pejman up the hill was crying out
in a panicky voice, and then Hassan bellowed. But he wasn't worried. There was still plenty of time. He left the boom box and ran

away from it through the creosote and bitterbrush. He had got only about twenty paces away when something knocked him off his feet. The noise was stupendous, and he found himself flat on his face, spitting out dirt. His arm stung and he glanced over to see a sliver of black plastic poking into his forearm. Then he was engulfed in a white cloud, breathing in the choking aridity of flour.

After a moment of coughing and spitting he heard footsteps. "You're such a daydreamer, Fari," Pejman reproached him. "You gotta stop being like that."

"I'm okay." He sat up and brushed at himself, stirring clouds of white dust as Hassan looked down at him with a crooked smile and shook his head. Again he wondered about the bag of flour and what it represented.

"The coffee is pretty good here, but we might have a little trouble getting served."

"Really?" Jack Liffey perked up, as if sensing a challenge.

They sat at one of the little outside tables at Nu-Age, a cafe across the street from the Braille Institute in Los Feliz. L.A. City College was just up the street, and what they could see of staff and clientele both favored black turtlenecks and nose rings and other piercings, though there seemed a general exodus inside just as the he and Aneliese sat down.

Jack Liffey got back up and poked his head inside the door. Little knots of the black-clad folk chatted away languidly here and there. "Two coffees, outside, black," he called, loud enough to wake a few vampires.

One girl who stood bent over a table looked up at him and waved in an ambiguous way, so he rejoined Aneliese de Villiers. He had phoned and asked her to have coffee with him because he had an intuition it might be a good idea to talk to her away from the boy. And it seemed to him a pretty good idea to talk to her under any circumstances, since his imagination was already working overtime on her body. She looked a lot different in her business suit. Formal, younger for some reason, more confident. Her hair was pulled back severely, and her big eyes, one of her best features, bulged as if a warm soul inside were trying hard to burst out to get at those outside her to comfort, soothe, tend, love. Wishes working overtime, he thought.

" 'I didn't like the ugly way the whites talked about the blacks,'" he quoted her words from memory. "That got my attention."

"I honestly don't know where that feeling came from. My parents were racists—it was just natural there—and all my friends, too. I'd like to say it was because I had a wonderful black friend, but I didn't have. I might have, had I been raised in the city, in Lusaka, but the social gulf was just too wide out in the dorps. Do you say 'boondocks'?"

"It's a bit old hat."

"The countryside, then. The African kids my age were all children of peasant farmers, and only a few ever went to school past standard six. Plus there was a war of independence on, and we all had to insulate ourselves from blacks a bit. Oh, too much is coming back." She shook her head as if to shake off the oppressive memories. "That horrible butcher's fridge in the market. Northern Rhodesia had stamped out rinderpest and tsetse, so we had beef coming out our ears. There were white packets of chops, minced beef, frying steak, stewing steak, and then over at the side of the cooler there were always two more rows of packages—dogsmeat and boysmeat. I can still see those horrible handwritten labels. Can you guess what boysmeat was?"

"I'm afraid I can."

"Our 'boy' was about sixty and lived in a little concrete hovel called a *kia* out back when he wasn't cooking and cleaning for us. It didn't even have a door, just walls that wrapped around like a public toilet. One cold-water tap, stuck on the outside, and no electricity. That's why I had to get out. How could anybody not see that was all wrong? I left for England by myself when I was fifteen. I say by myself, but my future husband left at about the same time and we ended up at the same school in Birmingham."

A couple of retro hippies in sandals and tie-dye strolled out the door and past, agreeing intensely about Herman Hesse. Three or four blocks of Vermont Avenue here in the lee of the Hollywood

Hills had been trying to upscale for years, centered on the Los Feliz Theater, one of the oldest art houses in the city. Jack Liffey remembered that there had once been a terrific independent bookstore next door, Chatterton's, but it had died under the onslaught of the giant chains and later come back as the Skylight, but still had a ways to go.

"I think I'd like some coffee," Jack Liffey mused, since it was becoming clear no one was going to show up. He went inside and no one had stirred, so he went behind the counter to the brewer, fetched two cups from a wire tray and poured from the pot. "Two cups, black," he announced and carried them out.

"I guess they don't serve old geezers," he said, when he delivered the coffee to Aneliese de Villiers.

"If we got nose rings, we could probably come here more often," she said.

He smiled. He liked the "we" part. "I don't really understand all this self-mutilation. I don't like sounding like some old coot, but a lot of those spots they use are *tender.*" He couldn't help remembering the aging movie star he'd known who had had nipple rings, a tongue stud, and another piercing off center on her vagina. She'd been old enough to know better, too.

"Is it self-mutilation? Or just a stab at being more interesting? No pun intended."

"I can't imagine getting that bored," Jack Liffey said.

They both sipped. The coffee was strong and good, though it might have been fresher.

"I think sometimes the kids just need a little attention," she offered. "You know why Billy got so upset last night?"

"I guess that's what I came to talk about."

"He admitted that he'd been in love with Becky. He asked me why we're always so attracted to things that are bad for us."

She waited, and her eyes sought him out as if it had been a real question. "If I could answer that," he said, "they'd make me king."

She smiled ruefully. "And if I knew, I'd never have fallen for Billy's father. Anyway, according to Billy, she played the two of them against each other, Billy and Fariborz, until she worked out which of them had money. Then the best she'd offer Billy was a sort of brother-sister friendship."

"That can be rough."

"I knew her, Jack. Though it is hard for any adult to know a teenager very well. I don't think she's quite as bad as—" she tilted her head as she considered—"as one might be led to think from some of the given facts. Though maybe that's my forgiving nature. She's going to grow up a strong woman. Did you ever read Stegner's *Crossing to Safety?* I just finished it."

He nodded.

"She'll probably end up like Charity Lang. Willful and domineering, but that's not the very worst measure of a person. Nobody's all one thing. She'll have a kindhearted side—she might just apply herself to something positive and use all that power in her to get things done. If she'd been born a man, I think people would just say she's determined and ambitious."

"Like Stalin."

She smiled. "Or Churchill."

They both looked up in surprise as a big black stretch limo came up the street backward. It was a Lincoln Town Car, moving fast, and if you looked closely you could see that the body had actually been reversed on its chassis so the driver sat at what should have been the rear window as he drove. A magnetic plaque on the door said: *s'omiL s'treboR.*

"There's something you won't see in Northern Rhodesia," Jack Liffey said. "Or just about anywhere else."

"It's called Zambia now."

"Second apostrophe is wrong, too, or the first one, I guess," he corrected.

They watched the *omil* out of sight. "There was something Billy wanted to pass along to you," she said softly.

"I'm all ears."

"Just before Becky disappeared something was up. The Iranian boys were abuzz with it and very secretive, and so was she. Maybe in a different way for her. Nobody was sharing anything with Billy by then, but Becky did tell him that she intended to teach them a lesson."

"Nothing else?"

"No. But it all centered somehow on Fariborz, not the other boys."

"Yes, I think so, too."

"I have to get back now, Jack. There's a staff meeting in my department."

He liked the way she said his name. "I don't think we're going to get the check, somehow." He went inside as the staff seemed to be gathered around a table, debating semiotics.

A rail-thin girl said something, fiercely, about postwar structuralism being nothing but a lot of fetishizing of linguistics.

"But reality always invades with a bigger army," a boy countered.

Jack Liffey thought of saying something nasty but he was feeling too good about himself and instead he found a wall menu that listed coffee at $1.50 and he waved three dollar bills overhead before setting them on the shelf of the cash register. "Two coffees!" he announced. "I tipped myself generously."

Outside, he walked with Aneliese de Villiers down the block, past a dress store with long dark Lady Dracula gowns, a shop that sold artifacts of the '60s like kidney-shaped coffee tables, and a reptiles-and-amphibians-only pet store, and then they crossed Vermont in a loudly chirping crosswalk for the blind toward the blank fortress of the Braille Institute. Not much point in windows there, he thought, but he didn't say it. Obviously they had some sighted employees. She seemed to be brooding on something as they walked, then she touched his shoulder softly once.

"Would you like to come to dinner sometime, Jack?"

He thought of a lot of snappy answers, but, with his heart, he said instead: "Oh, yes. Soon."

Nine

At the Crossroads

"Arturo, any luck on that question I asked about?"

"Uh . . . you might say that." Art Castro's voice sounded strange on the other end of the line. There was something pretty squirrelly in his tone, and Jack Liffey sat up and paid attention. "You were asking about the Sheik of Leeward Street. Well, Jack, if they made a documentary about this guy and his associates, they'd call it *Don't Fuck with Us, We're Crazy.* Remember the size of my office? I am told if I ever utter his name around here again, I'll be working somewhere else entirely, and it won't be a place anywhere near this comfortable. It'll be somewhere like Terminal Island or Boron. Do you get me?"

"Those are federal pens."

"This is not a joke."

"Oops."

"Oops it is. That is right on and exact; it is the authentic and real deal. This is an FBI-type thing, Jack. You know, a big ongoing post–9/11 investigation. As in, federal offense, don't butt in. Does that warn you off?"

"It'll do. I hope I didn't mess things up for you."

There was something like a laugh at the other end. "That'd be hard to do right now. Maybe if I pushed the old man into a vat of molten lead, things would be worse, but I doubt it. Wanna come over, see the Dodgers this week?"

"Not particularly." Art Castro knew the way he felt about baseball.

"Okay, well, I'll find some other way to make you suffer."

It was Jack Liffey's turn to laugh. "How about I hire Rosewood for some real work? Nothing to do with that sheik. Would that help you out?"

The line went silent for a moment. Jack Liffey figured he could get Auslander to pay for it. "Explain."

"I'm sure you've got a reciprocal agreement with some outfit in Tijuana or Ensenada, right?"

"Oh, sure, Jack. The sun never sets on our eye."

"I want to find out if an eighteen-year-old gringa from Bel Air showed up there about two months ago with a bit of money and rented a luxury apartment. My guess is Ensenada. But there's a lot of Americans living up the coast along Rosarito, too. Could be there. Maybe she moved in with a student from the university. I can get you her picture."

There was another long pause with the electronic hum keeping him company. Loco came up and nuzzled his legs, and Jack Liffey bent to scratch the dog behind the ears. For some reason, the aloof half-coyote was slowly turning into a real dog. Then all of a sudden Jack Liffey realized that Art had been subtly offering him a leg up, for all his professed loyalty to Rosewood and the FBI: "the Sheik of Leeward Street," he'd said. That was probably enough to find him himself, if he wanted to. "You still there, Art, or you on your way to some federal pen?"

"We can go two ways with this. I can send it upstairs to management, and they contact *Cervantes Servicio de Investigación* in Tijuana. That's gonna be full price plus, and in my current state of repute here, it doesn't buy me very much slack, anyway—not really. Or I can go to my brother's wife's cousin, who's a cop in Ensenada and it's maybe half price and it keeps me in good stead with that branch of the family. Just in case I need to run away some day."

"A Mexican cop. Is he honest?"

"*Jack!* Shame on you."

Jack Liffey waited.

"Jaime has a base pay of thirty-eight dollars a week. You ever been to New York? Do you go around asking people there if they ever jaywalk or double-park? If everybody in New York obeyed every law, the city would break down. If it comes up, you ask your friends there if they ever break *real* laws, like extortion or murder. Everybody turns up just enough corners of the page to let the grease leak under so things will run."

It would have taken a long time to sort through all the layerings of that mixed metaphor, but he knew perfectly well what Art meant.

"Jaime won't screw you, at least not if it means screwing me. And he knows the town."

"How much to turn up the corner of Jaime's page?"

"I'll bet five hundred bucks would go a long, long way."

Right after he hung up he called Dicky Auslander, who agreed to messenger a check and a photo of Becky to Art Castro. When you got anywhere near the high end of things in L.A., Jack Liffey had noticed long ago that pretty much everything was done by messenger.

"How's your arm?" Pejman asked.

"It was nothing; praise belongs to Allah." Fariborz cranked his shoulder around to show the simple Band-Aid where he'd plucked out the plastic fragment of the boom box. Certainly nothing in comparison to Iman's hand.

They carried the tuna sandwiches and lemonade they'd made to Iman, who was just waking up and still groggy. He sat up on one of the mattresses that lay on the floor of the back room, and he very nearly rubbed his eye absentmindedly with the bandaged stump before he caught himself. Then he glared at it and grunted angrily. He'd been taking refuge recently by doubling up the painkiller and sleeping a lot.

Hassan was away somewhere. He'd said he was going to the store for supplies, but they suspected there was more than that going on.

"Iman, how do you feel?"

"How am I supposed to feel?"

Even an oblique reference to the martyred hand inaugurated a certain seriousness among them.

"Sorry, man."

"Would you like tuna?" Fariborz offered the plate, and Iman's eyes glared at it.

"I would like a trip to Mecca and I would like the whole world to acknowledge the might and oneness of God."

"And that Mohammed, may the blessings and peace of God be upon him, is His messenger. I'll leave the sandwich. We need to talk about what's going down here, Iman."

"So, talk."

Fariborz settled on one of the other mattresses and wrapped his arms around his knees. Pejman stayed on his feet. "I'm worried about this radio thing. When we were making our own bombs, we used black powder and we knew exactly what we were going to do with them. But C-4 is a lot bigger deal, and these guys won't tell us anything."

"You didn't use very much C-4, and the burst wasn't in a confined space. If it had been, you wouldn't be here. Or your hand would be visiting the martyrs, like mine."

"I don't like the bag of flour, Iman. We don't know what it represents."

"Maybe it'll be paint. Or some stinky chemical. Maybe they have the same idea we did. They're going to point an angry finger at corruption and exploitation. How bad could it be in something that small?"

Fariborz sighed. "I'm not going to do a single thing more until Hassan lets us know. We have a right to know. You guys should see this."

He stood and hurried out of the room. Iman and Pejman glanced at one another. "He's going softheaded," Iman declared. "He wants to go back to his girl."

"I don't know. I think going to the girl is pretty much out of the question, don't you?" Pejman said with a shrug.

They heard Fariborz bang something on the outside of the shack.

Soon he stomped back in and set down a gallon plastic bottle of pills. They'd apparently been bought in Mexico, since the label was in Spanish, but it was clear from what they could read that they were generic potassium iodide, plain white oval tablets.

"The bottle was hidden in the water-heater cabinet out there. And this right next to it."

He showed them a folded sheet of thin yellow paper, a page torn from the yellow pages. When he handed it around, they could see a listing of the names, addresses and phone numbers of synagogues in 310, the West L.A. area code.

Iman looked up, but his eyes hadn't softened. "You just worried because your mom's Jewish?"

"Are we going to start hurting Jews? Is that what we've come to?"

Iman raised the bandaged stump of his arm, as if that refuted any argument whatever. "We've already hurt a Moslem. You have to learn that the Moslems constitute one united brotherhood, and we show no weakness to our enemies."

"Allah best knows your enemies," Fariborz quoted, "and Allah suffices as a Guardian."

Just as Jack Liffey settled in at his dining table for a session of his do-it-yourself meditation to try to calm his nerves, the annoying door ringer clanged away at him. He'd been meaning to replace the mechanical contraption for years. It was a big brass key on the outside, right in the middle of the door. The visitor cranked the key around to jangle a brass bell on the inside. He peered through the fish-eye lens. Since he lived in a guarded complex and the guard hadn't phoned to announce anyone, it meant either a burglar checking out who was at home, a local kid trying to sell him chocolates or magazines, or somebody who simply didn't have to ask the guard's permission. The dark suit suggested the last option.

He opened the door on a tall man in black, with very shiny shoes. The city cops called the feds "Shoes," but they could just as well have called them "Creases." The man looked like he'd just picked up his dark suit from the cleaners. He was attracting a following, too. Behind him, Jack Liffey could see a whole gaggle of black kids peeking curiously from bushes and around corners.

"You've been made," Jack Liffey said, nodding to the boys, a few of whom giggled. "But these kids would have made you even if you weren't wearing your neon sign."

"Mr. Liffey." It wasn't a question. "I'm Special Agent Johnson, FBI. Could I come in so we can talk?"

"At least show me the badge."

It was actually a wallet, but the ID card looked pretty official. He made a point of peering closely at it. "You guys all seem to be *special* agents. Is there, like, a *regular* agent, and then, maybe, a step up, a *very* special agent?"

Jack Liffey stepped back and the man almost smiled as he came in. "Thank you."

Poor Art Castro, Jack Liffey thought. The request really had touched a nerve.

"I hope I haven't got him in trouble," Jack Liffey said.

The agent frowned a little, betraying incomprehension, and Jack Liffey decided it would be a good idea to keep his mouth well shut. Maybe the man was just collecting for some federal pension fund.

Loco started to growl—he had a fine nose for enemies—and Jack Liffey had to shut him into the bedroom. When he came back he said, "Can I get you anything? Coffee? Soda? Truncheon?"

The curtains were open out onto his patio, and many of the one-inch gaps between the fence palings were filled now with eyes. It was like jacklighting deer in the woods at night.

"No, thanks." The man wouldn't be drawn. They sat and Jack Liffey settled into his Mad Dog stare. His composure lasted all the way up to the second word the man spoke.

"Your daughter—are you aware of where she was today?"

Still, he decided not to give an inch. "How do you even know I have a daughter?"

"We've had a file on you for a long time, Mr. Liffey. Don't take this wrong. It's not necessarily a hostile file, at least since you left the Vietnam Veterans Against the War, but it is thorough. Your shadow has crossed a number of our open investigations. There was that business about organized crime and gambling in East L.A. several years ago. Then the Lee Borowsky kidnapping. The dumping of toxic waste out on old U.S. 60 in the Mojave. The Hillside serial killer in Orange County. They had an FBI profiler on that one. There was even the matter of those white racists in the Pledge of Honor movement who died mysteriously in the riots last year, connected somehow to you."

"You said something about my daughter."

"I can't believe that you would purposely put your daughter in harm's way." Then he stonewalled a bit.

"Please."

"There's an unofficial mosque and compound in a corner of Mar Vista that has been under surveillance for a long time. Just a kind of preemptive surveillance, you might say, since we missed the bet on 9/11. So we naturally were a bit surprised when two young girls started peeking into the compound with binoculars."

He experienced a chill, imagining his daughter climbing some great big chain-link fence toward a coil of barbed wire and then a guard dog rushing up and yapping away. In his imagination, the dog wore a black leather collar with spikes on it like the ones in cartoons.

"And we were also watching when the girls got in trouble with two young men who came home and surprised them. The girls were hiding on their roof. Your daughter and a friend of hers. All of this was unknown to the people of the compound, luckily."

Jack Liffey bent forward and put his forehead in his hand. "Got in trouble, you said."

"Oh, nothing too bad. Basically the boys just embarrassed the girls, but we'd rather not have them—or you—near that compound again. Luckily, the compound's residents were out of the picture the whole time."

"I can promise to discourage my daughter. To my knowledge, I've never given the Bureau any trouble—not on purpose—and I don't plan to start now."

"Do you know why the girls were there?"

The boys outside were waving over the fence, trying to draw their attention. The two men did their best to ignore them.

"I'm afraid so." He didn't like the odds in trying to bamboozle the FBI. He told the agent that he'd been hired to find Becky Auslander, and to do that he was also looking for the missing Iranian boys. In his search he had been told that the boys had once gone to Sheik Arad for spiritual guidance. And, unfortunately, he had told his daughter all of this because she was nosy and because he had made a deal with her that she would stay out of it if he told her everything that was going on. In fact he did not have an address for the sheik, so she must have found that out on her own. He didn't mention that Art Castro had just given him a street name.

"So she broke her word," the special agent suggested.

"It does appear that way, on a kind of preliminary basis, yes. You could make double sure we all stay away from the sheik if you were to tell me that those missing boys are not at that compound."

"The missing boys are not at that compound," he said drily.

"Cross your heart?"

He smiled finally. "We're not usually in the business of disseminating information, Mr. Liffey, but I will tell you, if you were to go to this compound and break in, you would find it entirely empty. It's been empty for several days, and for a variety of reasons we expect it to stay that way now."

"Thank you. Do you know where the boys are, or Becky Auslander?"

"No, we do not know. And, if you find anything out about that, we would appreciate a telephone call. *First*—before calling your employer." He dug a business card cleanly out of his breast pocket.

Everybody wanted to know *first*, Jack Liffey thought. It was like some kind of treasure hunt, and he was the only one in the game who didn't know what the hell was hidden three paces east of the big oak tree. The card reiterated that his guest in the apartment was Special Agent Robert Johnson, and gave an address and phone number in the Federal Building in Westwood.

"You must stay away from the sheik, and keep your daughter away. I can't emphasize that enough. For your own safety."

Robert Johnson, he thought. One hell of a bluesman. "So you're

the guy that legend says traded his soul to the devil at the crossroads for the ability to play the blues."

"So I've heard."

"I always thought you were black."

He smiled. "My current state of whiteness is just temporary."
He was the first FBI man Jack Liffey had ever met who had anything approaching a sense of humor. On his way out, with the
condo's kids dancing around him and asking if he was going to
arrest anybody or shoot anybody, Special Agent Robert Johnson
sang a little:

> I went to the crossroads, fell down on my knees,
> Asked the Lord above, Have mercy, save poor Bob, if you
> *please.*

Maeve was weeping copiously, clutching her little suitcase in the
front seat of his VW as he drove. He felt terrible, forcing himself to
stay angry at her, but this time he knew he simply had to.

"What am I going to tell Mom about coming back suddenly?"
she sniffled when she had calmed down enough to talk.

"You could tell her you broke your solemn word and made
me upset."

"I'm soooo sorry, Daddy. I really am."

"I know you are, hon." He'd almost broken down and offered
forgiveness, and he stopped talking and drove in silence for a
block or two. Causing his daughter pain tore at something really
deep in him. He had so little in life, anyway, he thought, that
hurting her really pressed on the bruise. But it was always the
things you needed so very desperately that you had to beware of.
"I need to be able to know I can trust your word. Let us both
think about that for a few days, and then we'll talk about what
we can do about it."

She nodded vigorously. "Okay. Honest, Daddy, really, I was just
looking things over. I didn't think I'd get involved. I didn't think
anything would happen."

He turned and stared at her and she fell silent.

The noisy VW engine was their only company for several more minutes until they were a few blocks from her mom's place.

"Dad . . . I have to tell you. I *did* find out something. I know I shouldn't have gone there and all, but I saw a map through the window and I copied it. Maybe the boys are hiding where the map shows." She held out the business card she'd drawn her copy of the map on.

His window was down in the heat. He took the card from her and, without looking at it, crumpled it in his fist and tossed it straight out the side window. She gasped and turned to follow it with her eyes.

"Maybe that will convince you about giving your word. That map is what lawyers call 'the fruit of the poisoned tree.' We'll find a way to start fresh without it. Okay?"

She nodded glumly. "I'm sorry."

"Okay, that's enough self-righteous scolding from me. We've both made mistakes in our lives, and we both know what's right and what's wrong. We'll get past this, hon."

She leaned in, across the shift, and gave him a hug. He stopped in the uphill driveway, yanked on the parking brake, and found that it needed adjustment and wouldn't come fully on.

"Call me in a few days," he said.

"I will. I love you, Daddy."

It looked like she was about to skip away from the car, but then decided that it might be more appropriate to maintain a show of distress, so she trudged slowly up to the house.

It took him only two minutes to get back to the palm tree with the big scar on its trunk, just past the Chinese elm. He was glad he'd made a mental note of the trees because the parked gold Mazda that had been there had driven off. The crumpled business card she'd given him lay in the gutter on a windblown pile of little Chinese elm seeds, like disks of cellophane with tiny almonds embedded in them.

Ten

The Fragility of Things

"There was nothing I could have done, staying there, I mean being white. I'd have had to buy into the whole racist system." Aneliese de Villiers set out some nicely browned roast potatoes and a pitcher of water on the lace tablecloth.

"Looks great."

A cheerful African dance tune percolated softly from the living room. He had asked to hear some music from back home that she loved. It reminded him strangely of mariachi music, and he wondered if the dance music of the rural poor was similar the world over.

She had told him her son was staying at the Kennedy School for the night, which was convenient, and he wasn't going to ask just how unusual that arrangement was. He could not help noticing how far ahead of her she had to carry the heavy roast to keep the trencher from riding against her breasts. And then he chastised himself a bit for sinking to the level of Beavis and Butt-head.

"Meat and two veg," she said. "Very British fare."

"Looks wonderful." Part of him meant the food. He noticed again that inner warmth that made her eyes bulge and come alive.

She fetched serving dishes of carrots and rolls, and then poured herself some wine. He waved it off, happy with the water. He did his best to carve the roast, not something he knew a lot about. He'd done his share of turkeys, but Kathy had never been big on red meat, and Marlena had cooked mostly Mexican.

"Zambia got its independence early, but Rhodesia had a lot more whites, and they held out. Toward the end they came up with this desperate referendum scheme. It was a ridiculously complicated plan, meant to appear democratic but really just to delay black rule as long as possible. Some percentage of blacks would get the vote once they owned enough property or made a certain salary. Little by little over the decades, or over the centuries, the blacks would creep toward parity with the whites on the backs of their elite. It was so fantastically devious that they had to send teams of earnest social workers out into the locations with a big flannel-board to explain to the Africans how the plan would benefit them." She laughed. "They were really astounded when all these unlettered blacks just sat there mute and raised handwritten signs saying *one man—one vote*. In the end they crushed the referendum 100-to-1."

"People are not dumb."

"Please have some carrots."

"Not my strong suit, but I will." He distributed rare roast beef, and then shoveled some boiled carrots onto his plate. The music changed tempo, and two male voices seemed to be singing a lively back-and-forth duet, one voice almost comically deep and boomy.

"I went back to Zambia and Zimbabwe much later for a visit, after what they call black majority rule. A redundancy, of course. It was refreshing to see Africans running things, but most of the whites had gone and there was no place for me. Still, Central Africa is rooted very deep in me. I miss it terribly."

"I hear that from other exiles."

She smiled and a kind of light filled her from inside. "There's an amazing unfiltered sunlight that soaks the land there, the flat-topped trees out on the plains, the breathtaking sight of a flame lily. Oh, that smell of rain on a hot tar road. And all those wonderful animals—African animals are always the best, everyone knows that—lions, zebra, elephant, giraffe." She looked at the wall for a moment, as if waiting for a wildlife film to unfold there. "And the open way Africans laugh, their warmth and small kindnesses. I may go back yet, but Billy won't. He's an American through and through. It's so strange to be a different nationality from your own child. He doesn't know what *boerewors* is—the commonest kind of sausage to me—and he asks me questions about things like the Lone Ranger that I can't answer."

"I'm a different nationality from my child, too," Jack Liffey offered, "and we both grew up in the same *town*. I haven't got a clue where the expression 'da bomb' comes from. Do you?"

She smiled and shook her head and then reached over to press softly on his hand for an instant out of sympathy, or maybe something else. It sent fire all the way to his toes. This night was going to be something, he thought. He could barely eat. He wondered, why on earth do we look forward to this so much? It's terrifying.

They ate as much as they could, which was not much, and they moved to the sofa and held hands and talked about losses they'd experienced, about being single parents, about giving back in life and a lot of things like that.

"My God, I feel like I'm sixteen again," he said.

"I'll bet it's sincerity that does that."

"That and feeling just how politically incorrect I am when I can't help thinking you have the largest breasts I have ever seen in my life."

She burst out laughing. "They're very sensitive, too," she said as she undid the top button of her blouse. They started on the sofa and eventually retreated to the bedroom, leaving a trail of rumpled clothing. He discovered that much of her body was just as sensitive as her breasts. She had no trouble at all enjoying herself.

"It's been so long," she whispered against his chest.

But he had trouble for his part, and it threw a genuine pang of alarm into him, which only made it worse. Whether it was the way he had been imprisoned by sorrow for weeks now, or some new desperation about wanting things to be utterly perfect with Aneliese, or some other deep-rooted fear that he could not even identify, nothing that she did seemed to have any effect on his small boiled shrimp. She tried her best and then he stopped her. He lay back staring grimly at the ceiling.

"It's not you, I'm sure of it," he said.

"It'll all work out. It's fine, Jack, honest. This was wonderful."

He rubbed his eyes hard, his upbeat mood falling in like a house of cards. Just cut my wrists now, he thought. Put me out to pasture. This, he thought, was exactly where Hemingway ate his shotgun.

There was no sound of Loco scrabbling at the other side of the door when he got home at 2:00 A.M., and Jack Liffey wondered if this was another sign of the animal's newfound domestication, the dog finally taking human comings and goings in stride. But when he opened the door, his heart started pumping, and he knew in an instant that it was something else altogether. His world had been invaded, the condo tossed and ransacked by somebody who didn't care that he knew it. In fact, somebody who *wanted* him to know it.

The first thing he saw was the back of his sofa knifed out, and white cotton stuffing coming off the cheap frame underneath. He looked back quickly at the door but there was no sign of forced entry. The patio door was closed and locked. A couple of videotape cassettes that he happened to have—Maeve's favorite movies, in fact—had been ripped open in pointless vandalism and the brownish tape lay spaghettied on the floor. The drawers of a cabinet had been emptied out and the drawers themselves tossed into the heap.

Then he saw a partially gnawed raw steak at his feet and felt a new chill. He went straight to the closet in the back room that he knew Loco favored for refuge, ignoring further devastation as he went, and there the dog lay. Its flank was still warm as he knelt but the dog was terribly still, and then he saw it inhale slowly with a little raspy sound. He gathered the body up in his arms and carried it down the hall, then set it down on the sofa long enough to toss the steak into a plastic bag which he slung over his arm. He carried the dog to his car and drove like mad to the twenty-four-hour animal hospital on Sepulveda.

"Please, please, please. . . ."

A bored overweight girl with bad acne took the dog in ahead of a Siamese cat in a box on an old woman's lap, and a few minutes later a skinny old guy with a cigarette dangling from the corner of his mouth came out to tell Jack Liffey that since Loco was still breathing and the dog's heart seemed strong, it was probably only something like Thorazine, but they would keep the animal under observation. They had no facilities to analyze the gnawed meat, but they would freeze it in case it became necessary.

He left his name and address and went out to the small porch in front, watching the dead street and dark storefronts across the way. He stayed like this for a long time, so long that it began disturbing him. He knew he'd wound down to some kind of stasis in front of the animal hospital, and now it was hard to force himself to move again. A big sedan came north very slowly, with its brights on, the driver probably drunk and beating an overcareful retreat home. A sea breeze gusted between the buildings, and he could actually smell the sea, though the Pacific was several miles away.

Poor Loco, he thought, finally turning from coyote into dog and rewarded like this. But that was the way of the world's rewards, wasn't it? He felt the self-pity stalking him and shut his mind to it, to thinking at all. He heard animal sounds from behind the veterinary building breaking up the deep quiet, a faint howl of protest, a moaning, some kind of bird chatter. There was a soft drone overhead. A couple of late, late airplanes droned high above, probably transpacifics, inbound to make the big turn over the L.A. River and then descend westward on their final approach into LAX. Everybody was homeward bound, except him. He didn't want to go back to his apartment and have to deal with all the disruption.

Home—whatever that had come to mean.

It was amazing how fragile everything was, he thought. Only the day before, his general outlook had seemed to be picking up, and he'd had the evening with Aneliese de Villiers before him. Then—when the moment had come—he'd broken down like a fifty-three-year-old jalopy dropping its transmission in the road and refusing to go an inch farther. On top of that, he'd lost the refuge of home.

He tried again to move off the little porch, but discovered that none of his limbs obeyed. His legs were in full revolt, sending back petulant refusals. There was no point to doing anything, they insisted. Pools of street light picked out little windblown slips of paper, sparkles of insects on the air, driven east by the breeze. He felt woozy and disconsolate, completely unhinged. Even the battered VW parked at the curb seemed a pretty dismal mode of transport for a grown man.

He took a deep breath, told himself to buck up and just *knock it off,* and drove home in a daze. He wrapped an artificial numbness around himself like a cloak and held it there to seal out the real numbness.

Thank God Maeve hadn't been in the apartment, he thought. He kicked detritus around on his carpet and examined the destruction. What had they been after? he wondered. He realized this thought heralded the return of a semblance of reason—to look for a reason. About half his books had been swept off the shelves in the bedroom, but luckily no one had touched the big *Oxford Companion to American Literature,* which was in its usual position. He took the large book down and opened it up. His .45 automatic pistol was still nestled in the hollow where he had cut away the pages. At least there wouldn't be a weapon out there with his fingerprints on it, holding up liquor stores. Unless, in the fragility of things, he decided to get into the act himself.

Like so much Tijuana construction, the window latch didn't quite meet its slot, and he was sure he could jimmy it open. Even at the luxury end of things, Baja buildings seemed to start decaying even before they were completed. Fariborz didn't know why that was, but he had a feeling it was something to do with contractors shorting everything by just a little extra profit margin—less sand than needed in the cement, too few rebars, not enough labor time to get things right.

He had wanted to like Mexico the summer he had lived in T.J., in this very apartment, but the sense of ubiquitous shoddiness and decay had soured him a bit. He had read about the Shakers and how they had built their homes and furniture simply and slowly and sturdily, to the glory of their God. Fariborz himself instinctively understood that, felt deeply that every act should be a kind of tribute to God.

But now he had begun to realize he was no expert at all on how to perform an action meant for the glory of God. Everything he had tried to do had gone wrong. Somewhere in his recent reading, there had been a striking passage: When you find yourself a long ways down the wrong path and you're finally sure of it, you have to act as soon as you can. So the evening before, he had gone out the window of the rural compound with his flight bag while Hassan and the other boys had been praying in the next room.

He had walked to a minimart and discovered he was in a hamlet called Campo on Highway 94 halfway from San Diego to El Centro and he had then hitched west to the improbably named Thing Road, where he had walked two miles south to the border crossing at Tecate. He had crossed on foot with no problem at all. On the Mexico side, there was no bus until dawn and he had eaten three wonderful soft tacos—grilled *carne de res*, his first meat in months, like a repudiation of some kind—from the vendor beside the bus station, and then slept fitfully on a pile of smelly cardboard behind a cantina.

In the morning he caught the packed and tipsy westbound bus on Baja's Highway 2 to Tijuana. He had stood the whole way, pressed against the back doors, tossed back and forth along with everyone else by the ragged road. It was an easy walk up from town to Colonia el Paraiso, near the country club, out in the eastern districts of Tijuana which he knew well, just a long jump across the foul T.J. River from Otay Mesa and all the *maquiladoras* that surrounded the airport and stretched out endlessly to the east, American and Japanese factories that assembled almost anything you could name.

The latch finally gave to his penknife, and he slid the aluminum window open and listened. He doubted anyone ever stayed in the company apartment, except an occasional business visitor. Mahmoud disdained living on the Mexican side of the border and had a fancy house up at Imperial Beach south of San Diego. There were no signs of recent habitation, and Fariborz went straight to the stripped bed and flopped down to try to sleep. Being on the run was incredibly exhausting, he decided, physically and morally. But after a few minutes his eyes opened wide; he was too keyed up to sleep.

He could not go back to his father; he had burned that bridge two months earlier, with a startling and unexpected assist from Rebecca. But he couldn't stay with his friends and the sheik's people any longer, either. He had no confidence that Hassan had any sense of right and wrong whatsoever, though the man seemed bright enough and actually talked about moral issues. Fariborz was certain that it was time to start doing something right to make up for everything he had done wrong—even if you could never really make up the balance. There was no one he could approach to talk it out, and he knew he had to face all these moral and political choices alone.

"Jack, Art here."

"Hi, there, Arturo." He had found the ringing telephone by hauling its cord hand over hand out of a pile of books and papers, elementary detective work. It was nine in the morning, but he still hadn't got it together enough to tidy up. He sat down on an overturned drawer. "Things looking up for you at the office?"

"They haven't taken away my file cabinet yet. That's something."

"That's something."

"I may have news for you. Jaime wants you to come down to Ensenada."

"Has he found her?" Jack Liffey straightened his back and alerted all his senses. That would be a shift toward the positive, after a very bad day.

"He didn't want to talk about it on the phone. In fact, I think he was on a pay phone."

"What would that mean?"

"I have no idea, dude. But he had a healthy little quaver in his voice. Go today. The police station is at Obregon and Second, right in the heart of things, but he says to stay away from there and meet him near the big flag at two."

"The big flag?"

"You'll know, Jack. Take my word."

"How will we recognize each other?"

"You're both detectives, aren't you? What do you want him to do, carry a rose in his teeth? If I know Jaime, he'll be in a cowboy shirt. He's scared of something, Jack."

"Man, I'm going to a place where I don't speak the language, not much at all, and I don't know any of the rules. If he's scared, I'm *really* scared."

Eleven

Talking to the Dead

The last thing he did before heading off for Mexico was memorize the map on the back of the crumpled and then flattened business card, and then mail it to Art Castro with a note to hold on to it for him. He had no idea if that had anything to do with what the apartment wreckers had been after, but there was no point having it on his person. He drove straight down to Tijuana and followed the toll road south from there to Ensenada. He hadn't wanted to use the toll road, but larcenous road signs just over the border had sent him to the toll road by default, calling it the "scenic route" but not mentioning any other.

Art Castro was absolutely right about the flag. The road skirted around a rocky point and into town, and there it was, on a flagpole as tall as a twenty-story building. The huge Mexican flag, billowing inland on the sea breeze, was so ludicrously overlarge that it virtually reduced the good-sized city in the basin to a toytown.

The big flagpole turned out to be in a plaza next to the sleepy harbor, and parking nearby was easy. He sat on a bench for half an hour, listening to the eerie *flup-flap* overhead like the landing approach of some malign Flying Dutchman. He had never noticed before, but there was something inherently nightmarish in very

large things that made noise. Perhaps he was just attuned to night-
mares now, having spent his short night's sleep retreating block by
block as a flood slowly inundated the town he had grown up in. He
didn't even want to speculate on what it might mean.

Finally a man in a cowboy shirt approached across the cement
expanse. He had his black hair slicked back in a pompadour and he
wore expensive-looking cowboy boots. It was either the cop, or
Jack Liffey was about to be offered a bag of dope.

"Jack?"

"Jaime?" They shook hands.

"You can call me James if you want. James Torres." He spoke
nearly perfect English.

"I can get my mouth around 'Jaime.' "

"Come."

The cop nodded and began to stroll toward the harbor and he
followed, noting a bulge or two at odd points under the man's
clothing. "Your English is very good."

"Garfield High in East Los," he said. "My parents sent me up
there to learn about your country and get my education. Our public
schools, I must admit, are not very good."

Jaime Torres looked around now and then, as if suspecting a tail.
It seemed strange for such a chunky, stolid-looking man to act so
skittish. They turned onto a harborside promenade lined with
mostly sport-fishing boats nodding gently on the placid water. On
the land side were dry docks and closed-up restaurants. There were
several little knots of strollers, heading both ways. Jaime's cowboy
boots had taps that clicked and clacked on the cement, which didn't
seem particularly advisable for a cop, but what did Jack Liffey
know about Mexican police work?

"Let me tell you a tale."

"Oh, sure."

"Two months ago, a college student in town comes to a real
estate office to buy a nice house. Up on Chapultepec Hill. He's got
it picked out, and he closes the deal right away. This is in the neighborhood of $100,000 U.S. In cash—used hundreds. Now, this real
estate lady doesn't say too much because cash has been used in this

town before. Large amounts of cash are not unheard of in Baja California. Some of the *narcotráficos* buy nice homes here and in Rosarito with cash, to get their families out of the horrors of Tijuana. And there are legitimate ways of coming up with North American cash, too, of course. Especially in the tourist trade."

They approached two men in work clothes peering into a trash bin, as if it might contain something interesting. "Galleons have been stopping in this bay since Cabrillo." The policeman switched subjects without missing a beat. "It is the only sheltered bay on the whole north coast of Baja and I'm sure you will find it's a fascinating town."

"Nice flag, too."

The cop was silent for a while until the two men were well astern. "Now the real estate lady notices something else odd. This college boy isn't really the one to move into the house, she discovers. It's a very nice house, I might add. It is a *norteamericana* moving in, maybe eighteen. She calls herself 'Betty Olson,' and she looks a lot like the photograph Art sent on the fax, except her hair is bright red now. She is seen several times at the El Gigante supermarket stocking up on food, and buying some furniture over on Juarez, like somebody planning to stay awhile."

They had to come to a stop as a bell clanged and the sidewalk lifted all of a sudden ahead of them like a drawbridge. A beautiful two-masted wooden yacht began to wheel seaward across their path in a dry dock, freshly varnished. Men yelled at each other to direct the operation. "If you look at those islands out in the bay, those are the Islas de Todos Los Santos. They are supposed to have buried treasure from the galleons. Your Robert Louis Stevenson lived in San Miguel up the coast for many years, and those islands are supposed to have inspired *Treasure Island*."

"He isn't really *my* Robert Louis Stevenson, I don't think, but I *did* like him as a child."

Jaime Torres crooked his neck as a signal and they turned around and headed back along the promenade.

"It was the connection to the college boy, information that Art passed on to me—well, I think that is what made my search successful so quickly. I suppose the other people looking for this girl did not know about that."

"What other people?"

"Do you know who the *judiciales* are?"

"Maybe you better tell me."

"They are a federal police agency. They have a certain reputation."

He glanced at Jack Liffey as if trying to decide how far to trust him.

"I don't think it's a big secret, but maybe you better tell me the reputation, too."

"They have been known to be very close to the *narcotráficos*, to protect them, to act as bodyguards for their drug shipments, and to do their *tareas*—their dirty work, I think you say. Some parts of my English are rusty. But who knows, perhaps in this case, the *judiciales* are only cooperating with your authorities. They must do *some* legitimate police work, after all. Your federal agencies have this girl listed as a class-one offender. That is very bad. It means they really, really want her."

"And you found her. It sounds like you earned your money."

He nodded. "And it was enough money for me to report to you and not them. And also because Arturo is my good *carnalito.*"

Jack Liffey noticed that the policeman hadn't actually told him anything yet, except the name of the hill. He wondered if there was going to be a surcharge. A deep horn bleated out in the bay and he saw a sleek white cruise ship rounding the breakwater with a lot of people on deck.

"In forty-five minutes this town will be overrun with your countrymen asking the way to Hussong's, and trying to buy a human skull made into an ashtray. There is one thing else, *amigo.*"

"As long as it's not my skull made into an ashtray." Here came the *mordida,* he thought.

"I paid a visit to my *adivina* this morning. My fortune-teller. I asked about you, because I knew I was going to have to do business with you, and she said you are honorable, but you have a rare thing, a duplicate out there in the world. No, I wonder how to say 'doppelganger'?"

"It's 'doppelganger.' " Jesus, Jack Liffey thought. He really was an outsider here. In his wildest fancies, he couldn't imagine a Culver City cop telling him he'd dropped by the palm reader that morning to ask about him.

"Okay. She says only a few of us have this doppelganger somewhere in the world who is a complement of our soul. Normally we never meet him in the journey of our life. But if we do, there are explosions and surprises. Our soul struggles with this other, and some bad shit goes down. Or very good shit, but not very often. This is what Madame Sosostris told me."

The name seemed familiar, and then he remembered that the name was from Eliot, from *The Waste Land*. Super-duper, he thought, personal messages from a Mexican soothsayer who had named herself out of one of the great English poems of despair. It didn't do much for the dread he had felt ever since Jaime Torres had mentioned the *judiciales*. They troubled him a lot more than any doppelgangers. "Did Madame Sosostris say where she got her information?" he asked to be polite.

"She talks to the dead."

They were almost back to the flag, and he heard it flupping again, beating and whapping the air. Something big and bad descending from far above.

"Fuck the dead," Jack Liffey said, suddenly tired of all the non-sense. "What the hell makes her think the dead tell the truth? They probably lie just as much as your ordinary Joe. Are you going to tell me where the girl lives, or am I going to have to pay extra?"

"Go down to the bus depot. It's on Calle 2a, but you won't find any street signs saying that. Go north on this street and it becomes Alemán and takes you up the hill. Keep going to the pink house with the dolphins on the posts."

"Thank you, Jaime." He was relieved.

"See those two men by the food stand? Don't look directly."

There were two preoccupied-looking men in dark suits, with white cowboy shirts a lot like Jaime's. They seemed to be eating tacos.

"So you know what *judiciales* look like. *Buena suerte, amigo.*"

* * *

They might have been dolphins, but they might as easily have been big concrete tunas sitting on their bent-under tails, or even bass. The house was on the flank of the hill and looked out over the entire basin, with the huge flag smack in the middle of things since the coast curved out again behind the flag. There was probably meant to be an automatic gate on rollers between the guard fish, but it didn't seem to be functioning yet and sat open. Everything looked brand-new, just built. He parked in the courtyard, where the cement had been stained red and grooved to suggest tiles. There was a spiffy new purple Toyota RAV-4 with *Frontera* plates.

She opened the massive antiqued door right away to his knock, with a big silver revolver pointed straight at his face. "Who are you?" Her voice was very jumpy.

"Relax, Becky. The guys to worry about won't struggle up your hill in an old VW." He opened his jacket to show there were no guns in his waistband.

She seemed to be trying to hide her face behind both fists and the big pistol, but a lot of bright red hair stuck out all around.

"How do you know my name?"

"Your father sent me to find you. Don't worry. I never take anybody back if they don't want to go. I just need to find out if you're okay."

"My *fucking* father, the jerk-off," she said contemptuously.

"Right, the fucking jerk-off. Could you put the pistol down, please. It makes me nervous."

"Me, too." She lowered it but kept it ready. He could see she was a lot more attractive than the photo. She had one of those faces that relied on mobility, and freezing its expression in a single instant would never do it justice. She was wearing a Mexican peasant blouse and a big skirt—protective coloration.

"Let's sit down," he suggested, "and talk a bit so I can reassure your father, and then I'll get out of your life. Is that satisfactory?"

She didn't say anything but she beckoned him through the living room, out glass doors onto a rock patio that looked out over the town and the monster flag again. She left him for a moment and then brought out a tray that held the pistol, a pitcher of lemonade, and two handmade deep blue glasses. Judging from the barrel, the pistol used some odd oversize ammunition—maybe a .44.

"Hold the gun," he said, waving it off. "I'll just have the lemonade."

She smiled just a little, but remained very nervous. "What's your name?"

"Jack Liffey."

"So my tool belt of a father hired a private dick to find me. *Mierda!* Like, do you know how aggravating that man is?"

"I think I know a bit of it."

She sat and poured them some lemonade. She seemed to relax a little.

"When I was growing up, I'd, like, *do* something, and he was always, Why are you *doing* that? And then he'd *tell* me why I was doing it. He, like, couldn't stop digging at me."

He took his glass and sipped. It was bitter, but refreshing.

"I mean, all the time, *at* me. Interpreting. Inspecting. Like, cross-examining. I couldn't get in a word edgewise about my own motives, before he was making me the absolutely perfect object lesson in some goddamn *theory.*"

"And his theories are nowhere near as bright as he thinks they are," Jack Liffey offered.

She focused on him all of a sudden. "Huh? Yeah. That's exactly true. It's nice to have somebody agree with your reality. Did he annoy you, too?"

"Some. Not enough for me to screw up my whole life out of spite."

She grinned. "Well, that's your opinion, *Jack.* You're not his daughter. And anyway I feel pretty good these days. Wanna go inside and get down, a little recreational sex, feel like it? This is Mexico—all things are permitted."

It wasn't a serious offer, just showing off, so he didn't have to deal with it. "Could you tell me how you can afford all this?"

"I'd rather not."

There was a hoot from the harbor, echoing between the hills, and a second cruise ship came slowly around the point, looking top-heavy with so many decks.

"How about the idea of going back with me, maybe just for a visit?"

She laughed. "You don't get it, do you? This is, like, a done deal. I can't go home. Why do you think I've got red hair and the horrible name 'Betty Olson'? Wasn't she something in the Archie comics?"

"I don't think so. It's best not to keep any of the same initials, you know. I know it's comforting but it can be a giveaway, just a hint that catches the observant eye in an otherwise-featureless list of possibilities."

"You're an expert on disappearing?"

"*Finding.* It can amount to the same thing. I'm on your side here, but I think you'd better tell me who the bad guys are. I found you. You can bet they will."

"Oh, shit!" That realization seemed to be dawning hard on her, and she picked up the pistol again for comfort. "Damn, damn, damn! You're right, of course. Stay here." She climbed a staircase up to a widow's walk on the roof and surveyed the road that climbed the flank of the hill, then came back down.

"You think anybody might have followed you?"

He shrugged. "This isn't my country. It's hard to tell. I've only had one lesson on what *judiciales* look like."

She shuddered. "That would not be good news. Okay, I'll tell you what happened, like, just the newsbreak. Film at eleven."

She settled back into the wood chaise, sipped at the lemonade, and made a face. "This is *awful,* isn't it? Contrary to what people may have told you, I was deeply in love with Fariborz Bayat, really, really in love. He was a wonderful guy, thoughtful, smart, kind and passionate, with an amazingly dry sense of humor. I was head over heels. Right up until that religion stuff got its hooks into him. Well, he was still all those wonderful things, he just directed it elsewhere and his gurus made him, like, cut me off cold. I wasn't Moslem, wasn't moral, wasn't a good influence." She smiled. "We *did* get it on some, and the Prophet seems to disapprove of that, just like Jesus.

"While this is going down, without us knowing much about it, his dad is, like, sinking into deep economic doo-doo. The market for new housing in Southern California is in the tank, nobody's building anything, and consequently, like, nobody's buying his ugly fake rocks."

"So, something has to give. I think the bright idea to solve his cash-flow crisis comes from his number two, Mahmoud. You meet him?"

"Uh-huh."

"Mahmoud talks to some guys in T.J. who specialize in . . . importing stuff across the border. Mr. Bayat shudders and says no. He's not a bad guy—a lot like his son—but Mahmoud has already made some arrangements and you don't back down on these guys. So finally, I think to save Mahmoud's neck as much as anything, Mr. Bayat Senior says he'll do this thing just one time, and that's it. Unfortunately, this comes just as the boys are getting all holy at Kennedy. Fariborz found out about his dad's deal. Which is part of how I found out about it. Fariborz had worked down at the plant in T.J., and he's a bright boy."

She poured herself some more lemonade. There was a look of relief on her face, telling her secret to someone at last. Jack Liffey guessed most of the rest, but he sat silent.

"The Kennedy Four decide to, like, liberate the money and trash the dope, to the greater glory of Allah. The dope money would buy a lot of prayer rugs, or whatever. They sneak into the warehouse in Bev Hills and find it's not so easy to trash the dope. It's sealed inside hundreds of those fake rocks." Jack Liffey recalled the sloshy feeling of the rock with fluid inside. "It's dissolved in some solvent used for the purpose, but it would take them all night to empty the rocks, one by one. They do get the money in their surprise raid, though; a big pigskin suitcase full of cash. Lord knows where the buy-money would be now"—She grinned—"I blindsided them while they were busy trying to empty out the rocks. They're just boys. It took me three solid hours to count the money when I got it away. Almost two million dollars in used bills: hundreds, fifties, and twenties. I'd been wanting to run away and, like, what better nest egg, huh?"

"I can think of a lot better one," Jack Liffey said. "A nest egg that doesn't belong to the Arellano *drogistas.*"

"I didn't have much choice."

"You know, they tend to machine-gun everything in the area on general principles and sort out who's who later."

She shrugged. "Everybody disappeared at once. The Mexicans probably think Mr. Bayat took them off, or some L.A. gang took *him* off. Mr. Bayat probably thinks his son took it, so he's not going to squeal. Only the boys know *I* took it. I'm not afraid of them."

"There's a cop in this town who found you pretty easily, when I asked. He says the Border Patrol and the *judiciales* have Rebecca Auslander listed as a class-one offender. I think they reserve that for serial killers and the heads of drug cartels. It's just a measure of their seriousness in looking for you. I wouldn't count on cheap hair dye going very far."

"Did your cop pal tell the *judiciales?*" Her eyes were as big as saucers.

"Not yet. They'd be swarming up the hill right now. You can bet there's a hell of a reward, though, and I can't promise he won't. As I see it, you've got two choices. Come back with me now. I'll protect you and try to find a way to return the money to mollify the narcos. Or run. Now, today. Abandon everything, leave the car, dye your hair black with shoe polish and take the bus out of here, and don't look back. I'd head for Europe, get out of this hemisphere completely. Or Australia. You'd probably be even better off in Idaho, though our own feds are looking for you, too. I'm not sure why."

"Shit!" She stared out over the town. "I guess it was just a false sense of security, wasn't it? Like, I hardly got settled. Wanna buy a nice house with a view for $2.98?"

He laughed. She was pretty self-possessed for someone her age. Her father must have done something right. "Come back with me. I'll do everything I can. You can probably go into witness protection."

"I don't know a thing that would make the FBI bargain with me. I just, like, grabbed a bag of money and ran. I think you'd better go now."

"Sure?"

"The longer you're here, the more dangerous for me, right?"

He told her his P.O. box number and asked her to write, and promised he would forward stuff to her father with no return address.

"Sure, sure. Beat it. Wait." She considered. "Tell Dad I'm growing roses now. He'll know what it means."

"All the luck in the world."

"Go straight back to the States—okay?—so nobody can torture my location out of you."

"Yeah, well, you be gone in a half hour, and then I can tell them everything I know before I lose all my fingernails. I'm no hero."

He stopped at a bright-colored roadside place called El Mirador on the sea cliffs halfway back to the States and had a Coke on a patio that overlooked a steep drop-off to the surf below. Now that he'd found Rebecca Auslander, he finally knew why wanting to talk to her *first* was such a big deal. The first one to get to her got the brass ring, the two million bucks. He decided he'd tell her father, and that was it. The FBI could do their own hunting, and he certainly wasn't going to snitch to Bayat Senior, since that would bring on the *drogistas*.

That seemed to be all he had left to do, really: Report to her dad that she was okay, and hopefully she would be in touch. She was growing roses, he remembered. Whatever that meant.

It was a real letdown he felt there in the Mirador, the job suddenly over. A moroseness settled over him as he sipped the Coke, and he thought of Aneliese, wondered if he ought to buy some Viagra on the way back. You could buy anything at all over the counter here. But, Jesus, he wasn't an old man yet. He was just under some kind of psychological stress, just knocked off balance.

Below him the water crashed and foamed, trapped in a rocky inlet, a fair analogue of his troubled psyche, he thought. Various kinds of dread and distress banging one way and another in there. Was he just afraid of getting old and ending up alone, tottering home from the convenience store every day with tiny frozen dinners? He registered that the Coke tasted better than the ones across the border, fizzier and less sweet, more like the Cokes of his youth. Nearby, Mexican children played recklessly on the cement walls. He was about to go shoo them back when a heavyset woman bellowed at them and they scattered with squeals of delight. The men's room demanded a quarter before it would let him in to pee.

The wide toll-road from Ensenada circumnavigated the west side of T.J., up the coast, and then it ran due east hard along the border for several miles. Scores of bored-looking men lounged against the steel border wall right next to the road, as if waiting for the moment to make their break for it. Coming down the slope earlier, he'd seen over the high wall into the U.S., and it was clear that jumping the border fence wouldn't get anyone very far right here. The rolling scrub beyond had been cleared of any trees or cover for miles, and big white-and-green four-wheelers from the Border Patrol held lookout on all the hillocks. In between, other agents putted about in those three-wheel dune buggies, or whatever they were called. And then you'd have to wade through what was left of the Tijuana River as it flowed out north of the border into the sea, which would probably etch your shoes right off your feet. Finally, you'd have to cross twelve lanes of I-5.

He'd read that Tijuana was the busiest border crossing in the world, and one of the few where the Third World met the First directly. The road to the crossing carried on straight and dusty, the ugly graffiti-filled border wall on the left and a continuous barrio to the right. Most of the exits into the barrio were walled up, but here and there a road left at an angle up into a dismal-looking shopping street. At one of those breaks, a beige Jeep with a light bar on top appeared abruptly and hustled up to keep pace with his VW, right behind him. He checked his speed and kept it well down.

Glancing nervously into his mirror, it was as if a UFO had landed—he'd never seen so many flashing lights on a vehicle. Red and white flares chased back and forth across the roll bar, a steady red light on each fender and a spinning blue light behind the windshield. They pulled alongside as he slowed, and a man in a dark suit pointed to the next opening ahead into the barrio. A sign said COLONIA CASTILLO and took him into a narrow *calle* of shops. He hadn't had time to read the legend or the seal on the Jeep's door, but it looked official enough.

He parked and had the presence of mind to pocket his car keys. He got out and two men in dark suits came toward him, one grinning and the other frowning darkly, as if to make up precisely for the grinner. They were wearing off-white cowboy shirts, and the grinner sported a string tie.

"*Manos arriba, señor,*" the frowner said. "The hands op."

"Was I speeding? I'm sorry."

They patted him down thoroughly, but he wasn't crazy enough to bring a gun into Mexico.

"*Manos* . . . behind they back."

The grinner was carrying a roll of duct tape, and he tore off a strip and lashed Jack Liffey's hands together behind his back.

"Run out of handcuffs?"

"*Si,* we run out of handcuffs. Now, welcome to Mexico, shut the fock op."

Another strip of tape went over his mouth, and he panicked for an instant until he satisfied himself he could breathe easily through his nose. A third strip of tape went tight over his eyes, and he could tell it was going to hurt coming off—probably take his eyelashes and some of his eyebrows with it. He felt himself pushed into the back of the Jeep, and they drove away, making no attempt to avoid potholes as he bounced in back like a big bag of doorknobs.

He wasn't sure of the time, but he was pretty sure it had been about an hour since he'd left Becky. He hoped she had taken him seriously. He was not going to be able to hold back much when the *judiciales* started asking questions in earnest.

Twelve

As Much Demon as Man

It hadn't been a short trip; he knew that much. The vehicle had jog-gled over its share of potholes, banging his hip hard against the steel floor, and they hadn't climbed any hills of note, as far as he could tell. Occasionally he had gone into breathing panics, since his hands were immobilized and there was absolutely nothing he could do about the tape across his mouth, but he had forced himself to inhale long and slow. Each time, eventually, he had calmed himself again. His abductors had spoken to one another in Spanish, which hadn't helped him very much. The word *buscar* or *busquen* a few times. Finally they had braked to a stop with a jolt and he'd been manhandled out of the vehicle and marched forward blindly across dirt then up some steps onto a smooth hard floor. The echoes of their footsteps seemed to suggest a cavernous building; next he heard the unmistakable rattle of a roll-up door descending and banging shut.

Somebody kicked the backs of his knees to send him down again to where he could smell dusty cement. His ankles were taped to immobilize him completely, and then the footsteps faded. A door shut, apparently to leave him alone with his thoughts. They weren't very happy thoughts. His abduction was seeming less and less like police business, even if the abductors had been *judiciales,* and he doubted if he was in anything remotely like a police station. He could smell some plasticky chemical in the air. If he listened hard, he could hear machinery somewhere not far away. One sound was intermittent, a pounding like a stamp mill, and the other steady, like a big air-conditioning unit, but the room he was in was not cool. It was hot and stuffy and seemed to be getting hotter.

Eventually he heard a door come open, boosting the machinery noise, and then he heard the approach of several men. Without warning, the tape was stripped off his eyes in one hard yank. His cry of pain was muffled by the tape still across his mouth, but that went next. His first sight from where he lay was the grinning cop, balling up the silver tape between his palms into a compact mass. He lobbed it in front of himself and soccer-kicked the crude ball sideways. The frowner was there, too, but Jack Liffey's eye went quickly to a third man, who was new.

He was immensely overweight, straining a very large polo shirt in every dimension under an equally large expensive-looking linen jacket. The fat man wore mirrored sunglasses in the dimly lit room, like a caricature of a Tropical Bad Guy. He kept the left hand of his treelike arm buried in his jacket pocket for some reason, and beckoned with his free hand. The frowner got him a folding chair immediately. Sweat prickled the fat man's forehead, as if just standing up in the big room were a terrible exertion, and he sat hard to spill off both sides of the chair. The frowner quickly brought him a second chair and, without embarrassment, the fat man shifted his large rump to rest on both of them, side by side.

The grinner squatted to tug out Jack Liffey's wallet and handed it to the fat man, who riffled through it.

"Liffey. Jack. Culver City. Fascinating. Do you know that was the home of the great Laurel and Hardy?" His English was not just good, like Jaime Torres's, but perfect, although it had the faintest accent. He had obviously lived much of his life north of the border.

"Not where they lived," the fat man corrected himself. "But the Hal Roach Studios, where the movies were made."

In fact, Jack Liffey had once been shown a location on a side street of tiny bungalows fairly near his condo, where quite a few of their short films had been shot. Stan Laurel had died in an ordinary apartment not far away in Santa Monica, but he said nothing.

"I have a sixteen-millimeter print of *Tit for Tat*. That is the one where the greatest of all comedy teams are selling Christmas trees door-to-door in July." The fat man chuckled, increasing the strain on his taut polo shirt. "The famous James Finlayson with his big mustache is their foil, and he reacts in scorn and slams his front door on their tree, which of course cuts off the top of the tree. So Hardy knocks again and, after pointing out the damage to the tree and giving his wonderful slow burn, he retaliates by tearing off Finlayson's porch light. Then he nods with that finality he has. In due course, the exchange of destruction continues until Finlayson has destroyed their car and they have broken up the house and even thrown a piano out the window. They display the true Mexican spirit, in fact. Always get even. *Segundo,*" he called.

He handed the wallet back to the grinner, who took out the cash before putting it back in Jack Liffey's pocket. He didn't get much.

"You have been searching for Rebecca Auslander." The fat man enunciated the name carefully.

"Yes. Her father hired me to find her."

"Why did you look in Ensenada?"

Trussed up on the floor, Jack Liffey did the best he could to shrug. "Her family had gone there a lot. I heard that she liked the town."

The fat man turned and glared at the frowner. Then he strained forward and reached out to slap the frowner's head quite hard with his right hand. Still, his left was caught up in his pocket, as if holding onto something it could not let go. "See, *Primero*. The way a *professional* does it." He turned back to Jack Liffey. "Culver City is also the home of the Keystone Kops."

It wasn't, but he didn't say anything.

"Our federal police have been known to make mistakes, but they are not the Keystone Kops, Jack Liffey. Don't make that mistake. Every taxi driver and vegetable seller—even the barefoot little Indio girl who insists you buy her Chiclets—reports to them and they know everything, absolutely everything, sooner or later. In this case, however, it seems to be later." He glared at the frowner again, who did his best not to flinch away.

Jack Liffey wasn't going to be able to do much more than delay them. He knew that.

"Did you find her?"

"Yes," he admitted.

That perked them all up.

"How did you do that? Does her family have a vacation house that our efficient police also didn't find out about?"

He wanted to leave Jaime Torres out of it, if he could, though it was probably Jaime's searching through town that had stirred them up. "I showed her picture around town. At El Gigante, someone knew who she was. After all, she was a new gringa in town, and pretty."

"Very pretty," the fat man agreed.

"I know she took some money that belongs to someone else, probably to you. She's very frightened about it. I think I convinced her to give it back, but she wants me to bring her father down here first so she can talk to him. I was on my way to get him. Why don't you let me bring him down here? She may have hidden the money away in some offshore account that you'll never find without her cooperation."

When he risked a glance, the fat man was smiling. "Very entertaining, your imagination. Where does this girl live?"

"I don't know the address." He hoped Becky Auslander had taken him seriously and fled—he wasn't about to risk a bout of determined persuasion by these thugs. "It's the house with the dolphins on Chapultepec Hill, but I'll be happy to take you there and negotiate with her."

The fat man pointed to the frowner and made a telephone signal, a fist with the thumb and little finger stuck out, brought up to his mouth. The frowner nodded and went out a door, boosting the growl of machinery noise, which died down as the door sealed shut again. The cement floor was getting more and more uncomfortable on Jack Liffey's hip, but he didn't want to call attention to his level of comfort in any way. It could only get worse.

"So you were going to get her to give our property back?" The fat man took out a handkerchief and mopped his brow.

"She didn't know what she was doing. I don't think anybody wants to make enemies of very powerful people."

"Very powerful and very vindictive people, you might say."

"I didn't."

"That is discreet of you, but it's true nevertheless. We'll just wait a little and see if my friends can speak to the girl."

They waited for a while, and the grinner spoke in Spanish to the fat man. The fat man seemed a bit exercised and snapped back at him. The grinner went out and came back a minute later with a large floor fan trailing a long cord, which he set up to blow across the fat man.

"Your English is very good," Jack Liffey said.

"Michigan State University. The Spartans," he explained proudly. "Not the Wolverines. State was also where the great SDS met in 1970 and began to come apart. I was proud of that once, because . . . Well, just because."

Jack Liffey thought it might be important to keep him talking. "Because?"

"Do you know about the Mexico Olympics in 1968?" the fat man asked, with an edge in his voice for the first time.

"Two black Americans raised their fists and had their medals taken away."

The fat man smiled, but there was no humor in the expression. "I suppose that is what a North American would remember. Like a Mexican remembering that General Santa Anna had a cold the day he visited the Alamo. I was a student at Mexico City in 1968. Just before the Olympics, we were protesting for more democracy in our country. The government didn't like the embarrassment in front of the world press, so at first the army shut down the university, and then they fired on a demonstration at Tlatelolco Square in the center of the city. Three hundred students were shot down and killed. That's officially—I think more."

"I remember some of it."

"There were thousands in jail, and I became the treasurer for a group that collected money for lawyers and bail. The police arrested me and wanted to know who had contributed to the defense fund. I wouldn't tell them." For the first time, he took out his left hand. He displayed it casually and Jack Liffey winced: The back of his hand was scarred grotesquely, as if it had been larded with gobs and strings of pink clay. "They held my hand over a gas burner for a long time. Still I didn't tell them. When I got out of jail, it was prudent to leave the country and finish my education somewhere else. In fact I couldn't come back to Mexico for a long time. I missed my country a lot in those years, or I thought I did. But, you know, you don't really long for your country when you're in exile. What you miss is something in yourself that you can't have anymore."

"What did you long for?"

"That is none of your business. Relax now." He chuckled. "Enjoy what Albert Camus called 'the benign indifference of the universe?' It may not always be so."

Fariborz realized he'd not eaten since the morning of the day before, but he stayed on his knees on the small frayed carpet in the center of the bedroom floor. He needed to continue to pray and fast, and fast and pray, until he was given some sign. At the moment, there was only a silence and the stillness of the spirit that disturbed him deeply.

He prayed for guidance and for absolution for his mistakes, prayed to have a sense of rightness again, prayed even for the merest sense that Someone was listening. He bent forward and pressed his forehead to the carpet, repeating the formulaic Arabic prayers, feeling the blood drain into his face and flush it warm. He heard traffic outside and a horn now and then, the voices of children squealing at each other as they passed. That world out there was no longer his. He felt he needed help to reenter it, to feel as if he belonged.

He tried to frame explanations for his actions—but for whom, he wondered? All he had wanted to do, all along, was take a few small actions that would advance him along the *Sunna,* the right way. He asked sincerely if that wish had perhaps been vanity, if he had been following some voice in his own mind rather than the voice of God, and it was the vanity that had poisoned what he had done.

God is greater, God is greater.
I witness that there is no god but God.
I witness that Mohammed is the prophet of God.

He had tried to separate himself from the mores of a society that he had come to see as utterly godless and irreverent. But he did not want to punish any individuals—even the godless. He had wanted simply to draw a bold line around the lusts and venal indulgences he saw, around injustice and cruelty, the cheapening of love and affection, around intoxication and exploitation, around that terrible obsession with buying commodities and the whole invisible bondage of the cash nexus. His only purpose was to call impassioned attention to what lay inside the line he would draw so everyone might see it. He had not expected everyone to change overnight, or maybe at all, or even to understand what he was doing, but the act of witness would be enough for him. It should have pleased God.

Instead, everything had gone wrong. People had been hurt. Iman had lost a hand. Their group's hopes to finance their plans had vanished in an instant. They had become isolated from the school and their friends and families. And there seemed nothing but more hurt in store for them. He did not know for certain what Hassan and Sheik Arad were planning, but what little he had seen made him profoundly uneasy about their designs. So he had run away. And now Fariborz Bayat felt utterly alone in a cold and silent world.

His prayers went on and on until he felt the tears rolling along his cheeks, and then on still more. Something boomed outside. Once, twice, three times—either a truck backfiring or a gun. The walls of the building shook with it; the windows rattled. He collapsed and rolled onto his back on the floor of the apartment, surprised that he was even alive. God had let him live through his

crisis. God, in fact, had sent explosions to stir him out of his immo-
bility and carry him to a calmer place, into the eye of the storm.

The booming sounds had broken into a culpable drift of his
attention: he'd been thinking of his short tenure as a bodybuilder
in the Kennedy School's weight room. In his mind, the gym coach
had been telling him insistently how muscles were built—through
failure after failure. There was no such thing as a slow accretion
of muscle tissue, the coach had told him. You worked a particular
muscle, harder and harder, worked through the pain, until it
failed and the tissue broke down. And then, if you ate protein and
kept in good health, the muscle tissue grew back bigger and
stronger where it had failed. He sat up: It was a revelation. Maybe
what he had been doing was exercising his moral and religious
muscle. He had taken them past the critical point, he had failed—
but, like a muscle, this failure may be exactly what he needed for
moral growth.

Others had been hurt, and he could never really pay off a debt
like that; but he could set his whole life, right now, against some
tangible evil. Arriving at this thought seemed to increase the light-
headedness that he felt, but it seemed to ease his burden.

His father's corporation had become enmeshed in the evil of
narcotics smuggling. He was certain that Mahmoud was responsible. He could not believe it was his father's doing. Working in the
plant the previous summer, Fariborz had seen enough of Mahmoud to distrust him in all things. The man had cut corners at
every opportunity. He had bribed Mexican officials. Every payday
he had cheated the workers out of at least a few minutes of their
wages, in his office he had sex with one of the women workers,
and he drank tequila every afternoon with his Mexican watchman.
Fariborz had tried to tell his father, but his father had cut him off
and refused to listen—far too trusting and loyal to Mahmoud for
his own good.

Fariborz lay on the floor, inhaling and exhaling slowly. If he
could only disrupt the smuggling—one simple and direct action—it
might constitute the beginning of a kind of penance for any vanity
that had led him astray. He still had the door code to the factory.

He would wait until late, break into the LA ROX *maquiladora* and somehow thwart the terrible evil that dwelled there.

It was even possible, he thought, that Mahmoud was as much demon as man. He did not believe literally in demons—only that there were people who had inexplicable selfishness and evil within them, and Mahmoud was as good a candidate as anyone he knew.

The frowner had come back and was chattering away in Spanish. The fat man was rubbing his own chin, as if trying to remember if he'd shaved. Fear and anxiety had exhausted Jack Liffey so thoroughly that he had actually dozed for a few moments on the cement—he wasn't sure how long. The conversation went back and forth for a while, with the frowner insisting hard on something.

Finally, the fat man turned back to his prisoner.

"The girl is not waiting in her house to meet her father. Are you quite sure that was the plan?"

"Yes. I was on the way to the border to get him."

"Where do you think she would go?"

"Maybe to the store."

"Maybe to the store," he repeated. "I am not an idiot, Jack Liffey. My people have been inside the dolphin house, and there is very little clothing there. Some of what is left is laid out on the bed. As if she packed hastily and did not have room for everything."

"She must have panicked. Where could she escape? You must have friends watching the border."

The fat man spoke to the frowner, who left the room again. Then he sighed and seemed to settle in to wait. The grinner began to whistle a tune, and the fat man silenced him with a single word.

"Is your family name Arrellano Felix?" Jack Liffey asked.

He smiled. "Half-smart, like your newspapers. It is true, of course, that my industry is a special instance of monopoly capitalism. Only the commodity is different. We don't deal in cars or canned corn or CD players; we deal in illegal substances. But the way the business works is the same. When we were all reading Marx and Lenin in 1968, the simpleminded students in our cell all thought that the expression 'monopoly capitalism' meant there was only one big company running things, but the world is never so simplistic. Never. Marx never predicted that. It is enough that there are a handful of big companies, and sometimes they compete and sometimes they cooperate. But all in all, their economy of scale and the way they gobble up competition is sufficient to keep out the little guys. Yes, Arrellano Felix is the best-known monopoly by far. Let's say I am only Avis, and they are Hertz."

Thanks for the lecture, Jack Liffey thought. It was not very reassuring to know he was being held prisoner by someone who might feel that he had to try harder.

"I think now you should tell me whatever you know about the girl. It will be good for you in the long run. The world's benign indifference is about to end."

"The girl is running. If she was planning to do that, you know she wouldn't tell me where she's going."

"Maybe you are in cahoots with her. Maybe you are going to meet her, or arrange a false passport for her. Who knows? Money can buy many things. I need to be sure you don't know."

"I don't know a thing, believe me."

"But, you see, I need to be *sure.*" He barked at the grinner, who went out for a minute and then returned, followed by a new man who waited in the doorway as a hulking silhouette with the sounds of machinery leaking around him, the clattering and hissing in the building beyond. The fat man turned to the silhouette.

"A temporary layoff has been ordained," the fat man said. "Shut the plant down now, for the night."

"We're just starting swing shift. They haven't been in an hour yet." Jack Liffey could not get a good look at the man, but the voice was familiar.

"Oh, Lord, don't let him argue. Send them home now."

"I need to keep a warehouse crew for the shipment to Phoenix." Now he knew who it was. Mahmoud something, Bayat's man in the *maquiladora*. What word had they used to describe his duties? Fixer? Expediter. Now Jack Liffey knew where he was being held, though it did him no good.

"Everybody goes home. You, the warehousemen, supervisors. You have ten minutes to clear the building."

There seemed to be a staring duel for a moment, but the other man—if it *was* Mahmoud—finally seemed to decide where the power lay. "I hope you're loving this, my friend," Mahmoud said.

"It is my profession."

Jack Liffey had no idea what was going to happen, but it frightened him so much that there was a spasm in his leg. Only the fact that his ankles were taped together kept him from thrashing around on the floor like a jumping bean. The fat man no longer seemed to feel that he needed to hide his mangled hand.

"What a long, strange journey it has been, hasn't it, Jack Liffey?"

"What?"

"Me, I mean. A Marxist-Leninist student who began by demanding democracy in Mexico City, and is then driven out of his country by the *federales,* who studies six years in Michigan, USA, to get his MBA. And now I buy *federales* wholesale." He chuckled. "You know why *federales* often go in threes in our country? No, of course you don't. The first *federale* can read, the second *federale* can write, and the third is assigned to keep an eye on the two intellectuals." He laughed and glanced at the frowner, who did not seem to have followed the joke.

The fat man went on like that for a while, but it was becoming hard for Jack Liffey to listen. Something bad was about to happen, and he could think of nothing he could possibly do to fend it off. He tried again to insist that he knew nothing about Rebecca Auslander's whereabouts, but the fat man just waved the objection away, erasing his words out of the air.

Then the grinner came back and nodded. They untaped his ankles and lifted him to his feet.

"I must tell you, my friend, the world is about to get very interested in your predicament. Existentialism is now extinct." He sighed theatrically. "This is just a kind of insurance policy, you know. So we're all happy that you're truly in the dark."

The two *judiciales* frog-marched him out the door between themselves, past a lot of silent machinery with large vats and tubes and some kind of pneumatic jacks that looked like they were meant to slam parts of the machines together hard. Probably injection molds for LA ROX, he thought. Then the bulk of his attention did a paradigm shift into the kind of panicky fizzing that came with utter helplessness. They turned a corner at a tidy orange line on the floor and went into a lunchroom that looked exactly like a lunchroom in an American institution, with Formica tables and vending machines, a microwave, a fridge, and a stove. The only difference was that the vending machines seemed to carry nothing but varieties of burritos.

The two *judiciales*—if that's what they were—pushed him hard up against the stove and turned on one of the burners, and his mind went woozy with fear as he saw the little ring of flames. Each blue flame swelled to red, then tapered to yellow at the tip. They untaped his wrists and the *judiciales* held his right arm as the fat man gripped his left with both of his hands. The fat man gave off an overpowering aroma of rosewater.

"Jack Liffey, I lied to you a little. When I said I didn't talk. I mean, when the soldiers burned my hand. I'm afraid I told. I told the soldiers every name I knew who had anything in any way to do with the defense fund. I probably got two dozen other people arrested and tortured. There is no honor in this kind of persuasion, believe me."

"I believe you. I don't know where she went. I don't."

"Maybe so. Now we find out." And his hand was wrenched around and pressed down into the flame with incredible strength.

He kicked and thrashed around and screamed from somewhere very deep inside his body.

Before very long, he told them he was the one who had suggested that Rebecca Auslander run away, and he had suggested, by name, just as examples, Europe and Idaho. Anywhere but Mexico. He even told them she had said something about roses. If there was any honor at all in resisting that kind of persuasion, he did not mention Jaime Torres. He passed out before he could.

Thirteen

La Libertad

He woke to a searing pain in his left hand, someone rasping it down to the bone with a cheese grater. In fact, one peek revealed a real person bent over his hand, a young man, rubbing a cold wet goo onto the unbearable wound. He clamped his eyes shut again, engulfed by a visceral desire to return immediately to the world of sleep and blot out the pain, but it had so thoroughly invaded his busy dream-state that even there some terrible wolverine-like animal had been chewing on the hand. No, he was awake now. He discovered that his ankles were still taped and his hip told him he lay on cement. His shoulder was being shaken gently. Jack Liffey opened an eye again to see a delicate hand, slim pianist's fingers.

"Can you swallow, sir?"

The boy was maybe seventeen or eighteen, darkly handsome, and knelt beside him offering a glass of water and two pills.

"It's codeine. I put Xylocaine on your hand, from the first-aid kit, but it's probably not strong enough to help much."

Jack Liffey took the pills from the boy's palm and swallowed them with a sip of water, and the boy scurried around to strip the tape off his ankles. A pennant of the same tape fluttered from his good wrist, waggling a little as he sloshed the plastic tumbler for no particular reason. Freeing his hands must have been the boy's first act, after first pushing aside that angry beast gnawing on his hand.

The boy settled back on his haunches with an earnest, concerned look, and Jack Liffey studied his face. He had an olive complexion, but he did not look very Mexican, at least not in the round-faced mestizo-Indian way he was familiar with. His voice had sounded American. Of course, he might have been upper-class Mexican, fitted out with a few more European genes, the people who used to call themselves "Spanish" in L.A.

"I heard those men talking about you before they left. You found Becky."

Jack Liffey's eyes snapped back to the young man's face, studying it for clues. Pain made his thought process stiff and refractory, but he managed the leap of logic. "You're Fariborz."

The boy nodded. "We have to get you out of here. They'll come back tomorrow to question you again. I heard them say you passed out too soon and they couldn't get you to wake up again. Your body must have a really strong defense mechanism."

"A really strong defense mechanism would be asbestos skin." He thrust his fiery hand into the glass of water and closed his eyes. "Oh, Lord!" The relief was immediate, almost total, but within a few seconds he could tell it was not going to last. Pain gathered, the wolf padding forward again to gnaw at the wound, tear off chunks.

"Soon the pills will make you drowsy."

"Then let's get going now."

"We can't leave until that light turns red." He indicated a tiny green glow showing on a metal box by the door.

"Why?"

"The alarm is off because the manager came back. He would see us now. I think he needs to finish some work the Mexicans interrupted. He'll leave soon. He never stays late."

"Will he come in here?"

"No. He doesn't want any part of them or what they did to you. I think he's scared of the big Mexican."

"So am I. My name is Jack Liffey," he offered. "I find missing kids. I was hired by Becky's father to find her, and I talked to your father, too, and to some of the people at your school. Where are the other boys?"

"They're not here. That's all I can say."

Jack Liffey's hand was throbbing. He had displaced most of the water from the tumbler and there wasn't enough left to wet the whole wound. "What on earth is this all about?" Jack Liffey asked. His question offered Fariborz the latitude to explain just about anything he wished. "Everyone said you were a good boy."

The boy looked rueful. There was a distracting pop-bang up on the metal roof, and they both glanced up quickly. But it was probably only a heat contraction or a big bird settling on the ribbed aluminum.

"A good boy," Fariborz repeated, as if testing the words for some secret meaning. "Yes, I was trying to do good. The *Sunna,* the straight path, if you're Moslem, but I don't think you have to be Moslem to appreciate the idea." He smiled grimly, as if there were some joke at his expense. "It's harder than I thought."

"Congratulations. That sounds like the beginning of wisdom." Jack Liffey glanced toward the door, but the tiny glowing lamp was still green.

"Or a step straight into cynicism, Mr. Liffey. I don't want that to happen to me—it's cheap and ugly."

He felt the boy's sincerity reverberate and he tried to give him his full attention. "Sure. Tell me more."

"I was looking for a way to behave morally in a world that offers almost no moral paths."

"I don't think you're completely alone on that expedition. A few people before you have tried to do the right thing, within their lights."

"None of them seem to be in charge of anything much that matters these days."

Jack Liffey chuckled, then grimaced as the pain redoubled. The pain seemed to have the quality of intensifying all experience, including his perceptions of Fariborz, who seemed to carry a hazy aura of piety around himself. He'd met one kid before who had embarked on what Kerouac had called "the holy boy road," but this young man seemed to have a bit of humor about him, which, in the end, might just save him.

"I've read Gandhi," the young man said. "You can't just be passive, you can't just keep your own hands clean. You have to take positive action for the good. Anyway, that's what I thought."

The pain charged back into the center of Jack Liffey's consciousness and made it hard to concentrate. Still, it helped for the young man to talk away. At first Fariborz spoke in evasive generalities but finally he broke down and told him about some grandiose plan he had worked out to draw attention to conspicuous nuggets of vice that were afoot in America—such as paint-bombing *Hustler* magazine's headquarters on La Cienega.

The boy had been saving newspaper articles about likely targets: the one industrial block in Studio City where most of the country's porn production was centered, a neo-Nazi storefront, a notorious sweatshop downtown, etc., etc. He had pictured himself as something like Mexico's popular hero Super Barrio, an actual caped character who showed up from time to time to twit the rich and powerful. He figured the press might pick it up and start following his exploits, a new Zorro or something. With the right publicist, it was almost wacky enough to have worked.

Fariborz employed the first person insistently, taking the whole plan on himself, but Jack Liffey figured his friends had all been in on it.

"But somebody got hurt. It was my fault. I prayed and prayed to discover the name of my sin."

"Could you get me some more water?" Jack Liffey asked.

"I don't think it's a good idea. Mahmoud's just down the hall." The little light was still green.

It was the first time the boy had used the man's name and Jack Liffey realized the boy knew the setup here pretty well. He nodded dully and waved his hand a little. "My generation was luckier than yours," Jack Liffey said. "We actually got to stop a war. That's pretty amazing when you think about it."

He clamped his eyes closed. There was nothing to do but try to talk through the pain. He heard himself saying, "Of course, the

Vietnamese had a lot to do with stopping the war, too. But I think it was rebellion spreading through the U.S. Army that finally put the fear of God into the government. I was just a tech over there, monitoring a radar, but we all had peace symbols and strings of beads on our scopes. I heard more than one time about platoons taking their officers prisoner at gunpoint and refusing to go out on patrol, and lieutenants just clamming up about it to prevent an ignominious end to their careers. Who knows."

They heard a door slam and both looked over, but the light was still unchanged.

"Of course, a lot of kids got a big head about it all. They'd driven out a president and built a rock-'n'-roll culture and they thought they could change everything, overthrow the whole system. That was pretty crazy. America is a big, rich, deeply conservative, almost immovable country. A lot of those kids hurt themselves— psychologically, if not physically—trying to do the impossible. I have to deal with them and their children every day now. It's best to know the limits of the possible."

"But you have to try, no matter what the limits seem to be," the young man protested. "How else can you know what's possible?"

"I can't walk through that cement wall, and I don't have to keep throwing my shoulder into it just to make sure."

Fariborz shook his head, unconvinced. "Maybe one day the atoms will all line up just right and you *will* be able to walk through."

Jack Liffey tried to laugh, but the pain ambushed it. "I think that's probably excluded."

"Mr. Liffey, the people who wanted democracy in Czechoslovakia were beaten in 1968. What if they'd given up? They went into the streets twenty years later and won."

He felt addled and unhinged. Perhaps this was the wrong time for a simple political discussion. "Times were different; I don't know. Maybe every generation *does* have to try. I'm not blaming you."

Jack Liffey flexed his hand, grimacing, unable to concentrate. What he wanted to tell the boy was that the kind of heroism he was talking about wasn't something a single person could just will on the spot—that even a Gandhi born a century too early would have been irrelevant. When it worked, it was a relationship between a single will and a special time that made moral action possible. But he didn't want to argue any longer; he didn't even want to hear his own voice. It seemed to him futile—even a little distasteful—to argue against a boy's idealism. And then there was the pain, always the pain.

"You came here to disrupt a tiny corner of the drug trade, didn't you?" Jack Liffey guessed.

The boy nodded warily. Drugs had not been mentioned before then. "How did you know?"

He sighed. "It's a manageable goal. You have my permission to save my life, too. That's also a nice small, manageable goal."

The young man nodded again slowly, and there was a deadpan aspect in it that Jack Liffey missed at first. "Perhaps you're worth saving. Just barely."

Jack Liffey laughed softly, despite himself. This was one confident kid. Then Fariborz hissed him quiet. *"There."*

A tiny red pilot lamp had come on and begun to flash beside the green. In a moment, the green went out and the red turned steady.

"We'll give him a chance to drive away," the young man said.

"When we get out there, I think we're going to have to avoid just about everybody," Jack Liffey suggested. "The *judiciales* have informers everywhere."

"I'm on it," the boy said. "If I'm going to be charged with saving your life, you're not going to be going the gringo route. I'll be your coyote. That means your unofficial guide across to *el Norte.*"

"I know what a coyote is. Have you ever crossed illegally?"

"No, but I know how it's done."

"I hope you do." The codeine was starting to fuzz him up now, without doing all that much for the pain. He caught himself looking up at the ceiling and groaning. "Did you do anything here to disrupt the drug business?" Jack Liffey asked. It might interfere with their escape.

"There's no evidence of it here anymore, nothing."

"Did you have anything to do with the shipment that was hijacked in Riverside?" He remembered it had been grotesquely violent, with somebody executing the driver.

"No."

Dark armies, fighting in the dark. Maybe that was just an object lesson, from someone in one camp to someone in another. He'd probably never know. Jack Liffey's impatience swelled with the pain. "Let's go *now.*"

The young man helped him up and turned out the room light before leading him into a hallway where there was only blackness and a pulsating silence. "Follow me. Touch the wall to keep going straight."

"You're the boss."

They tapped their way along, and before long they came around a corner to where they could see, far ahead, a faint haze of light from an emergency lamp, and they could walk a little faster. At the outside door there was another code box on the wall. The boy punched in a series of numbers and a green light came on, then punched what seemed the same numbers again and the red began to flash. "Go!"

Then they were outside, blinded by the glare of a security light overhead as they hurried across a parking lot toward the street. In the distance, the whole sky was orange with town light, and the road showed the taillights of a single car, a big low-riding American sedan, diminishing.

"Do you think you can walk for an hour?"

Jack Liffey looked at his watch for the first time and saw it was only 9:45. "I have to. I do what I have to. Does that get us across?"

"No. It gets us to the right *colonia. La Libertad,* where many people wait to cross."

Jack Liffey wondered if the name was somebody's idea of a joke—for the neighborhood where illegals waited to cross the border to take up their miserable underpaid jobs in *Norteamerica.* Better *La Peonage, La Serfdom.*

The industrial street was dusty and curbless, rutted at the edges with weeds, and a footpath snaked alongside it, where people had worn away the weeds, like a well-used game trail. As long as he fought the wooziness and kept moving, he found the pain in his hand almost manageable. A big doubly articulated truck ground slowly out of a driveway behind and crept past them.

"*La Libertad* is a sad place. People used to wait in the river zone next to it, which was even worse. But that whole colonia was bulldozed to build a shopping center and apartments. It was called *cartolandia*—cardboard-carton city."

"How do you know so much about Tijuana?"

"I worked here last summer and made friends with a lot of students and artists. Tijuana is a wonderful city if you stay away from the tourist area. It's full of energy and a great hunger for decency. Many, many people just try every day to get a little money honestly to live." His face seemed to glow under the waxy yellowy streetlights.

"I remember only *Avenida de la Revolución,*" Jack Liffey said. It was the street of bars, brothels, and trinket vendors, cheap serapes, pottery, and leatherware, and he hadn't seen it in ten years, since Art Castro had taken him there to the *jai alai* fronton.

"*La Revo.* The locals say it's a magnet that pulls two ways. All of America's losers are pulled there to be preyed on by all of Mexico's crooks."

"That's convenient," Jack Liffey said. "In America, the crooks have to make more of an effort."

They walked between big silent factory buildings like raw concrete fortresses, several of them automatically igniting their security lamps as they passed. Here and there a little cluster of beat-up sedans in a parking lot suggested a night shift. The road rose and fell shallowly, and at one crest, a bit higher, he could see the solid metal wall at the border, a scar running for miles, and maybe ten miles on the other side of the wall a mirage, the lit buildings of downtown San Diego like the unattainable Emerald City.

A sound swelled behind them, first just a rumble and then it erupted into a crackling roar. He ducked involuntarily as an old Mexicana DC-9 passed low and incredibly loud on its landing run. The little jetliner sank out of sight beyond some buildings, presumably touching down on an invisible runaway. It roared with reverse thrust.

"This side gets the landings," Fariborz said. "*La Libertad* is on the other side of the airport and gets the takeoffs. Then the planes go right across the border. I bet it's the only airport in the world where you take off into another country."

A police siren approached them from behind, and they stepped back into shadows. It turned out to be a beige Crown Victoria, many years old, its multicolored light bar flashing away like a gambling casino.

A big truck pulled blindly out of a plant ahead, forcing the cop car to brake hard, backfiring and lighting up everything around it for Christmas. There was a noisy skid and a policeman's head leaned out into the night: "*¡Ándale, pendejo!*"

The police car skirled around the truck, clipping dirt on the far shoulder of the road to stir a cloud of dust, and accelerated away.

"Move on, asshole," the young man translated.

"I guessed that."

Apparently the police car had been a forerunner. Coming up fast was a truck crammed with soldiers, grim round-faced teenagers standing up in back clutching their automatic rifles and rocking in unison. They looked put-upon and sleepy.

"What's that about?"

"Could be us, or looking for guerrillas. Sometimes they think guerrillas are everywhere. The army is terrified of the big bad Subcomandante Marcos in Chiapas." They waited in the shadows as yet another troop truck whisked past.

The military convoy had stirred in Jack Liffey some adrenaline which seemed to push back his codeine sleepiness a bit, and he tried to keep the boy to a fast pace. Pain still dogged him and he closed his eyes from time to time, drawn along in the wake of Fariborz's voice as he talked about living in T.J., his trips down to Sonora, Mexican rock groups he'd met, but not about his father or Becky. Some inner self had retreated into Jack Liffey's core, watching out his eyeholes, separating a little from his unruly body. There was the sound of a gunshot somewhere ahead, bringing him back to the present to discover they had trekked into an area that looked much less industrial. Cantinas that might be open or closed, seafood restaurants, and locked-up car-repair shops with ramshackle wooden fences, even a few dark homes. An old man hobbled toward them. His aluminum crutches dangled bulging plastic bags filled with bottles and rubbish, which all swayed with his steady pace. Fariborz greeted him politely, but the old man was spooked and shied away.

Then they neared a ramshackle disco in full swing, with polka-like music banging away and men in silky black shirts and cowboy hats spilling outside into a dusty parking lot to posture and hit each other's shoulders. *Anatolio's Jet-Set Go-Go*. One group of men appeared to be sniffing glue out of a paper bag, and another was showing off with knives, slashing the air in a mock fight. Well before they reached the disco, he followed the boy to the opposite side of the road to give the place a wide berth.

Jack Liffey was reminded of what life was like for the *real* outsiders: for blacks in any of the big American cities until very recently, for illegals even today. No cops to call if something went wrong. No taxis, no ambulances or hospitals, no banks, no safety net.

Now the commerce gave way to rickety homes, and the main road descended into a valley of rolling hills, scarred by dirt cross streets that climbed hillsides choked up with shanties. The whole world here was adobe bricks and salvage, reused plywood, cardboard boxes, and black plastic, even opened-out tin drums. Up the slopes, in pools of weak light, he could see that homeowners had terraced their plots with old tires and salvage. The urge to beautify was astonishing. In each old tire there was a geranium, a beavertail cactus, a dark green chili plant.

At an open corner lot business was flourishing under bright lights. Small men were loading big silver propane tanks onto beat-up fender trucks from the 1950s. The bustle was all clangs and crisp calls on the night air, and he marveled that so much infrastructure carried on amidst such poverty. But of course, it had to. There were irreducible minimums for urban life, and even the poorest needed a way to cook and heat.

"Turn right here."

They skirted the tall fence at the edge of the airport and trended north on a dirt street into the colonia. Soon they crossed a four-lane highway, dodging the slow-moving semis that rolled steadily out of the industrial park toward the twenty-four-hour border crossing. The boy led him into another mesa of shanties that crowded up hard toward the big metal fence ahead. *La Frontera* itself.

"*La Libertad?*" he asked.

"Yes."

Things were livelier here. Knots of men and women stood or squatted where they could, some tending barrel fires, and the air seemed thick and hostile. There was a stench on the faint breeze, smoke and fire ash and ordinary dust, plus piss and rot. A big jet blasted into the air above them, seeming to hurl itself right out of the shantytown, and banked into a hard turn to cross the border wall. Aeromexico markings, an old four-engine 707 that he hadn't seen in years. He smelled kerosene now, jet fuel.

With his eyes still skyward, he noticed tiny shapes skittering against the clouds lit orange by city lights, moving herky-jerky, like bats. They probably *were* bats. He had never minded bats, but he remembered the only camping trip he'd taken with his wife, and Kathy's going hysterical about getting them caught in her hair. He wondered whether there was any rational basis for that. He flexed his hand. Something was working to take the pain down a notch.

There were shouts ahead. The boy seemed to recognize some peril in them and grabbed his sleeve to tug him up a smaller unpaved side road that ascended the hillside. Both sides of the narrow road were a solid tangle of makeshift housing, punctuated by banana trees and old cars.

Ahead, several men were gathered around a campfire in a bare lot, reduced to silhouettes in the glare. If the boy were to disappear suddenly, Jack Liffey thought, just yanked heavenward in some Persian Rapture, he, Jack Liffey, would be irretrievably lost, marooned in *La Libertad* for the rest of his natural life. "*Buenas dias*" and "*gracias*" would not get him very far toward safety.

And he wasn't sure how long that natural life would last. He guessed he would be a pretty soft target for any toughs hanging out in the busy night, waiting to feed on the gentle souls from inland Mexico who were hoping to cross, waiting for a coyote themselves, or just waiting for some miracle to make their lives a little better. So why not mug a rich gringo?

And why not? he thought. American jerks came down here every day and threw their weight around, took up all the best property along the coast, had no respect for the culture of Mexico, ran wild at fiestas, expected to skim off all the premium foods and goods as their birthright. And then they climbed back into their Winnebagos and Porsches and hightailed it for the border whenever they felt like it. In the right mood, he could mug a gringo himself.

A gang of squat figures drifted slowly down the hill toward them.

"Wait here." The young man went up to a house and spoke softly to a man who lounged in the doorway. A voice barked something and then slammed the flimsy door on him. Fariborz stepped over a row of oil cans that marked the edge of the front garden and knocked at the next house, light spilling out through chinks in its crude construction.

The group coming downhill was resolving itself in the half-light into teenagers in white T-shirts with some similar homemade marking on each. They banged fists on one another now and then, drifted slightly apart and then back, reminding him of a shoal of fish, looking to feed, and Jack Liffey was pretty sure he was in the food chain, and pretty far down into it.

"Come over here!" the young man called out to him, none too soon, and Jack Liffey hurried to the opened door, where a stocky old woman in an oversized housecoat studied him in abject fear. She held up a carved walking stick, as if fending them both off.

"For a price, she will let us rest here."

"One of the cops took my money." He thought it better not to say the word *'judiciales'* in front of the woman.

"I have some."

Fariborz handed her some cash and she let them step inside. The stick barred them any further until Fariborz counted out more money. One weak bulb hung from bare wires over a card table, where a single propane burner rested beside several empty cans. Jack Liffey tore his eyes away from the propane ring, his hand crying out in recognition. Everywhere else his eyes moved there was trash and debris, lumpy, stacked on top of itself, and mostly unrecognizable.

"She wants us in the side room."

Jack Liffey followed them into a dim lean-to chamber where he had to duck his head. The door closed hard behind them. He did not really feel trapped because a good kick would have knocked out the outside wall. They were in nothing more than an add-on shed made of packing crate wood, raw corrugated iron, and delaminating plywood. A mattress lay against the wall, covered by an unspeakably soiled chenille bedspread, and the rest of the floor appeared to be many layers of flattened cardboard carton that had dampened and dried so many times it was spongy and matted into a single piece. The only light came in threads and triangles, gaps in the outer wall.

"We shouldn't cross until three o'clock, so you might try to nap," Fariborz suggested.

Involuntarily, as he sat on the mattress, Jack Liffey recalled his tormentor's chatter about his favorite film stars. "This is another fine mess you've got me into," he said. The young man laughed softly, as if he understood.

Fourteen

The Piñata

"What's the time?" His own voice surprised him with its scratchiness. He guessed he had slept for a few minutes, maybe as much as half an hour, but he didn't feel the least refreshed. Earlier, after a lot of entreaty through the locked door, the woman had brought a shallow pan of water and his hand now marinated soothingly in it. From outside somewhere, they could hear competing strains of tootling and clangy music.

"It's just after midnight."

There was an intermittent clatter and bang out there that had invaded his hectic dream-state in odd ways. He only had to roll onto his side on the smelly mattress to look out through an oblong gap between a sheet of corrugated iron and a big square of stained plywood. A flat patch of land across the road was now bathed in light from several bulbs that dangled from the sickly-looking trees, and a dozen men were dismantling two very new cars. They had no power tools, but they scurried over the cars—a silver Toyota Camry and a red Trans-Am with California plates—like soldier ants, unscrewing and tugging at parts. The hoods and trunks were propped open in silhouette like arms thrown up in despair, and the strippers were sorting and stacking body panels and drive-train parts into piles. This is where his VW, parked in another border *colonia,* would end up in a few days, he thought.

He could imagine the parts being transported across town, and then mixed and matched to be reassembled into new hybrid vehicles: pickups with Cadillac fins, minivans with long sports-car hoods. But, in fact, he guessed the choice components would go into the inventories of auto-parts stores all over northern Mexico and the western United States.

Fariborz knelt to peer out his own aperture, a hole poked through a stiff cardboard poster for Bimbo Bread. "I've never seen a chop shop," the boy said, after watching awhile. "It's like a nature film with piranhas swarming over an animal carcass."

One of the radios offered a pounding banda polka in weird counterpoint to a wailing North American girl singer on the other, but the outside world had lost its interest for him and he turned away. Beside his bed, there was a splayed-out stack of decomposing newspapers, all with the bold masthead *¡Alarma!* The photos he could see were of gore and crushed cars and gunshot victims and the newspapers smelled heavily of mildew, which mixed with dust and piss smells heavy on the air. There was also a single orange plastic wheel that he recognized from a Big-Wheels tractor.

"Have you always been so confident?" Jack Liffey asked. The boy's cool had impressed him at several points, though he had found it fairly typical of rich kids. He lifted his hand experimentally, but it stung and he plunged it back into the pan of water.

Fariborz had settled into a crouch, and he clasped his knees with his arms. He was lit faintly in stripes, and he pursed his lips, emoting deep thought. "That's hard to answer without sounding like one big fat ego. I had a happy childhood, and I had loving parents who paid attention to me. When I look at my classmates, I think that's mainly what gives you a feeling of confidence as you grow up. But maybe I'm just not imaginative enough to picture things going wrong."

Somebody outside hollered at the top of his lungs, as if he'd just struck his thumb with a hammer, and the boy made a face. "Whatever I look like to you, I feel like a total outsider. Not just as a Persian.

I don't want to feel at home in all the sinfulness I see. Sometimes it seems that the main purpose of education is to get you to accept all that as what's normal. I don't quite mean sinfulness as the word to use. I mean something like selfishness and greediness and just looking the other way when bad things happen."

All that *is* more or less normal, Jack Liffey thought, but he didn't say anything.

"When I peeked at that big fat Mexican, I could see he was really evil." The boy's face was overworking itself to suggest difficult, or just painful thought. "It's funny. For some reason, he didn't scare me. I don't know. Maybe I just trust Allah to protect me."

"I don't want to mess with your religion," Jack Liffey said softly, "but I think it's a good idea to get over that sense of invulnerability. That's youth. Sooner or later, it's going to hit you that it's entirely random whether things take a wrong turn."

"I think I learned that—I mean, things did go wrong for us. But it didn't really change me. I mean, it changed my life, for sure, but it didn't change how I am. I guess it's like those girls who grow up with a fat self-image—no matter how thin they get, they still feel fat."

The boy went on for a while talking about his moral struggles at Kennedy. Jack Liffey could see he had been self-absorbed with this for a long time, spoiling away inside, bouncing around in a fragile ethical wrangle of his own construction while dealing like a trooper with the outside world. His own thoughts subsided toward the much simpler relentless pain in his hand. The burn made anything else an effort.

"Didn't *you* have a happy childhood?" the boy asked.

Jack Liffey tried to drag himself back toward the boy, who probably needed him more than he knew. "I grew up white and suburban in the fifties. That was probably the most fortunate daydream in world history, but it was a freak. We had so much fun playing with our model airplanes, we never looked around at things."

"What do you mean?"

"Racism is the obvious one. The Dulles brothers destroying

Central America because their family owned United Fruit. Vietnam was under way; then somebody went and shot King and the Kennedys. And Malcolm. Suddenly every single stone got turned up, and there was something deeply nasty under every one."

It was the pain in his hand talking. He decided not to say any more. Fariborz was still young, and it seemed vaguely disgraceful to interfere with the idealism of the young. Maybe it was still possible in the boy's worldview for Shane to ride into town and fix everything. And Jack Liffey knew perfectly well that every once in a while, unpredictably, he could not refrain from trying to act out some Shane drama of his own.

"I don't think moral blindness is my problem," the young man said.

"No, you were born way too late for that. Think of the change. My TV sitcoms all had perfect moms and slightly goofy dads who wore cardigans and did their earnest best to help their kids stay out of trouble. Yours are full of dysfunctional parents screaming insults at each other."

"I don't watch TV."

"It's kind of a metaphor. We've left you a world stripped raw of illusions. You don't have to be a Moslem, you know, to recoil from the pain that shows through."

"I know. If I thought that, I'd have to leave America. No matter what anoyone's religion is, they have the capacity to add to the good side of the balance."

"Well, just now, you get to save my life. That's not a bad goal, on any moral level. I have a hunch you're planning something to help your friends, too."

Fariborz shook his head quickly, as if refusing any conversation about the other boys. He started to say something more when a gunshot slammed into the night, quite close, rattling and buzzing the flimsier panels of the shack. They went to their peer-holes to look out into the dark busy world. The car breakers were still at work, oblivious to the shot, and the light from their workshop poured across a gang of teens and preteens in the middle of the street. What must have been the gang leader had a slightly older teen down on his knees at gunpoint. All the gang members wore white T-shirts with a big 18 drawn on the front with Magic Marker, in that angular, vaguely Aztec lettering of Latino grafitti. "Eighteenth Street" was the Latino supergang of Los Angeles, but in L.A. they didn't wear it on their shirts. These were wannabes or copycats.

The boy on his knees wore a too-big trench coat and was whimpering as the others shouted at him and the tiny mean-looking gang leader held a cheap automatic pistol to his neck. Strangely enough, the car mechanics just went on working. In the background the Trans-Am had been stripped of all its body panels, which were set aside now like big red flower petals.

"They want him to do something I can't figure out," Fariborz whispered.

The boy in the trench coat pleaded and whined and finally acceded to something, as several of the gang boys danced from foot to foot. One skinny boy at the side breathed fumes out of a paper bag and then bellowed up into the sky.

Poverty doesn't necessarily ennoble, Jack Liffey thought, keeping it to himself and realizing that it was not a particularly profound observation after a century of various genocides by one group of the desperately poor against another. Yet these were just boys. Groups of boys, thrown together, seemed to get in touch all too easily with a warrior ethos, eternally re-creating bands of Visigoth raiders.

Two of the kids were dispatched on errands by the tiny leader with his Saturday-night special. The boy on his knees chose a different gang member as the object of his pleas, but the other boy just made rude gestures at him, clutching his own crotch like a rap singer, and laughing. Not laughing, really—the sound was a ghastly bray, like a distress signal from whatever soul remained within, the boy throwing his head back and opening a wound to the sky to dispatch that horrible sound.

Then one of them trotted back, holding at arm's length a big mangy cat that was kicking and boxing against the air. The boy with the paper bag generously offered the cat a whiff, and the cat yowled and kicked harder. Two boys decided to push the trench-coated victim back and forth on his knees in a demented shove-o'-war. Inevitably it got too rough, and he went over onto his side.

One of the strains of competing music stopped suddenly, and it was like a toothache abating. What remained was ordinary North American rock, dark and angry lyrics over a wailing guitar, somehow fitting for this horrible scene. Across the dirt road, two men rolled a hoist toward the Trans-Am and prepared to winch the engine out of the remains.

A second errand boy came back with what looked like a small dog, a Mexican hairless. It, too, objected to captivity, yipping and writhing, and the trench-coated boy called out to the dog plaintively from where he lay.

"It's his pet," Fariborz explained unnecessarily.

Jack Liffey had no idea what was about to happen, but he had a feeling that it was going to be something he didn't really want to see. Yet it had the morbid fascination of a train wreck, and he didn't look away. The boys produced a thin rope—maybe ten feet long—and tied the animals' tails to each end of the rope. The boy in the trench coat launched an appeal on deaf ears.

Two of the gang members swung the animals back and forth on the rope like pendulums, the animals objecting with increasing wails. The leader counted off, and the boys hurled their living bolo into the air. Jack Liffey noticed now that a power line—probably an unofficial one—dangled slackly over the dirt street, just low enough so a big truck coming up the road might snag it; but no big trucks would ever come up this road. Neither animal passed over the power line, though that seemed to be the intent. The boys scrambled to catch the rope in midair, halting the free fall of the animals so suddenly that after a moment of shocked silence there was a renewed clamor of yelping and cries. The tiny dog seemed angrier and more feisty than the cat. The gang boys leapt in the air and hurled up their fists and cheered in celebration of something.

The second toss put the heavier cat over the power line, and it jerked to a stop with a screech five feet above the dog, which swung and kicked at shoulder height, a living pendulum. One boy cupped his hands under the dog and boosted it upward, the rope slacking to let the cat descend a few feet. A taller boy leapt to boost the dog again until both animals were just about at equal height, up at the level of a basketball rim, and the original errand boy took a running leap and batted at the animals to set them swaying. The gang members hollered encouragement to this sport as the taller boy jumped again and again to redirect the animal trajectories until the cat and the Mexican hairless finally met upside down in a clash of tiny gladiators. The boy in the trench coat covered his eyes and sobbed.

"Aw, shit!" Jack Liffey said.

On its next pass, the cat wriggled around and slashed with all its legs, and the dog squealed shrilly in pain. The boys set the little gladiators swinging again, and at the next pass, the dog got in a good neck bite to set off a screech from the cat. The cat then doubled itself up at the top of its swing and, judging its aim well, struck home with all four paws on the dog's nose. The dog went into that rapid battle gargle that dogs give.

It was eerie that the car-breakers continued their work only a few yards away, as if they and the street gang existed in parallel universes unaware of one another.

Jack Liffey finally wrenched his eyes away from the tiny oblong window. It was a nastier sight than he could tolerate. The boys' voices went on shouting and rooting, punctuated by abrupt animal noises, while he studied a large print of the Virgin of Guadalupe tacked to the inner wall, imprisoned in her full-body spiky golden aura. It was posted on what was formerly the exterior adobe wall of the house, spiked in place with huge bent nails as if crucified. After another burst of yowling, Fariborz pulled back from his window, too. The young man's face seemed to have gone white, but it was hard to tell in the striped dimness.

Jack Liffey watched in surprise as the boy crawled over and hugged him, resting a forehead against Jack Liffey's chest. He felt the young man tremble. People are so damn complex, he thought. He had just been thinking the boy tough and brave, and though he might yet be, he was certainly not stonyhearted. Outside, the wailing and yipping went on and on. It was hard to tell which animal was getting the worst of it.

"How can boys do that?" Fariborz complained.

"We don't know what was done to them as children."

"I knew a boy at Kennedy who was beaten by his father every single day, and he's sworn never to harm a living creature."

The contest outside seemed to quiet down. One could always hope the boys had grown tired of tormenting the animals.

"In the religion I supposedly grew up in, they talk about turning the other cheek, but that seems to be a pipe dream," Jack Liffey said. "We used to have Gandhi and King and a lot of men like that. I think the world's just run out of saints."

Then there was a sustained outpouring of yaps and screams, followed by a police whistle that cut through all other sounds. Then more whistles, coming from all over the compass, as if the *colonia* were being invaded by soccer referees. The music cut off ominously. They went quickly to their peepholes. Jack Liffey saw that the car dismantlers were gone, just vanished into the night, the gang boys as well. The animal combat had displaced the rope so that the lighter dog hung about a foot above the cat, just out of reach, and both ropes swung gently together, enforcing a truce. The animals still wriggled now and then as the ropes swayed, but they seemed exhausted and resigned.

A khaki-colored open truck roared past up the hill packed with soldiers carrying automatic rifles at all angles. The soldiers looked little older than the gang members. One soldier craned his neck curiously at the dangling animals passing just at eye level. The truck skidded to a stop nearby, and an amplified voice from the truck barked orders to the community, then went on up the hill and repeated its commands farther up.

"A *gringo* is wanted for violating a little girl," Fariborz translated softly for him. "He raped her viciously and then killed her. There is a reward. It's you they describe."

"Oh, wonderful!"

Fariborz went immediately to the locked door and spoke through it, then slid an American twenty halfway under the door.

He talked some more, waggling the currency, and after a moment, the money disappeared. He came back and sat with his back against the pile of *¡Alarmas!*

"Don't worry. Nobody ever believes what the soldiers say. I told her you humiliated the lieutenant by kissing his wife in a cantina."

"Hmm."

"It's something she can believe. I told her there was no reward from the army, but there was plenty more from us. She's seen the color of our money, and she knows if she turns us in I'll tell the soldiers she has it."

Jack Liffey stared at the boy in wonder. "You don't quite live in a pristine universe after all."

He made a grim face. "Fear is always understandable, in everyone."

"You're way past recognizing an old woman's fear. You used it. Bribery and blackmail."

"I still see it as bad. But would you rather I hadn't?"

"My daughter calls that portable ethics." Jack Liffey grinned, but the boy was not amused by his own compromises.

They heard another commotion outside and went to their portholes. An army platoon was working its way slowly downhill, dropping soldiers off to each side to pound on doors and push inside. Several of them looked terribly earnest and intense—schoolboys doing their best at dress-up—but others carried their automatic rifles haphazardly, as if they hadn't had the lessons yet. One soldier took note of the animals overhead, still swaying head-down and exhausted. The soldier rapped a companion's shoulder with the back of his hand.

There was laughter, then exhortations and pointing. A few of the gravest round-faced, dark-eyed soldiers looked away, but most gathered at the spectacle. Jack Liffey heard the word *piñata* on the air and then an eruption of laughter. Two soldiers grabbed the arms of the shortest and darkest squaddie who carried only a short carbine and had a big old-fashioned radio strapped to his back. They dragged him toward the animals and somebody produced a bandanna and tied it over his eyes. Soon he had been relieved of the radio, and an NCO snatched away the carbine and reversed it to hand him the barrel end to use as a club.

The tallest soldier, a real beanpole recruit who would have been playing basketball anywhere else in the world, stepped on the locked hands of a comrade and boosted himself upward briefly to grab hold of the rope just above the dog. The renewed activity set both animals protesting as the tall soldier leapt to the ground, holding the dog out away from himself and then sawed the rope up and down to set the hapless cat bobbing up and down above the blindfolded soldier's head. The cat quickly regained enough energy to complain shrilly and slash at the air.

Two troopers spun the blindfolded soldier around and turned him loose to flail at the space over his head with clumsy roundhouse swings of the rifle butt. The calls and cheering intensified and more soldiers descended the hill to watch. The world was not of a single moral opinion though, Jack Liffey noticed. About a third of the soldiers seemed embarrassed and disapproving and moved away with their backs turned.

"This is inexcusable," Fariborz said softly.

Jack Liffey desperately wanted to turn away, too, but he felt he had to keep watch on the soldiers. He became aware of the pain in his hand—amazed he had forgot it for a few moments—and readjusted his position to get his hand back into the pan of water.

The blindfolded soldier seemed to be taking cues from the shouted directions of his comrades as his big swings with the rifle never strayed far from the cat. The cat itself seemed to sense that something dire was up and it began to loose mewls of terror, one burst after another. One swing clipped the cat's paw and set the animal twirling with a shriek like a steam whistle. The dog was yipping now, too, and it tried to curl itself up to nip at the tall soldier who clung to the rope only a foot above the dog's tail. The dog's assault must have unnerved the soldier because he stopped yanking all at once, which left the cat in easy reach, and one off-balance lunge of the rifle caught the cat square on the head. There was a horrible *thwop* on the hot air like a hardball coming off a bat, and several soldiers ducked away from gouts of cat blood.

Jack Liffey's stomach sank. For a moment the platoon seemed chastened by what they had done. The cat's carcass hung limp, swinging in long pendulum sweeps to spatter blood in arcs across the road, but then they braved themselves up with new cries: *"El perro! Ahorra el perro!"*

A far whistle sounded and they looked uphill, warning one another, *"Prisa!"*

"El teniente!"

"Allah, please, not the dog, too," Fariborz objected softly. "Leave the dog alone"

The beanpole grabbed the other end of the rope and began yanking the dog up and down. They spun the blindfolded man again and set him to flailing at the poor dog, which seemed to know what was happening and let out a terrified yip-yap-yip as it wriggled in desperation.

Miss him, miss him, miss him, Jack Liffey begged, but he could not look away. He had seen unpleasantness before, and usually the ugly images dimmed out with time, but he figured this one would probably stick.

The blindfolded soldier swung so hard he stumbled and fell to his knees, and they had to lift him to his feet. Anxious to get it over with, the beanpole lowered the dog into the regulation strike zone and they steadied the blindfolded man into a baseball stance. The dog noticed the ground so much closer and clawed toward it with its forepaws.

"Beisbol, beisbol," they chanted. "Strike! Strike! Dodg-airs!"

The blindfolded soldier wound back and fidgeted the rifle over his shoulder for a moment like an old hand at the plate. When he brought the bat around and connected, it was only a glancing blow and so much more terrible for it. A soggy thud marked a swipe to the tiny dog's hindquarters that slung it hard around the butt of the rifle to tangle in its rope. After a stunned instant, the dog emitted one howl that was much too loud for such a small animal. Then the officer came storming down the road, berating and cursing, waving his arms in the air. He was much older and had a bushy mustache and an air of great contempt. The troopers looked sheepish suddenly and backed away, and the tall soldier let go of the rope to leave the bewildered and blindfolded batter standing there alone with the tiny yelping dog strapped to the butt end of his rifle.

The officer drew a .45 automatic from a woven leather holster at his waist and put it against the dog's head. Even as an act of mercy, the gunshot was intolerable in the night, a sacrilege. Much of the dog just disintegrated in a wet rain, and the blast echoed back and forth several times among the shacks. The officer shouted angrily and pointed around the compass to send the soldiers off on their duties. He stared sadly at the slack remains of the hind half of the little dog for a moment as if the officer might have been an animal lover in another life, and then he holstered the pistol and turned to stare straight at the house where they hid.

Jack Liffey felt an electric jolt go through him. Not only was the officer staring directly at their shed but the stocky soldier, the *piñata* breaker, was now unblindfolded and heading for their shack with a sense of purpose, as if he had a lot to make up for.

"Here," Fariborz whispered. At his direction, they tugged the filthy mattress eight inches away from the wall and Jack Liffey wedged himself into the gap. His hand immediately began to throb, but there was no way now to keep it in the water. The young man tugged the reeking bedspread over him and lay on the bed himself to block any view of what lay in the gap.

They heard a hammering at the front door that was followed immediately by shouts. The old woman must have opened because they heard her and the soldier blustering back and forth. The building shook as heavy boots came inside. Jack Liffey felt a chill course through his limbs. He knew it was only the woman's expectation of more American currency that stood between him and another experience of torture.

He heard the bolt on their inner door clatter, and the door squawked open, and then the soldier shouted into the room. Fariborz said two words very softly. The door slammed and after a while, the young man whispered, "It's okay. The soldier was an idiot. I mean literally."

"I'm petrified. Literally."

"We're all right now. The woman was good to us," the young man said. "I'll give her more money."

Fariborz lifted the smelly bedspread off him, and Jack Liffey emerged slowly from his niche and thrust his hand into the pan of water. "Ooooh. I'll pay you back when I can."

"If you can sleep, we've got a couple more hours to kill."

"Sleep?" His chest shuddered in an attempt at a laugh. "I doubt it. Even my karma is quaking in its boots."

"How is your hand?"

"That, too."

Fifteen

The Rat Patrol

"They're early risers, working people," Fariborz observed. They were making their way across the shadowed *colonia,* and a dozen scattered windows had faint lights burning. One man trudged along the dirt road crossing their path with a paper sack under his arm and the glow of a cigarette stuck in his lip. "Some of them travel for hours on buses to start at six or seven."

It was three-thirty, and the military sweep had pretty much combed the surplus humanity out of the *colonia.* Jack Liffey was feeling a bit woozy and light-headed. Since he'd had a nap, Fariborz had allowed him a second dose of codeine just before leaving their hideout at about three, the lights over the car-dismantling lot and the remains of the cars themselves completely gone, and the neighborhood sunk into a uniform obscurity. A quarter moon was just rising now out of a banana tree atop the dusty hillside and the moonlight might help them when they got across *la linea*—or hurt them.

There was a four-lane road just ahead, slicing through the heart of the *colonia* away from the industrial zone toward the border station and there was enough traffic on it now to hold them up for a minute, big grinding semis, beat-up Chevys carrying six and seven men to work, pickups with men crouching in back, and even a few taxis. Just after they crossed the airport road, he could see where the abrupt gray scar of the big wall itself showed between rows of the slightly more prosperous homes and shops that nestled down on the flat of the mesa. Funny how it was the better-off who lived on the bottomland in Latin America, he thought, and the poor who lived up the slopes, while it was just the opposite in most of Norte America.

His hand still throbbed dully, but he felt a strange exhilaration as well. Finally he was on the move. And the codeine was kicking in as well, freeing him from self-absorption and fear so he could appreciate that he was treading in the footsteps of hundreds of thousands of others, and he was about to commit the archetypal Southern California crime: He was going to become a wetback, an illegal.

The ebb of pain also freed him up to look around—almost a tourist—at the clash of dimly seen shapes and textures in the *colonia*. Softly eroded mud bricks, pebbly concrete blocks, plywood with oblongs of paint that offered evidence of previous lives, cloudy plastic tacked over window frames. One whole wall of a home was made up of old doors nailed one to another, and an alcove at the end of another house appeared to be a Maytag box, sealed against the weather with shiny resin. A kerosene lantern flickered in a kitchen window where a round old woman in a scarf was busy patting tortillas between her hands, a genuine icon of Mexico.

Nearby a car stammered and coughed, trying to start. The eerie moonlight shone along the unpaved side streets to the east, silvering the hardpan that was dotted with weeds and motionless animals. Then suddenly they arrived. The road sign along the wall said Cañon Emiliano Zapata and rubbish had piled up against the ribbed steel as if a tidal surge had swept through the town and deposited its burden at the limit of the flood.

"It's made of construction panels from the Gulf War," Fariborz explained. Looking up, Jack Liffey could see the top of the wall was a single strand of that newest sort of razor wire, intolerably sharp little slice-your-finger-off tabs sticking up every inch or so. The whole ugly structure was about ten feet tall and had been hit with a lot of graffiti and dented with rocks and other aimless pounding of resentment. Rust seemed to have proceeded at different rates from panel to panel, suggesting they were of different ages, suggesting in fact an unremitting struggle between one set of people wrenching panels loose and another rebuilding. A little farther west, someone had worked loops of wire onto the rivets holding the wall together and run a washing line flat along the metal for thirty feet, where pennants of underwear and children's bright T-shirts dangled in the still night. He had to admire the resourceful housewife making practical use of the monstrosity.

A block to the east, a burned-out wheelless pickup truck was abandoned right next to the wall and Fariborz led him that way. A fist-sized hole had been punched through the metal two feet above the roof of the cab, and someone had impaled a large gunnysack of rags on the razor strand immediately above the makeshift step. Obviously the *colonia*'s designated crossing point for that night, or one of them. He wondered if they had all gone before, or they were still waiting for something; cloud cover, fog, or their own coyote.

Fariborz clambered onto the truck roof as Jack Liffey kept lookout. No one seemed to be stirring. The young man peered through the hole into his other country and waved Jack Liffey up.

"Gotta go, T.J.," Jack Liffey whispered. "Sorry. It's been fun."

He helped boost the boy up from the single foothold to the sack of rags at the top, which he bellied himself onto. Fariborz was very agile. He found handholds on the ragbag and swung his legs out sideways and then over, like some trick on a vaulting horse. Jack Liffey heard him drop and land on the far side with a grunt. He peered through the hole into a surprising vision of emptiness. Behind him in the *colonia*, he could picture the miles and miles of houses crowding right up to the *frontera*. But on the other side, there was only a bulldozed hundred feet of no-man's-land, plowed and poisoned to dead weedless soil, and then an even higher mesh fence with the top third angled toward Mexico. Beyond this second see-through fence there were gently rolling knolls and far away a handful of concrete warehouses and other structures. The very United States. It was the first time he'd ever seen it like this, truly from outside, this forbidden land, promised land—a place tantalizing with jobs, wealth, a future, but only beyond a tribulation zone of great danger. Dirt trails cut here and there on the rolling land just beyond the no-man's-land, obviously well-traveled by motorcycles or three-wheelers, and portable light towers were scattered here and there. There was not a tree or shelter to be seen.

Time to go. He planted his foot in the hole and clawed his way up the ribbed metal so his chin was just over the bag of rags. He took a close look at one of the razor-sharp tabs beside the burlap, the size of a fingernail, and realized even with the padding he was going to have to be careful or risk serious injury. He got a grip with both hands where the rag was thickest and tugged himself up slowly, his arm muscles screaming in complaint, until finally his waist rested over the top, his legs sticking straight out behind. At one point the padding was a bit thin and he could feel a tickle of danger in his belly. There would be no fancy vaulting dismount for him. He leaned forward more and more until he felt himself start to go and then he tried to somersault forward into the USA. He didn't come fully over, though, and his back hit first with a wrenching jolt, and then his buttocks and legs slammed down ahead of him, knocking the breath out of him.

Fariborz squatted beside him, looking concerned.

"Oh-point-five," Jack Liffey said, his diaphragm barely obeying his effort to speak. "Degree of difficulty." He had scraped his sore hand coming down, too, reanimating a little of that terrible pain, and now he shook it hard. It was probably the codeine keeping him from real pain, and contributing to the goofy amusement he felt at himself. The boy shushed him with a gesture and pointed. A quarter mile away, a green-and-white INS truck was parked facing them right in the middle of the dead strip. The agent inside seemed to be asleep or distracted.

"Let's go."

Fariborz led in a bent-over Groucho Marx duck walk across the dead zone to where a rag had been tied to the next layer of fence. It marked a slit in the stiff expanded metal lattice. Somebody had gone at it with a metal cutter up to chest height, so all they had to do was pry it open and slip through. He nicked his wrist, but made it easily.

Beyond the second fence, the rolling land was cut up by dry ravines that would offer a little cover if he could talk himself into scrambling down into them. There was an overwhelming reek of human shit rising out of them. A mile or so ahead there were a few well-lit warehouses and parking lots separated by blank patches of pitch dark. He knew the official border crossing—the road that became I-5—was a mile to the their left, but it was hidden by a low rise.

"Are we technically across?"

"I think so." They descended into the nearest of the fetid arroyos and fell silent when they heard the burring of a light plane advancing low along the border. It probably had infrared going, or night scopes, and they pressed back into the moon shadows on the east side of the arroyo until the faint outline of the high-wing spotter plane passed, replaced by the sound of crickets chirping away in the ravine.

"*La Migra,*" the boy said unnecessarily. "That's just the beginning. The INS has helicopters and four-wheeler trucks, and Humvees and those fat-tire desert-bike things."

"We've got one advantage," Jack Liffey said. "We're actually legal. We could walk in singing 'Dixie' if we wanted to, but I'd much rather get out of here unseen. I don't know if some Immigration officer wouldn't hand me back to the *judiciales* in a little quick-and-dirty extradition—'just a little mistake, señor'—for the extra cash. Maybe they're using that rape story over here, too."

"And there's the *patrullas ratas,*" Fariborz warned. "Rat patrols, some really nasty gangsters who rip off the illegals. We're not home yet."

They followed the arroyo for about a quarter mile. Here it was shallow enough that by climbing a few feet they could see the end of Interstate-5 at the border crossing, lit up like a mirage. There was a twenty-four-hour strip mall and a set of yellow MacDonald's arches bright as a picture postcard in the vast, dark no-man's-land. He hadn't really thought through what to do once they got across, but now was the time.

He knew there was a trolley stop at the crossing, and the trolley would take them directly into downtown San Diego. But there were plenty of dangers getting there—overzealous INS agents, the rat patrols, he'd even read of bands of right-wing thugs out of rural San Diego County who liked to come down to the border with baseball bats and powerful flashlights and help the INS defend the American Way of Life by bashing a few wetbacks.

"What do you say we circle around a bit through these arroyos, and come into the trolley stop from the north?" Jack Liffey suggested.

"Sure."

While they caught their breath, they saw far away a big 747 rising out of San Diego on four throbs of light, like normality waving from just out of reach. He wondered what flew that early— maybe FedEx or something military. Nearby there was a sudden screech out in the darkness, followed by the triumphant cry of a bird. In the moonlight, he could just make out a hawk rising on labored wings as it carried a small kicking rodent in its talons. This was about as emblematic as he needed things to get.

Behind them an engine growled. He saw the silhouette of a big-tire Border Patrol truck riding a ridge, a Chevy Blazer or something similar with the body so high it looked like it could wade through anything. A swivel-light on the roof stabbed around into the canyons like a finger trying for a sore spot. The light fastened briefly on a mangy yellow dog that ran hard out of the sudden illu-mination. Rabies, he thought—one more thing to worry about.

When the truck went its way, they moved on northward and found the arroyo deepening until they could see only narrowly straight ahead. They weren't the first to come this way. Moonlight showed a discarded packet of Alas cigarettes, and another for Canel's gum, unfamiliar brand names. Here and there the sides of the ditch were scooped out into minicaves, apparently to harbor a few border-crossers for a layover of a few minutes or a few hours. The smell of excrement was much stronger near the hollows.

Fariborz hissed and they both froze. There was just enough moonlight so Jack Liffey could see the young man pointing to the ground ahead, the V-bottom of the arroyo. He wrinkled up his forehead as if willpower alone could intensify his vision, and then, because of the slight movements, he finally made it out in the silver light. A tarantula bigger than his fist was pacing right across their path, languidly lifting two legs at a time and placing them down experimentally beside its hairy body.

"Tarantulas have the right of way," Jack Liffey insisted, and they waited to let it go its unhurried way. The spider didn't worry him much, with all the other perils out there. As far as he knew, not many people were killed by tarantulas. A rattler would have been a different story. He'd stepped on a diamondback as a ten-year-old hiking in the hills above San Pedro and still had a vivid tactile memory of that rubbery hose of a snake under his shoe. He had run all the way home, periodically flagging in exhaustion, but then picking up the pace again when his imagination flaunted the snake right behind him, right *there*, flailing along frictionlessly, its jaws open to bite.

Fariborz gave a little cry and Jack Liffey's pulse thundered as the tarantula leapt straight up in the air and then just vanished out of their universe. They both patted frantically at themselves to make sure the spider wasn't clinging to their arms or chests. He'd heard tarantulas could leap prodigiously, but it was still startling.

They took a moment to comfort one another and then went on, accompanied by the unremitting stench of human shit and rotting foodstuffs. A flying insect began to make passes at their heads and they waved furiously to shoo it away, Jack Liffey imagining on what offal its tiny feet might have rested only moments before. At a rock outcrop, the ravine took them through a hard right bend and then straightened north again.

"I thought this crossing would be easy," Fariborz said. "But it's turning out to be pretty weird."

"You know—I've been thinking about that, too. But in a sense it's not strange at all." Something was making him talkative, probably just relief at the sense of escape. "There's probably a million Latinos in California who've come this way, or something a lot like it. We never really think about it, sitting in our nice homes, do we? I can imagine terrified mothers holding their children's hands in this very arroyo, or lonely teenagers who know ten words of English. These are damn brave people. And then I think of my suburban neighbors who look right through them every day, mowing their lawns or washing their cars."

"It's true," the boy said with a hint of chagrin. "My dad has gardeners, and I don't even know their names."

"God strike me dead if I don't show more sympathy for them after this night," Jack Liffey vowed.

"Please don't blaspheme."

"Sorry. If I don't believe in God, I shouldn't use His name, should I?"

"Really? You *don't?*"

Jack Liffey's companion was actually shocked. It was a long way out of his recent experience to run into someone for whom religion held such heartfelt and immediate consequence. He didn't want to upset the boy, but he didn't want to lie, either. "I guess you'd say there's a God-size hole in my world." Jack Liffey smiled to himself. Maybe it was the codeine, still tickling his fancy. He figured that was a pretty fanciful image for a devout Moslem to wrap his mind around.

"So you're trying to stuff up the hole with good deeds, like finding lost children?"

He chuckled. Smart kid, Jack Liffey thought. "Perhaps you've nailed me." What he didn't want to tell the devout teenager was that the hole would always be just that, a great emptiness that went on and on, no matter how he tried to fill it. Mostly it didn't bother him, but there was no denying it.

Fariborz gave a helpless shrug. "I worry sometimes that I've moved so far away from Him that He can't hear me anymore. But I *know* He's there." He glanced at Jack Liffey. "How can you not believe in God and be a good man?"

"I don't think the two have anything to do with each other. Right is right and wrong is wrong. God didn't look out at the world one day and decide, 'Hey, I think I'm going to declare that human cruelty is wrong!' It's either right or wrong, and even a God can't change that."

Jack Liffey twisted his ankle slightly on the uneven ground and winced. "Let's talk about it again when we've slept this off."

They slogged on for a while over the broken ground in silence. There was another big jetliner high above, oblivious of them, and then they heard a dull thudding noise and Jack Liffey took the young man's arm and tugged him against the dirt bank. A helicopter lolled past overhead, spraying a superbright searchlight left and right.

"Screw you, *Migra*," Jack Liffey said softly and Fariborz chuckled.

"From me, too."

When the chopper was gone, Jack Liffey scrambled far enough up the bank of the ravine to get a look around. Their progress was disappointing. They'd only gone about three hundred yards north from the border fences and were now about parallel with the little shopping center, still a bright oasis to the west. He slid back down and pointed forward like a weary pioneer. They trudged on uneventfully for a few minutes, a tiny expedition into the promise of North America.

"*Alto, pollos!*" The voice erupted out of the darkness, as shocking as an evil thought. A flashlight dazzled them. The source of the light was up on the crest of the ravine and the man came diagonally down toward them, the light bobbing beside him.

"*Manos arriba!*"

Jack Liffey decided his best bet was to declare his nationality right away. "*Arriba* your own *manos*. We're Americans, and get that light off us."

The man stopped where he was and lowered the flashlight beam to their feet. As the dazzle ebbed, Jack Liffey could see the silhouette of their would-be captor, a man no more than five feet tall. Something was wrong with the whole situation. There had been no vehicle sounds at all.

"*Jou* pay me for pass," the man demanded. Now that he was speaking English, his accent was thick as molasses.

So, he wasn't *Migra* at all, Jack Liffey thought. For some reason, the unprepossessing little rat *patrullista* didn't frighten him at all, even though he carried what might have been a pistol in one hand. Jack Liffey looked around quickly for confederates, but there didn't seem to be any. It was too dark to see his facial expression.

"What sort of pass you selling? Disneyland? Hail Mary?"

"*Jou* no pay, I kill *jou* dead *now*. I find *jou* home over big San Diego, find *jou* muzzer, kill her, too."

"My mother died of cancer, asshole. Look, I'd like to oblige you, but the *judiciales* took all my money already. You can have my credit card if you want. It's a very nice platinum MasterCard but it's over the limit."

Jack Liffey got a better look at the man as he sidled closer down the slope and his face turned to the moonlight. The small man's cheeks were covered with pustules, and a smell of putrefaction emanated from him. His mouth hung open and his teeth looked rotten, too. He wore a strange white thick-soled shoe on one foot, as if that leg were shorter than the other. It was like being mugged by the organ grinder's monkey.

"Take off *jou* clothe-es. *Jou pollos* always got hide stuff."

"Fuck you. Here." Jack Liffey unstrapped his wristwatch and held it out. "Take my watch. It's a Rolex, worth a thousand bucks."

The man tucked the flashlight under his arm and reached out for the watch. Without warning, Jack Liffey grabbed the man's wrist and yanked hard, putting all his weight into it. The small man was so lightweight that he came flying past, shrieking, and the flashlight fell with a clunk and died. Jack Liffey kept his hold on the wrist and went with him into the ravine bottom. He hated even to touch the man, but he wrenched the arm around and knelt with a knee in the small of his back.

"No hurt! Please, señor! No hurt!"

Jack Liffey grabbed for the other hand to make sure the gun was gone, and it was, if there ever had been a gun. He wiped his hand on his shirt after touching the man's clammy hand.

"Should I break his arm?"

"No, *don't*," Fariborz said quickly.

"How much money have you got on you, Mr. Rat?"

"I got no money! Poor, poorest. Many brother, many sister, much sick mother. All poor. All hard on."

Jack Liffey chuckled to himself. "Your whole family is poor, I know. The cook is poor, the gardener is poor, the chauffeur is poor."

"What you say?"

"Beat it. If you run fast, I won't call the cops. *Vamos.*"

The small man scrambled to his feet and scurried away. He let out a strange insane sound as he got beyond their reach that Jack Liffey finally decided was some kind of sniggering laugh. "*Jou* soft in head! *Pinche gringo pendejo!* Ha ha ha." He scampered away, running hard.

Fariborz found the man's flashlight and managed to get it to work and searched the bottom of the ravine with it. Jack Liffey wasn't sure he wanted a good look at the damp lumpy rubbish they'd been hiking through. In a moment the boy found the pistol and handed it to Jack Liffey. It was old and rusted, and the ornate tracery spelled out *Hoppy Special* on the crude barrel. He pulled on the hammer, and a metal compartment dropped open where you could stick in a roll of caps. He hadn't seen anything like it since his youth.

The flashlight beam went back to the ground. "I'm looking for your Rolex," Fariborz explained.

"It's a Timex. Nineteen-ninety-five at Kmart, and the date window died last year."

"Waste not, want not." The boy retrieved the wristwatch and rubbed it off before handing it over.

"Better turn off the light," Jack Liffey suggested. But he could already hear a gasoline engine approaching. It seemed to be a ways off, but it was coming fast. There wasn't much point running because it sputtered like one of those fat-tire ATVs that could go just about anywhere, fast enough to catch anyone on foot.

A glow became visible on the lip of the arroyo above them, and then a QuadRunner heaved into sight, decked out with a lot of lights. It growled once as it slammed on its brakes to send a shower of dirt down over them.

"*Alto. Manos arriba!*"

"We've already had the *arriba* business," Jack Liffey said cheerfully. He was really enjoying this codeine aura, if that's what it was. "Don't wear it out. And your Spanish is *really* awful." This one was certainly *Migra*.

"You two Americans?"

"Oh, yes indeed we are."

"What the hell are you doing here?"

"We're FBI agents. We're decoys sent here to catch people victimizing border crossers."

That gave the man pause. "I haven't heard anything about a sting. If you're FBI, let's see some ID."

How often did life hand you a straight line like that? Jack Liffey thought. "Badges?" he said in an absolutely appalling Mexican accent. "We don't got to show you no stinking *badges.*"

The INS agent burst out laughing.

Sixteen

More Borders

"Do you mind if I fade out a bit? I haven't slept."

"Of course not. I'm going to stop at a drugstore and buy you a wet bandage for that hand. I know a little about burns."

Jack Liffey closed his eyes and his head slid along the headrest toward the passenger window, where the shuddery road vibration punished his temple a little. He was still too wired to go off to sleep immediately. A team of INS agents had questioned him and Fariborz separately for an hour or two, and then together, until almost ten in the morning. Then—within five minutes of their release from the federal office building at the border—Fariborz had disappeared, just vanished out of the air like the leaping tarantula. Jack Liffey assumed it was because the young man had some agenda of his own, to do with saving the other boys.

He had ridden the trolley up to San Diego, woozily and alone, but had arrived at Amtrak too late for the last train to L.A. until late afternoon, so he had just given in and phoned Aneliese de Villiers at the Braille Institute. She dropped everything to drive down to get him, and she found him at about 1:00 P.M. nodding off at the little mission-style Amtrak station on Kettner.

He awoke with a strange feeling that a big clam was sucking on his hand. When he peeked, he saw that it was in fact a wet white bandage of some sort, and that the hand was resting on his own thigh. Aneliese was driving efficiently northward through the endless yellow hills of Camp Pendleton, the only real nature between San Diego and L.A. No one was running the surprise INS checkpoint they had built across I-5 sixty miles north of the border, so they blasted on through without slowing. Generally a myopic agent forced you to slow enough to peer in the windshield and decide if you looked sufficiently Anglo to avoid harassment. More irony, he thought, in his woozy state. He actually *was* a wetback, albeit a light-haired blue-eyed wetback.

He drifted for a moment and then opened his eyes to see the giant concrete breasts of the San Onofre nuclear power plant. His eye was drawn to the danger sirens that he knew hovered over the hillsides and then over the housing tracts for the next ten miles.

"I wonder what those good folks would do if the sirens went off one day," he said idly. His throat felt scratchy and dry.

"Sirens?"

"See the one up there. They're just like the old fifties air-raid sirens, but it's for the nuclear plant. For the day it goes critical, like Chernobyl."

"I've never noticed them. Did that atomic-bomb business traumatize you when you were growing up?"

"I think reports of atomic fear are vastly overstated. We had drop drills in school, but I don't think anybody believed it would really happen. We used to joke that we were putting our heads between our knees so we could kiss our ass good-bye. In the fifth grade, I was much more afraid that I'd never get picked for the softball team."

"You weren't good at sports?"

"I didn't like them, and that's almost the same thing. It's truly the only thing American boys value at that age."

"It was the same in the white schools in Zambia, believe me, and my brother says it's very much that way in Australia, too. I wonder if it's being out on the periphery of the British Empire that leaves you stuck with values like that."

"I hate to disillusion you, but we don't think of ourselves as being on the periphery of the British Empire."

She laughed. "Okay. But it's a similar thing. We're nearer the frontiers of civilization somehow. Closer to some imaginary barbarians who are trying to overrun the margins."

"I *like* barbarians," Jack Liffey said. "Loosely speaking. Maybe I *am* one. Anyway, I have a lot more appreciation now for the people who sneak over the margins."

They talked wistfully of their childhoods for the rest of the way back, and he found himself growing so tender and affectionate toward her that he developed one of those wooden, unstoppable erections and had to readjust his pants surreptitiously. He wondered if it had started opposite those big domes at San Onofre. It was okay for him to joke to himself about that now, he thought, as long as the apparatus seemed to be working again, but in the back of his mind he feared another limp collapse.

Aneliese had to go back to work to finish some project at the institute, so she agreed to drop him near Auslander's office. He went to a big plastic egg-shaped phone booth on La Cienega, and Auslander agreed to meet him at the end of his office day, at 5:30 after his last patient. Jack Liffey didn't want to panic the man about his daughter by expressing any particular urgency. It wouldn't have done either of them any good. Then he called from the booth and had Art Castro call him back right away to put the call on Art's dime.

"Please pass many thank-yous to your brother-in-law in Ensenada. He earned his keep, but I've got to send him a big warning, too." He recounted some of the events of the last two days and described the fat drug lord.

"Man, that sounds a lot like Frankie Miramón, *jefe* of the Sonora cartel. He's said to be tight with the *judiciales*. You're lucky you're alive. Nobody even knows where the guy lives. They say he sleeps in a different bed every night."

"Just tell Jaime to watch his back. And if there's any way he can rescue my VW in T.J. before it gets melted down to make ashtrays, I'd appreciate it. I'll be happy to meet him in San Diego to pick it up and buy him a huge steak dinner. I'm not crossing that border again in *this* lifetime."

"Understandable."

"I don't even feel very safe on *this* side."

"Jack, I gotta tell you something."

"Uh-oh."

"It's not that bad, but you know that little map on the business card you sent me for safekeeping? Or for backup, or something."

"Or something. The mail got there pretty fast."

"Well, look, the feds came around to see me again—about this Sheik Arad guy. He's like something they can't get off their shoe. And this map of yours just showed up right as they walked into my office and it's got this clumsy Arabic copied on it, it just screams 'sheik' all over it, plain as day, and I kind of needed something to help me out in my career, here."

"You gave it to the FBI."

"I let them make a copy, just in case there's something special for you about *this* one. I'm sorry if I screwed something up, Jack, but it don't pay to go against the feebs. They got a long reach."

"You probably did right. I hope it buys you something."

"At least I won't be sent down to the basement. I don't even know if the Bradbury *has* a basement."

"I'm sorry about everything, Art."

"Hey, if you can't ruin your life for a friend, what's it all worth?"

Jack Liffey tried to offer him a laugh and hung up. He hadn't decided yet what to do about LA ROX and their drug connection. He hadn't even thought very hard about it. Maybe he should go to the FBI about them, too, but he rather liked Farshad Bayat, and he had a feeling the man had been forced into something that he didn't want to do. Probably by his expediter, Mahmoud. And the man was also Fariborz's dad, and he found he liked the boy a lot.

A grizzled man in a striped referee shirt came along the sidewalk, his neck cranked up toward the sky. His palms were raised over his head and his biceps were flexed a little, as if he were holding up some huge invisible weight—maybe a blimp that floated just above his head. Both hands bobbed a little as he moved along, and he never took his eyes off the immensity above him until he stubbed his toe on the sidewalk and had to glance down briefly. Apparently something had happened while his eyes were averted. He had to grab for the blimp and tug it back down again.

Jack Liffey watched him out of sight down the block, but there was no change in his deportment. He hoped he got it home safely, whatever it was.

He had his own blimp to carry around and he couldn't worry about a stray one just then. He could tell he was still frazzled by the last few days and the lack of sleep, not to mention the ugly wet clam that clung to his hand under the dressing. And there was something else weighing on him, making his knees tremble a little. He didn't know if it had a name, but he knew what it was, all right: When you had been so completely at someone else's mercy, when you'd been abused helplessly, something inside you tore open a little and it didn't repair easily. The whole world seemed a lot more fragile now.

Suddenly he realized that he had become pretty much an illegal alien in a number of respects: cashless, jobless, and carless in the city of cars. He was also exhausted and anxious, standing right in the heart of the famous city of mellow. Sports coupes and SUVs with solo drivers drifted past him just as an evil orange smog was settling over West Hollywood, trapped by an inversion. The reclaimed Timex told him it was 3:30, so he could nap for two hours before Auslander would see him. But he had no way to get himself the five measly miles home and back, and where else but your own home would they let you sleep in a big modern city? There was a furniture store on the outer rim of the Beverly Center mall across La Cienega and in the front window he eyed a king-size bed enviously. He strolled to a park down La Cienega, but it had just been watered and the turf was soggy.

He glanced around in a daze of bafflement. Temporarily home-less, he thought, and the proposition didn't actually seem so strange. It was as if he'd found his level at last—permanent disequilibrium. His fate would be to stay out here in the elements permanently, his beard growing out slowly, his hair tangling and knotting to dread-locks, his clothes rotting away to tatters. He could barely keep his eyes open.

Where could you go in a city to be inconspicuous, to cause no bother and avoid encroaching on anybody else's precious space? It was a strange side effect of civilization, he thought, that the sim-plest natural acts that you could have performed anywhere in a forest, such as peeing or sleeping, say, required a specialized and hired space in a city. He had a strange sensation that all the build-ings around were receding from him, locks and latches fastening firmly. He could almost hear the clicks and slams.

Before his bewilderment could lead him to do anything truly weird, he set out briskly into a neighborhood of two-story Spanish homes, as if he had a purpose in mind. Here and there a guard dog barked to shoo him onward. Several of the homes seemed to be in the process of being remodeled, and the dark eyes of dead windows glared at him. One was pretty much gutted and surrounded by a hurricane fence. There were no workmen about, so he headed straight up the driveway, as if he belonged. The grass in the back-yard was long dead, and a fishpond was empty, its concrete bed cracked up into hexagons like a mudflat.

He saw just what the doctor ordered: A stained and ruined sofa, abandoned for some reason, lay up against the detached garage. It had once been Danish modern, the kind you saw in cheap furnished apartments with loose cushions resting on plastic straps. Some of the cushions were missing, but by flipping down the extras from the back, he had a complete bed, even one extra to prop up his head, and he lay on his stomach and let out an audible sigh of delight. Just before he fell down a dark well, he realized he had an erection—so springy and uncomfortable under him that he had to roll onto his side. He was thinking warmly of Aneliese.

"Failure to appear," a voice challenged darkly in his ear. It sounded just like the FBI man Robert Johnson. "Failure of duty. Failure of periphery."

"Guilty," he replied, but he was out cold.

* * *

Fariborz hid behind a bushy castor bean on a hill not far away from the Campo house. Nobody seemed to be stirring, and no vehicles were parked there. He worried that the Arabs' plans might already be under way somewhere, whatever they were, and he was too late. He saw a helicopter far up, but the house was only a few miles from the Mexican border, and it was probably just an INS patrol.

He was just about to sneak up closer when he saw a dust cloud boiling off a vehicle that was coming up the dirt road fast from the west. Something made him look east, and there was a second dust-tail approaching. He burrowed himself into the big-leaf castor bean as he heard the helicopter descending.

The vehicle coming from the east resolved itself into a desert-camouflaged APC, a low wedge-shaped military vehicle that had huge knobby tires. The vehicle crushed a wire fence under its big tires and crossed into the square of unkempt yard, where he'd stood only a few days earlier. It slammed to a stop a few feet from the shack. The second APC approached even faster and stopped with a dramatic skid near the first one as the helicopter went into a small noisy orbit very low around the house, raising even more dust.

An amplified voice called for anyone inside to come out, but they didn't give it a lot of time to work before one of the APCs revved its engine and lunged forward to smash open a corner of the shack. The vehicle backed off to leave a listing ruin with a big ragged hole at the corner. He thought of Waco, but nobody here was firing in or out of the house. A ramp door dropped down from the back of the second vehicle, like a UFO opening up to emit its Martian invaders. Fariborz felt his heart pound when he saw that was just about what emerged.

Two men in space suits, each carrying a little white suitcase attached by a hose to a bubble helmet, came down the ramp and walked gingerly across toward the shack. One carried a rifle of some kind, but the other went straight for the opening knocked in the corner of the shack, holding an instrument of some kind out ahead of himself. He thrust the small machine into the shack, studied it for a moment, and then went inside.

Fariborz couldn't help thinking of the water-heater panel and the giant jar of potassium iodide he had found. But what did they mean? The back door was thrown open from the inside, and the second spaceman went into the shack warily with his rifle ready. Soon one of them came out and made a high fist-pumping gesture to the vehicles. A third spaceman came down the ramp of the APC pushing a big red wheeled container ahead of him. There was a big symbol on its side: three separate pie slices with a circle in the middle. Fariborz recognized it immediately from chemistry class at Kennedy—the radiation symbol.

He settled down to wait. They would probably be there for a while now, and he didn't want to get caught trying to slip away. It was more important than ever for him to find his friends, probably back in L.A. now, to do his best to foil whatever it was the sheik was up to. He felt a terrible responsibility for his own misplaced devotion. He wondered if he should have stuck with Jack Liffey, rather than dropping him so quickly.

His arm had fallen asleep but he managed to use it, pins-and-needles and all, to drag himself out of the deep pit. Loud music was banging away. He opened his eyes to a stucco wall and wondered where on earth he was. Then slowly he recognized the brown cushions, the derelict backyard. The music came from a house directly behind, some kind of thumping electronic rock. His watch said 5:25, and he marveled that the sleep guardian had managed to wake him just in time.

Jack Liffey sat up woozily, as the tatters of a busy, overwrought dream fled. A man yelling at him, an electrical plug that he had to lug through a huge complex city looking for a mate. He desperately had to empty his bladder. He would have climbed the fence to hunt down whatever was left of the bathroom in the empty house, but he was only three or four blocks from Auslander's establishment.

He strode down the driveway, a building inspector having completed his task, and headed for the psychologist's office. He realized that once he told Auslander about his runaway daughter, the job would be all but done. She was on her own now. Just looking for her again would endanger her. All he had left after Auslander was dealing with LA ROX and Farshad Bayat, and he had no idea how to approach that. He felt some responsibility to the boy, too, wherever he was.

Rush hour was clogging the streets. A giant billboard over La Cienega said *Experience Drive-Through Hi-Colonics. Relief Without Waiting.* There was a picture of a satisfied-looking man in the front seat of an expensive sedan. It didn't even bear thinking about, but he was pretty sure it was a joke.

A furtive-looking woman with dark hair stole quickly away from the little blue clinic as Jack Liffey came across the street. The side entry was locked, but Auslander must have seen him coming. He opened the front and beckoned.

"First things first." Jack Liffey found the bathroom and relieved himself with great pleasure, wondering why it was that his kidneys always took sleep as a signal to drain every last drop of fluid from every corner of his body into his bladder. The chronic prostate irritation probably didn't help, either, but he had no money for doctors.

Auslander was waiting in his interview room, shuffling papers and making a few desultory notes.

"Hi, Jack. I guess you've got news."

"You may not be wild about it, but it's basically good news. Given the possibilities." He made himself comfortable and told Dicky Auslander that he had seen his daughter and she was very much alive and very rich and on the run. He explained that she'd seemingly taken off a drug cartel for over a million dollars and gone on the lam with it. He didn't mention the Bayat connection.

"I suggested giving it back and I'd try to square things with them, but she refused. She's probably right about that, you know—they're not a forgiving sort. She seems to be pretty resourceful, so I think she'll be all right in the end. She underestimated them at first, but she knows better now. I know this isn't what you wanted to hear, but if I brought her back to you, she'd be dead in a week. I think I can guarantee that."

Jack Liffey peeled back the wet bandage and showed his hand. The psychologist flinched when he got a good look at the ruined skin. "The *drogistas* tried to use me to find her. Luckily I'd already advised her to take off for parts unknown."

"That's nasty looking."

"Try it from this side. These are real evildoers, Dicky. The guy's name is Frankie Miramón, I think. They say he's head of the Sonora cartel. I don't even know if *you're* safe. Don't entertain any illusions about the government's riding to your rescue. All the resources of the DEA can't do a thing to these guys, and the Mexican federal police are on his side of the table, some of them anyway, and he has a bottomless supply of money. I didn't like it much, but I thought telling Becky to run was the best thing I could do. She has a million bucks to play with. That'll buy a lot of run."

"Where can she go?"

"I suggested Europe. It's farther from the cartels, and she ought to be comfortable there." He shrugged. "If you send someone to try to find her again, please remember that there will almost certainly be people tracking *him*. I won't do it. She said something about roses, that that would let you know where she went, but I wouldn't count on it. Misdirection is her pal now."

Auslander stared gloomily at the carpet for a while. "Molly and I raised a strange little girl, didn't we?"

"I like her. She has spirit." He hadn't liked her all that much, but it was the least he could do for the man.

Then Auslander talked of going to look for his daughter himself, and Jack Liffey had to take him through the whole thing all over again. "Look, lots of daughters leave home and don't write. She's alive—I'm not shitting you about that. She's in command of herself, and she's well fixed for money. Give it a year or two at least, then look for her. Maybe the *drogistas* will forget."

By then the trail would be so cold, he'd never find her, Jack Liffey thought. Finally, Auslander sighed and seemed to give in. Oddly, he took a few notes about something in a notebook. "So, how are you doing through all this?"

Jack Liffey held up the bandaged hand. "How do you *think* I'm doing? I *liked* this hand a lot—I had a use for it."

"I mean psychologically. Aren't you pissed off that the author of your story wrote in such an ordeal?"

"Aw, Jesus, Dicky. Not *this* again."

"You might as well. You look like shit. What did this thing do to you psychologically?"

Jack Liffey glared for a while and then shrugged. "It shook me up. Okay? A lot. My car's gone—there's no way I'm going over there to get it. My confidence is just about gone. I'm getting older, and some parts of my body aren't working very well anymore." He wasn't going to get specific about *that*. "I've had a wife and a near-wife leave me. I had to bawl out my daughter. And some sort of secure space I used to live in has been violated."

"Tell me about that part."

"You know, the outlines of your own body are kind of sacrosanct. It's a kind of minimum of space you need in the world. Some sonofabitch comes and breaks through that boundary, and it really gets to you. I think the violation hurts more than the fucking burn." Oh-oh, he thought. He felt himself losing some kind of control, his voice shuddering a bit. "I don't like it, Dicky, I don't. It's too goddamn upsetting."

He went silent for a while, struggling back toward some kind of quiescence. Any kind.

Finally Auslander told him, "That's a fairly common reaction after a rape, the sense of violation of your personal space. Aren't you mad?"

He wondered if he could get across the room in two strides to punch Auslander, or if it would take three. "Christ, yes, I'm mad. If you're the fucking author, why did you do it? Go on, if you're gonna play this goddamn game about my personal pain, you tell me why I've got to have all this happen and end up feeling like the world's biggest leftover part."

"Long ago, when you first started to separate from your mother—"

"*Stop it*, Dicky, right here. Jesus, I don't want any more of your *Psychology Today* eyewash. I know exactly what's hurting me, and I know it's burning its way through me like acid. This is your game, man, you invented it. You play it right. I want to know *why* this shit had to happen. Why does shit like this have to happen to *anybody?*"

"I guess I really don't know."

Seventeen

Solutions in a Nightmare Are Not Solutions

"Please don't worry about it. You've had a traumatic experience."

He stared at the oil painting of surf over the foot of her bed. There was just enough ambient light through the blinds to make out the scene, and he wondered if it was her work. Though amateurish, the painting had captured something of the power and anger of the ocean, a white wave crashing down across craggy rocks. There was a way in which your intent sometimes still counted for something in the world, he reflected, even if you didn't have what it took just then to bring it off. At least that was what he wanted to think.

"When I was scared and alone on the floor of the *maquiladora,* I didn't want to think about what was going to happen to me, so I tried to think about your body. Tried to think of running my hand over it like this."

"Mmmm. More."

"It's even more beautiful than I remember."

"*It?*"

"You. I'm not trying to objectify. Something is all too obviously going wrong in me, I'm sorry. Maybe I want this too much; maybe I need it too much."

He felt his face burning with humiliation.

"I would be supremely happy just to snuggle up, Jack. Honest."

She rolled onto her side and he spooned against her. Unfortunately, the position made him acutely aware of that small flaccid mass of tissue pressed against her buttocks. "It's odd. I seem to feel cut off from everything right now, even my own body. Like I'm somewhere outside, watching, and everything is moving very slowly."

Actually, he was even losing touch with having spoken aloud just then. Maybe he'd just imagined that he'd spoken to her. He wanted to ask her if he'd just said something, but he was afraid to.

She rolled over so they were nose to nose and placed a palm gently against his cheek in the near-darkness. "Lighten up. You're trying to hold up the sky."

He felt a rush of tenderness toward her. He wished she could meet Maeve.

"I felt your cheek puff a little," she said. "Did you smile?"

"That was something Mao said, as I remember. 'Women hold up half the sky.' "

"You're trying to hold it *all* up. What is this passion men have for duty? And strength? If only John Ford had never made those horrible movies, boys would be a lot better off."

"*High Noon* was Fred Zinnemann," he said. "That was the one where Coop said, 'A man's gotta do what a man's gotta do.' "

"*See?* You've got to get everything exactly right. A grain of sand falls in the wrong spot, and you need to tidy it, adjust it. You're responsible for it."

"You're right. It's funny, I thought I knew how to live with a certain level of untidiness. Thanks, Aneliese. You've been wonderful."

"I don't like that past tense, Jack."

"It doesn't mean anything. You *are* wonderful. You will be wonderful. You could be wonderful. You ought to be wonderful. You wouldst be wonderful. I've run out of tenses."

"Then you're nowhere near perfect. There's the subjunctives, all the continuous tenses, conditionals."

He put a hand over her mouth gently and then kissed her forehead. Sex or no sex, he didn't want to talk about grammar.

* * *

"Jack, are you all right?"

He wondered why her voice was calling out to him, asking him that, and then he wondered why *on earth* he had gone to sleep on the floor of her bathroom with colored-plastic shampoo bottles lying all around him. He sat half up and saw that one of the plastic bottles was even floating in the open toilet. There was simply no logical explanation for this.

"Jack!" Yes, that was Aneliese's voice, full of concern, a room away.

"I'm fine."

But was he fine? He noticed that his elbow hurt and then he saw quite a bit of blood trickling down his arm. His eyes went immediately to the bandage on his hand, but that was still in place, still pure white. The very first priority here, he thought, was to sort out what the hell was going on. This was not a dream. He was recovering a vague memory of coming into the bathroom to empty an overfull bladder in the middle of the night. He had fumbled the seat up and peed to his great relief— he was quite sure of that—and then he had flushed. He had felt his cheeks burn. Perhaps there had been a wave of nausea, too. He wasn't sure.

He looked around again and the conclusion was unmistakable, though astonishing: He had just plain fainted, pulling down a shelf of her toiletries with him. He looked at his elbow and saw it was badly gashed, probably by the doorstop screwed into the wall. He had no memory of falling down, not even a clear memory of dizziness. He must have gone down like a sack of old tools.

"Oh, Jack." Aneliese squatted in the doorway in a filmy wrap, watching him.

"I often sleep on the bathroom floor," he said. "Give me a moment to think up some witty reason."

She knelt and studied his elbow. "This'll need stitches, but I've got some butterfly bandages for now. What happened?"

"Aneliese, honestly, I would tell you if I knew. I think life just finally caught up with me. Or maybe it's got a bit of a lead."

"Sit up and let me clean you up. You've had a bad couple of days."

"Thanks. You're a peach." Had he just said that?

He hadn't noticed it before, but Ruth Bayat had a way of fishing about with her eyes when she talked to you, as if something was going on just behind you. He still thought her quite handsome in that wonderful Persian way, with regular dusky features and thick shiny hair cascading over her shoulders. An expensive-looking dress. "He's by himself, listening to music and writing poetry. Saturday morning is his retreat." He followed her across the too-white house.

"You don't go to synagogue?"

"In terms of manifest devotion, I am about as Jewish as Farshad is Moslem. I don't mean we've rejected our religions. We are both what we are, deeply and culturally, but not the other. I guess you'd say we're heartfelt but secular. Thus our son turns religious to rebel. I wonder if we're doomed to alternate generations forever, with Fariborz's children becoming secular again, and their children finding a renewed God."

"I've seen similar," he said.

"I suppose life was a lot easier when we all knew who we were."

"Are you sure? None of us really remembers a time like that."

"I do and it *was* easier. I didn't say better." She made a contemptuous wave of her hand. "I will never again allow men to force me to wear the *chador*. What monstrous patronization! Have you noticed that democracy never survives for long in any place where a significant number of people—women, for example—are denied equality? It happened in your own South, with colored people."

"Yes. And the South is still paying for it."

"Farshad." She knocked softly. Jack Liffey could hear Beethoven through the door. He'd expected something more exotic.

"*Bija tu.*"

She opened the door and ushered him in as Bayat rose from a pillow, holding a leather-bound notebook, and smiled insincerely. He didn't really want to be interrupted. Jack Liffey took the offered hand.

"Welcome, Mr. Liffey, welcome. You always catch me in my Persian sanctum. I'm afraid you're going to think I wallow in nostalgia."

"It's a pleasant place."

"I'll bring tea," Mrs. Bayat said and sealed them in with the soft music.

He displayed his notebook, unlined paper half-filled with elegant lines of cursive Arabic. "Persian is written in Arabic characters," he said. "It's a bonus you get with a language with such calligraphy. You're trying to write beautiful words and they *look* beautiful, too. I can't think of another art that's two arts at once."

He gestured and they settled onto pillows, Jack Liffey uncomfortably because of his wounds and a certain stiffness left from his fall the night before. Nearby he noticed a parrot in a freestanding cage made of ornate wrought iron, like something out of a musical comedy. He was certain it hadn't been there the last time. The big green parrot paced and bobbed restlessly, as if it wasn't quite sure it belonged, either.

"I found Fariborz," he said abruptly, so there would be no more reflections on the arts or long discourses into polite blather.

Jack Liffey didn't quite get the reaction he expected. It was a kind of vigilant regard, showing neither surprise nor delight. "That's very good."

"I know we're all supposed to carry on here and be super-polite for a while and kiss hands and things—what was the word?"

"*Taarof.*"

"But I found out about your drug deal, too, so I think we can dispense with the sweet talk. And maybe the moral posturing, too."

Bayat looked quite pained, as if he'd just been hit by an abdominal spasm. "That's not quite fair."

The parrot emitted a low squawk and then it left a single word hanging on the air that sounded like *lot-fan.*

"As I remember, you put on a big performance about being one of those guys whose feet never touches the crooked path. I distinctly remember a lot of talk about that, and then I go and find out there's a bunch of dilute cocaine hidden in those LA ROXes of yours. Look here." He peeled back the bandage to show the back of his hand. "One of your confederates questioned me. On *broil*. Maybe you should take a wild guess why I haven't already called the DEA."

"Probably because you don't have any evidence. *No*, I'm sorry, please let that go. That's not the attitude I wish to take."

The parrot repeated its word, sharply and impatiently, then seemed to lose interest and turned its back like a disgusted preacher in a frock coat.

There was a knock, and Bayat clammed up while his wife brought in the tea. The parrot perked up though and watched her closely as if she might hold something for him, too.

"I'm going to Bahameen's," she said, and Bayat nodded. "I'll see if she and Kamran want to go to the Greek for the music thing next week."

He watched her out the door, then watched the teapot for a moment without decanting any of it. Vapor sashayed gently over the spout. *"Lot-fan, lot-fan,"* the parrot croaked.

"That's 'please' in Farsi," Bayat explained. "I'm holding the bird for a friend and I have no idea what it wants, or if it even knows that the word has a meaning."

Bayat poured the tea and set a cup in front of Jack Liffey. "It was known we were in trouble. Somebody brought the deal to Mahmoud and he brought it to me, half-cooked already. I should never have entertained it, of course. But Mahmoud had already said 'maybe' to these men, and it is very difficult to back away from men like that." He huffed a little bit, then sipped at his tea. "The Miramón cartel employ some very frightening gunslingers."

Jack Liffey didn't think he'd ever heard anyone use that word in a serious conversation. The bird screamed all at once like an impatient child, and both men reacted a little. Bayat got up and tugged a thick tailored cloth cover over the cage, then stood staring at the rock wall of the room as if some answer lay there.

"Will you go to the police and put an end to it?" Jack Liffey suggested.

Bayat turned and his eyes showed real fear. "Mr. Liffey, I can't, I really can't. Mahmoud is scared. I'm scared. I'm worried about my family. You know what they did to you, just trying to get a simple answer. From me, they want money that I don't have."

He sat again, and the bird very distinctly shrieked *"Fuck you!"* through the cover. Bayat did not try to pass it off as Farsi.

"I think I finally convinced Miramón that the girl ran off with the money, but they still hold me responsible for the full amount, and I don't have it. Just as a reminder, they hijacked a load of our rocks, burned it all, and killed the driver. I believe there is a Western proverb about supping with the devil and needing to use a very long spoon. I have learned that nowhere is there a spoon long enough to sup with the Miramóns of the world. What would you do in my place? Let them kill my wife? Please walk a short distance in my shoes, Mr. Liffey."

Jack Liffey remembered his own resolution never to cross the Mexican border again, never to get near the Miramón crew. "I'd probably lock my doors and go armed."

Farshad Bayat lifted the pillow at his right hand, also hoisting his expressive Groucho eyebrows. There was a 9mm Browning pistol under the pillow. "I hate weapons, I left Iran in part because there were far too many children with guns, but I will defend my home and my wife to the death. This is a true nightmare. What else would you do? Stay in my shoes a moment, please. Whatever you try to think of, I believe you will see I am doing it already or have done it."

"A bodyguard company."

He shrugged. "You saw the little signs out on the lawn. Dickless Tracies, I believe they're called. A minimum-wage teenager with a pistol drives up in a Dodge Neon ten minutes after someone has blown up your house."

"Pay Miramón. It's only a million and a half, right? That shouldn't be so much for you."

"I made this mistake in the first place because I was in a cash-flow crisis. I'm mortgaged beyond any rational limit. Anyway, he's doubled what I owe him. For his 'inconvenience,' he says. As if there was no inconvenience to me in all this. The only people I know who will lend me what I need under the circumstances demand twenty percent interest. Per week."

"The only thing left is the feds."

"If it was just the American police agencies, I would do it, but they have no jurisdiction in Mexico. You can't seriously expect me to go to the Mexican federal police. That's like going to Frankie Miramón's uncles and cousins. I might cooperate in setting up a sting over here, but I don't think he's stupid enough to cross the border for it. Mr. Liffey, for over a month now, I have lived every day side-by-side with mortal fear." It almost looked like there was a tear in his eye. "Solutions in a nightmare are not solutions, but only another part of the nightmare. Can you tell me how to save myself and my family?"

He couldn't even save himself, Jack Liffey thought. "I came here to ask you to call this guy off me, but I guess that's not very realistic." Jack Liffey thought about it again, went all around it, but came up with nothing new. "I found the girl, too," he said. "But she's skedaddled with what's left of the money, so I wouldn't make any big plans for that."

He shrugged. "It hardly matters. Now that Miramón's doubled the stakes, giving back the original amount wouldn't be much use."

A rhythmic banging started up in the covered cage, as if the parrot were hammering its head against the bars. Bayat glared at the cage as if considering some sudden and terminal fate for the bird. Jack Liffey tried to stay very still deep inside himself, tried to tune himself into Bayat to see if he could tell if the man was running some game on him, but his host seemed genuinely stricken by his predicament.

They both felt the tremor in the slab floor. A light fixture on a cord began to sway gently. Their eyes met. "Earthquake," Bayat said. It was quite mild or far away, and there was no sequel. "I wonder if that's what was disturbing the bird. They say animals can sense them coming."

"*I* can sense them coming," Jack Liffey said. "But it doesn't do me any good, because they're always coming."

Eighteen

A Half Gram of Death

The turn indicator stalk snapped off in his hand and he stabbed at its hole in a brief flurry of panic, trying to reroot it, and then he just rolled the window down and stuck his hand out the window, still holding the stalk, to signal his turn into the veterinarian's.

Rolling Wrecks had rented him the old Chevette at a ridiculously low rate. The odometer had died long ago, along with most of the gauges, and a lot of the plastic interior trim was hanging loose or missing. The plastic seat had given up one layer of its color in patches. Just sitting in the car, you could feel the dejection and contempt of everyone involved in its manufacture. The executives had wanted to make something with more profit, the engineers with more pizzazz, and the line workers had all wanted to be home in bed with their hangovers.

"He's accomplished a complete recovery, Mr. Liffey." The cheerful assistant vet bobbed up from the counter and plucked a key off a rack. She led him outside to where dozens of dogs in separate runs started to go mad to get his attention. "But he hasn't been happy here. He's not an enclosure sort of dog, is he?"

"Loco's not any sort of dog. He's basically a coyote."

When she pulled the gate open and dragged out the semirigid

animal, Loco growled and snapped at her for a moment and then its yellow eyes found Jack Liffey and it went catatonic with wrath. The beast had reverted to those flat wild eyes that he'd known so well when they'd first been hobbled to one another.

"Sorry, boy. But *you* went and ate the poisoned steak. Let that be a lesson to you. Be more discriminating."

"It was probably Thorazine. It's one of the easiest heavy tranks to get your hands on."

Jack Liffey shook his head sadly. "He took it from a complete stranger, as far as I know. In most moods, he won't even take ground sirloin from me." He stooped to hug the reluctant dog and felt a tremble in its flanks. "Loco, I'm sorry. I recognize the terrible irony for you. You were just beginning to get over the call of the wild and become a pet. I had hopes you might learn to fetch my slippers."

On the way home, the dog lay in the rear seat with its shivering back turned away. Jack Liffey talked to the dog gently and sadly the whole way, recounting his adventures in Mexico, though leaving out any mention of the poor Chihuahua and cat. The front door of his condo released a musty breath of neglected garbage, and the dog broke away from him and scurried straight to its old hidey-hole in the rearmost closet.

There were two calls on his machine:

"Daddy, I'm sooo sorry. Really I am. We need to discuss how I can worm my way back into your good graces. Please call me, please, please. I'll never ever be a pest again. Cross my heart and hope to die."

That wouldn't be too hard to deal with, he thought, his spirit lifting a little. The machine announced a wildly inaccurate time and date, and then squawked forward to the next caller.

"Jack, this is Arturo. Our friend down south tells me you're lucky to have got home alive and with most of your organs still functioning. J. is okay for now, but Miramón's homies are on the warpath and tearing a wide swath through Ensenada, trying to pick up any trace of the girl. Apparently she got away clean. He says he can't touch your car right now, but maybe soon, if nobody drives it off and strips it. Something big is going to go down in the cartels—he can sense it, he says, like elephants rumbling off in the jungle. Don't call me, I'll call you, hey. Tomorrow I think I move back upstairs."

Jack Liffey went and got his hollowed-out *Oxford Companion to American Literature*. It felt curiously animate as he lifted it and the heavy .45 shifted inside. He set it on the end table for comfort, like Farshad Bayat with his Browning. He settled back into his favorite chair, losing a little more of its stuffing every time it flexed, and he tried to will himself to stillness. The building creaked a little; a toilet flushed somewhere. Alcohol would be good about now, but he had enough will left to resist that, and besides there was none in the house.

He chanced a peek under the bandage on the back of his hand and winced. The burn ached in a dull, persistent way now, and the flesh was veined and multicolored, disgusting looking, like some kind of deep-sea sponge. It would probably need to be debrided, the strange word that the burn wards used for sadistically ripping off your old flesh, and it would probably stay a real mess of scarring unless he had skin grafts, to join his growing collection of detective-business wounds like the metal plate in his head and the star-shaped bullet wound in his left shoulder. Sooner or later, he could join a sideshow as Mr. Scar, Eighth Wonder of the Medical World.

He tried again to make himself relax. In a sense, the job was over now, he told himself. When Auslander finally calmed down, he might even pay a bonus for finding out that Rebecca was alive. He'd found the Bayat boy, too—but, really, he'd failed to close out either case. He hadn't brought either of the kids home. That was part of the simmer that kept everything from settling down into a kind of end-of-job quiescence. That and the fact that the Miramón drug cartel was still very much on the rampage. And something was still afoot with Fariborz and his conscience-driven fervor. Then there were his own problems underlying it all like quicksand, especially that particularly humiliating one with Aneliese.

Far too many loose ends, too many anxieties, like sores on the roof of his mouth that his tongue couldn't stay away from.

Probably just the nature of things, he thought. You could never really close anything out. All you could do was tweak one strand running through the complex skein of billions of strands and pluck it a little and hope at point B down the line, things would be a bit more satisfactory for that strand.

It was probably something like megalomania to think you could do more than that, he decided. Life was just plain untidy. He did his best not to think about his dysfunctional libido—a euphemism, obviously—but it was hard to avoid. He wondered if he'd just finally got so lost in the immensity of things that he was unmanned by his own insignificance. He was sure it had never happened to Philip Marlowe or Sam Spade. He touched the spine of the fat gun-laden book for subconscious comfort. That other penis.

Loco wandered out and lay across his feet. In Jack Liffey's current state, the dog's affection touched him so deeply, it almost brought tears to his eyes. The dog began to snore, breaths grating in and out. Here was a beast as worried about life as he was, he thought, just as consumed by his otherness, yet so desperately lonely that he would violate his own coyote species-being and cozy up to the Great Betrayer.

The awful-sounding doorbell shrilled abruptly at him. Loco didn't even stir. Complete moral exhaustion, he thought. He got up and peered out the fish-eye to see the natty FBI man—what was his name? Devil at the crossroads. Robert Johnson. The man was standing well back from the door, probably some procedural training to avoid being dragged unexpectedly into the deep shit, and in his right hand he carried a large black boom box by its flip-up handle, as if he'd just taken it off the kids who hang out in the complex.

Jack Liffey opened the door.

"Mr. Liffey."

"Mr. Johnson. Here to show me your blues style?"

The FBI man moved forward without invitation, and Jack Liffey backed away ahead of his bow wave to let him in. They sat exactly where they had sat before, and the FBI man placed the boom box gently on the low coffee table. This time there were no kids bobbing up and down at the patio fence.

"Surely my daughter hasn't been sending ripples through your equilibrium again?" Jack Liffey said, still hearing her voice on the phone with its forlorn promise to be good.

"Perhaps *you* have. 'Ripple' would understate it some."

"Uh-oh."

"We share information from time to time with Immigration and Naturalization and with the Border Patrol. They believe but cannot prove that you and a young Persian-American crossed the border illegally from Tijuana two nights ago."

"We're both citizens. I shouldn't think that was illegal."

The FBI man squinted at him a bit. "It's illegal, all right, but we don't need to get into that right now. All things being equal, we're not really interested in you at all. We'd like to talk to the boy, if he's who we think he is."

"He disappeared on me. Maybe I'd better tell you the whole story." His eye went to the black plastic boom box, and he couldn't help wondering what it was for. The brand name was Sonovox— one of those tech-sounding names they churned interchangeably out of Chinese factories. Was the man going to play him some incriminating tape recording? Surely the FBI had higher-class pocket recorders for that, mini-Uhers or DATs.

"Maybe you'd better tell me."

He told the man pretty much the whole tale of his misbegotten adventures in Mexico. The only place where he got a bit coy was in whether or not Farshad Bayat knew in advance there had been drugs in the ROX. For some reason Jack Liffey started feeling a throb in his neck, as if his heart had climbed up there and begun banging away for escape.

"Where do you think the boy has run to?"

"He's a good kid," Jack Liffey insisted. "Really. He got a bit wrong-footed, but he's the son we'd all like to have. Earnest and trying very hard to do the right thing."

"Uh-huh. But the question is, where is he trying to do the right thing at the moment?"

Loco stirred awake and glanced up and almost did a double take when he saw the FBI man. There was a little vestigial growl in the

back of the dog's throat, but weariness took over again, and he
flopped back onto Jack Liffey's feet.

"I don't know. I have a hunch he's trying to foil some plan that's
started to embarrass him. Probably something to do with his
schoolmates. I have another hunch it also has to do with that thing
there on the table. Would I be within hailing distance?"

The FBI man made a face. "My colleagues tend to call that a
ghetto blaster, unless they get to thinking report-wise and politically
correct, and then they use expressions like 'portable stereophonic cas-
sette tape player.' Actually, some of the older agents in the office call
it a nigger-blaster when I'm not around. But they know I'd squash
them like a bug if I heard it. I don't know why I'm telling you all
this, but my wife is an African-American, Mr. Liffey. A wonderful
woman, and we have two fine children who the world also con-
siders African-Americans. I want you to realize that the Bureau has
changed a lot since the benighted days of Mr. Hoover."

"Got any gay agents?" Jack Liffey asked.

"Not to my knowledge. But to get back to your question. . . ."
He seemed to have a big conversational hump to get himself over,
for some reason. "What do you know about plutonium?"

Jack Liffey felt a chill on his spine. "It's bad news. The Nagasaki
bomb. Breeder reactors. Cancer."

He nodded. "It's a heavy metal. We don't use it much in reactors
in this country, except mixed with uranium oxide, but it's nowhere
near as dangerous as most people think. Unlike radium and some
other radioactive materials, it's not a gamma-ray emitter. It emits
only simple alpha rays—unless you have enough mass for it to go
critical, of course, and then it blows up your city. But in smaller
amounts, a piece of paper will stop all the radiation it gives off.
The only real way it's dangerous is if you breathe it in a powder
form. . . ." He shrugged.

"Like Karen Silkwood."

The agent didn't acknowledge the name, but Jack Liffey knew it
was widely suspected that Kerr-McGee had purposely contami-
nated her several times for being a whistle-blower about lax safety
at their plant before eventually having her car run off the road to

kill her. The film had starred Meryl Streep, if he remembered right. Not that any of that mattered.

"Inhale about half a gram, and it'll kill you quick," he said in a flat voice. "But that's far less lethal than a lot of other substances. Arsenic, for instance. Twenty milligrams of inhaled plutonium will kill you in a month. Anything less and you're just upping the statistics for getting cancer one of these days."

He paused for a moment to let Jack Liffey think it over.

"Take a good look at that boom box."

Jack Liffey extracted his feet from under the contented dog and got up to look closer at the tape player. He touched the CD lid and instead of the lid coming open, a much bigger section of the top popped up. It was cleverly done along the seams of the plastic case. There was a fat white paper bag about the size of a half brick under the lid.

"That's not? . . . " he said.

The FBI man shook his head. "Ordinary Globe A-1 wheat flour. There used to be a little C-4 explosive under it, just enough to scatter the flour into the wind. We're pretty sure this was a test device, for what the press is calling these days a 'dirty bomb.' You use a tiny bit of explosive to spread around something nasty. Plutonium-oxide powder is heavy—twice as heavy as lead—and that compartment would hold maybe two thousand grams."

"Are there more of these?"

"We think we've seized all the prepared tape players save one, and we also seized a map that locates many of the synagogues in the L.A. area. There's a cell of fundamentalist Islamic fanatics, mostly Sudanis and Algerians, who were apparently going to set these little dirty bombs off indoors on the Sabbath. They were meant to kill as many Jews as possible, and make it necessary to close down the synagogues for quite some time."

"Where the hell did they get plutonium?"

The FBI agent shrugged, but not really as if he didn't know. He just wasn't going to talk about it. Jack Liffey stared in horror at the bag of flour. Robert Johnson leaned forward and flicked the little switch that turned the radio on, and a jazz station started playing softly, ominously.

"Who would have suspected that this innocent-looking thing playing Stan Getz could decease quite a lot of people?"

Jack Liffey was pretty sure 'decease' wasn't a transitive verb, but he didn't bother pointing it out. Maybe in FBI-speak it was. "I can't believe the boy is involved in that."

"He may not know what he's involved in. We need to speak to Fariborz Bayat as soon as possible. I think you can appreciate that."

"Oh, yes. Believe me. I have nothing at all against synagogues, or my own lungs. I get chills just looking at that thing."

"So do we." He shut the radio off and closed the top and looked like he was getting ready to go.

"Can you do anything about the cartels and the boy's father? That might help me bring him in."

"We knew something, but not much. You can see why it's of secondary importance right now. We can't do very much for him if he doesn't come forward." He smiled a little. "On the other hand, if he *does* come to us, we still probably can't do very much for him, and then he's up shit creek with the narcos. I recognize that. I'll talk to some friends of mine and let you know. In the meantime, think of plutonium. And see if you can remember something about the boy. You've got my card." He paused. "We'd like everybody in this country to be able to live out their dreams in peace."

Jack Liffey grimaced. "Most of my dreams are about being in French class and discovering I forgot to put any clothes on."

The Greyhound rumbled north with a kind of ponderous swaying that had been set up when it changed lanes too quickly and the driver overcorrected a little. Back in San Diego, he'd got the last free seat, over a wheel well, and his legs kept cramping up now. There were only so many ways you could scoot your legs at angles. He'd wondered at the time why the elderly Latina had ceded him the window seat right away, but now he saw that she could straighten her legs out into the aisle.

Through the windows on the inland side of the bus, across from him, he saw a long palisade of empty yellow hills that showed that the bus was passing through Camp Pendleton. On the ocean side, he caught glimpses of blue green water and surf. Then there was a high wall on the sea side and through a gap he glimpsed a covey of Marine hovercraft, parked like taxis. A colorful sign on one end of the big wall said, *No Beach Out of Reach,* and at the other end, *The Swift Intruders.* Mean-spirited stuff, Fariborz thought, imperialist stuff. Though he didn't usually think in terms like that.

As an exercise in empathy, he tried to imagine himself a U.S. Marine, spit-shining his shoes to a glow, getting tattooed and shorn, stalking through town arm-in-arm with his pals and glaring at longhair peaceniks, the whole dollar standard of macho posturing, but he couldn't quite do it. Still, he told himself it was no uglier than *Death to the Great Satan,* the slogan that his father's countrymen were always out chanting in the streets at the drop of a hat. There was so much hatred, so much ugliness and cruelty.

He hoped he was done with hard-heartedness now, as surely as if he'd had a religious conversion, a bolt of revelation on the way to Damascus. He didn't know why he hadn't seen through all his ferocious self-righteousness sooner. Even if you were certain that some pious doctrine was right, utterly right beyond any doubting, it was obvious that you couldn't bomb your way to converting the doubters. Even the silly and harmless stink bombs and paint bombs that he and Iman had planned. That kind of action damaged only your own heart.

The final moment of his conversion had come, curiously enough, in the shabby INS interview room that had only been 100 yards north of the Mexican border. He had sat at a table made out of some kind of nicked and dented hard black rubber, across from a kindly gray-haired interviewer who had seemed more bored than anything, and Fariborz had gone on and on refusing to give a name or address. He had broken no law, he insisted, and, following Jack Liffey's whispered suggestion while they were being herded toward the green-and-white Ford Explorer out in no-man's-land, he kept denying that he'd come across the border at all. They'd just been wandering lost near the border for half the night.

"You look like a lucky kid," the agent had said to him. "I don't know, something about the way you sit up straight. I wish my own kid had your stuff when he was growing up."

"I'm not a kid. I'm an adult."

"Joey's a construction flagman over in Phoenix. Said he couldn't stomach community college to try for something better. You in college?"

It was such a clumsy attempt to gain a little more information that Fariborz just smiled. The pen lifted, checked something, and wrote a few words.

"I've got to ask," the avuncular man said, almost apologetically.

At dawn the exhausted man had spoken at the door to an equally weary-looking woman and given her some money, and soon a white paper bag appeared with two coffees in McDonald's cups and two Sausage-Egg McMuffins. He couldn't touch his sandwich, of course. It contained pork. But he did accept the coffee.

His McMuffin sat there the rest of the morning on a sheet of notepaper, leaking grease that congealed into a graying pool. As loathsome as the food was, it touched Fariborz deeply that the man had bought it for him with his own money. The old man was polite and gentle. He had never once tried physical intimidation, never threatened him in any way.

The manifest decency of the old man, just doing his job without causing a ruckus, made Fariborz want to weep all of a sudden. He looked from the horrible egg-and-sausage McMuffin to the kindly grizzled face and decided, all at once, that much of mankind was basically good. In that instant, he realized he wanted only to love his enemy. He knew it was a weirdly Christian sentiment, phrased that way, for he was still a Moslem beyond all doubt, but he sensed a spirit of amity washing through him, and then out toward the whole human race.

For the next hour in the interview room, he had felt curiously at peace with himself, as if a fever had broken. He was sure that Mohammed (may the blessings and peace of God be upon him) must have felt exactly the same way at some time in his life and encouraged his followers in that direction, but he couldn't recall any quotes touching on it from the Koran. That just showed his lack of study, he thought. The feeling of generalized love waned a little when a new man took over in the morning and pushed him a little harder, but he didn't let the new man spoil his new feelings. Imagine, he kept reminding himself with a strange wry self-consciousness, a religious epiphany set off by an egg-and-sausage McMuffin. It *must* be something powerful.

And he felt the glow still as he rocked hypnotically in the Greyhound, surrounded entirely by poor people and people of darker skin. His own inner feelings told him clearly that Islam demanded he find the path of gentle truth and peace. Now he had to find his best friend Pejman, little Yahya, and poor maimed Iman, and convince them of the same truth before the sheik and Hassan got them into real trouble. He didn't know what they were up to, but the man and his people obviously had much in common with those who had attacked the embassies in Africa and blown up the World Trade Center in New York (may peace be upon all the fallen), and Fariborz guessed their plans had to be bad ones.

And then all of a sudden a memory made his face burn with shame. He had sat with Becky on the turnout up on Mulholland Drive, the spot they had visited many times because it looked south over the whole of L.A. and then by turning your head 180 degrees you could see north into the Valley, too. He had often played his acoustic guitar on a big rock there, as if he were serenading the entire L.A. basin, picking out Becky's favorites, "Guantanamera" and "Here Comes the Sun" on the gut strings, deceptively simple-sounding tunes but actually quite complex and lovely.

He closed his eyes in mortification at the vividness of the recollection. "I could never marry a nonbeliever," he heard his own voice telling her, avoiding the charged word *infidel*, but still unbearably sanctimonious as he tried for a tone of utter emotional neutrality. "I couldn't be sure of the purity of such a woman's heart."

How had he been such a priggish idiot? And worse—he was sure now that it had been this rejection up in the Hollywood Hills that had driven Becky into her own transgressions. That was as good an example as he would ever need of the insidious damage you caused by following a rigid code.

He thought of how easily and painlessly Jack Liffey had offered his one simple insight: that even God couldn't make right wrong. It had never occurred to him before, but it seemed so obvious now. Becky or anyone else could follow *safa* for the same reasons he did, whether she believed there was a God wagging a giant finger at her or not. The thought warmed him inside, as he formed a new all-encompassing notion: that all people were brothers and sisters, all capable of the same struggle to behave with decency.

Ahead, he saw the two big domes of the nuclear power plant, the northern edge of the U.S. Marine base, and he realized he was about halfway to L.A., halfway to Jack Liffey. He had been wrong to ditch him. The man's presence drew him powerfully now. It was as if he needed to be with the man to talk it all over again, test the sea changes that had gone on in his psyche, maybe even to complete something in himself. And, of course, he needed the man's help to find his friends. After all, Jack Liffey was a detective.

Jack Liffey was startled at first when he opened the door, expecting the FBI man back for some further horrifying revelation, or a gaggle of kids from the complex trying to sell him the world's very best chocolate bar to earn a trip to camp. It was twilight and the bulb in his alcove was out, as usual, so it took him a moment even to recognize her.

"Hello, Jack Liffey." There was a little trepidation in her voice, but a hardworking brazenness overrode it. "You never called me."

She came straight in wearing a beige belted trench coat that went perfectly with his earlier flight of fancy at Taunton School about her posing in a Nazi cap for the cover of a man's magazine. Finally the name came to him: Rebecca Plumkill, headmistress.

"Mrs. Plumkill."

She extracted a bottle of wine from her overcoat. "Ms. But it's Rebecca, *please*. May I call you Jack?"

"Sure, of course. Have a seat."

"I require two wineglasses."

He hadn't had a drink in six years, but he searched out two glasses that he had once loved, elegant black-stem crystal numbers forgotten on the top shelf of the cupboard, between the unused Osterizer and the Joe Namath Butter-up popcorn popper. He hunted through a drawer for a corkscrew, and finally found an old two-prong number to open the cabernet. He hadn't forgot how, but opening the bottle was complicated by the way any pressure on his left hand disturbed the burn and sent a scream of pain up his arm.

"Was I supposed to call you? I'm sorry."

"I waited for it every night," she said in a strange throaty voice. He wasn't sure, but he thought he felt her hand drag very lightly across the back of his neck as he tugged at the cork. He poured the two glasses, still not sure whether he would drink his. Something so odd was going down that he couldn't get a grip on things. Was he dreaming this? He thought of Aneliese, but chased the thought away, like stamping his foot at a pest. Things like this only happened in 1940s movies, he thought. But things like *what?*

Loco was curious, too, sitting up by the sofa staring at them both. The animal gnarred a little. Without looking straight at her yet, Jack Liffey said, "Do you realize that in the last four thousand years no new animals have been domesticated? And I'm still failing with this one."

He heard a hearty laugh. The laugh made him feel good—actually, to his surprise, aroused him sexually. He turned with a wineglass in each hand to see that she had taken off the trench coat and looked marvelous in a short black dress. He recalled a quote he had read in a science-fiction novel as a teen, the first line of print that had ever aroused him: *Looks like that dress will come off easy.*

He decided to go ahead and sip the wine. *Wow,* he thought. The first shock was a little harsh, but then a mellowness flooded over him. It was only wine. He'd have only the one glass.

"To what do I owe this honor?" he asked.

She grinned broadly and he realized she was already a little drunk, probably something imbibed earlier for Dutch courage.

"Chemistry," she said. "Better living through. This was so damn hard for me, Jack Liffey. Every woman, *absolutely* every woman, desires to have a man who is slightly roguish and makes her laugh."

"Is that me?"

"Why do you think I got myself half drunk to come here uninvited?"

And for the first time since Marlena, he turned out to have no trouble at it at all.

Nineteen

Defending Abstract Expressionism

"Jesus Christ," Jack Liffey murmured, and then corrected himself. "Jesus *H.* Christ."

Cool air wafted across his body, discernible at several sensitive points because he was completely nude where he lay on his back in a tangle of sheets on his bedroom floor. An opened bottle of Wesson oil lay on its side beside him, making a terrible mess where it had gurgled onto the carpet. A pillow was torn open and had coughed out its shredded foam to add to the disorder. He had no idea how *that* had happened. He didn't see how he could have done it because his left hand was still swathed in bandages and hurt like hell. He would need some more painkillers soon.

"How did we tear the pillow?" he asked, but there was no answer.

Rebecca Plumkill breathed evenly, deeply asleep in her own nudity, diagonally across the bed. Her small breasts, flattened now to near-invisibility as she lay on her back, had been fantastically sensitive, as had various other spots on her. And on him. He had no idea what time it was, or if he'd been dozing for long, but it was still dark. He had no idea where his watch was, either. He'd fantasized about evenings like this, but he hadn't really thought he had any left in him at his age.

An empty wine bottle lay on the floor, too, and two stemmed wineglasses lay on their side with a haze of red liquid pooled in the low spots. He did not think he had had very much of the wine since he did not feel very buzzed. It had been his first drink in six years, and it appeared to have been worth it. The world was amazing, he thought. All the wearying absurdity of things seemed to have evaporated off him. He looked at the woman's slim body again and felt himself smiling like an idiot. It was as if he'd skipped forward in time, far past the predators, and landed in an age when everything that had wanted to eat him was now extinct.

He was just drifting off again when he was startled awake by his raucous doorbell. He wondered if the FBI man was back with another tale, another demand, another caution. It shrilled again, insistent and chilling, and a tremor took his shoulders. He pictured the fat Mexican drug lord standing darkly in his alcove, attended by a choir of *judiciales*. There were still predators after all.

Wrapping the sheet around him, he made his way toward the front door like the sorry leftover of a toga party. Loco stirred a bit, too, one yellow eye opening with a lazy regard to watch the fluttery white apparition pass by. He wondered if Loco had lapped up any of the wine. Normally, the dog was wound so tight that it snapped erect at the slightest cooling pop in the walls.

He peered out through the fisheye to see in the shadows, lower than he expected, Fariborz Bayat. The boy looked exhausted and disheveled, and he was just reaching up to ring again. Jack Liffey moved quickly to forestall that terrible noise, clapping the flat of his hand over the exposed bell to muffle it, and then tugged the door open. A blast of cool air ran up under his makeshift toga. The boy looked startled.

"Don't ring. Come in."

"Sorry, sir."

"You look done in. Sit down over there while I put something on."

He went back to the bedroom where he contemplated again the

gloriously nude Rebecca Plumkill, headmistress of Taunton
Academy, lips slightly parted as she gave a light snore. She hadn't
budged an inch. If he hadn't seen a single hand twitching like a
cat chasing its dream mouse, he would have feared he'd killed her.
He covered her with the sheet and put on the pants and a shirt he
rescued from a wad in the corner.

By all rights, he should take Fariborz Bayat by the nape of the
neck and convey him straight to the FBI, but he went to the kitchen
and put on hot water instead.

"How did you get here?"

"I took the Greyhound to the station downtown, but then it
was tough. They've frozen my ATM account. You're in the phone
book, so I hitched out Wilshire to La Cienega, and I had to walk
from there."

"That's four or five miles."

"I've been walking for two hours."

"How'd you get past the guard?"

"He was asleep."

So much for his last line of defense against the *drogistas*. "You
could have called me."

"I'm sure your phone is tapped. Just like they've been watching
my ATM. I always used a different one miles from where I was
staying just to run them around."

"You'd be better off coming with me to the FBI."

"*No.*" The boy stirred as if he was about to leap up and run. "If
you even suggest it again, I'm out the door."

"Hold your horses. I don't turn people in. Do you want some
tea? And what's this visit about? I thought you were finished with
me at the border."

"I'd love some tea. I think I need your help."

It was nice to be needed, Jack Liffey thought. He hadn't actually
been doing so well lately as Mr. Fix-it. He went back into the
kitchen where the little flip-number clock built into his stove said it
was 3:30 A.M. Which was plus or minus an hour, depending on its
mood. From the kitchen door he watched Fariborz and wondered

how much he knew about his comrades. He was slumping to one side, obviously exhausted, hardly able to keep his eyes open. He felt an immense affection for this boy with his fierce longing for rectitude. His resourcefulness at the border hadn't been bad, either. Quite a kid.

"Stay awake a bit."

"Oh. I don't know what the sheik's people are planning to do, but I think I need to get my friends away from them. I got them into trouble in the first place. Even Iman"—he shook his head—"he always had a tendency to go overboard. You always think you can't tell Iman anything, but I knew when we argued he'd be listening even when he pretended he wasn't. Maybe later he'd come around. But now he's been hurt very bad and I'm afraid it's probably made him supercommitted. It's like shooting the father and eloping, getting the whole pregnant enchilada. Iman lost his hand."

Trying hard to explain, but not being quite coherent as he drifted.

"Do you know what they're up to?" Jack Liffey asked.

"They didn't really trust any of us, you know. Something about a radio with a little explosive charge in it. Like you'd use in a stink bomb or a paint bomb. Also, I found a big bottle of potassium iodide pills."

"I see," Jack Liffey said.

The young man tried to come alert. "Do you know what it means?"

"Be right with you." He caught the kettle just as it began expelling a thin soundless mist, an instant before the whistle, and turned it off. He poured scalding water into two mugs with tea bags and brought them into the living room, where Fariborz was listing precariously to the left again. Loco had adopted him and lay across the boy's feet.

The dog was developing pretty good taste, he thought. There was probably a single domesticated gene working its way like a virus through his bloodlines.

"Don't drift off yet," Jack Liffey said. "Here." He handed the boy the tea so he would have to concentrate enough to stay upright. The boy sipped the tea and sighed.

"They're dirty bombs, meant to spew out some radioactive powder, maybe plutonium," Jack Liffey explained. And he told the boy most of what Special Agent Robert Johnson had told him. Fariborz appeared horrified, intent, angry, troubled—emotions scudding across his weary face like cloud shadows on a prairie. Then they were both quiet for a while, contemplating the enormity of it.

"I guess that explains the big *X-Files* episode I saw," Fariborz offered. "I went out to Campo, where they'd kept us all cooped up for a week. The government had the place surrounded with tanks, and there were men in space suits walking around with radiation containers. I think I remember reading in school that if you take a lot of potassium iodide, it protects you from radiation poisoning. I saw their list of synagogues, too." He sighed. "Those imbeciles, targeting ordinary Jews. That's *stupid*. It makes us look terrible; it makes Islam look bad. I wasn't into hurting anyone, honest. Damn their bigotry, these guys out of the desert."

"That's edging up on bigotry itself."

He gave a rueful shrug. "Most of the other kids at Kennedy thought *I* was an Arab. 'Little raghead,' they called me behind my back. Sand nigger. What's that all about? All those prep-school boys with razor haircuts and more pocket money than a Third World country. How does anybody think it accomplishes anything to call people stupid names?"

"We can't solve that one right now, but we'd better find your friends. Do you have any ideas on that?"

He nodded. "Do you want to start looking right now, tonight?"

Jack Liffey shook his head. "Neither of us is up to it. I'll make you a bed on the sofa, and we'll head out in a few hours."

"Plutonium," the young man said as Jack Liffey stood up. "I had no idea, really. Maybe I should have guessed something terrible."

"Don't worry," Jack Liffey said. He ruffled Fariborz's hair fondly as he went by; he couldn't help it. "Just remember what we've learned from all the movies about fighting a heavily armed enemy. You're really in no danger at all unless you tell people you're planning to retire in three days. And then only if you show around a picture of your wife and kids."

The boy thought about it glumly for a moment, but just when Jack Liffey figured the boy wasn't up to getting the joke, Fariborz almost smiled. "I think you also have to talk fondly about a particular stream to go fishing the day you retire."

Jack Liffey chuckled softly; he'd understood perfectly. You might call it some sort of doppelganger effect here, he thought.

"Jack, Jack, somebody's there!" The voice was urgent in his ear, a woman's, rich and wonderfully throaty. He woke, opening one eye to see the frizz of her short blond hair, which was colored too evenly to be real, her big greenish eyes. She propped herself up in his bed on an elbow. Rebecca Plumkill, he thought. Will wonders never cease. He remembered that he had straightened her out longways and covered them both with bedclothes rescued from the floor. He felt vaguely scalped, as if pain had been distributed mildly but evenly across the whole surface of his head, so he figured he'd had his share of the wine after all.

She pointed urgently at the closed bedroom door, and he listened to a murmur from the living room. His conscious mind, coming alert, could account for one of the voices, but not the other. Bright light bled in at the curtains, so it was probably already well into this exceedingly complicated morning and time to get up and deal with it. Something about the timbre and rhythm of the second voice made him smile.

"Don't worry about it," he said. "The voices belong. How are you feeling this morning?"

"Pretty good, if I do say so, Mr. Jack Liffey. Sore here and there, tender." She patted around her chest and flanks. "A bit sticky. *Whoa!*"

She'd caught sight of the riot of shredded foam on the floor.

"Did we do that?"

"*You* did that," he said. "I think. Don't you have to be at school?"

"It's Saturday." She nuzzled up next to him and he started to get aroused. "Mmm-mmm." He'd lost track of the days. Saturday explained the other voice in the living room.

"I'm sorry," he said, disentangling gently. "Duty duty duty. I'll block the view down the hall if you want to make a dash for the bathroom."

He took a couple of old codeine pills that he had and then dug around in the closet until he found the bathrobe somebody had given him years ago, an expensive kimono that had been slit open and westernized with buttons. He'd never worn it, but now seemed as good a time as any. She came up to him before he could put it on and held his penis hard for a moment, like a jack handle.

"I'd like some more of this. Quite soon."

"I wouldn't call it the impossible dream."

When he went out into the hall and stood to block the view, Fariborz was sitting up on the mussed sofa, wrapped primly in a blanket, and Maeve sat in the chair opposite, with her legs tucked under her in that way only women did. The two seemed to be deep in a debate on the merits of abstract expressionism.

"Most of them don't have enough going on in the picture to challenge you to look for very long or even think very hard," Maeve was saying.

"Good morning, punkin'. I see you two have met."

Maeve leapt up and ran to hug him. He kept a bit sideways to hold his erection out of contact, and to keep her from noticing the bandage on his hand. "Daddy, hey! I love you to pieces!"

Abruptly they could all hear water start splashing into the bathtub.

"You've got somebody here!" Maeve exclaimed delightedly.

"There's lots of somebodies here," he evaded. "Have you figured out that the somebody right over there is the one you got in trouble over?"

She turned and looked hard at Fariborz.

"Maeve was spying on your pal, the sheik," he explained for Fariborz's benefit. "Helping me out, and the FBI nearly popped her for it. We had a bit of a disciplinary discussion about that, and she's not quite out of the woods yet." He wasn't ready to give up the last shreds of leverage it gave him.

"Fariborz Bayat—Maeve Liffey. I'm going to try to get some breakfast together for all of us, and I don't want anybody talking business until I'm done. Understood?"

Maeve nodded and then indicated the bathroom. "Who's in there?"

"You'll meet her."

Going into the kitchen of his suddenly jam-packed condo, he experienced a comforting paterfamilias mood that he hadn't felt in years. He delved in the freezer and found a cardboard tray of rock-hard English muffins. One jar in the fridge held about an inch of marmalade. Another was full of reddish jam, some indefinable homemade berry kind that probably hadn't been touched in a year.

"But it's all been emptied of content," Maeve's voice rose in the living room. "It's the quintessential art of the Cold War. It turned its back on the world on purpose, so it can't be accused of saying anything at all. And it's proud it did that."

"I agree in a way," the boy said. "I think decoration is immoral if it doesn't have a spiritual purpose."

Where on earth did she learn a word like "quintessential"? Jack Liffey thought. There was a half carton of milk that smelled okay. He set that on the counter. Cereal from the cupboard. He got out the canister of ground French roast and started to make a big pot of coffee.

"You could say abstract expressionism is in flight from meaning." That was Maeve, in that hectoring too-old voice that he found quite touching, with somebody else's quotation marks in her speech. Maybe even his. Though he rather liked abstract expressionism.

He leaned around the corner into the living room. "Kids, I've never heard such doctrinaire crap," he interjected. "I grew up with abstract expressionism, and I love it. A painting isn't a novel, *you*, and it isn't a religion, *you*. Before you both shut it completely out of your universe with some ridiculously rigid theory of what it *ought* to be doing, why don't you open yourself up to what it actually does? Let it work on your *perceptions* and feelings instead of your tiny little left brains."

They both turned on him, eyes big, uniting in instinct against Authority, just as he yanked his head back into the kitchen, grinning.

"Dad, that's not fair at all! You're just arguing ad hominem."

My, we *are* getting sophisticated, he thought.

"We have every right, sir, to ask art to have a meaning."

"Don't just hit and run, *Dad.* That's such grown-up arrogance!"

He let them argue at him for a while, but he had planted the seed he wanted to plant. Maybe they'd recall it one day, before some one-track outlook solidified in their psyches to wall out a whole enriching experience of life.

Then, in a lull in all the good feeling, he realized if things kept working out with Rebecca, he was going to have to tell Aneliese de Villiers something. She was so decent and he wanted to like her so much that it made the hair on his neck stand on end. He'd even had fantasies of Maeve and Billy as step-siblings. They'd have liked one another. Why did life have to be famine or flood? And what was it that had defeated his libido with one and not the other?

Soon he called the kids in and set them to preparing what there was of the breakfast, defrosting the muffins in the microwave and laying out the table, and then a glistening Rebecca Plumkill emerged in a fresh sheath dress that she had conjured magically. He introduced them all around.

When Fariborz took his turn in the shower, Maeve did her best to embarrass her father by asking Rebecca how he had been in bed.

"Ssst, Maeve"—he cut her off—"have you got your cell phone?"

"Sure. Mom would kill me if I lost it."

"I need to borrow it. Right now. And when I say, 'I have to take the garbage out,' I want you to keep Fariborz occupied for a few minutes, just make sure he doesn't follow me."

Her eyes went wide. "You're not going to turn him in!"

"No, I'm not, but I am going to have a talk with the folks who made such a mess at Ruby Ridge, and I don't want it to spook him. I'd do it now, but I don't know how long he showers."

And just then, the water went off. Maeve hurried to her back-pack by the armchair and got him the phone. Jack Liffey went into the kitchen to forestall any further talk that the boy might overhear, and to open a can of dog food for Loco, who was finally stirring from his deep sleep.

"You know what's got this dog worried about his food?" Jack Liffey asked them all.

"No, Dad, what's got Loco worried about his food?" Maeve parroted with a pretended singsong annoyance in her voice. "I know a Jack Liffey straight line when I hear it coming."

"Alpo's over a buck a can now. That's seven dollars in dog money."

Rebecca Plumkill laughed, and he decided right then that she was a keeper.

Twenty

The Library Tower

After hastily downing coffee and a muffin, Rebecca Plumkill had rushed off to attend to some school business, but not before a whispered promise to return very soon and a long kiss that turned his gizzard inside out. He'd explained away the bandage on his hand to Maeve as a minor burn, and now the kids were deep in conversation. He showered with his hand covered by a plastic bag and then stood in the middle of his mussed bedroom with a curious new ease at inhabiting his own body, a consoling kind of clarity about life.

He recognized it immediately as an illusion, but the kind of illusion worth hanging onto for all you were worth. The opposite of truth—he remembered the words of the great nuclear physicist Niels Bohr—was clarity. But who wanted truth? Not if you could have clarity like this. Or was it just the codeine?

As he dressed, Jack Liffey whistled a tune, or at least took a stab at it. In that happy state, his psyche received faint, worrying messages in the form of a murmur from the front room, and little by little he felt the top layers of his contentment spalling away like old, curling paint. Pay attention, and you'd see that there was always a lot of unpleasant stuff undone.

He dug into his T-shirt drawer and found the tangled mess of leather straps at the bottom. He had bought it at a gun swap meet back in the days when these semilegal bazaars had been held weekends in alleys behind most of the gun shops in L.A., and now he threaded his arms through the two big loops and tugged and wriggled until the breakfront holster hung straight down in his left armpit. He had rarely used the shoulder holster since he had no more right than any other civilian in L.A. to carry a concealed weapon, but this seemed about as good a time to break the law as any.

He had brought the *Oxford Companion* back into the bedroom with him, and now he flipped open the cover and lifted the Ballester Molina out of its hollow—the Argentine copy of the army .45 he'd bought at the same swap meet—and tucked it into the holster. He tugged it out a few times just to make sure he could. It was a little like carrying a toaster under your arm, but a loose jacket would shroud it enough so that polite—or easily alarmed—people would pretend not to see it.

When he came out, the kids had moved on to a discussion about pop music, names and styles that meant little to him, though he tried hard to keep up.

"Maeve, you'll need to look after yourself for a while. Fariborz and I have some work to do."

"Uh, Dad. I haven't told you my good news yet."

Somehow he didn't like the sound of that.

"I got my license this week, and I've got Mom's old Toyota now."

"Congratulations," he said dubiously. It had been coming for some time, and he realized now that he should have asked how she'd got herself there bright and early Saturday morning. "And the downside?"

"If you don't let me come along and help, I'll just follow you around. I'm a big girl now."

"You just turned sixteen last week. When you're eighteen, you can move out of both of our houses and do what you want. *That's* a big girl in the law."

"Since when have you been a stickler for the law? Fari and I decided that I could be a real help."

Jack Liffey looked at the young man and he could tell this was the first the boy had heard about it, too, but Fariborz didn't seem to want to contradict Maeve. If he left her at the condo, she probably *would* try to follow him, and it would be next to impossible to give her the slip in the gutless Chevette. Short of putting a couple of rounds through the tires of her Toyota, he figured the best thing to do was to tell her she could come along and then put her out of the car with cabfare home at the nearest Denny's.

"Where are we going?" he asked Fariborz.

"I'd rather direct you. I want to be there, too, and I have a sense you'd leave me behind if you knew."

"*Everybody* wants leverage!" Jack Liffey complained. "All right, I give up. It's a school outing. I've got to take out the garbage first."

He caught Maeve's eye and she had understood. He actually did pick up the dampish kitchen bag and head out the door into a gust of Santa Ana wind that was warm and dry and gritty on his face. After tossing the bag into the big green Dumpster off the parking lot, he took out Maeve's cell phone and dialed the number that said "direct line" on Robert Johnson's business card.

"This is me," came the answer.

"Who me?"

"*Who is this?*"

"We could do this all day. *I* called. *You* identify."

"Johnson. Is that Jack Liffey?"

"Uh-huh. Listen, the kid came to me. Fariborz Bayat. But he's going to spook and run if I try to bring him in. He says he's going to lead me to the other kids, which probably means to the sheik's cell. I'll make a deal with you. I'll stay in touch and tell you where we go, if you tell me what's going on with these Arabs, as far as you know. I don't want to walk into a big cloud of plutonium."

"You really ought to bring the boy in."

"Don't even go there. I've been having leverage battles all morning, and I'm just barely on top here."

He heard a sigh and a kind of electronic buzz. They were probably trying to trace him, but he'd be gone in five minutes. "We picked up most of Sheik Arad's group yesterday. All the boom boxes are accounted for, except two, and one of those seems to be a mangled mess on a hill not far from their country retreat down near the border. It was probably a test. It sure put the fear of God into the agent who found it until the 100-meter circle of powder tested as wheat flour. One guy called Hassan Osmani is still on the loose and he's got one boom box. We don't know if it's armed and loaded, but we have to act as if it is. Where are you?"

"Don't know yet." Jack Liffey clicked off. He was about to head back to the apartment when he had a second thought. Through directory assistance, he got the number of the FBI in the Federal Building and he even let Maeve's mom pay the extra charge for the dial-through.

"Federal Bureau of Investigation, Westwood. How may I direct your call?"

"You may direct it to Special Agent Robert Johnson, thank you."

There was a long pause. "May I ask where you got that name, sir?"

"No, you may not. Just give me his direct line."

"I'm sorry, sir. There is no Robert Johnson in this office."

"How about some other office?"

"I'm on the Bureau computer, sir. We have no special agent in this area by that name. May I direct your call to another agent?"

He hung up with the granddaddy of chills scurrying up and down his spine like a yo-yo. He stared at the card in his hand. The ID the man had shown at the door had looked pretty good, but Jack Liffey realized now that he should have wondered about an agent showing up alone. In his experience, Shoes always went about in pairs.

Who the hell was Robert Johnson, and how did he seem to know so much? He thought immediately of the Mexican *judiciales,* but their interest was in the drugs, not the Arabs, and Robert Johnson hadn't been interested in drugs at all. Could some other agency be involved here, an agency that didn't want to leave footprints? The CIA was forbidden to do domestic surveillance, as were the military intelligence groups, if you took anybody's word. It couldn't have been some L.A. agency because the Campo house was in San Diego County, or maybe even Imperial. And no local police would have the resources to deal with plutonium, anyway. But Johnson sounded like he knew the score, and what other choice did he have?

He came back up the steps from the Dumpsters, and two little girls skipped past, carrying a doll between them by the arms. "All fall down," one of them said to him. Or that was what it sounded like. Then a crow cawed softly up on the eaves. Enough with the omens, thank you, he thought.

"Bus is leaving," he called into the house. They had been holding hands when the door swung open. He'd caught a glance of it, and then they came out sheepishly and trooped toward the parking lot. He felt like a scoutmaster herding his charges to the trailhead. Maeve deferred the front seat of the Chevette to Fariborz with a hand gesture. He hadn't seen her at such a loss for words in a long time.

The trashy car just barely started, the engine turning over reluctantly several times before catching. "Which way?" Jack Liffey asked.

"Right on Jefferson," Fariborz directed.

He pulled out of the condo, swung in front of a slow motorhome and the boy began looking for addresses as the old bucket gathered speed.

"Oh, gee," he said.

"Are you going to enlighten me?"

"I didn't realize. We could almost have walked. It's probably right up there."

He pointed to a self-storage place that had gone up a year earlier, on the lot where the city had once tunneled down to get at L.A.'s main sewer outfall and replace it, a job that had annoyed the neighborhood with stinks and rumbles for years.

"Might I know what it is that's right up there?"

"The group has a storage locker. I saw the address on a shipping label that was taped to the radio cartons. I know the locker number, too. Don't you think it's worth checking?"

Jack Liffey thought about it. They were virtually there. So much for booting Maeve out somewhere safe. "I want you two to stay in the car."

He parked in front of the office. There was what appeared to be an apartment above the office with tidy blue awnings. Past a big draw-gate, a series of ugly storage buildings stretched up the shallow slope in the lee of the same weedy hills with oil wells that loomed over his condo. As he looked, a tumbleweed whipped hard into the chain-link fence in the distance. Many others had piled up there already.

"What's the number of the locker?"

"I'll show you."

Still, the leverage.

"Okay, but Maeve Mary stays *here*. Are we agreed?"

He had put his most forceful tone of voice into the admonition, using both her names, and she seemed to take it as a sign to acquiesce. She nodded, and he and Fariborz trooped to the office. Inside, an immensely fat man in a wheelchair sat behind the counter. A nasal cannula wrapped around his cheeks to poke its little tubes up his nostrils, and the hose ran to a big aluminum canister beside him that hissed now and then like an atomic bomb in a cheap movie.

"Hi. I'd like to check out one of your lockers. You got an open one?"

"Any idea the size you're gonna want?"

He hadn't counted on that. "I'll look at what you've got and think about it."

The fat man set a clipboard on the counter. The top sheet of paper seemed to show a blueprint of different-sized lockers and a lot of fine print about conditions.

"We've got us A's. Those are like a two-car garage, and the B, fifteen-by-ten, and the C, that's ten-by-ten, and D, the five-by-ten, and a few E's, that's five-by-five, upper and lower. Most people think of the lockers as, like, the closet size or the garage size, and go from there. Now what you probably want—"

He didn't have the time or patience for this.

"Just let me look. I've gotta visualize it. Tell me a middle size that's open."

"You ain't got no idea of what you need stored?"

He was about to pull out his .45 and wave it around. "Do you want to rent a locker or not?"

"You're the boss, sir. C-25 is a five-by-ten, about the size of a deep walk-in closet. Building C is the third one up. The room ain't locked, and I ain't had it swept out yet, either. Guy pulled out this morning with some printing equipment in a U-Haul, so there might be a smell."

"Great. Fine."

"You can walk in through that door. Don't got to drive in."

Jack Liffey led the boy out the side door of the office that put them inside the complex, and they headed up the access roadway that ran beside dozens of swing-up doors.

"I thought he was going to try to explain what a cubic foot was."

"What was that tube he wore?" Fariborz asked.

"Oxygen. Probably emphysema. Don't ever start smoking. The upside for us, it means he's not going to be following us around. Give me a number now."

"D-53."

Each building seemed to specialize in one size of lockup. The first had garage doors, and the second had a series of evenly spaced room doors, like a windowless motel. In the third, the doors were closer together. D was identical to the third building, and locker 53 was around on the back side, so they'd be out of sight of the office if the manager happened to want to watch them.

Coming up he saw the big padlock on the door, so there was little chance of finding Hassan Osmani camped out here, or a cleaned-out locker with a forgotten treasure map on the floor. But he knocked anyway, just to feel he was doing his job.

The boy reacted first. Jack Liffey could see him perk up, so he knocked again and put his ear to the door. Sure enough, there was some kind of muffled noise in there, like a caged animal stirred to fright.

"Iman!" Fariborz shouted without warning, nearly deafening Jack Liffey.

The noise inside became rhythmic, a regular chug that sounded a lot like his rental car trying to start. It was almost certainly human, probably somebody gagged with duct tape.

"Iman, if it's you, be quiet for five seconds, then make noise again!"

He did exactly that.

"Stay and reassure him," Jack Liffey said.

He trotted back to the office and burst in on the caretaker. A skin magazine quickly went under the counter, and he wondered cruelly if there were specialty magazines for oxygen-tank sex. They stared at each other for an instant and then Jack Liffey took out Robert Johnson's card and showed it.

"I'm working with the FBI. You can call this agent if you want to confirm it. Right now I need to get into a locker. There's a kidnap victim inside."

The man did his best at an elaborate shrug. "We ain't got keys. That's the point. You use your own lock."

"And when people don't pay and leave their padlocks on your doors, you don't have a big bolt cutter here to break in?"

"I don't know, man. I can't go letting anybody break in our lockers."

"There's a voice inside crying for help. You want to come check?"

"We oughtta just call some cops."

"In five seconds, I'm going to rip the oxygen line off that tank. One . . . two . . . three—"

"Sure, sure, guy. Okay." He had it right there under the counter, a huge bolt cutter with bright red handles and lots of little scars on its jaws.

"Give me five minutes, and then you can call all the cops you want."

"Sure, sure. I ain't lookin' for no trouble, mister."

The wind swept a big flapping sheet of newspaper toward the fence as he hurried back to the locker and he saw the paper plaster itself flat to the chain-link fence, dimpling and bellying through the little diamonds. The Santa Ana was picking up. He could feel the desert air drying his sinuses.

"Stand back," he said to Fariborz. "The bolt cutter might throw a bit of metal." As he pressed, there were warning twinges in his hand but he worked through them.

The hardened jaws of the cutter went through the hasp easily with a satisfying little *chomp* at the end. Fariborz plucked the remains of the lock off the door and wrenched it open. A whiff of some peculiar smell, like the ionized air off electrical equipment, was sucked out of the dimness by the wind. The first thing he saw was three boys lying on their stomachs on the cement, hogtied and gagged with duct tape, and then he saw, with a renewed chill on his spine, a big finned container of black metal with the universal radiation symbol on it. Fariborz knelt and began ripping tape off the biggest boy, and the narrow room filled with gagging sobs.

Jack Liffey went gingerly to the container, a fat lid propped open, and without touching it, he peered down into it. There was a thick, slit-open foil liner that had been peeled back, and then a layer of foam peanuts. Then a second foil liner that was also cut open. Inside the inner barrier, his eye came to rest on a number of square metal boxes, each the size of a half brick, marked

"Depleted Pu oxide. Do not open containment. Acute radiation hazard."

He had seen something the same size before, inside the boom box that Robert Johnson had shown him. But he doubted that these contained sifted flour. More ominously, there was an empty space right in the center of the top layer, where a box should have been.

His spine crawled at the thought of the evils of whatever substance was packed in those metal boxes. He used his elbow to tip the lid back down.

The first of the freed boys sat up, and a second began to sputter as Fariborz worked on his tape. Jack Liffey turned to the boys. "Where did he go?" he demanded, and he had no doubt they knew exactly who he meant.

"*Allah-u akbar,*" the largest boy said.

"You have five seconds," Jack Liffey said. "Or I will personally tape you back up and shove your nose in that container."

"Tell him!" Fariborz insisted.

For the first time, Jack Liffey noticed that this stocky boy seemed to be missing a hand, his stump bandaged and apparently tender, as he cradled it with his good hand.

The next boy sputtered and coughed. "Hassan went downtown," he said. "You've got to stop him. He tied us up because we wouldn't help him."

The biggest boy glared and then seemed to come to a decision inside himself. "We were away from the *madrasa* with Hassan when the police raided it and caught everybody else. But Hassan got mad at us when we wouldn't help him fight back."

"Iman!" Fariborz demanded. "Where did he go?"

"He said he'd get the whole town. He said we're all infidels, and he meant you and me, too. We've been in the West too long and been corrupted. He said he'd go to some high-rise downtown and set the thing off on the roof and scatter that dust into the Santa Ana wind. What is it?"

"Is he armed?" Jack Liffey asked.

"He's got a little machine gun."

"Shit! Take care of them and *don't* touch that box," he said to Fariborz, sprinted back to the office, and banged in through the door. The manager was on the phone, his eyes going wide in fright.

"I hope that's the cops. Call the FBI, too." And then he was out the front door, hurrying to his Chevette.

"Dad, what is it? What?" Maeve stepped out of the car. He was astonished that she had obeyed and waited there.

"Fariborz needs you. *Now!* Hurry!"

He could tell she was suspicious, but she went hesitantly to the office. As soon as she was in the door, he started the car. In the mirror, he saw her come back out and stare as the car accelerated sluggishly down the ramp to the street. His heart thudding in his chest, he dialed the cell phone one-handed, peering at Robert Johnson's card.

"Who is this?"

"Johnson?"

"Liffey?"

"Look, I'll trade you. You tell me who the hell you are, and I'll tell you where a guy named Hassan is going with a can of Pu-238. I know you're not FBI—I called them."

"Lighten up there, Liffey. You don't need to know exactly who I work for. You pay my salary every April 15—that's good enough."

"Do better or I hang up."

"I'm part of a team put together years ago for just this dirty-bomb and biowar contingency. Okay? Our headquarters is Bethesda, just outside D.C."

"Assuming you're telling the truth and you're not on this guy's side, he's heading for a high-rise in downtown L.A., and he threatens to set off one of those boom-box bombs on the roof, right into the Santa Ana wind."

"*Shit!* But don't get too worked up. It's not as dangerous as you think."

People had been saying that for years and Jack Liffey simply didn't believe him.

The man was hollering something unintelligible, apparently to other agents with him. "I'm heading for the Library Tower," Jack Liffey said. "I don't know how many men you've got, but you can concentrate on the other big buildings downtown, or you can waste your time trying to arrest me. That's up to you."

The Library Tower was the tallest building west of Chicago, and well known in town for it, seventy-some stories and over 1000 feet, a real New York–scale high-rise, and he figured that was where Hassan would go, though there were a half dozen others pretty near it in scale that would do just as well. The tower had been built in 1990, taller than normally allowed, as part of a deal to help finance the rebuilding of the old landmark central library next door after a disastrous fire. Even now he could see the building's fluted circular top ten miles away as he drove, clearly visible in the wind-scoured air. It had been known briefly and unpopularly as the First Interstate Building until that bank had been swallowed up in merger mania, and then had quickly reverted to its original name, the ugly giant advertising I's taken off the roofline.

Robert Johnson still seemed to be on the phone. Jack Liffey told him where the boys had been tied up and about the big opened container in the locker. "Where the hell did they get their hands on this stuff?"

"Liffey, don't get your ass caught up in this. Take my word—it's not that dangerous."

"I don't trust you. I don't want my family glowing green at night."

He hung up.

Twenty-one

The Boom Box

It was sinking in, the ghastly notion of a powder-cloud of radioactive plutonium. Maybe Johnson was right and it wasn't that dangerous, blown up into the wind and diluted, but how could he believe him? The atomic agencies had been lying for years about the dangers.

He could see the skyscrapers of downtown a few miles ahead. Choose one, a burst up there and then a whitish billowy cumulus spreading outward, maybe faintly yellowish, maybe almost colorless— welling steadily, wisps ripped ahead of the main mass on 80 mph Santa Ana gusts, the cloud growing fainter out at the expanding rim, reaching right toward him, until particles, sparkling with radiation in his imagination, began to settle gently earthward over the car he was driving east on Adams.

He could picture the old black lady on the sidewalk, with her shopping cart, inhaling, drawing in the sparkles. Particles would enter the lungs of penniless Latinos selling oranges on the on-ramps. Movie moguls working overtime trying to peer down their secretaries' blouses. Grocers in aprons sweeping their sidewalks, guys reading comics in the glass booth at the gas station. Maeve, Kathy, Rebecca

Plumkill, and Aneliese de Villiers. He felt a chill as his thoughts acquired names.

Then just for an instant a wise-guy corner of his mind made him smile. At least the radiation would get to that fucking lawyer with the little mustache—what was his name?—who had once banged into his car and then sued *him* for negligence. Parking too close to the corner.

Reality: The radioactive cloud would do something to the grim woman driving the station wagon beside him, and the little girl she was scolding. And it would even get the two guys standing at the curb ahead in weird space-alien masks, all pale greenish rubber and almond-shaped Whitley Strieber eyes. They held up a banner that said *Open Up Area 51, Display the Alien Remains.* An unexpected tangle of traffic behind a bus stalled him right in front of the banner, and he wondered why space travelers only made themselves known to schizophrenics, guys who used dating services, and families who kept their fridges on the back porch.

And he wondered how it would feel to come down with radiation sickness in a cuckoo costume like that, off on a cuckoo crusade. Probably, he realized, not much worse than catching it in a three-piece suit, selling short 100 shares of IBM. Abruptly, the alien-lovers stooped to wave shyly and spookily in the window at him, their arms in eerie sync like windshield wipers, probably attracted by the beat-up look of his car, though it might have been some subtler emanation of outsider-ness that he was broadcasting.

That only added to his unease. Alien was an elastic concept. It took in everything from the stocky little Salvadoran holding up a bag of fruit at the corner, to Farshad Bayat writing Farsi poetry in his Persian cave. The outer reaches of the concept even took in the sensibility of a surplus aerospace worker who couldn't hold his girl-friends and couldn't find a place in the world to settle into.

His mind kept spinning away from the reality of what he faced. He wondered if he should take a quick detour up to curse Dicky Auslander as the Author of the tragedy. Why write in something as ugly as plutonium? Why not a little dynamite? Why not something even more harmless, a damp squib that would pop off ineffectually in the bright autumn light of L.A.—like all those perils in '50s sci-fi movies that succumbed in the end to something homely like loud noise or stray ultraviolet rays?

The greenish corona at the top of the Library Tower grew more menacing as he approached, looming over the other buildings around it. He headed north on the Harbor Freeway, past the green bulk of the Convention Center and then past Staples Arena, looking more than ever like a giant oven knob, and dropped off again at Fifth. He tried to remember how the one-ways ran and guessed right, taking Grand up to a curving little road called Hope Lane. The narrow lane edged nervously up Bunker Hill and there it was: a drive-in portal for the Library Tower. He had to crane his neck out the window to make sure it was the right building.

A sign announced some exorbitant parking price for every fifteen minutes, and he took the dark driveway down at speed, like an animal diving into a burrow. As he turned hard right to follow the tunnel, the Chevette engine roared suddenly in the confined space, as if it had muffler trouble. This was it, he thought with a chill: Ahead of him, the wooden barrier arm had been snapped off, three-quarters of its red-and-white length lying on the ground. He touched the butt of his .45 to make sure it was still there under his arm.

He slowed at the parking kiosk where there were two bullet holes in the glass and no attendant in sight. Hassan must be running on adrenaline, starting to lose it. All he'd had to do was take a ticket.

Jack Liffey tried the cell phone to alert Robert Johnson, but surrounded by concrete and steel, he couldn't get a dial tone in the garage. A parked Mercedes ahead of him had been sideswiped recently, the rear fender creased and the shattered remains of its big taillight on the ground. That told him which way Hassan had gone, driving like a maniac—toward the big *Monthly Reserved* sign.

Then he saw a panel truck abandoned at an angle up ahead. The driver's door hung open to leave the interior light glowing faintly in the garage. He came up cautiously and cut his engine to drift toward the van. The .45 was heavy in his hand as he stepped out of the car. He heard the crackly buzz of a fluorescent going bad, and its flicker from overhead pressed on a raw nerve. Air-conditioning machinery kicked on and started to blow air out a big vent.

No one was in the van. In front of the van there was a freight elevator with a set of keys dangling from the switch on the wall. He wondered where the man had got the keys and how he knew how to use them, but it didn't matter now.

He twisted the elevator key, like starting a car, and was a bit shocked when the heavy door trundled open slowly. He stepped to one side, aiming his pistol self-consciously into the wide cargo elevator. No one was there. It must have been programmed to return on its own to the basement.

The walls of the elevator cabin were padded with big gray grommeted quilts that hung from brackets, and someone had left a wheeled bucket and mop inside. He studied the double row of buttons that ran from B-4 up to B and then from L up to 82. Above 82 there was a square button labeled R. It didn't take a genius to work out what that probably stood for. He pressed the R and the doors exhaled once and closed sluggishly, and then—as if to rebuke the indolence of the doors—the elevator jolted hard and shot upward faster than any elevator he'd ever used. But he supposed if workers were meant to go up 1000 feet on company time, somebody would want them to do it pretty fast.

He marked his progress by the lighted numbers counting off above the door, pinging at each decade. The door was almost the full width of the big elevator cab, but there was a small wall-space on the right side for the controls. As the indicator entered the 70s, he pressed his back against the wall to stay as far out of sight as he could. He was so scared he felt woozy, felt his vision tunneling down to a small central vortex, and he was giddy with unformed thoughts—awareness of the .45 in his hand, memories making him almost catatonic with anger: his drugged dog, his daughter staring at his receding car, a sparkly mist spreading over the city.

The car stopped so suddenly that much of his weight went airborne. His stomach was just settling back into place when the door groaned once and started its dawdly withdrawal. Bright light and warm dusty air flooded in, along with muted traffic sounds, swelling as the heavy door retracted. There was no question he'd reached the roof, with the elevator giving directly onto the outside world. He had the pistol up in both hands and his heart thudded like something trying to burst out of his chest. Jack Liffey counted to three. Just as he whirled around to dive out the door, something swung fast into his field of vision and the side of his face seemed to explode.

He went down hard across the threshold of the elevator clutching his jaw and he felt himself howling in pain. It felt as if a dentist had broken through suddenly into a rotten tooth, and his left hand had scraped something and started acting up again, though the bandage still seemed to be in place. He spat out blood and pieces of tooth. The pistol was no longer in his hand. He clasped his jaw hard and rolled onto his side to see an olive-skinned man in a billowing white robe staring at him over an ugly little sub-machine gun.

They stared at one another. Then the man leaned down, grabbing Jack Liffey's shirt and dragging him out of the elevator along the rough roofing surface. He seemed very strong and he gave off a strong aroma of some sweet male perfume. When he let go, Jack Liffey ground his remaining teeth to see if anything would help the pain. It didn't.

"Who are you?"

The little submachine gun must have been what smacked into his jaw. It came around to aim right between his eyes now and he'd seen enough Navy SEAL movies to recognize an MP5, the little black collapsible-stock submachine gun that looked more like a leftover part from an oil rig.

The man snapped out something angry, probably in Arabic.

From where he lay, Jack Liffey could see above him a huge green glass flute that he recognized as part of the crown at the top of the Library Tower. Opposite was a low parapet, and beyond the parapet, deep blue autumn sky and a lone seagull soaring happily. No other buildings were visible from where he lay. He was atop the big one.

Jack Liffey tried to imagine himself into that seagull, setting off for some destination far, far away, but he couldn't. Gusty wind tugged at his clothing but he knew he'd never make takeoff speed.

Then he saw it and his heart sank. A black boom box sat on the parapet, about twenty yards away. For some reason, it had been wrapped around and around with silver duct tape to seal it tight.

"Don't move one centimeter." The gunman backed to the elevator and dragged the mop bucket out to wedge it into the door just as it was starting to close. The door trundled slowly into the plastic bucket, a bell rang, and then the door opened about halfway, thought it over for a moment, and tried to close all over again. This went on and on in unhurried repetition, *ding . . . whirr-whirr . . . whump, ding . . . whirr-whirr . . . pause.*

The sounds from the door irritated everything that already hurt, like a thumb on a bruise, so that his jaw gave an extra throb every time the heavy door rammed into the plastic bucket. It was like a lighthouse of pain, flashing regularly out of some private inner darkness.

"Now nobody comes."

"This is not going to be Islam's finest hour," Jack Liffey managed to say. "There's babies out there. There's even a lot of devout Moslems."

The man glanced around at the boom box and then back at Jack Liffey with a flat panicky look in his eyes, as if part of his mind were somewhere else.

"You fucking people kill babies in all the wars you fight against us. You say you got smart bombs, but they're not so smart. So mine's not smart either."

"We're not at war, man."

Wind yanked and fluffed the robe the man wore. The elevator door went on and on, like a madman set a single task: *ding . . . whirr-whirr . . . whump, ding.*

"Course we are. You been sending armies to beat on us ever since the Crusades."

From somewhere there was a faint whistle like a piccolo, the Santa Anas tooting over some antenna on the building, punctuated by the elevator's indefatigable *whump, ding.*

"Listen, I'm just speaking for myself here, not America or anything else." Jack Liffey winced at a sudden spasm of pain. "I don't care what you think of our leaders, I don't like them much myself, but there's a lot of little kids out there who never did a thing to you and your people."

The man took two quick steps and plucked the boom box off the ledge. He banged it down hard where Jack Liffey could see it. The timer in its little window said 11:56. The radio fizzed away softly, the volume turned to minimum.

"No stopping now! Twelve o'clock noon!"

"Oh, shit." This was absolutely real. Up until that instant, it had still been inconceivable, like the bomb drills in grammar school, waiting for the lumbering Russian planes that had never come over the horizon. "Man, at least slow it down so we can talk."

"Shut up."

Jack Liffey shivered. "Take it apart. You don't need the bomb. You can open the package and throw the powder up in the wind any time you want."

"I said shut up!" Hassan's jaw set fiercely, and his eyes started to go odd again. The readout flickered to 11:57. Suddenly Jack Liffey resented the accuracy of digital clocks. There wouldn't even be any leeway, no possibility of a few extra seconds after a big hand lined up over a little hand. It would be accurate to the precise digital stinking instant.

"What about you? It'll get you, too."

"I'm ready! *Allah-u akbar!*"

"Calm down, man."

There was a small noise, like the squeak of a tennis shoe on a slick surface. They both heard it. The man froze and then half-turned, his robe billowing like a big nesting bird.

He threw his head back and started chanting something in Arabic. Jack Liffey thought of lunging for the boom box, but what would he do if he got it? The top was so sealed with wads of duct tape, he would never get it open in time. And for all he knew, flicking the off switch would trigger the charge instantly. He seemed to remember Robert Johnson's suggesting something like that. His attention switched to his immediate surroundings. Wind. Brightness. Threat. The elevator door seemed to be banging a lot slower, though he figured it was just time itself slowing to a crawl. He certainly hoped so.

11:58. Jack Liffey felt himself go jittery with something approaching panic, even a peculiar sensation of sexual arousal, clouding his perceptions. Two minutes to stop this bomb. It might not even be very dangerous, but how could he take the risk? It wasn't a task he wanted on his plate, and there was nothing he could see to do.

An inexplicable spasm of nervous energy swept through him, and he nearly laughed: At least if it killed him, it would kill his toothache.

The man thrust the little spray gun straight up over his head and squeezed off a burst of shots, exulting. The gunshots made Jack Liffey's teeth hurt even more. Hassan began to chant again in Arabic, bobbing his head hard and belting out something in a furious rhythm that made it seem like his final outburst of apocalyptic energy. Jack Liffey could feel his own psyche grow more excitable with the chanting, his perceptions changing, seeing color fringes, a kind of molten border to things, hearing phantom squeakings.

His eye went to the timer. Still 11:58. He rolled his head away from the clock and what he saw sent an electric shock through his whole body. He knew it had to be a hallucination, a brief near-death dream, a wild, weird wish—that glimpse of Maeve sneaking up behind the robed man with a fire ax in two small hands. The ax had been too big and heavy for her, one of those implements you saw hanging on big metal brackets behind glass in hallways. He was afraid to look back to check his perceptions.

But just in case it was a real Maeve and not the psychotic hallucination it had to be, he kept his face to the boom box so that he wouldn't give her presence away. 11:59! He hadn't seen the number trip. Less than a minute to live in good health and think you had a future.

The man's rant picked up in volume, with a single word interjected repeatedly, screamed out louder than the others. Jack Liffey chanced another peek and the Maeve-like chimera seemed real enough this time. Tiptoeing up behind the bellowing gunman. How did she get on the roof? How did she get there at all? But who cared? Hurry, he thought. If you're not just a crazy desperate wish imprinting itself on my consciousness, *please hurry.*

As if hearing his entreaty, the putative Maeve swung the flat of the ax at the gunman. In that instant he had to smile inwardly: it was the real Maeve, all right, squeamishness and all. His own imagination would have gone for the sharp end.

The big tool was far too heavy for her. Its inertia resisted, and the flat of the big ax-head only made it to the man's shoulder. At the punchless impact, he took a step and spun around in a swirl of robe, firing a three-round involuntary burst that sprayed the air. Then Fariborz was there, too, running forward to tackle the man!

But Jack Liffey didn't waste any more time watching. He grabbed the boom box and came woozily to his knees. He almost passed out in a pink haze as he launched himself for the elevator. How much time did he have?

He kicked the mop bucket aside and slapped indiscriminately for a button, any floor. The door seemed to sigh in satisfaction and began to close the last few feet with its maddening lethargy, a molasses-slowed nightmare, and he clutched the boom box and watched the man swing his submachine gun around toward the elevator in a swirl of fluttery white cloth. Jack Liffey hurled himself into the shielded corner of the elevator just before three rounds splatted into the back wall, then three more slammed into the closing doors. The door chunked shut as three more bullets hit outside. The floor seemed to drop out as the elevator started its descent just as abruptly as it had risen.

Jack Liffey slammed his hand into the bright red *Emerg Stop* button, and he hurled the boom box away from himself across the big cab. A honking alarm went off in the confined space just before a concussion hammered him off his feet and something hard hit him in the chest. His jaw hurt terribly, his arm, his whole body, and he started to cough where he had crumpled in the corner as the air in the small, loud room had grown viscous with dust.

It was too much to take in all at once, and his consciousness decided it would rather not be in attendance. He dropped straight into a noisy, urgent dream of flying away from the skyscraper without sufficient support.

Twenty-two

Alone with the Dust

"Do you think we could come up with some even more imaginative indignity?" Jack Liffey suggested.

The nurse offered a very thin smile. "Breathe in and then cough, Mr. Liffey. Then we'll try the suction one more time."

He was propped up in bed, retching into a little metal basin, and she was about to stick the hideous long suctioning tube back down into his chest again, making him gag and giving him another spell of breathing panic. The act of retching stirred up the pain in his jaw and in his left hand, as well.

He was teasing the nurse to keep his mind off the warnings he had absorbed over the last day from whispered conversations near him: having one lung collapsed, it was all too easy for the other to fill rapidly with fluid and drown him.

"Woo."

"Has anyone ever taught you real breathing?"

"My mother?"

She shook her head. "You just use your chest muscles like most people. I'm going to show you how to draw from the diaphragm and then expel almost all the air from your lungs."

"Great! Have you got something to replace it with?" He knew it was just a question of getting the foreign stuff out of him, but after two full days of suctioning and other unpleasant procedures, and coughing and retching phlegm, he was getting pretty tired of it all.

In the fateful elevator in the Library Tower, stuck just above the sixty-seventh floor, he'd been summoned back to consciousness by a disembodied voice speaking to him out of a little metal grille. The voice had to pace its words to fall between the buzz-buzz of the *Emerg Stop* alarm. "Are you . . . hurt? Liffey . . . are you hurt?"

He had looked around and seen a thick film of dust on everything. When he touched his chest, a powdery puff billowed up. He came slowly to his knees. Everything he touched whiffed in the same way. In the corner there was the mangled remains of the boom box, much of the top blown away. Luckily, most of the small blast seemed to have been directed upward.

"Liffey," the tinny voice went on insistently. "Are you hurt?"

"No," he had managed to reply. "I don't . . . think so."

"Pull out . . . emergency . . . button."

"Can't. Danger. Plutonium." Words came with difficulty.

"We know. Pull it. Trust us."

He had given in, as much because the honking sound was driving him nuts, and grasped the fat red button and yanked. It popped out to afford an instantaneous blessed calm. The elevator didn't move, and he sat down on the floor and leaned against the padded wall. A lot of him was sore, particularly his jaw now. He didn't think it was broken, but several of his teeth were, and the right side of his jaw was probably all bruise.

"Your daughter's all right, and the boy," was the first thing the man's voice had told him once the alarm stopped. Mentally he thanked whoever the man was for his consideration.

"Is the elevator car filled with a fine gray powder?"

"Oh, yes."

"Okay, my name is Dr. Mourelinho. First, we want to congratulate you for confining the air burst in the elevator. It was a brave thing for you to do and might have saved lives if the boom box had actually contained plutonium, as you thought. I don't quite know how to tell you this." There was a silence for few moments and all of the hair on his neck and shoulders stood on end. "We have them all in custody now, so we don't need to keep up the masquerade. I work with Robert Johnson's group, and it was our organization who sold the terrorist cell that canister a month ago. It contains mostly ground granite—basically, just silica, very very fine sand. We had one sample pack with enough alpha emitter in it to convince them, but it was bait-and-switch."

"Oh, shit!"

"You *will* be all right."

Sure, he'd thought. He probably had just experienced the most thorough exposure to black lung of anyone since the early days of coal mining. But somewhere inside he believed the doctor's comforting voice.

The man talked to him for a while, telling him his daughter and Fariborz were already in a nearby hospital being treated for some bruises, but otherwise quite okay. Maeve's car had been parked up the block, and she had driven them to the building, on the same hunch he had had. The kids had come up the passenger elevator to the floor below and climbed the service stairs to the roof.

"Try to sit still, Mr. Liffey. We're going to bring you down to the lobby level now."

"I'm having a little trouble breathing," Jack Liffey said. It was odd, as if something wasn't working quite right inside him.

"We'll see to that. Try not to stir up the powder and breathe any more of it than you have to."

Powder, he thought. What a nice innocuous word. Like fresh light snow, baby talcum, a woman's face color. The elevator ground down slowly, in fits and starts, unlike its trip upward, almost as if a few brawny men were heaving it down by a big rope.

It stopped eventually and a tall, thin man with a stethoscope and a graying crew-cut shook his hand with a kindly frown.

"Mr. Liffey, I presume. I'm Dr. Pedro Mourelinho." He pronounced it, Pehd-ro, in Portuguese fashion. He led him out into the marble lobby, where two men in white coats took him to a child's inflatable swimming pool with red seahorses all over it. They stripped him and sprayed him down with cold water, then they gave him a set of green hospital scrubs and a respirator mask hooked to an oxygen cylinder which made his battered jaw hurt like hell, but soothed the breathing panic that was beginning to set in with gasps and gulps. He couldn't help thinking of the man with the oxygen cannula in the self-storage office. He hoped he hadn't been too hard on him.

Before long they had him in a private room at a small downtown hospital he didn't even know existed on South Grand.

"The X ray shows one of your lungs has collapsed, but don't worry too much," a nurse told him. "It's fairly common. It happened to Roman Gabriel once, in football practice. It will take care of itself."

"And if it doesn't?" The respirator mask had big holes in the sides and he found he could talk with it on; it just made his voice sound like it came out of a soup can.

She smiled reassuringly. "Don't you worry, Mr. L. These gentlemen from Bethesda know exactly what they're doing."

Later they would tell him Bethesda was the home of the Armed Forces Radiobiology Research Institute. Biowarfare, in other words.

An hour later the gentlemen from Bethesda themselves showed up. Robert Johnson waited calmly to one side with a newspaper tucked under his arm while Dr. Mourelinho gave him an injection, and poked and prodded at him, peered into orifices, pressed a cold stethoscope against his chest, and asked some perfunctory questions.

"Am I going to make it?"

Johnson laughed. "We certainly are optimism-challenged today. Not many people are hit with breathing that much silica all at once, but it ought to work its way out of your system pretty quickly. One of our colleagues was once exposed to the real thing—depleted plutonium dust—and Pedro married her last month. She's got a damn sight more life in her than you do."

"Did she sink her face in five pounds of it?"

"Exposure is exposure. The nurse been making you cough?"

"Endlessly."

"Good, well, you cooperate with the nurse, Liffey, you hear me, and you'll be around in six months to get you a presidential medal."

"I'd rather have a big house with a view, if somebody's in a giving mood."

The doctor was already on his way out, but Robert Johnson stayed. "You did a fine and noble thing, Mr. Liffey, even if nobody knows it but us, and even if it wasn't plutonium."

"You know the old mental poser that you hear," Jack Liffey said. "You see a burning house and you run in and you can either save a kitten or a Van Gogh? I thought of that for just a split instant as I dived into the elevator."

"So, which is it?" Robert Johnson asked.

"Damned if I know. Maybe I thought I was saving my daughter. There's never much of a question about that. I'd probably doom the whole West Side to rescue Maeve. Is she going to be able to come see me?"

"By tomorrow, I think. Just us professionals for now."

"That's gloomy."

"Do you read Spanish?" he asked out of the blue.

Robert Johnson untucked the paper he was carrying, a particularly garish ¡*Alarma!* and showed it to Jack Liffey. The front page was a full-page photo of the courtyard of a hacienda with dead bodies lying all around, including some women and children. The headline screamed: *Guerra de Drogas!* Just the sight of the magazine made his hand start hurting again.

"I barely read English."

"Early in the A.M., two days ago, a squad of professional hit men with automatic weapons burst into the Miramón family rancho just north of Guaymas and killed everyone they could find—the paterfamilias himself who called himself Frankie, the wife, kids, aunts, cousins, and henchmen. Twenty-three in all. That fat one lying there is Frankie. You may not recognize him in this posture, but I bet he's the one you had your little trouble with. Just another drug hit, I suppose. But you could probably go get your car now without looking so hard in the rearview mirror."

"Maybe Becky can come home now, too."

"The IRS will be on her like a coat of paint, but who knows? Any of Miramón's guys left alive are running to the forests of Chiapas about now. Life's tough, but it's a lot tougher if you're stupid and your side just lost a gang war."

"Frankie Miramón wasn't stupid," Jack Liffey said. He told Robert Johnson some of the man's history as a student activist who was tortured by the police. "He could probably have done something useful with his life, but who knows what it is that kicks anybody out of orbit?"

"Yeah, who knows?"

Jack Liffey wondered himself how easy it might be to take a step or two across the line someday and then just get lost and never find your way back. You'd have changed your whole settled view of yourself and what was possible.

"This Hassan is more my speed," Robert Johnson said. "No ambiguity at all. A good old fanatic, and the guy is so proud of it, he's over in the federal lockup right now singing like a thrush."

"In your line of work, I'd think a thrush'd be a yeast infection."

He smiled. "Doc Pedro handles that end. I'm responsible for tracking the human vectors. You know, this is the first-known terrorist attempt to use a dirty bomb."

"So I'm into the *Guinness Book of Records?*"

"Oh, in a couple of ways, Liffey."

"If my one good lung doesn't fill up with fluid and kill me."

"There's always that."

The next morning he woke up short of breath and with a scratchy throat, and was engulfed immediately in a wave of the blackest panic. He rang for the nurse and she peered into his throat with a tongue depressor and declared that he was a bit dehydrated. She tut-tutted and said he should be drinking more water. She upped the oxygen and switched him to a nasal cannula, which made life a lot simpler, and then gave him more painkillers for his hand and his jaw. They were going to see about debriding the burn soon, she promised. By the time he'd eaten his soggy hospital breakfast one-handed, he had calmed down and noticed there was no phone in the room and he wondered if they were isolating him for some reason.

The nurse brought him more pills and a note that she said had been approved by "the men from Bethesda." The note said Dicky

Auslander had heard from his daughter, indirectly, and he was so relieved and thankful that he was offering a huge bonus. "You can take Maeve to Europe and show her the sights," the note suggested.

His mind immediately started toying with the idea. He couldn't think of a cheerier prospect than sitting at a Left Bank bistro with Maeve, sipping espressos and watching leggy well-dressed Parisian couples drift past—except maybe having Rebecca Plumkill walk up to join them at the table, and then dropping Maeve at a museum for the afternoon and rushing right back to their quaint-but-comfortable hotel room and . . .

Rather than dwell too much on that, he switched to imagining confronting Auslander one final time in his office, giving him hell as the "Author" of the whole terrorist incident on top of his private hell in T.J. Why me, Dicky. For God's sake, the world's first victim of a dirty bomb! My hand hurts. My jaw hurts. I can barely breathe. Enough is enough.

Hey, man, Dicky laughed at him. I could have made it *real* plutonium, and then there'd be guys in lead space-suits launching you out to sea on a raft for the very short rest of your life. You could really wallow in being an outsider *then*.

He put the reverie away and was just beginning to enjoy a sense of calm that had come over him from somewhere—maybe the pills—when suddenly he realized he had to talk to Aneliese de Villiers, and *soon*. He knew he'd be seeing Rebecca Plumkill now, it had all felt so good and so right to him, even his libido seconding the nomination. He owed Aneliese a call, not to leave her dangling, he owed her an explanation before she came hurrying to the hospital with flowers. His gloom rushed back in.

"I'm sorry, it's the only loose phone we have. We shut down a pediatric wing."

The men from Bethesda had given permission for a call and she plugged in the Mickey Mouse telephone beside his bed, Mickey's cheerful gloved hand holding up a bright blue handset. Only three fingers, he noticed with a frown, like all cartoon characters.

"What if I were calling someone to report a terminal disease?"

She lifted one eyebrow. "I could cover Mickey's face with bandages, if it would help."

"Let it go."

He called information for the number. His little address book had gone somewhere during the ordeal.

"Hello," a boy answered.

"Billy, this is Jack. Can I speak to your mom?"

"Ma! It's Jack Liffey! We saw you on TV!"

That set him back a little. The local news must have had something on him.

"Jack!" she said breathlessly, and he could instantly picture the fullness of her, the eyes that wanted so much to burst out of her and *help*. "Are you okay? Billy called me in last night to see something about you on the TV, but there was nothing in the paper."

"Nothing serious, just banged up. Aneliese, hold on, let me speak." And say what? *Let's be friends*. Jesus, how could you do this and not sound like a soap opera? "I've really loved knowing you. Really."

Mickey was grinning like an idiot at him. I'll strangle you, you stupid plastic hunk of sentimentality, he thought. He could tell from her breathing that she knew where he was going. How could she *not* know? People had plenty of radar tuned up for this stuff. "We both know our bodies were trying to tell us something, or mine was. It just wasn't working—I don't know why. You're a great woman; it's not personal. I didn't plan it to happen, but I met somebody else."

After a few moments of silence, he heard her make some sort of indecipherable sound. These British types were pretty held-back, he thought. He was hoping for that. "And your body worked fine with her, did it?" she asked, with a tiny edge.

"Yes. Could we still be friendly, or is that excluded now?"

Then she said something that really threw him, not what he expected at all. "Jack, you're a living, fucking treasure-trove of neuroses." She laughed, maybe half-genuinely. "It's all right, really it is. Call me when everything settles down for you, but not before."

"I will. Honestly. I'd like to. . . ." But she had hung up, and he wondered just how angry she really was. She hadn't quite kept her composure, but she hadn't started screaming at him, either.

Mickey was still grinning idiotically, but Jack Liffey's eyes were
looking right through the big mouse, focused much farther away, as
if hoping that somewhere out there, just out of sight maybe, there
was some spartan and fundamental truth to be discovered that
could settle the human condition in such a way that he would never
again have to make a phone call like that.

He was overjoyed after lunch the next day when the nurse
announced that Maeve and Fariborz were going to be allowed in to
see him. Maeve first peeked in and then came straight to the bed
and put both hands on his arm under the sheet. "Daddy, we were
so scared about you."

She had saved his life once before and still he didn't quite know
how to express his gratitude. "If you keep disobeying me to save
my life, I'm going to have to rethink the whole question of paternal
authority."

"I don't know how adventurous I am anymore," she said, the
line above her eyes crinkling up. "Fari told me what those guys
were trying to do, and it gives me the creeps. I don't like the idea of
radiation at all."

Fariborz took a step closer and thrust out his hand. Jack Liffey
shook it.

"Thanks to both of you for tackling that guy. He seemed to me
about the size of a mountain right then."

"The cops were right behind us."

The young man had something behind his back and he brought
out a deep red rose and gave it to Jack Liffey. "There is an old Persian proverb. If you have two loaves of bread, sell one and buy a
flower. Thanks to you, sir, for carrying that bomb into the elevator.
It might have hurt us."

He didn't quite know what to do with the rose in his hand. "It turns
out the bomb wasn't all that dangerous after all. You brought me
safely across the border, son. There's something quite biblical in that."

"Mohammed had a guide when he had to flee Mecca. Abu Bakr,
one of his first converts. He was a rich man who gave much of his
fortune to ransom slaves."

Jack Liffey poked the rose into a drinking glass on the table. "How is your faith doing?" he asked the boy.

"Bruised a little, but I'll be fine," Fariborz said shyly.

Jack Liffey took the boy's arm for a moment. "When I was in Ensenada, a man told me I was about to meet my doppelganger. Do you know what that is?"

"I think so."

"Most people think it just means a double somewhere in the world, but it's a little more sinister than that. A doppelganger lurks in your shadow and chats with you and slowly adopts your traits until it becomes you."

He smiled. "I promise not to lurk, sir."

They all laughed, and Jack Liffey told Maeve about Auslander's bonus and the possibility of seeing Paris. "Are you game?"

"Wow, is a bear Catholic? Does the pope pee in the woods?"

He grinned. When he had last offered that fractured pair of aphorisms, within her hearing, the pope had been *shitting* in the woods. How like her to sanitize it a little. She was a good kid, he thought.

They talked some more, and suddenly Jack Liffey noticed that Maeve was crying silently. The tears were just welling out of her eyes.

He took her hand. "Hon, it'll be okay."

She nodded, but she went on wiping away tears, and he wondered what they had told her at the nurses' station that they hadn't told him. After a while, the nurse threw the kids out, but at the door, just as it was shutting, he glimpsed Maeve leaning in to hug Fariborz, her head tucked into the boy's chest as if she needed consoling. Uh-oh, he thought. Somebody must think it's worse than they're telling me. He was suddenly so exhausted he closed his eyes, wondering where the lethargy had come from, and he drifted off into a doom-laden sleep.

When he opened his eyes, the room was much dimmer and a nurse was standing over him. "Can you see your wife?"

It took him a moment to focus, drag himself out of a collapsing pit of sand and dust. Kathy? He hadn't seen her in a over a year. At least she probably wouldn't tear into him while he was in a hospital bed.

He nodded, and the nurse brought in Rebecca Plumkill in a

frumpy housedress. She dragged an uncomfortable plastic chair next to the bed and sat.

"I died and went to heaven," he said, after the nurse left. His throat was truly scratchy, and the collapsed side of his chest was frightening him again; but he forced himself not to think about anything but the immediate, the glowing woman sitting there.

"Oh, Jack!"

"Bec. It's good to see you." She leaned toward him and kissed him on the mouth. He had a little trouble getting his breath afterward.

"I had no idea I could come to want someone so much again," she said.

"Did you really need that Sears dress?"

She shrugged. "Shouldn't a 'wife' look a little matronly? They wouldn't let me in unless I said I was your wife."

Her palm pressed briefly against his erection which had come forth dutifully under the covers.

"Oh, soon," he said.

"I want us to do other things, too. Read great books to one another late into the night."

"If we're not too busy," he said.

"We can do both, I promise." She kissed him softly on the cheek, but the emotion must have taken the last ounce of energy he had. He drifted off to sleep again, pillowed up on fields and fields of red roses.

In the middle of the night he awoke with real panic clutching him, gasping for air. He wriggled around and draped his upper body over the side of the bed, coughing compulsively at the floor. Even the good side felt heavy as lead now, blocked. The obstruction wouldn't clear with coughing, but by hanging head-down and switching the nasal cannula into his mouth, he found he could slowly suck some oxygen into the good lung and ease the panic. He studied the streaky pattern on the white linoleum. He saw little rubber wheels, a tiny slice of the closet door. Wood grain, Formica—everything in the room carried a terrible inhuman coldness, belonging to no one, made only to be cleaned easily or moved easily or changed easily.

He was so weak that he didn't even know if he'd be able to get back up onto the bed. This is what being alone really means, he thought. Every soul was a stranger at the end of its days, as the rest of the world went its merry way somewhere. Truly walled off, inside yourself, hearing the gallop of death.

But that was nonsense. He had it all going his way now, he thought: a wonderful new lover, bonus money coming in, a trip to Paris in the offing with a sweet, bright, loving daughter. He could enjoy it all to the fullest if he could only get in one good breath, only cough away whatever it was constricting his good lung. But he couldn't.